The Lanzis:
The Boundless Shades of Life

The Lanzis:
The Boundless Shades of Life

Giancarlo Gabbrielli

iUniverse, Inc
New York Bloomington

The Lanzis:
The Boundless Shades of Life

Copyright © 2009 by Giancarlo Gabbrielli

All rights reserved. No part of this book may be used or reproduced by
any means, graphic, electronic, or mechanical, including photocopying,
recording, taping or by any information storage retrieval system without the
written permission of the publisher except in the case of brief quotations
embodied in critical articles and reviews.

iUniverse books may be ordered through booksellers or by contacting:

iUniverse
1663 Liberty Drive
Bloomington, IN 47403
www.iuniverse.com
1-800-Authors (1-800-288-4677)

Because of the dynamic nature of the Internet, any Web addresses or links
contained in this book may have changed since publication and may no longer be valid. This is a work of fiction. All of the characters, names, incidents,
organizations, and dialogue in this novel are either the products of the author's
imagination or are used fictitiously

ISBN: 978-0-595-52699-4 (pbk)
ISBN: 978-0-595-62753-0 (ebk)
ISBN: 978-0-595-51896-8 (cloth)

Printed in the United States of America
iUniverse rev. date: 7/28/09

Preface

During the Great War—which saw France, Britain, Russia, and Italy oppose the forces of Austria, Prussia, and the Ottoman Empire—the Italian front was located in the northeastern part of the country.

Roberto and Luisa Lanzi and their two sons lived in a small villa near the center of San Donà del Piave, which had been, until then, a tranquil town located just north of Venice. Roberto, a chemical engineer, had recently lost his job due to the war. Luisa, several years younger, was looking after her sons with the love and devotion that only a person of faith and great moral principles can.

Her eldest son was Riccardo, and he was just nineteen. Despite his aversion for violence, he had volunteered to defend his country from aggression. His parents, though very proud of him, were in constant fear for his life. The younger one, Lorenzo, was only nine years old and was at home since all the schools of the area had been closed. In fact, with the approaching war front, the city authorities, like many others with a place to hide, had suddenly disappeared, leaving the town to itself.

On October 25, 1917, after the collapse of the Italian front—known as the rout of Caporetto—the war fell upon the southern plains of Veneto with unsuspected ferocity.

By early November, Italian and Austrian soldiers were entangled in murderous hand-to-hand battle in the outskirts of San Donà, and the waters of the Piave River became tinged with the blood of the youth fallen from both sides.

- I -

1917

Luisa Lanzi had just begun to prepare their meager daily meal when suddenly, around noon, the Austro-Hungarian quick-fire batteries started hammering the town, plunging over fifteen hundred shells onto it in a matter of minutes.

At the first blast, her thought went to her son Riccardo, who was fighting in the nearby Piave Line. Then, as the explosions seemed to get closer to her house, she grabbed her nine-year-old son Lorenzo by the hand and raced toward the concrete stairway, calling to her husband while running. "Roberto, Roberto, where are you?"

"Run!"

Between the blasts, she kept calling. Calling and praying, while sheltering her young son with her body from the avalanche of falling debris that rolled down the stairs. They lay tightly in the far corner, shuddering at every blast. At last, there was a deafening explosion, and the house collapsed over them with a dreadful crash. The acrid smell of cordite and the dense cloud of dust filled every pore of her body, while the vision of death almost paralyzed her. Oddly, in her state of bewilderment, she found herself considering whether she was alive or dead. Then she was suddenly aware that something budged under her body. "Lorenzo," she cried, coughing dust. "Lorenzo," she repeated in astonishment, "we are alive; we are alive." She began to crawl out from under the stairway and over the wreckage, pulling her son behind her, his face a mask of dust lined by two streaks of tears.

Desperately, she called to her husband again, as her bloodied hands lifted the rubble and pieces of shattered furniture. "Roberto … Roberto!"

No answer ever came back to console her in her desperation.

*****

At the same time, a high-caliber mortar shell hit the forward Italian positions in the west dugout section. It killed a dozen soldiers and wounded many more. Second Lieutenant Riccardo Lanzi, who was walking behind his new commander as he inspected the trenches, was knocked to the ground by the force of the explosion. He was dizzy, disoriented, and then surprised to realize that he was unhurt. He paused for a moment on the ground before leaning against the mud wall and slowly starting to rise. Through the smoky air and his watery eyes, he began to see the degree of devastation around him and smelled the nauseating, sweet odor of blood. Body parts were scattered through the four-meter hole carved by the blast. Arms, legs, and heads were severed from the rest of the bodies; thick, dark blood ran through the muddy ground like rivulets after a downpour.

Resting in a puddle of water was the captain's entire left arm. The three golden stripes, sign of his rank, sparkled, strangely unsoiled, on his jacket sleeve. His wristwatch was still running. The rest of his body had been pulverized.

Poor man! Killed two days after his arrival at the front. Only yesterday, Riccardo had seen him in a corner of the shelter, writing a letter to his mother. *Poor woman! She'll briefly rejoice at the sight of his letter, only to be crushed by the news of his sudden death.*

Riccardo heard the cries of the wounded and noticed pale, frightened soldiers ready to jump over the standing parapets, ready to desert. He noticed others, although unhurt, sprawling motionless in the thick mud or resting against the trench wall. They seemed shell-shocked, exhausted by the long sleepless periods, or simply overwhelmed by the cruelty and senselessness of war.

Oh my God, he thought, shaking himself from that moment of bewilderment, *the captain is dead; I'm in charge now. I must act immediately!*

Though barely nineteen, he was already a veteran of the war. He knew that even a brief hesitation could turn that critical moment into an uncontrollable disaster.

He ignored his bowel, which seemed on the verge of dissolving, and at the first gap in the shelling, he fired a shot in the air. For a brief instant, it was as though time stood still. The blast reverberated throughout the trench. The wounded men quieted down, while the able soldiers descended from the parapet, picked up their weapons, and resumed their positions.

"Soldiers!" Riccardo shouted. "We're the only barrier between the

Austrians and San Donà. After the shelling, they'll attack, so make your bullets count!"

Many of the men were from that area, and they threw longing backward glances toward the town, where dense columns of smoke had begun to climb toward the gray sky.

"My family …," lamented an old, unshaven corporal.

"Damn the Austrians," said another. "I can't stay here while my people are killed."

"We haven't slept for twenty-four fucking hours …"

Others soldiers said nothing, but their pale faces and mutinous silence were just as eloquent.

"I'll shoot the first man who moves in the wrong direction," Riccardo said, with a voice that sounded like the extension of his blast. "My family is there too," he added, nodding toward San Donà, "but running away is not the way to protect it. Haven't you heard what happened to other towns that fell in the hands of the enemy? Are you so stupid to think that your presence—even if you ever made it there— would save them? Come on, men, let's close ranks and be ready to give those bastards the welcome they deserve. Let's show them how we can fight to protect our families and homes."

He was aware that any of those desperate men—standing in knee-deep mud, hungry, and discouraged to the point of desertion—could have raised his rifle and shot him. Several junior officers had recently been found at the bottom of a trench with bullets in their backs.

If I have to die, Riccardo thought, swallowing the lump in his throat, *it will be doing my best and defending my family and my town.*

"Come on, men," he said, placing his Beretta back in its holster and lifting a fallen sandbag to the edge of the trench. "Let's give them hell."

His calm demeanor and steady stare seemed to infuse the men with courage. He climbed onto a step carved on the trench and stole a look toward the enemy lines. No movement was visible from the Austrian trenches. He looked at his thinned line of defense and wondered how they were going to resist. Just west of his position, he noticed a large depressed area completely flooded by the recent rain. *Even if the place was passable,* he thought, *the attackers would have to slow down considerably.*

"Sergeant," he called, "have all dead soldiers moved in front of that flooded area. Make sure they and their weapons are visible to the enemy. Position a few sharpshooters among them, but move all other able men and the two machine guns to this position."

The sergeant hesitated. He did not seem to grasp the reason for the order.

"On the double, damn it!" Riccardo shouted. "We don't have time to spare."

This is where they'll come, he told himself, *and this is where we'll have to stop them.*

Then, certain he had done all he could for the moment, he snatched a backward glance toward the town. A pang crossed his heart as he saw an ominous column of black smoke rising from an area he judged was close to his own home.

Oh, God, he silently prayed, *please spare my family.*

*****

A more violent barrage fell upon the Italian trenches.

Soon they'll attack, Riccardo thought. He raised his field glasses and scanned the opposite field; there was no movement yet. He thought of previous fights, the carnage of Caporetto, his family.

I have stayed alive so far, but will I survive today? Please, God … He sighed, soon regretting his thoughts. *How can I invoke Your name? Ask to be saved the very moment I'm preparing to kill others?*

The hail of Austrian shells passed over the trenches like a rain shower pushed by the wind and began to hit the rear.

This is it, he thought, while a thunderous wild cry gushed out of the Austro-Hungaric trenches and a tidal wave of gray silhouettes sprang out of the earth's bowel and began to rush toward the Italian lines.

"Signal our artillery to start firing!" he yelled.

Physics and mathematics had always been Riccardo's best subjects. And the service in artillery, in addition to his use of these abilities, often allowed him to "depersonify" the war—not to see the faces of his enemies—and pretend that the shooting was just an exercise in accuracy. Today, however, the death of his superior had compelled him to fight in the trenches.

The order was repeated into a field telephone, and in a matter of seconds, the shelling began to hit the no-man's-land area with a furious intensity. Riccardo saw many men drop to the ground, bodies and body parts flying through the air, but the gray wave broke through smoke and fire and continued to advance.

One hundred meters, Riccardo estimated. *Soon I'll make out their faces; they'll become more real. Youth of one country, placed by ill-fated circumstances of place and time in the inescapable position of fighting and killing the youth of another country in order to survive. War!* He thought. *Now, like yesterday. Like tomorrow, like ever and ever.*

He looked toward the flooded area and saw Austrian soldiers stuck in the mud to their waists. They were easily picked off by Italian sharpshooters, fell, as if in slow motion, and disappeared into the sludge as though they never existed. The ones behind them assessed the situation and veered toward his position, but even they, while they changed direction, made an easier target.

At least this worked.

"Tell our artillery to shorten the range!" he yelled. His command was repeated on the phone, and soon the Italian shells fell fifty to seventy meters from his position, some even closer.

What irony it would be to be killed by one of our own shells.

The enemy still advanced and was now at rifle range.

"Shoot at will!"

The command echoed along the line, and the cracking of rifles and machine-gun fire tore the air to shreds and hacked into the advancing soldiers. Gray tunics with shiny buckles fell to the ground; helmets rolled on the mud, uncovering blond manes and boyish faces. Still, many moved toward the Italian line, their sharpened steel bayonets sending sinister flashes through the smoky air.

Soon they'll be close enough to throw hand grenades.

Riccardo raised his pistol. Almost trembling only a moment ago, his hand was now firm, his grip secure. He fired point-blank, and the closest uniform fell forward, a silent cry stifled by the mud. Feelings such as humanity, fear, and abstract notions of reason and justice suddenly abandoned him, replaced only by cold determination and a wild instinct of survival.

It's either us or them.

Am I afraid to die?

Then a new, alarming voice emerged from the bottom of his heart: *What if I'm badly wounded?* it said. The picture of thousands of youths, mutilated and disfigured, flashed through his mind, but the enemy was now too close to allow distracting thoughts. Riccardo shot once more, and then again and again. He reloaded his pistol and kept shooting until the pistol become hot in his hand. Soldiers were dying on both sides. The gaps in the Italian trench grew wider, while the mound of gray uniforms piled up only meters away. The lament of the wounded mixed with the explosions as wave upon wave of Austrian soldiers continued the attack. Some of them came within meters of Riccardo's position, but the line held, and toward evening, they were finally thrown back.

*****

Meanwhile, despite the ongoing bombing, Luisa kept on digging desperately among the rubble of her house, helped by little Lorenzo, while her hope of finding her husband alive was quickly fading. Her heart was stirred by the thought that Riccardo could have been wounded or, may God forbid it, even killed under that infernal fire. Warm tears streaked her dusty cheeks, and her hands were red with blood.

Over the rumbling roar, one could still hear the crying and wailing from the immediate neighborhood, punctuated by the whistling shells and thunderous explosions. All around, as far as one could see, there was nothing but smoke, wreckage, destruction. Only late in the evening were a few neighbors, moved with compassion, finally able to convince Luisa and Lorenzo to desist from their valiant but fruitless toil. They took them to the damaged basement of the cathedral, where many homeless people like them had found temporary refuge. Fortunately, despite the suggestion of the authorities, the archbishop had refused to follow their example and abandon his herd, and he remained there, sharing the food that he was able to scrape together.

In addition to the torment of her husband's death, given the magnitude of the destruction and the lack of news from the front, Luisa lived those early days with the additional terror that Riccardo might have perished in the onslaught. However, she needed to be strong in front of little Lorenzo who, despite his young age, had already witnessed so much horror.

It was with immense relief that a few days later, a wounded soldier sent back to the back areas brought her a short note from Riccardo.

Dear Mother,

I received the sad news of Papa's death from a soldier from San Donà who rejoined my unit. I wish I could be with you and my little brother in this heartbreaking moment. I'm sorry for the house as well. I know how much you and Papa sacrificed. Thank God, however, that you and little Lorenzo came out alive. I too have so far survived the onslaught, and I promise you that I'll do my best to come back in one piece. I know there will be more tough fighting ahead, but the tide may be turning, as the weight of the American intervention will soon be felt.

Give a hug to my little brother for me. All my love to both of you.

Your loving son,
Riccardo

He didn't tell her of the fear experienced during the ordeal. Nor did he tell her of his field promotion and the citation of his battalion.

Repeatedly, Luisa read and kissed that letter before hiding it in a corner of the shelter where she had gathered the few things saved from the ravages of her house.

Thanks to God, Riccardo and Lorenzo were still alive. That was the most important thing, as they were the stimulus and the reason to wipe her tears and keep living.

Her husband dead and her house destroyed, Luisa had to find the strength to overcome her sorrow and protect her nine-year-old son. She had to pull up her sleeves and face squarely her new life as a widow, without a roof and without a job.

For several months, along with dozens of other homeless people, she and Lorenzo remained sheltered in the basement of the semi-destroyed clergy house. They shared the scant food supplied by the bishop, who fortunately had remained with his herd.

Hopefully, her Riccardo was right, and the inhumane war would soon end.

*****

The war finally ended in 1918. As Riccardo had predicted, the weight of the American involvement had helped break the spine of the Germanic armies.

Unable to salvage her bomb-ravaged home, Luisa walked for days, without food or rest, throughout the shambles that had been her town, searching for better accommodations. At night, she returned to the shelter and devoured the remaining crumbs of stale bread to still the pang of hunger. Finally, after endless, desperate weeks, she was rewarded. She luckily found a two-room apartment in a battered dwelling that had somehow escaped total destruction. Despite her desperate situation, she had the courage to urge Riccardo—honorably discharged from the army as captain and winner of a bursary—to complete his studies.

"I'll go abroad, Mother. I hope you don't mind."

"Abroad? Why? Where?"

"Because there is nothing near that is suitable, mother. And as far as where," he continued with a pained expression, "I've chosen Germany."

"Why there?" she asked, with resentment in her voice.

"Mother," Riccardo answered evenly, "I know what you think, but the war is over. I've chosen it because I've studied the language … and because the technical disciplines I am pursuing are more advanced there."

For a long moment, the two stood looking at each other silently, and then, finally, Luisa spoke. "Go on, son," she said, teary-eyed. "Go and fulfill your destiny. You are right; there is nothing here for you."

"Thank you, Mother," he said. "I know this is a sacrifice. It will be hard for both of us, but I promise I'll do my best and come back an engineer, like Papa wanted. Farewell, Mother. Good-bye, Lorenzo. Be good, my little brother."

After Riccardo's departure, Luisa searched for work in the nearby town of Mestre, where she'd heard a few job opportunities were available. She was finally hired as an estimator by a small supplier of pylons and other wood products that he provided to the nearby port facilities of Venice.

She said, "At least we'll have a roof over our heads and enough food to stave off hunger."

- II -

Riccardo completed his studies in four short years. However, given the poor economic situation in Italy, his mother encouraged him to remain in Germany and continue his research work. In fact, although it was now almost six years since the war had ended, Italy, perhaps more so than the other participants in the conflict, was still reeling from its great human and material losses.

Though ultimately victorious in the battlefield, the country's initial hopes for adequate compensation were soon dashed, as the Treaty of Versailles saw primarily France and England share in the spoils. Following the news from abroad, Riccardo was saddened to read that Italy, with its ineffectual leaders and little international influence, received only insignificant reparation and was left to lick its wounds. This factor added to the detriment of its economy, the atrophy and degradation of its internal politics, and the growing unrest of its people.

It is not an easy world in which to survive, Luisa wrote to her son, *particularly for a widow like me.*

As conditions worsen, the discontent among our people grows, and at times, our poor country seems to slip toward absolute chaos. There are frequent strikes, workers' occupation of factories, peasants' seizure of land, and riots. Stay awhile longer, Riccardo. Hopefully, matters will eventually improve ...

Finally, amid this bedlam, a scarcely known man, who had fought in the Great War and knew firsthand the frustration of the common people, took advantage of the situation. He seized the opportunity and created a new political movement. He did this with the help of industrialists and the Church, which feared the growth of bolshevism and anarchy, and with that of disgruntled war veterans who had fought and risked their lives for three long years and were now jobless and unable to adjust to a conventional life.

This man was Benito Mussolini, soon to be known by the popular pseudonym *Il Duce,* from the Latin word *dux,* for chief or leader.

What's happening now, Mother? Riccardo wrote, reading the news. *Are Italians really taking to this movement?*

My dear son, she replied, *Mussolini promised the Italian people jobs and a vigorous leadership. So strong are our hopes and desire to improve our condition that, yes, many Italians have readily embraced his movement. Personally, though, I have my doubts ...*

By the mid-1920s, despite Mussolini's promises, matters had not significantly improved. Riccardo's mother, like many other Italians, still struggled to survive, sustained only by her unwavering faith and the love for her sons.

*****

One Saturday, Luisa Lanzi waited for the Venezia-Mestre commuter bus among the usual crowd of workers. She felt more remote than usual, as she was battling a strange feeling that had suddenly taken hold of her like an albatross, a premonition weighing heavily on her spirit. She had experienced this eerie sensation twice before. Both times, dreadful things had soon followed.

When the worn-out vehicle arrived, she sprang forward, boarded it, and dropped down on the front seat near the window. *Dear Lord,* she prayed silently, *if something harmful is going to happen, let it not be my children. They're all I have left.* It was the same irrational fear she had felt when receiving the letter that called Riccardo to arms … and the morning her husband was killed.

She gripped her worn leather bag, which held her meager pay. Her sharp, mathematical mind itemized the most urgent bills to pay and calculated the essential food provisions she and Lorenzo needed, enough to get them by until the next payday. She also started to sketch in her mind the letter she would write to Riccardo after attending Sunday mass.

Although used to her presence, the people around her always seemed intrigued by the charm of this woman in her forties, with gleaming jade green eyes and noble features. She usually answered politely to their salutes, but avoided any protracted conversation. Like most of them, she was returning home after a long, hard day at work.

Finally, everyone was aboard, and the rundown vehicle, after a few coughing bouts from its rusty muffler, moved with a jerk. Thirty minutes later, it came to an abrupt stop in Piazza Indipendenza, and Luisa leaped off and began to walk.

Six long years had elapsed since the end of the Great War. Yet here, as in many other parts of San Donà, many buildings still stood like unhealed wounds inflicted by repeated bombing on the town during the hostilities.

Another fifteen minutes and I'll be home, she thought. Instinctively, she quickened her pace, as if by doing so, she could escape from those frightful war recollections. She tried to dodge her anxieties, filling her mind with thoughts of ordinary day-to-day-living matters.

I'll stop at the butcher, she thought, *to see if they have a small piece of meat for Lorenzo's supper. Then I'll do the laundry and iron my old silk shirt to wear to tomorrow's mass. Then I will write to Riccardo.*

Dear God, she thought, *please give me health and the strength I need to fulfill my duties and to see my children through.*

She had barely expressed that notion when she heard someone call, "Mother, Mother!"

It sounded like Lorenzo's voice. "Oh my Lord," she said, while crossing from Piazza Indipendenza to a side street that led to her rooms. *Is it him? And why is he here?*

Alarmed, she looked around and spotted him running toward her, waving a brown envelope. She felt her heart leap. Had something happened to Riccardo?

"It's from a notary in Florence. Look." Lorenzo showed her the sender's address. "It must be important; the postman made me sign for it."

A moment later, she looked up from the contents of the envelope. "Oh my God, It's a death notice …"

"Whose?"

"My old aunt in Castelvecchio. Poor woman, with all our troubles,

I forgot she even existed. She died two weeks ago," said Luisa, noticing the date of the letter. "Even if we wanted to go, it'd be too late to attend the funeral."

"I don't even remember her."

"Let's sit here for a moment," said Luisa, considering the length of the letter. She took a few steps toward one of the new wrought-iron benches. Lorenzo sat at her side and waited.

"I can't believe what I'm reading," she said, turning to the second page. "My aunt—whom I haven't seen in years—has made me the beneficiary of her modest property. Poor soul." She then sighed. "One must reconcile to the inevitability of death."

In amazement, she read the letter again, and beginning to grasp its positive implications, she raised her eyes heavenward and added, "It must be a sign from God that she thought of us."

"But what is it, exactly, Mother?" Lorenzo asked. "A house, a piece of land, money … what?"

"It's not clear. It just says 'property,' but there is a key at the bottom of the envelope." She dug out a small key with black iron scrolls and continued speaking in a somber tone. "The notary's comment and his trifling offer makes me think it's not that significant. Perhaps we shouldn't get too excited about it."

"Where is Castelvecchio, Mother?"

"In Tuscany. Somewhere between Florence and Pisa, on the banks of the Arno River. Let's go now," she said, putting the key and the letter in her bag. "We'll do some shopping and then go home to eat. After supper, we'll write your brother about this news."

She put an arm around her son and began to walk at a fast pace.

*****

Luisa tore the envelope open as soon as the postman left. She read Riccardo's telegram.

I know it will be a sacrifice, Mother, but if I were you, I'd go to Tuscany and appraise the matter personally.

Love, Riccardo

Luisa groaned inwardly.

What if it's a broken-down apartment in need of repair? Or mortgaged to the hilt and with unpaid taxes? What if the inheritance isn't worth the missed wages, the train fare, and all the other incidental expenses? It has been so hard to save a few pennies for the future. Now, she thought, *I'll risk squandering the lot on this trip of doubtful value.*

She was also apprehensive about the special fascist squads, or *squadristi,* who organized "punitive expeditions" against towns or associations that they branded as "subversive" solely because they did not support il Duce's regime. That year alone, they had burned and destroyed over forty headquarters of opposing parties, cooperatives, and workers unions. Innocent bystanders had been caught in these battles as well.

"Under these conditions, I don't feel too comfortable traveling in unfamiliar areas," Luisa told Lorenzo.

"I'll come with you, Mother, if that concerns you," he replied. "I'm sixteen years old now; I can protect you."

Luisa smiled kindly. "Yes, my dear," she agreed unconvincingly. "I should be all right with you by my side." *And you won't mind missing a few days at school,* she thought. "Yes, you'd better be with me."

Reluctantly, she arranged for a short leave of absence, notified Lorenzo's school, and bought the tickets.

"God willing," she said, boarding the train with her son, "the cost of this trip will be justified. Let's go visit these Tuscan chattels, whatever they may be."

*****

The journey was initially uneventful. However, when they reached Bologna, there was clamor and confusion on the station's platform as a long column of young fascists boarded the train. Rowdy and undisciplined, they shouted slogans: "Down with the communists! Kill the bastards! Viva Il Duce!" They pushed and shoved their way through, and scuffles soon ensued with angry civilians.

"You are a horde of ignorant brats," shouted an older man who had been pushed aside by that turbulent human tide.

"You are wrong, old fart," a youngster yelled back. "We are the *Figli della Lupa*—Sons of the She-Wolf. We are the future of Italy."

"Poor Italy," the old man replied.

"Poor us," echoed Luisa.

The Figli della Lupa was a fascist youth organization, named as a tribute to the old Roman legend that claimed that Remus and Romulus, the alleged founders of Rome, abandoned by their mother in the wild, were found, fed, and survived thanks to a she-wolf.

Several of them started singing one of their favorite tunes, whose words emphasized their importance in the party and their determination to be the scourge of the communists:

Allarmi, allarmi.
Allarmi siam fascisti,
Terror dei Comunisti …

At first, the fascist youth tried to resist the security police, whose barking and admonitions were lost in the roar of the shouting crowd. They shoved back and threw stones toward the advancing uniformed men. An officer looked at the ticking clock of the station and, apparently fearing that precious time was lost, slid his revolver out of the casing, pointed it in the air, and pressed the trigger. The loud bang resonated under the pensile roof, and suddenly the yelling and shoving subsided. Additional policemen, clubs in hand, crossed over the adjacent railways tracks and came to the platform. They moved toward the young crowd, which gradually turned around in silence and boarded the wagons reserved for them.

Luisa made an effort to hide her anxiety from her young son, and when she heard the whistle of the station master, she finally let a sigh of relief and sat back in her seat.

In Florence, Luisa and Lorenzo got off the express train. The young fascists again began to sing and yell their slogans from the open train windows: "Viva il Duce—Long live our Duce!"; "*Abbasso i comunisti*—Down with the communists"; "*A morte i traditori*—Death to the traitors!"

"The closest station to Castelvecchio is San Romano," said Luisa to her son, consulting the departures, "and it's over an hour wait. Let's get out of here and avoid being caught in this turmoil."

*****

They left their luggage at the depot and bought a mini map at the newspaper stand. Walking out of the station, they crossed the square. Once they entered Via de' Panzani, she found the sober elegance of the shops a temporary distraction from her apprehensions.

They progressed into Via de' Cerretani, and the spectacular view of the cathedral came suddenly into full view. Its multicolored yet sober marble façade, resplendent under the midday sun, left Luisa breathless. She made the sign of the cross as if that vision itself held some elements of the divine.

"So that's Brunelleschi's Cupola!" Lorenzo exclaimed. "Isn't that something, Mother?"

Luisa nodded her agreement.

They walked quickly through the interior of Santa Maria Novella, Luisa stopping in front of altars and holy images. Lorenzo pressed on, toward the contiguous rooms, where he knew from his readings that many drawings and some of Brunelleschi's winches and lifting devices were shown. Then they exited and stopped to admire Giotto's bell tower and, lastly, Ghiberti's Baptistery doors.

"The Gates of Paradise," Luisa said in admiration. "Now I know why they call it that." She attentively examined the ten door panels, admiring the sense of depth gained through linear perspective. Lorenzo rubbed his hand casually on the miniature head of a saint protruding from a bas-relief, his attention taken by a group of attractive female tourists nearby.

"Come on, son," Luisa said at the end of her prayer. "It's time to catch our train."

As they walked back toward the station, they heard a sound of drums in the distance. It grew louder as they advanced, and suddenly, from around the corner of Via De' Rondinelli, a parade of fascists in black shirts, olive green pants, and shiny black boots came marching. Several *milizia* soldiers blocked the way to civilians, giving priority to the parade.

"Hurry up, Lorenzo," Luisa said. "I don't want to be caught in the middle of these bloody fanatics."

"Now, Mother …!" Lorenzo admonished under his breath. A few meters away, fascists with cudgels were pushing a slow-moving couple against a wall.

He didn't have to add anything else. They both knew that comments against the regime were not a healthy practice. Ostracism, ill treatment, and even physical violence were the common responses of the regime to its detractors. Like one of Luisa's longtime friends, who had lost her job just because of a casual comment against a local fascist Hierarch. Or the university professor in San Donà who had lost his job for refusing to enter the party and now taught preschool children in the local church, earning barely enough to survive.

Grudgingly, mother and son had to wait until the parade was through.

"Now we have to hurry if we want to catch our train," said Lorenzo.

As they boarded the third-class coach, Luisa was out of breath from running. The door slammed shut behind them, and the train started with a jerk.

"After four years in power," she said, gasping for air and pointing to one of the many posters picturing Mussolini, "he hasn't done much to create jobs or help industry, but he sure as hell makes trains run on time. Look at that, son." She pointed to the clock hanging from the pensile roof of the platform. "It's three thirty sharp."

- III -

The empty booth of the local train had the typical smell of all economy compartments: stale air mixed with the acrid residues of burned coal, cigarette smoke, and a pungent smell of disinfectant wafting from the distant latrine.

"Carbolic acid," said Lorenzo, twisting his nose.

"I wish it could be as effective against certain people," said Luisa under her breath, "as it is with other parasites."

Lorenzo did not reply.

She knew he shared her opinion, just as she knew that he saw no merit in being so upset by those people. He lifted his mother's bag onto the high rack and lowered the windowpane to allow fresh air in.

He sat quietly near the window, his eyes avidly absorbing the view.

"You know, Mother," he said, gazing at the receding cityscape beneath the hills of Fiesole, "one day, I'd like to live in this city."

"Who knows? Perhaps one day you will," Luisa replied. "Fate conjures up stranger things than that. We are in God's hands. Who could have said, only weeks ago, that we'd be here in Tuscany today?"

Tuscany, she repeated in her mind, and for a fleeting moment, she allowed her mind to consider the inheritance. Wondering if, whatever it was, it would help improve her lot in San Donà so that she could buy a new piece of furniture, a proper writing desk for Lorenzo, add a few lire to her depleted funds.

But what if it's nothing at all? she thought. *What if I missed my wages and squandered my little savings on a worthless trip, for a foolish yearning? Let's hope I'll still have my job when I return. I wish my Riccardo would soon be back from Germany.*

She tried to put the matter out of her mind by reciting a silent prayer, and she finally began to relax.

Temporarily relieved of her anxieties, she finally took pleasure in observing the countryside unfolding before her eyes. She was captivated in that momentary theatrical illusion that she and the train itself sat motionless, while the scenery, with its luxuriant geometric fields, raced past them.

Farther away, at a slower pace, moved the gentle, rolling terraced hills with vineyards and silvery olive groves, the summit studded with villas and the typical Tuscan cypress trees that looked like dutiful sentinels or, as Lorenzo put it, painters' brushes temporarily poised over nature's canvas.

"That's how unscarred and pristine our region was before the war,"

Luisa said, with longing in her voice. "How many more years will pass before returning to this state?"

Every now and then, farmers working their fields near the railroad straightened for a moment, their bodies bowed to the ground. They raised their heads, held their spades with one hand, and waved at the passing train; then they returned to their chores. The pleasant smell of freshly cut clover grass now coming through the open window swept out the staleness in the air and added to their sense of comfort.

At one point, Luisa noticed in the distance little white forms huddled over a green slope not far from the railroad tracks. When the train got closer, she realized it was a cemetery, its grounds studded with white Carrara marble tombs and headstones geometrically arranged around a tiny redbrick chapel. Her heart suffered a pang at the thought that she had failed to visit her husband's grave before departing San Donà.

Forgive me, Roberto, she now invoked in her mind. *You know that I had intended to come. I just ran out of time. Oh, how I wished you were here with me. Please help me from heaven.*

She began to recite a silent prayer.

The train chuffed to a stop at several towns along their route and finally arrived in San Romano.

*****

"For Castelvecchio," said a station attendant, "you need to take the *carrozza* that shuttles between here and there."

Just outside the station, a man in his mid forties stood by his horse, feeding him some hay. He was modestly dressed in gray woolen trousers and a worn but clean brown leather jacket. When he saw Luisa and her son, he took a few steps in their direction, shouted a loud salute, and took their luggage. He had a friendly manner and talked at full volume, like a person with poor hearing.

"How far is Castelvecchio?" Luisa asked the coachman, as he helped her up into his old carriage.

"My name is Meo," he answered instead, "but everybody calls me Meino. I lived all my life around here; therefore, if you want to know anything, just ask."

"Thank you, Meino," said Luisa, raising her voice. "I am Luisa Lanzi, and this is my son Lorenzo. How far is Castelvecchio?"

"About four kilometers, on the other side of the river. It's a tranquil town. And in these times, it's no small consideration, but …" He stopped, seeming unsure whether he should go on.

Luisa urged him on. "Yes?" she said.

"Like many other places nowadays, it's rather short of work and opportunities."

"I see. Sorry to hear that."

"Where did you say you're going?"

"Number 7, via Francesca North."

"Where?"

Luisa repeated the address, a bit louder.

"Oh, It's the Villani property, isn't it?" he said, after some consideration. "Are you a relative?"

"The one and only. Maria Villani was my aunt. She left it to us."

"I'm glad for you. Maria was a nice lady; I knew her well. I gave her rides from time to time, to the station or to Monte Falco on Sundays." He paused and then said, "Hundreds of people came to the funeral."

"Unfortunately, we didn't make it," said Luisa. "We didn't find out in time." She wanted to ask him about the "property," as he had called it, but then thought better of it, fearing to appear too greedy, or to be too quickly disillusioned. At the same time, she couldn't stop her mind from thinking of it: *Will it be small? Will it be large? Will it be easy to sell? How much could it fetch? But what if it is mortgaged or falling apart?*

Meino loosened the reins, made a clicking sound with his tongue, and the carriage moved with a jolt. Its wheels drew a wide semicircle over the dusty grounds and entered a boulevard that ran parallel to the tracks.

The large graveled roadway was lined with majestic cypress trees, whose dark green color intensified the contrast with the strip of pale blue sky overhead. After traveling a straight course of about one kilometer, they crossed over the railroad tracks and headed north.

Meino turned toward them and said, "My regular stop is the Piazza del Comune, but since you're my only customers and the next train is hours from now, I'll take you to the house at no extra charge. It's about half a kilometer outside town, north of the bell tower."

"Thanks, Meino. You're a nice man."

"What?"

"I said you're very nice!" she shouted.

Lorenzo covered his mouth to hide his laughter.

As they crossed the bridge, they came in full view of a massive redbrick edifice situated on the right riverbank. It was flanked by a pier that extended like an arm across the river, forcing the water to rush through two narrow passages, one on the north side and one in the middle.

"What's that?" Lorenzo asked, pointing his finger.

"The Arno River," said Meino, turning toward him.

"That I know," said Lorenzo. "I mean that large brick structure over there."

"Oh, that's the old mill. Built in the fifteen hundreds by the Medici of Florence. Later, under the grandson of Cosimo, that low section that spans the river was added."

"You're quite knowledgeable!" Lorenzo yelled.

"For a cabbie, you mean? Well son, I wasn't always a cabbie, you see. I used to be a schoolteacher. I lost my job on account of my principles."

"You see, Mother?" Lorenzo whispered. "What's the point of study-ing under this system?"

"Don't let me hear statements like that," Luisa answered in a low voice.

"Anyway," Meino said, "we call that lower section *pescaia*——be-cause the deep-water pool on this side of it is full of good fish."

The water was swift and strong as it passed through the narrow constriction of the weir and flowed sluggishly and redolently in the wider basin that followed. Instinctively, Lorenzo looked to the other side, where the river course continued within its high banks.

"What kind of fish?" he asked.

"You name it, son: carp, eels, sturgeon—huge ones at that. I should know; I've caught some good ones myself. The original reason, though," he shouted, "was to control boats and barges and charge them a passage toll! Death and taxes," he added with a sneer, "have always existed, son. Mind you, never as bad as now, under this fascist government."

No one replied, and he glanced cautiously over his shoulder, as if regretful of having spoken his viewpoint so openly to strangers.

Once again, Luisa would have liked to ask more questions, but she was afraid to reveal too much of her disquietude to her son; being away from her job and San Donà made her unsettled. Then, turning her attention to the river, she noticed how much that particular site resembled the place where she and Roberto met secretly before getting married. She could still feel, in her memory, his gentle touch, the sweetness of his first kiss. Was this a sign? Was it a subliminal message from her spouse? She shook herself from her reverie as the coach approached the other end of the bridge.

The horse started to relieve itself, and Meino pulled slightly to the right and stopped. The falling urine sounded like rainwater coming down from a broken water pipe, and it made Lorenzo laugh and then squeeze his nostrils because of its strong ammonia odor.

"When nature calls …," said Meino, as if to excuse his horse. He turned in his seat, lifted his arm toward the left, and said, "There, you can see the town." He cracked his whip in the air, and the horse began to move again.

*****

Castelvecchio came into full view about half a kilometer to the north. It was a typical Tuscan town, with redbrick tenements covered with red roof tiles, still enclosed by crenellated medieval walls. Being far south of the front lines, it had survived the war unscathed, revealing its original numerous turrets and a majestic square-sided campanile. The domes and the smaller bell towers of three or four churches emerged from the rest of the buildings and tenements that appeared to be roosting around them.

"This is Piazza Dei Caduti—the Fallen Soldier Square," said Meino, pointing to his left. "The township and a few wealthy families pitched in to build this memorial. A couple of dozen of our youth died during the Great War."

"A couple of dozen?" Lorenzo uttered. "There were hundreds of deaths in San Donà—just on the day my father died."

Luisa made a gesture that made him desist from further comments. Memory brought back in vivid detail what had been the worst day of her life: November 12, 1917.

Meino cracked his whip in the air, and the blast almost caused Luisa to jump out of her seat. She again shook herself from her memories and looked at the square. It was quite large, and tall trees lined its entire perimeter. Diagonal pebble-filled paths directed to the center, where a large lead gray monument was located.

"It reminds me of the *Pietà,*" Luisa said.

It did seem inspired by Michelangelo's *Pietà* since it portrayed a seated woman, obviously a mother, holding her lifeless son in her arms.

"It must be so heartbreaking," Luisa said, "for a mother to lose her son." *Please, God*, she added silently, *don't let another war happen.*

The coach wobbled over the ancient Pietra Serena slabs that covered the town streets, and the bell tower came into full view.

"It's much taller than I had guessed from afar," Lorenzo said.

It looked about forty meters high. The uniformity of its redbrick façade was interrupted three quarters of the way up by a white circular space housing a massive clock. Its long, spear-shaped hands and distinctive Roman numerals were forged in black iron. It was almost six o'clock.

As they went under the bell tower, which was one of the main passageways to the town, Luisa noticed that the side walls were plastered with fascist slogans and a few funeral announcements. She shook her head. The clopping rhythm of the horse's hooves was amplified as the sound traveled upward, carried by the acoustics of the arched ceiling.

"It sounds like a cavalry platoon," Lorenzo observed.

They left the town behind and came upon what must have been, until recently, open countryside. On the north side, one could see that some of the land had been parceled off for development. Some of the spaces between older houses were slowly beginning to fill.

"Whoa!" Meino drawled, pulling on the reins and coming to a stop.

They were in front of a medium-sized villa, known in the area as a *viareggina,* due to its resemblance to the ones built in the seaside city of Viareggio. It was one and a half stories high, and the lower floor was half hidden below grade. It was a graceful-looking building, its basic square shape enhanced by two stone terraces, one in front and the other on its west side. Two sets of stairways joined the ground level to the terraces that provided access to the elevated main floor. The terrace on the west side was large, round, and conveniently shaded by a pergola of wisteria. The large windows of the façade were divided by granite mullions and had green Persian shutters. Its front garden was covered with flower beds filled with a variety of plants and fruit trees at the center; the pathways were packed with smooth river pebbles.

"Here we are," Meino said.

Luisa and Lorenzo looked at each other in silence. Then, simultaneously, their eyes ran upward to check the street number. It was number 7!

"I can't believe it," Luisa exclaimed. "If this is the place, it's better than I could have imagined."

It's a castle compared to where we live now," echoed Lorenzo.

"Yes," said Luisa ignoring the comparison, "and to think that that notary offered nothing for it."

"It's a beautiful property," Meino said. He handed the luggage to Lorenzo and then asked Luisa, "Will you be moving here, signora?"

She hesitated, taken aback by the question she had not even considered.

"Don't you like it?" insisted Meino. He clearly couldn't understand her hesitation.

"Yes. Of course I do," she finally answered. "It's better than I dared to hope. It's just that I never thought of living here. I don't know anybody in Castelvecchio, and then my poor husband …"

"You'd better consider it, signora," Meino interrupted. "It's a beautiful place. Besides, given the times and the poor economy, even if you found an honest buyer, you wouldn't get much for it. It'd be a pity.

Anyway, send for me if you need to go somewhere. Everyone knows me, and I'm always on duty, day and night." He shook Luisa's hand, lifted his hat, and left.

"What do you think, Mother?" Lorenzo asked.

She did not answer.

My family lived in San Donà since time immemorial, she was thinking. *I've grown and lived there, and friends and family connections contributed, in many different ways, to the feeling that makes one call a place one's home.*

She was proud of her town. The new church and the main bell tower had recently been rebuilt in the likeness of the one sited in the famous Piazza San Marco of Venice. She was even more proud of the significant role the people of San Donà, including her Riccardo, had played during the final phase of the Great War.

She closed her eyes and saw the calm waters of the Adriatic Sea lounging not far from the eastern side of town … and at the end of a long stretch of fertile countryside, the towering Julian Alps in the West. She heard in her mind the low murmur of the Piave River and saw its waters reddened with Italian blood during the offensive of 1917 … its south banks … where the Italian army had finally regrouped and held the front against the Austro-Hungaric forces at the cost of countless lives.

It wasn't easy to abandon a land drenched with the blood of relatives and friends who had fallen while defending it from the enemy … the soil where relatives and forefathers were laid to rest. She thought of her husband, Roberto, and imagined him as if he were asleep under two meters of soil in the small cemetery of San Donà. She thought she saw him smile at her, and she shook herself from that odd, disquieting vision as if caught in the act of acquiescence toward a new lover. *Yet, she thought, this would be such a beautiful place to live … I could really fall in love with it.*

"What can I say, son?" she finally replied. "The place is beautiful, but you can't discount so quickly the place where you lived all your life."

Lorenzo shrugged his shoulders.

"Besides," his mother continued, "as Meino said, there are no opportunities here, and I don't even know if we could afford the maintenance or the property taxes for a home like this."

She sighed and climbed the stairs to the side terrace, inhaling the sweet fragrance of the flowering wisteria clusters that hung from the pergola. The adjacent countryside to the north was framed between the rolling green hills and the distant Apennine Mountains. To the south, immediately beyond the road, lay open fields. Perhaps no more than a kilometer away ran the horizontal grassy line of the Arno's high banks. There was a whistle, and the trailing white smoke of a locomotive revealed the parallel course of the railway. Beyond it loomed the irregular treed summit of San Romano Alto and Monterpoli's hills.

Quite striking, she conceded reluctantly, while her husband's memory yanked at her soul. The thought alone of moving to this place felt to her like nurturing feelings for a new lover … an outright act of infidelity.

For a moment, she silenced her conscience and indulged in the idea of living again in her own house, and a large one at that, with a front garden, an orchard, and a back section of land.

If I didn't find a job, she pondered, *could I not raise chickens and rabbits? Use the land to good advantage and make up for lost wages? This place would certainly offer some benefits and a sense of well-being. But,* she thought again, *it would be hard to leave my Roberto, San Donà, the Piave River, the legacy of my land ...*

"I know you love San Donà, Mother," Lorenzo said, as if hearing her thoughts, "but this place looks good."

"Yet, as Meino said, work is scarce here. There, at least I have a job, modest though it may be."

"On the other hand," Lorenzo said, "if the place is hard to sell, what are we to do, Mother? We can't just give it away. Riccardo will return soon, and he'll help. Besides," he added with enthusiasm, "can you imagine how good it'd be for all of us to have our own room?"

"Wouldn't you miss your school friends?" Luisa asked mildly. She couldn't rid her mind of the images haunting her: the cemetery where husband, father, and dozens of relatives rested ... the familiar places.

"I would miss them a little," Lorenzo said, "but I'm sure I'd get used to this place and make new friends."

"Yes, you would," Luisa said. "I'll tell you what, son: Let's tell Riccardo. See what he thinks about it. After all, it's a difficult decision, and the whole family should be involved."

In saying so, she took the key from her purse and unlocked the door.

- IV -

The interior was as pleasant as the outside, with rooms spacious and well lighted by large double windows and French doors. The main floor contained three bedrooms, a studio, a formal dining room and sizeable kitchen, plus two bathrooms and other small service spaces. Two of the bedrooms faced the front street, or south, as did the entrance hall, which was accessible from the stairs connected to the front terrace. The kitchen fronted west and was reachable from the outside through the stairs connected to the round terrace. When its Persian shutters were open, the ample glass panes on the doors looked into the neighbors' side garden and the east side of their house. Farther away, the horizon was partly occupied by the round hump of Monte Serra. The furniture was mostly solid walnut and cherry, except for the white marble top of the kitchen table. It was tasteful and in keeping with the sober elegance of the house.

Lorenzo ran up and down the stairs, crying with excitement, "Look, Mother, another bedroom. I think I'd take this one." "Come and see,

Mother; there is another kitchen in the basement." And a few moments later: "The attic is quite large; your aunt kept extra linens and other stuff in there. There is lots of it."

With every door they opened, and every new, pleasant detail, it was as though Luisa was discarding another garment and getting closer and closer to the moment she would fall into the arms of her new suitor. She did not reveal this growing determination to Lorenzo yet. There were legal matters to be addressed, numbers to add up, and many other practical things to consider. Lastly, there was her emotional attachment to her birth place, the friends and acquaintances, and, finally, her dear Roberto, buried under the soil of their native town of San Donà.

How could she possibly leave him behind—renounce her weekly visits to his tomb and her lengthy conversations with him, in which she imagined in the silence of her mind his subtle answers, his words of encouragement, his love? Who would bring fresh flowers to his grave? She had shed so many soothing tears over his last resting place.

*****

Upon signing the inheritance papers, the notary confirmed Meino's opinion.

"Signora," he said unequivocally, "even if you found a buyer, under the present economic circumstances the house wouldn't fetch half its value. It'd be a real pity."

"But from your letter, I thought you'd make us an offer …," she said, knowing this to be the last impediment beyond which she would consent to her lover.

"I know," the notary interrupted. "I didn't know you or your situation then, and I made a ridiculous offer." He looked into her eyes.

"Taking advantage of opportunities is part of what I do for a living. Now, however, I've met you; I heard your story; and I don't want to take advantage of you. I can honestly tell you that if I were in your shoes, I'd keep the house and live there. One day, we'll see better times, and your home will again have its rightful value. Your children will be grateful to you."

That night, Luisa did not sleep. She lay in bed weighing the pros and cons of her possible choices. The house was certainly beautiful. The few people she had met appeared friendly and decent. Despite Meino's inference, the fascist presence seemed less intrusive here than in the north. And if she didn't find a job, would the orchard and raising chicken and rabbits make up for the lost wages? *Perhaps,* she concluded. Besides, Riccardo was due back soon, and between her small pension, the orchard, and his contribution, she was positive she could make ends meet.

As she rationally considered all the facts, her mind began to tilt in favor of the decision that would ultimately change her life and that of her family.

- V -

April 1931
Six years later

For Luisa, it had been hard to abandon her town, her people, the Piave River … to forsake the relished visits to her husband's tomb, where she spoke to him as if he were still alive. Despite this, she had finally opted for a new life in Tuscany in the knowledge that her sons would eventually benefit from this choice.

Times were difficult, and job opportunities were scarce—especially for those identified as non-fascists like the Lanzis, who did not adhere to fascist ideals or belong to the party. But at least here in Castelvecchio, they had their own roof, and between the products of the orchard, the chicken and rabbits she raised, and her meager pension, Luisa was able to keep her dignity and feed the family without renouncing her principles and without having to join the party, which she despised.

Luisa was concerned about the indigent economy and the lasting nature of the unrestrained totalitarian regime. At least for now, though, she could do nothing but hope and pray that her sons, though upholding their own personal convictions, could stay clear of troubles.

*****

One late afternoon, the bell rang three times at the Lanzis' home. Three short tones played at equal intervals, like the distress signal of the Morse code.

Luisa heard it from the kitchen. *Too late for the postman,* she thought, looking at the clock. *Who else can it be, then?*

These days, unexpected calls could often be unwelcome surprises.

The bell rang again, its sound more urgent, more ominous to Luisa's ears.

She wiped her wet hands on her apron and walked toward the family room, whose windows afforded a full view of the garden and the front gate. She walked past the closed door of Riccardo's study. Her thirty-one-year-old son must be still immersed in one of his projects, oblivious to the outside world. *So talented and dedicated,* she thought, *and not a permanent job offer yet.* She shook her head in frustration and walked on.

She squinted through the Persian shutters, which were closed as usual, both to shield the furniture from direct sunlight and for much-needed privacy. Her eyes focused on the gate through the three slats at eye level; they were slanted to allow looking without being seen.

Her heart jumped.

"*Gesù mio!*" she exclaimed, making the sign of the cross. Her heartbeat accelerated. "And now what?"

Parked on the graveled area, a few meters from the gate, was an ominous-looking black *Balilla* car with a military driver. Three men in the black fascist uniform stood chatting by the gate, impatiently waiting for it to be opened.

This does not bode well, she thought.

Even without her glasses, Luisa recognized, by his prominent belly and bullish posture, the podesta of Castelvecchio, the equivalent of a politically appointed mayor. The others, however, who, judging from the deferent manners of the podesta, looked even more important, were completely unknown to her. This was an additional reason for concern.

For a moment, she had the urge to call Riccardo and ask him if he had said or done something against the system, antagonized the authorities. She thought of telling him to run from the house. But to what end? The arm of the regime was far-reaching and vindictive.

Therefore, she bravely unlocked the door, stepped onto the terrace, and, resting her hands on the stone banister, said with feigned nonchalance, "Yes, may I help you?"

The three men voiced the compulsory *Al Duce* greeting, while performing the Roman salute, which, since 1928, had replaced the traditional handshake by order of the regime.

"Signora," shouted the podesta from the gate, "these two gentlemen from Rome would like a word with your son!"

"I have two sons," she said, trying to gain time, "Riccardo and Lorenzo. Which one are you looking for?"

"We wish to talk to the chemical engineer … that's Riccardo, if I remember correctly. Is he in?"

She came down the stairs and crossed the garden to unlatch the gate. *What do they want from my son? Has he done something? Not my Riccardo; he always keeps to his work … Please, Virgin Mary, save us from these nefarious people.*

"Yes," she finally said, "he is at home, attending to his own affairs. Why do you need to talk to him?"

"Don't worry, Signora Lanzi, there is nothing to be afraid of."

"I'm not afraid," she snapped, starting toward the house. "I'm just wondering." Luisa asked them to sit in the entrance hall and went to call her son. She entered his study, closed the door, and leaned against it to regain her breath. "Riccardo," she whispered.

"What is it, Mother?" he asked, keeping his eyes glued to the drawings on his desk.

"*Who* is it, is what you should be asking."

There was a long silence before he finally put down his pencil and raised his eyes. "Well?"

"Friends of il Duce are here to talk to you."

"Yes?"

"Three of them. The local podesta plus two high-ranking officials from Rome. Is there something I should know, Riccardo?" she asked. "Is it something you've said or done? What could they possibly want from you …?"

"I have no idea, Mother," he answered calmly. "But let's find out."

As they walked into the hall, the three men stood up simultaneously and performed another Roman salute. They resembled marionettes.

"Please sit down, signori," said Riccardo, ignoring the fascist ritual.

The podesta's brief introduction confirmed Luisa's guess. The two men from Rome were presented: the tall one was the Minister for Labor and Industry; the shorter, more corpulent man was an army colonel in charge of Security and Political Affairs.

"Please sit down," Riccardo repeated with cold politeness. He took a chair as well and then asked, "What could you possibly wish to discuss with me?"

Luisa hovered apprehensively near the kitchen door. She silently began to recite another prayer. All eyes turned toward the man introduced as the Minister of Labor.

"Please allow me," he said, removing his hat and placing it on his knees. He smooth his dark, shiny hair with his right hand. "I am the bearer of good news, Ingegnere."

"Really?" Riccardo exclaimed with exaggerated puzzlement. "And what would that be?"

"I am sure you are familiar with the San Romano distillery," said the minister.

"How could I not be, given my profession?" he replied. "In fact, being so close, it's one of the places where I applied earlier on. I even left some of my research papers with them. No comment or reply was ever received. Nothing, as though I did not exist."

Everyone fell into an embarrassing silence, and Luisa bit her lip as if to choke back a groan of concern.

"Excuse my digression," Riccardo concluded in a more neutral tone, "but what bearing has the San Romano distillery with this visit?"

"The operation has been less than satisfactory. Presently, several years since its inception, the project is not yet—how shall I put it?—self-sustaining, and the investors are becoming anxious. We need to find a new director to reorganize the distillery and show some profit."

"New blood is necessary," added the colonel with a broad smile, "and for the right person, in addition to the technical management of the San Romano distillery, there are other interesting projects. Projects of even larger scale, to be built near the capital."

"From what we have heard," said the minister, "that person would appear to be you!"

Luisa felt as if a weight had been lifted from her chest. She silently thanked the Madonna for the escaped danger, and then walked toward the far corner of the room and sat quietly on a wicker armchair, waiting. She was not yet convinced these black devils were merely harbingers of good news.

Riccardo did not flinch. "Why is the present director unable to produce better results?" he asked.

"I am afraid he doesn't have the fundamental technical background," answered the minister.

"Why is he in that position, then?" he said mercilessly.

"It must have been a necessary political appointment," the colonel admitted flatly.

"Really?" Riccardo said under his breath.

Luisa hoped he would not voice the words probably crossing his mind: *Why don't you call it for what it is, you black-shirted bastards— nepotism, corruption …* Though enjoying the growing embarrassment of the fascist dignitaries, she was still worried about possible consequences.

"These things do occur sometimes," said the minister, "but now we are here, and we intend to remedy the situation."

"But," Riccardo continued after a moment of reflection, "how did you happen to think of me? It puzzles me to receive such an offer now, after so many refusals in the past. And since I have not modified my views, pray tell me, what on earth has changed now?"

"Well," said the minister in a calm, conciliatory tone, "your fortune has suddenly changed for the better."

"My fortune?" Riccardo exclaimed, as if the word had been a lashing to his face. "I am a man of science, I don't rely on 'fortune' or fiction. I rely on my own merits and on facts. Hence, forgive my insistence, sir, but I really would like to know why me … and why now?"

The three men looked at each other. Then the minister nodded, and the colonel opened his black leather attaché case. He lifted a white sheet of paper and handed it to Riccardo.

"Please read this," he said. "Everything will be clear."

*****

As he took the letter and looked at it, Riccardo recognized the writing of an old French colleague. He felt the emerging pull of a smile at the corners of his mouth. He covered it with his right hand and coughed lightly. Then, showing no other visible reaction he began to read.

Eccellenza:

I have been contacted on behalf of your esteemed government on a business matter.

This matter concerns the maximization of earnings related to the industrial output of an Italian distillery specializing in the utilization of dregs of pressed grapes.

It is an honor for me personally, and as a French citizen, to be considered an "expert" by no lesser personage than an official of your duce, Mr. Benito Mussolini.

However, I am also a little ... baffled by Your Excellency's inquiry requesting these services from abroad when you are fortunate to have in your midst the real expert in this field. The very person who, I am happy to state, taught me most of what I know on the subject matter.

Whether an oversight by your esteemed department, or an intentional political choice, under the circumstances, I am sure you will understand that I would consider it preposterous to accept your kind request, flattering though it may be.

Yours truly,
Jean Claude Dessault

P.S. If by any unfortunate circumstance you intentionally or unknowingly ignore the name of the person I refer to, please allow me the opportunity to enlighten you by supplying his name and address:

Ingegnere Riccardo Lanzi, Via Francesca No. 7, Castelvecchio, (PI), Italie

Riccardo smiled, savoring a moment of gratification. "Dear Jean Claude," he said, handing the letter back to the colonel, "such an honorable man!"

"Well, now you understand *why you*, Ingegnere Lanzi," said the minister.

"Indeed I do! And I also understand that my expertise is known and appreciated abroad but not in my own country. Nemo profeta in patria, as our Roman ancestors used to say. They were right; one can never be a prophet in one's own country. Particularly when the country is Italy and you don't share the prevailing views!"

"This is no longer so. Anyway, let's forget the past and concentrate on the present opportunity. Are you interested?"

A deep sense of uneasiness overtook Riccardo. He could hardly contain the loathing for these men in black shirts, who could, with identical ease and lack of scruples, cajole or threaten the people they encountered. He felt revulsion for the system they represented: one that allowed or even promoted the type of base, amoral person who could pervert any concept of social justice for the benefit of false creeds or personal aggrandizement. He felt abhorrence for a regime that filled any position, anywhere, with anyone—regardless of personal qualities, qualifications, and experience—just as long as he or she belonged to their damned party.

For a moment, it seemed that he was going to refuse the offer—to answer, *I am not interested.* Yet this was the chance of a lifetime.

A glimpse of the opportunities, challenges, and potential accomplishments within a project like this was appealing. Its scientific considerations, the commercial value for the area, and, last but not least, his family's benefits were such that … *But how realistic is it,* Riccardo wondered, *to expect to gain this commission, from these people, without making personal compromises, undesirable concessions, loss of self-respect?*

"Are you interested?" the minister persisted.

"I might be, but only if I had full control of the project. Please don't misunderstand," said Riccardo, noticing a reaction. "It's not for me that I ask; it is necessary for the effectiveness of the job. The technical papers I wrote on these matters explain why. They are not exciting reading," he added with modesty, "but their findings and recommendations have been considered valid and useful by many experts. Besides, I would be completely governed by them. They'll help you to understand my premise."

He paused for a moment until the others indicated their agreement. "The other thing I wish to make clear," he added conclusively, "is that I am a technician. As such, I am not interested in politics, and I take no part in parades or assemblies, local or otherwise."

There was a long moment of silence. Luisa bit her lip again as if, for a fleeting moment, she was almost sorry to have instilled such honesty in her son.

The podesta glanced at his superiors, his body language suggesting that he expected them to castigate this arrogant man. His anticipation, however, was soon dispelled, as he apparently detected a smile on the lips of the minister.

"We get the drift," said the hierarch, "but for your knowledge and peace of mind, please understand that this project has received clearance in the most eminent places." He nodded knowingly. "No need to mention names. Even politics, as you would probably call it, will be waived in this case."

Those were the minister's words. By his restrained expression, it was evident, though, that he resented anyone who was apparently immune to the fear he usually saw in the eyes of people he spoke with. It must have been hard for him to resist his desire to wield his authority and power, to verbally put this man in his place. He waited a moment before he spoke again. Then the obedience to his instructions and the objective in this visit prevailed.

"By the way," he added calmly, "I have two more questions for you. How soon would you be available? And what's your monetary expectation?"

"On a temporary basis, in a week. Permanently in one month," Riccardo answered. "As for your second question, you will find my recommendation for wages for all personnel contained in the papers I spoke about. Let me get you a copy."

He left and soon returned and handed out a pamphlet to each of them.

"Thank you, Ingegnere Lanzi," said the minister. "We will be in touch soon with all the details. This is my card. Don't hesitate to call me if you encounter obstacles in your way."

The three visitors stood up in unison, straightened their uniforms, and clicked their heels.

"Al Duce!"

- VI -

July 21, 1931

Ingegnere Riccardo Lanzi walked briskly to the front of the convening crowd of workers at exactly eight thirty, as established. His straight posture, open face, and energetic stride made him look like a field officer reviewing his troop.

He was dressed in his typical denim suit, a dark blue shirt, and no tie. A white slide rule stuck out of his front pocket. His unpretentious attire was in sharp contrast with that of his predecessor, Signor Pietro Ligato, who, clad in a showy three-piece suit, walked sheepishly several steps behind him.

Riccardo stopped at the center of the yard, in front of the ninety-odd employees facing the Arno River, and unceremoniously climbed on top of a drum of chemicals, using it as his improvised platform. The informal gesture provoked smiles and a few comments among the workers.

"Good morning to all of you," he said. "I am Riccardo Lanzi, the new technical director of this distillery. I apologize for not supplying you with a fancier location, or at least with chairs, but as you can see, I am sharing the Spartan accommodations with you." He noticed that some of the workers nodded in agreement. "It will be an additional incentive for me to be brief," he said, "and incidentally, conciseness will be the trademark of my tenure."

He paused to let his eyes roam around the crowd.

"The other trademarks," he continued, "will be complete dedication to my work, a determination to succeed, and the pursuit of the financial improvement of the distillery. I will only ask of you things that I'd do myself. I want to see the redistribution of earnings, starting with those who believed and invested in this venture, and filtering down to each and every one of you. Under my term, raises and promotions will be received strictly on merit. Please don't waste your time and mine in useless pressures or recommendations from powerful friends; they won't work with me! I believe in fairness and justice, not nepotism."

The workers, caught by surprise by Riccardo's straightforward words, were clearly astonished. However, surely those who were satisfied to collect their checks at months' end, thanks to their political connections, were not reassured by this man who seemed to mean what he said. Others, who had suffered the injustices of nepotism, certainly felt their day had finally come.

"With your help, I intend to make this company a profitable one," Riccardo said, "and I'm prepared to do whatever it takes to make it happen. What about you?"

There followed a sudden silence. Never before had the workers been invited into an open dialogue with management. The uneasy stillness was finally broken by an enthusiastic female voice who yelled, "Of course we are!"

Riccardo turned toward her. She was an attractive young woman, with dark chestnut hair and dark brown eyes. She was taller than most of the men beside her, and from the white coverall she wore, he assumed her to be from the chemical department. Her voice, clear and pleasing, had a ring of authority. Her natural demeanor seemed to transcend the common attribute of her working clothes.

"Aren't we all?" she loudly challenged, turning toward the crowd.

"Yes. Yes!" shouted a small chorus of voices.

Riccardo nodded his thanks and looked at the young woman again. What a smile! Their eyes locked for the briefest, yet timeless moment. He tore his gaze away from her face and let his eyes rove over the crowd.

"And now," he concluded with a candid grin, "let's return to work, for that is what we are being paid for."

*****

This was the position Riccardo had always longed for. It was the place where, once his theories were proven correct, he would have the power to advance the interest of poor farmers as his father had done before him, help agriculture, and to contribute, if in a small way, to the economy of the region. He could finally promote an industrial sector that had become stagnant and obsolete. If he could only keep in check his aversion for the regime and those who supported it, he could finally make his dreams come true.

He jumped down from the barrel and walked toward his office.

Signor Ligato, plainly stunned by the informal, if pointed, speech, and its abrupt end, looked at the already dispersing crowd, raised his arm, and yelled what, for the past ten years, had been the ritual opening and closing of any official speech or ceremony. "Al Duce!"

A lukewarm choir of voices replied, "Al Duce."

*****

A week later, Riccardo and Signor Ligato stood on the main floor of the office complex, five steps up from ground level. On the left side were the executive offices, and opposite was the accounting department. A travertine marble stairway led to the second floor, to the drafting section and the boardroom. The two men were to discuss, as Riccardo put it, a more appropriate allocation of space.

"Where will my office be now?" Ligato asked. He kept adjusting his jacket and pulling on his shirt collar, as if it had suddenly become a size too small.

Riccardo did not seem to hear him. His back was to the glazed entrance, which flooded the hallway with daylight, his long shadow projected over the shiny granite floor. His eyes shifted from one office to the next as if to measure, in his mind, the ideal positions of each desk and the least wasteful motions for its occupants.

Suddenly, he turned around and looked straight into Ligato's eyes. "Don't worry," he said tonelessly, "you can keep your office. I'm more comfortable in a frugal work environment." Then he nodded toward the adjacent office occupied by a voluptuous young lady who sat at her desk, dedicating great attention to her nails. "What other function does she perform?" he asked.

"She is my assistant," said Ligato, twisting his fingers and shuffling his feet.

"I had already assumed that. But what skills does she have?"

The other man raised his shoulders and said awkwardly, "It's kind of nice to have extra talent around you, you know?"

"Unless her 'talents' are directly applicable to the business of the distillery," Riccardo curtly interrupted, "you'll have to dispense with her services. This will apply to anyone else, male or female, related or not, party member or not. My own assistant," he said, staring straight into Ligato's eyes, "will be the best draftsman I can find."

"Yes, sir!" Ligato mumbled, while standing almost to attention. "I understand."

"One last thing. From now on, please confine your activities to strictly administrative functions and curtail unnecessary expenditures."

*****

The following week, under the pretext of needing to freshen up the dark walls of his office for better lighting, Riccardo removed the pictures of Mussolini, King Emmanuel III, and several framed fascist slogans. After the paint job was finished, he replaced the pictures with technical drawings and blueprints suitable to his workspace.

I hope I'm not overdoing it, he thought. And then: *Why are my principles so often in conflict with my self-interest?*

It was irritating, but he forced these considerations out of his mind and went forth with his plan. He had the common door to Ligato's office removed. Finally, he ordered a section of the side wall opened to allow the installation of an additional window From there, he could observe the vast yard with its several edifices and all the movements between them. He also had a clear view of the front gate, the incoming and outgoing traffic, and the scale where the loads of grapes dregs were weighed on arrival.

Now he felt ready to introduce the innovations he had planned and put into practice for his academic projects. *Hopefully,* he thought, *they won't stand in my way.*

- VII -

Since the day of Riccardo's introductory speech at the distillery, Patrizia Berti, the enthusiastic young woman who had yelled her support at the assembly, had not ceased thinking about the new young director.

She had previously heard "news" of a new appointment, but when Ingegnere Lanzi was mentioned, it didn't strike a note of recognition, and she wondered what kind of person to expect. It didn't matter anyway, as she did not have much respect for the stuffy Mr. Ligato, as she called him. His scarce technical knowledge, his loose administrative style and favoritism for party acolytes, and even his garish clothing were, in her mind, indicative of a mediocre, decadent mind. Although she had been firm in defusing his initial attentions and unsolicited compliments, she did not like the way he kept looking at her. Therefore, she always avoided any unnecessary contact with him. At one point, she had feared for her job, but fortunately, there weren't many people with her qualifications in San Romano or the neighboring towns.

At worst, she thought, *the change at the helm might bring a breath of fresh air, and perhaps, with any luck, even more honesty.*

During his short, incisive opening address, she had been positively impressed by this new man with a slight northern accent. She also liked his handsome, open face; slender features; and his exceptionally blue eyes. He had cold eyes, except for the moment they had locked on to hers—and she had felt her knees tremble under the weight of her body.

The first impression wasn't bad at all.

Later that day, she was told that a meeting with the "new boss" had been scheduled. She made a brief examination of her conscience and decided that she had nothing to fear. In fact, depending on her reading of the new director, she might even tell him some of her concerns.

No, perhaps it was too dangerous. That wasn't a good idea.

On Monday, moments before the meeting, she made a brief visit to the lavatory, and finding her frowning image reflected in the mirror, she laughed mockingly at her pensive expression.

Most of the time, when doing household chores and singing, or riding her bike down the hills of Monterpoli, or sitting at her desk preparing the gradation of dregs, she completely forgot about her appearance. She laughed when men told her that she was *bella,* or that she resembled a movie actress. She completely ignored the occasional whistle or the appreciative if vulgar comments men made as she pedaled her way home and the wind made her skirt rise above her knees. She never placed much importance in those comments about her looks. After all, her mother always told her that what counted most in a person was one's mind, one's heart, and one's actions. She believed that as well, of course.

Now, however, just moments before presenting herself to the new, young director, she found herself standing in front of that mirror, looking critically at her reflection; wrapped in that coverall, she felt it framed her like the white borders of a black-and-white photograph. Dissatisfied, she shook her head, took her brush from her pocket, and quickly arranged one side of her silky dark hair toward the back. Unsolicited, a daring thought crossed her mind: *How would he react,* she thought, *if I entered his office, put my arms around his neck, and kissed him?* She laughed and pinched her cheeks and applied gloss to her lips. The white marble-tiled walls still resounded with her laughter as the door of the lavatory slammed shut behind her.

After a few steps in the corridor, her expression was again unfathomable. However, her heart beat faster in anticipation, a mixture of hope and trepidation.

Patrizia was proud of the fact that she had been able to save the dignity of her impoverished family with her job. Proud that her position was owed solely to her qualifications and abilities and not, as in many other cases, to "friends" of the regime. But—and in that day and age, there always seemed to be a *but*—would the fascist apparatus allow the loss of control of preferential treatment for certain clients, kickbacks to the party? Would the new director really prevail over the old one? Would he really be as fair as he had sounded? Would she dare tell him those matters that had been troubling her? And finally, would he like her?

She knocked lightly, waited for a response, and entered Ingegnere Lanzi's office, as the inconspicuous metal door sign read.

"Good morning," he said, gesturing for her to sit in front of his desk, his lips sketching a fleeting smile.

He is even better at close range, Patrizia thought.

His smile, his uncontrived appearance, and his manners emanated a sense of purposefulness and power that inspired confidence.

"Ah!" he said in a tone of recognition. "I get to meet my first supporter in this distillery. I hope that we shall be allies."

He got up and shook her hand. A pleasantly firm handshake.

"You can count on it, Ingegnere," she replied, "if you keep your promises."

He acknowledged the hint and laughed heartily.

They sat, and after some introductory questions, he flipped a few pages of a file he held in front of him. "From what I see, all reports concerning you are very flattering, Miss Berti," he stated.

"Thank you."

As he raised his eyes and met her limpid, bold stare, his heart seemed to beat at a quicker pace. He tried to avoid those enticing brown eyes— that gaze so openly sincere, so innocent.

"Where did you get your training?" he asked.

"The theory at a Viareggio college. The practical part here, from my predecessor who retired two years ago." He made no comment and she continued. "When I heard of the job opening, I offered my services. For half of his pay, until I had proven my worth."

"I also see," he said, "that you are our … 'de facto' first-aid nurse." He raised his eyes. "It says that after the accident described here, you took care of several wounded people. What happened, exactly?"

"A bad accident. The main boiler exploded during tests, and several people were badly wounded. Scalding from boiling water, cuts caused by falling glass and other debris, bruises and contusions, a few broken limbs from falls. A fair amount of blood, confusion, cries … but at the end, it wasn't as bad as we had initially feared."

"An impressive sangfroid, if I may say so."

"*Merci,* Monsieur le Directeur," she replied, taking the bait. "I had some first-aid training, and blood doesn't scare me, so I helped."

"You are too modest."

"I am not modest, just factual. I took over because there was no other alternative and those wounded people needed help. So I cleaned their wounds, disinfected them, stopped or reduced the bleeding, applied bandages. I did whatever common sense suggested until the ambulance came."

"My compliments to you," Riccardo said. "Most people in your position would have taken the opportunity to inflate the importance of their involvement."

She did not reply. She lifted her shoulders, raised her eyebrows, and smiled.

"Do you like your job?" he asked.

"Yes, I do."

"What do you like about it?"

"The process itself, and the fact that I can work alone, and as long as I do things right, be my own boss. Even hum a song as I work," she added, smiling. "Besides, I do need it. For the money, I mean. I also have my mother to look after, and as you know, there aren't many opportunities in our area, particularly for women."

"Is your father not living?"

"No. He died in October of 1917, during the battle of Caporetto. Or, to be more precise, the *rout* of Caporetto."

"I'm sorry to hear that." He knew too well what it meant to suffer war losses. There was a moment of silence. His thoughts carried him far away.

"Is there anything you don't like about your job, Miss Berti?" he finally went on.

She looked straight into his eyes, her forehead producing a light wrinkle as she took a deep breath. She seemed on the point of saying something, but thought better of it.

"Well … not really."

"Go on, you can talk frankly with me." His tone was encouraging.

*****

Patrizia wondered if she was embarking on a dangerous course. She could not afford to lose this job. Should she tell him now or wait until she knew whether to trust him or not? What if he betrayed her confidence? What if Ligato, through his connections, took revenge against her, and even him? She wasn't sure which of the two possibilities was more disturbing.

She stared right back into that clear, blue gaze and felt as if she were looking into his soul. *Yes,* she concluded, *I'm going to tell him.*

"As I said, I need this job …"

"I hear you perfectly, signorina. You can trust me. Please go ahead."

"It's not really about my job as such. As I said to you earlier, I like my job."

"What is it, then?"

"It's that I am uncomfortable when people tamper with my reports," she blurted out.

"I don't understand."

"Sometimes, for the analysis of the dregs certain land owners, I am asked to sign my report without entering its alcohol content."

"Please go on," he encouraged her.

"Well, Ingegnere," Patrizia said, lowering her voice, "why on earth would they want me to sign an incomplete report, were it not to fill in whatever alcoholic gradation they wanted? And always for the same people?"

"I think we both know why, Miss Berti, but did you report this matter to my predecessor?"

It was obvious to her that he didn't want to mention him by name. "He is the one who forced me to do so," she said. Her eyes appeared glazed by tears, but her voice was firm, her head high. "Believe me," she continued, "I did consider telling someone else, but whom? I would have done it if I thought it would benefit the distillery. But whom could I tell? And then, with me gone, perhaps someone even weaker would have been installed in my place—someone who would have resisted the distortion of facts even less. I tried to reason with Signor Ligato, but to no avail. Therefore, my conclusion was that if I openly rebelled, I would have certainly lost my job—the only source of income for me and my family—and the distillery might have been even worse off."

Riccardo was mute, but his face now showed his internal rage. In addition to Ligato's incompetence, it seemed to say that he'd also dared to abuse his position. He was silent for a while. Then, as if touched by the trust she had put in him, his face softened and he said, "Miss Berti, when are your next reports due?"

"Next Friday. However, Salani is not due with another load for a couple of months."

"When they come, fill in all the correct information, and then we shall see ... Come to me if you have any problem." He looked at her again and added, "Anything else you wish to say?"

"No, thank you. I'm afraid I have already said too much."

In a way, she was glad to have relieved her conscience of an unwanted weight. On the other hand, she still feared the revenge of the people connected with the party. What would she do if she lost this job? How could she support her mother?

"Don't be afraid, signorina," said Riccardo, as if reading her thoughts in her darkening eyes. "No one will harm you while I am here. You have nothing to fear. You will do your job as you should," he calmly concluded.

He consulted his watch. There were a few more minutes before the next appointment. He should ask something aimed at revealing more of her life.

"Where do you live?" he asked. It didn't seem such an intelligent question. In fact, self-assured as he was in professional matters, he seemed to lack a natural talent for the chattiness required in casual conversation. His puzzled expression seemed to say, *With two university degrees to my account, is this all I can to come up with?*

"Two and a half kilometers from here," she said, "near Monterpoli. It's only about twenty-five minutes away by bike. Twenty, when I feel really energetic. The ascent to the hill is rather steep."

Before he could ask another question, the siren announced the lunch break. They rose from their chairs, and he walked to the door.

"It was very nice meeting you, signorina. Remember," he said, as they shook hands and their eyes locked once more, "you can come to me if you have any problem."

*****

When Patrizia left, Riccardo looked at his right palm, as if to find the traces of her hand. *Such strength,* he thought, *from such a seemingly delicate hand.* He was glad to have noticed that no ring adorned her fingers.

*****

In the corridor, Ligato's office door was halfway open. His flabby face peeked through. "I hope you are satisfied with your interview, signorina," he said with a sneer.

Patrizia's heart jumped inside her chest, and her legs felt unsteady. "Yes, I am," she replied. As she spun around to return to her office, she noticed his lips curl up into a mischievous smile, while his covetous eyes descended toward the lower part of her body.

"We shall see …," she heard him mutter.

"Yes, we shall," she whispered through her teeth.

- VIII -

Patrizia and Riccardo did not have the chance to speak to each other again for about two weeks. Riccardo was totally absorbed in his projects, and his heavy work schedule did not leave him any time to socialize.

Yet, to his surprise, the memory of their meeting lingered in his mind. He did see her every now and then from his window as she crossed to the guardhouse to pick up the bills of lading or when directed to his building to consign the analysis of the dregs. He liked her somber elegance and poised manners. *A probable residue of the college she had mentioned during her first interview,* he thought. He didn't remember the name or the place, and he regretted not asking more questions about her life when he'd had the opportunity.

He was surprised at his thoughts. He also realized that, regardless of his academic achievements, his social skills were abysmal.

On the business side, he had rectified the initial problems with the experimental equipment, and the laboratory tests for extracting oil from the seeds of the dregs had given positive results. Now, with the help of the lab, he had to render this oil edible. This supplementary process and the greater discipline and spending control he had established had transformed the money-losing plant into a profitable one. These factors were duly observed by the shareholders and by politicians in charge of the industry department in the capital.

For Riccardo, though, these were the less important, if more visible, results of a single experiment that confirmed his theories. He saw, decades ahead of others, the need to extract edible and industrial oil and create precious resources from unthinkable secondary or tertiary sources. But now it was time for him to leave the oil purification task to the lab and to concentrate on his other project—the one that would use every single part of the dregs, transforming them into another source of food, or energy, or chemical, rather than the expense of their disposal costs.

For this to happen, several important pieces of equipment needed to be designed. His vision was ambitious: he would need a new centrifuge to accelerate the separation of the outer skins from the seeds, an efficient method of reblending the parts after processing, and a super press and drier to eliminate every bit of remaining moisture. Finally, he would need a compactor to press the product into small bricks or briquettes for easy handling.

He hoped the end product would turn out to be what his preliminary experiments had shown possible. If so, in addition to supplying the distillery with free energy, the surplus briquettes could be sold at a lower cost than firewood and earn additional money.

*****

"Where is the equipment pledged for our program, Luigi?" Riccardo asked the board director, who had come to the distillery upon his request.

"It was agreed by the board and budgeted since the beginning of my tenure. However, though ordered in time, it has not been delivered as promised."

The two men were on the second floor of the office complex, in a rectangular room furnished with a large ash wood table surrounded by about a dozen black leather chairs. One of the smaller walls was almost entirely covered by a blackboard that still showed chalk residues of erased writing. Windows facing the river made up the entire opposite wall. Parallel to the table ran the longer wall, decorated with regional maps of Italy, indicating wine-producing areas and graphics related to yearly production. The room was used only for rare board meetings or, as in this instance, when Riccardo wished to be as far as possible from the indiscreet ears of Signor Ligato.

"So far," Riccardo insisted, "we haven't even been told when to expect it."

Luigi Baroni shifted his weight on his chair, pulled on the front of his beige jacket, and then removed invisible lint from his sleeve. "The money for the copper sheets to build your boiler," he finally said with a pained expression, "has been diverted."

"Why?"

"Because there are other worthy causes to consider, I'm told."

"What worthy causes?"

"Riccardo, why do you always ask *why? What? Where?* And all that?"

"Because it's my job, Luigi. I need clear and specific information if I am to perform as expected. In my field, generalities bring no results. So, unless you wish me to go directly to Rome for answers, you should give me more details." Riccardo stopped, placed his pen beside the writing pad, and waited. His body, clad in his usual dark blue denim jacket, cut a sharp outline against the white wall.

"Please don't tell anyone that I told you," said Luigi. "I'm not supposed to know it either, but I heard that the money was used to build a new sport arena in Leghorn ... but don't worry, we are pretty well positioned for the next allotment of funds."

"Fantastic," Riccardo said. "Mussolini's son-in-law builds an arena in Leghorn; another hierarch builds a boudoir for his lover or a bidet for his aunt. Meanwhile, the industrial progress of the country should patiently wait for the next allotment of funds."

"Shhh. *Don't* let *them* hear you say those things."

*****

Riccardo hadn't talked to Signorina Berti for weeks. That day, seeing her coming toward his building, he had the urge to open his office door. As she went by, he had a long, wistful look at her young, slender figure, which, though wrapped in the common one-size-fits-all white gown of the chemistry department, could not hide her beautiful feminine figure. She passed by his door without turning her head, and after a few moments of idleness, he returned to his work, thinking that he should have stopped her.

He turned his full attention to the drawings in front of him, but his thoughts were soon disrupted by a dissenting voice rising in anger. It was *her* voice. Riccardo got up and approached the door.

"These are the correct reports for Salani's load, and that's where I intend to put my signature," she said. "Not on a blank piece of paper."

Her voice, he thought, *musical as it sounds, also denotes a strong character.*

"I know I have signed blanks before, but I will not do it again."

"My dear signorina …"

"What's going on?" Riccardo asked from the doorway.

She turned around. "Good morning, Ingegnere," she uttered. Then she lowered her voice before continuing. "I think Signor Ligato should answer your question."

Still sitting behind his desk when Riccardo entered, the man leaped up as if propelled by springs. His face was red and his hands pressed on the top of his desk as if he wished to push it below the floor.

"It's a minor administrative matter," he said, "and in my capacity of commercial director, I can solve it myself."

Riccardo stepped into the room and quietly closed the door behind him. The deliberate slow action made his gesture even more eloquent. He turned toward Ligato, his expression unchanged.

"That is where you are mistaken, Mr. Ligato," he said in a low, calm voice. "As overseer and chief responsible for the welfare of this distillery, I don't consider myself above any details, or 'minor matters,' as you call them. Let's hear it, please."

Ligato's red face turned white. "Mr. Salani," he said, after clearing his throat, "is a well-known contributor to party funds. To repay him for his generosity, through an arrangement endorsed by local authorities, it was decided to concede a higher gradation on the dregs that come from his farms. Now this junior employee not only declines to sign the necessary papers, but even has the gall to raise her voice to me."

"How many 'well-known contributors' do we have the pleasure of counting as our clients?" Riccardo asked.

"About six or eight, I think."

"Mr. Ligato, math is an accurate science. How many, exactly?" His tone left no room for guesses.

"Twelve," he spat out. "But I assure you that they are all approved …" He couldn't finish the sentence.

"Sit down and listen carefully," Riccardo said. "You need to remember that my job is to increase profits, to create job security, to enhance—if only by a little—the benefits to poor, hard-working farmers. I thought I made this clear the first time. Obviously, I should have also spent a few words describing what I am *not* here for. Allow me to correct my omission."

He inhaled deeply. "I am not here to reward undeserving individuals, or to subsidize any party, or to create preferential treatment. The only people entitled to and deserving of any regard are the owners of the company, the very people who have invested their own money in this venture and who are paying for my work and yours. I want a full list of the beneficiaries of your generous treatment, and I want it stopped now. You shall process the Salani analysis as submitted by Miss Berti."

A scornful little smile surfaced to Ligato's lips. "You don't have the authority to do this. I'll talk to the podesta," he said with a shrill voice.

Riccardo walked straight to Ligato's desk and reached for the telephone. "Is that what you think?" He then extracted from his pocket the business card the minister had given him.

Riccardo was fully aware of the risk involved in his move. What if the minister was not there? Or worse yet, what if he sided with Ligato? Hell, he had pulled riskier stunts than this one as a young officer. He remembered that day on the Piave Line, when he'd removed all able defenders from a critical section of the west trench, ordered that dead soldiers with rifles be positioned in their place, and repelled the attackers with the very soldiers shifted from the previous line. He hoped to be as lucky in his present ploy.

"What are you doing?" Ligato asked. Curiosity, fear, and indignation rang in his voice.

"I am calling a certain minister in Rome. I am sure he would like to hear of my problem."

Ligato pressed the switch on the telephone's cradle. "It won't be necessary. There is no problem. I will do what you ask." His voice, shaded by arrogance only moments before, was now draped in resignation.

Riccardo returned the telephone. "Yes," he said in a low, cold tone, "and advise your podesta, and whomever else is behind these schemes, to play at their own games and stay out of mine. After all, Rome is only a call away."

Then, turning around, he said, "Miss Berti, please follow me."

*****

"Sorry for my little display of anger," he said calmly. He asked her to sit down and walked to his chair. "From now on, I will initial all your reports before you submit them to the administration. There will be no doubt as to their authenticity or authority. If you have any other problems of this sort, don't hesitate to see me."

"Thanks."

"No. It is I who should thank you for bringing this matter to my attention. Both for the trust you had in me and for the courage it took."

"Ingegnere, I appreciate your intervention, but—"

"But what? Speak freely."

"Don't you think you are exposing yourself? Risking too much with these 'party' people?"

The clear, spontaneous laugh that suddenly brightened his handsome face quickly seemed to dispel her apprehension. She smiled too. "I know it's not my place to give you advice. I am not that presumptuous, but I am concerned for you." Then she quickly added, "We need you here."

"I appreciate your praise and your concern, but I wouldn't worry so much. To use a well-worn cliché, these local fascists are only sheep in wolves' clothing."

"You are brave, but they can hurt you. I know it."

"Well, thank you for the compliment, but it's not all bravery, you know? While I am needed, they will not dare touch me. In fact, 'they' might even need me to build a model distillery in Ciampino, near Rome."

Riccardo should have been surprised at his gratuitous information.

What was he trying to do? Bragging was not his style. Was he trying to impress her?

"We shall see," he added reflectively. "Anyway, thanks again for your concern, Miss Berti."

"You are welcome, Ingegnere. And if I may be so bold, I wouldn't mind if you called me by my first name ... Patrizia."

He hesitated and then said, "I will be glad to do so ... Patrizia."

There didn't seem to be anything else to add. She got up, and when she reached the door she swung graciously on her heels and asked, "Shall I close your door?"

He was still looking at her. The blue of his eyes, which was like ice only minutes before, was now suggestive of a blue, sunny heaven.

"Yes, please," he said, smiling again. A soft, dull sound confirmed that she'd closed the door.

Inside his head, though, the warning voiced by Signorina Berti resounded loud and real. He knew of many people who had protested or rebelled against the system and were harassed, physically abused, or persecuted. Abuse of power, violence, and disregard for democratic principles were exactly the ingredients that had made him an unwavering antifascist—a condition that had, until recently, deprived him of a permanent occupation. Now he had a career, and the prospects for the future had suddenly improved. He knew all that. What he didn't know was whether his principles would allow him to keep it.

He inhaled and then let out a deep sigh. "Patrizia," he slowly repeated to himself. He liked the sound of her name.

- IX -

1931–1932

During the following months, Patrizia was often in Riccardo's thoughts. For the first time in his life, his longing for a woman was almost as great as his ambition for his career. His yearning for her was so intense that he began fantasizing of a life together.

But how was he going to find the time to develop a relationship? And how should he go about it? Suddenly, he realized that despite his age, his academic achievements, and position, when it came to women, his experience was limited to some casual liaisons during his university days. Nothing too serious … and nothing like this.

Throughout the long years of wait for a permanent occupation, he had stored up so many ideas, accumulated so many drawings, and had so much hope. Now, on the verge of realizing his goals and prove all his theories valid, his restless energy was ready to explode. He wanted to accomplish everything immediately, and he had to exercise restraint when circumstances held back his expectations; Signorina Berti must wait a while longer.

That week, there was more bad news.

"What do you mean there is another delay in the delivery of copper sheets?" he asked the purchasing manager during a weekly meeting.

"Just what I said. We have no power over the allocation of special materials."

"Who does?"

The people around the table looked at each other in silence.

"If you wish," Ligato said at last, "I can find out from my contacts."

"You mean your party acolytes?" Riccardo snapped. "Forget it. If there is no other way, I'll go to the ministry myself." Then he turned toward the purchaser. "Sorry if I raised my voice," he said. "We badly need to add one large boiler tank. I'm anxious to see results."

*****

In spite of his impatience, the three-plus-hour train ride to Rome was pleasant. Riccardo reviewed his drawings, read the morning papers, and told himself to exercise self-control at the ministry.

In Rome, outside Termini Station, several black Fiat taxis were queuing up along the nearest sidewalk.

"To the Ministry of Trade and Commerce," he told the driver, "via Fontana number 33."

It was a warm, sunny day and Riccardo, comfortably seated in the back seat, placed his leather briefcase beside him and indulged in the view.

He had visited the city before, yet he was always amazed at the traffic. Not to mention the casual manner pedestrians crossed the street wherever they felt like it, seldom waiting for the green light; the crude shouts of vendors; the overall high level of clamor. Despite the early hour, in some of the sidewalks of inner streets, one could recognize, by the provocative scanty attire, the odd prostitute. At night, everyone knew, these … women became more important than professional spies, as they were able to suck from the somnolent bodies of their customers even the most important state secret.

It hasn't changed much, he thought. *Despite its antiquities and Mussolini's rejuvenation program for some of its quarters, it doesn't have the feeling of an important, modern capital. It lacks Paris's charm, Vienna's imperial character, Berlin's vitality. Except for its history and archeological wealth, present-day Rome is more like a provincial capital. Or like a theater stage, decorated with recycled props and clattering streetcars.*

"Here you are, sir," said the cab driver, coming to a stop. "It's the building right across. It'll be twenty-two lire."

Riccardo crossed the street, climbed the dozen or so steps to the main floor, and asked one of the guards for directions.

"The materials coordinator's office is on the third floor, sir. You can catch one of those running elevators."

There were many people ahead of him. Some were sitting on the chairs placed against the peripheral walls of the reception area, reading the morning papers or smoking. Others were standing or slowly pacing the room. Riccardo stood near the entrance, and through the partially open door of the office, he could see part of a shiny mahogany desk,

Giancarlo Gabbrielli

a tan leather armchair in front of it, and a worn Persian carpet partly covering the marble floor. He heard people talk but could not make out the words.

About an hour later, he was finally in front of the person responsible for acquisition and distribution of strategic materials. He was a man in his forties, sporting a head of slicked-down, dark, oiled hair, neatly parted in the middle. It was reminiscent of the style donned by Mussolini's son-in-law and Foreign Minister Galeazzo Ciano. He was dressed in a dark green suit and black shirt. On his left lapel shone the emblem of the fascist regime. His desk was almost completely covered with stacks of files, and typically, on the wall behind him hung the profile pictures of Mussolini and King Emanuele III.

"Yes, yes, I got your telegram," he replied to Riccardo's question, "but I can't see what I can do for you."

"I'm told you have the power to expedite orders of urgency and importance," said Riccardo, letting the man see the drawings he pulled out of his briefcase. "We need to receive our copper sheets within two weeks if we are to complete this program."

"Look at this," said the man, ignoring the illustrations and pointing at his desk. "These are all solicitations for orders of urgency and importance, as you put it. What am I supposed to do?"

"But the success of a distillery, perhaps many, plus the betterment of an agricultural section, is certainly—"

"Agriculture, bullets, transformers, frying pans …," the clerk interrupted. "Everything is important to somebody. "The truth is"—he continued shuffling some of the papers on his desk—"Italy doesn't have the mineral wealth of other countries, and we must do with what we've got."

78

"What's the chronology of our requisition with respect to the others? Has at least that priority been respected?" Riccardo heard his tone getting colder and angrier. He did not know how to entreat him, but he knew that this wasn't the best way to succeed.

"These are internal matters that don't concern you," was the curt reply.

"You give me no other option but to appeal directly to the minister."

"Suit yourself. His office is on the top floor. Al Duce."

"Arrivederci."

Riccardo searched for the office of the man who, during his initial interview, had promised to help in case of difficulties. He was told to wait fifteen or twenty minutes, and he walked toward the tall window at the end of the corridor. He inhaled deeply and slowly exhaled, hoping to rid himself of the built-up anger. He leaned against the window ledge, his face close to the glass pane. Just below, he saw the quilt of red rooftops interspersed with the dark green manes of Mediterranean pines. On his left, at the end of a street perpendicular to the ministry, he noticed the short segment of a river, its water the color of cappuccino. Farther down, another segment appeared, and then another. The river seemed to wind itself capriciously around the city.

The Tiber River, he thought. *What happened to the brave men who fought invaders over those very banks, who built roads, bridges, and created an empire?*

He shook his head, and turning to the right, he saw that several sparrows had come to rest on the parallel electric wires stretched between two opposite buildings. From this distance, they seemed to be notes drawn over the black lines of a music sheet.

"Mr. Lanzi," a voice called behind him, "the minister will see you now."

*****

"Well, well, well," exclaimed the minister upon Riccardo admission to his office, "if it isn't the famous Ingegnere Lanzi."

"*Buon giorno,* Signor Ministro. I appreciate your seeing me without a prior appointment, but ..."

"Not so fast, Ingegnere. Please sit down and let me offer you a *real* espresso coffee. Then we'll talk business." He walked to an adjoining door. "*Attendente,*" he called, "two espressos, please, on the double."

"Yes, sir," replied a voice from the adjoining room.

Riccardo lowered himself onto the softness of a large leather armchair and crossed his legs impatiently.

The minister returned to sit behind his massive cherry wood desk. In contrast with that of the materials coordinator, his was completely clear of paperwork. Only a few elegant items floated on its mirror-finish surface: a black leather desk pad; a monumental inkwell shaped like the Altar to the Falling Soldier in Rome, capped by two golden pens; and a leather-bound diary. The walls, except for the one entirely covered by a library containing well-bound volumes, were covered with a green tapestry intersected with a silver geometric key pattern. They were decorated with the usual pictures of Mussolini and King Emanuele III. A third photograph pictured a group of Italian and German hierarchs standing in front of Berlin's Bundestag. Sheer curtains shaded the windows.

"What do you think of the décor?" asked the minister, following Riccardo's scrutiny.

The knock on the door and the arrival of the adjutant rescued Riccardo from answering. "You were quite right," he said instead. "This definitely smells like real coffee."

"Belonging to the party bears certain advantages. I wish you could partake of some."

If benefits offered by the regime mean that I must compromise my own principles, Riccardo thought, *then they mean nothing to me. I'll do without the coffee.*

"I appreciate it, Signor Ministro, but I am apolitical. I cannot 'belong' to any party." Riccardo tried to soften his voice. "My mind perceives right and wrong as attributes devoid of political leaning. Upon making a choice, I would naturally go where my conscience dictates. Given this, you'll agree, no party could appreciate my independence."

"It is a real pity. You have a good mind and the country needs people like you—professionally, I mean."

"Sir," said Riccardo in a barely audible voice, "I serve the country in whatever fashion I'm capable of, in my profession or as a soldier—as I did for three long years during the Great War."

"I know, I know. It's just that … Well, let's drop the subject." The minister drained his little cup and placed it on its saucer on a corner of the desk. He blankly stared at the wall in front. "I presume you wish to tell me the reason for your visit," he said finally.

"Sir, the San Romano project needs a super boiler to conclude the experiments and proceed with the final phase. Copper sheets and other materials were ordered in due time. So far, however, we have been unable to get the supplies or even reliable delivery information."

"Many people and many projects are after these limited resources, be they materials or the money to purchase them."

"That I've been told, sir. But what am I to do? Do you or don't you want the project to be completed?"

"I'm just trying to apprise you of our predicament. Your disdain doesn't help your cause." An edge of impatience colored the minister's tone.

"Sir, I didn't mean to be disrespectful. As I pointed out during our first meeting, I'm not interested in politics, and I'm not versed in diplomatic language. My training as an engineer only taught me to state matters briefly and factually. If I have become an impediment to your plans, I can resign."

"Damn you, Lanzi!" the minister shouted. He pounded his fist on his desk, and the demitasse cup danced inside the saucer. "Don't you understand? I'm just offering an olive branch, and you bite my hand." As he pronounced the word "offering," small spots of spittle were ejected from his mouth, and they fell like little bubbles on the mirrored finish of his desk. Finally, he let his body rest toward the back of his chair and let a long sigh. Then he said in a calmer voice, "Forget about resignations. We've just received the go-ahead for the Ciampino Distillery, and you are part of it. Our Duce wants to show the god-damned Germans that we can do something as well as they do."

This last piece of information alleviated Riccardo's mounting anger. What was he to do now? Apologize? Vomit a conciliatory phrase? Invent some compromise? He felt unable to do any of that, and he damned his nature for not allowing what most others would have considered a simple, convenient course.

"It's all up to you, sir," Riccardo heard himself saying. His voice did not convey an apology.

"It is and it isn't, my dear Ingegnere," the minister said. "I too must sometimes act according to other contingencies and follow orders. Your materials will be released, so … complete your project and be ready for Ciampino."

"I'm grateful to you, Signor Ministro," said Riccardo, getting up.

"Then show it," replied the minister. "Al Duce."

*****

Riccardo returned home with mixed feelings. On the one hand, he was happy for the positive conclusion of his meeting regarding materials, as well as the renewed promise of the Ciampino distillery. On the other, he was angered by the continued reference to his nonadherence to the party and other allusions. How long would it be before he got tired of all this? How long before someone less forgiving than the minister tried to harm him? He could not answer his own question, but he redoubled his efforts.

He now started his day at five in the morning with a cold shower and a frugal breakfast in order to be at his desk by seven. He worked without interruption until twelve when, as customary with almost everyone, he returned home for lunch. He listened to the one o'clock news on the radio and was back at work by two. In the evening, he was seldom home before eight. He read the papers as his mother prepared supper. At the table, they conversed about the progress of his work, world events, or the latest news from his brother Lorenzo who, after several years of part-time attendance, had decided to leave the university and dedicate himself to a business career.

"That son of mine," Luisa complained one evening, "just as smart as you, but surely not as focused."

"He is only twenty-four, Mother. He is still young," Riccardo said, trying to defuse her disappointment.

"You were young too, my dear, but you behaved differently. Maybe you should offer him a job at the distillery."

"Are you joking, Mother? Even if I did—and I don't intend to—he'd never want a clerical job with me. You know his dreams: money, travel, women …"

Riccardo didn't tell her that sometimes he feared his own impatience could lead him to react unwisely and lose his own position as well.

Nor, for that matter, did he tell her of his growing yearning for the young woman of the chemical department. In fact, he consciously avoided talking about her, fearing his mother—who had often longingly spoken about grandchildren—might seize the opportunity and help him into a decision before he was ready for it. Fond as he was of Patrizia, he wanted to know her better and be sure of his feelings and hers before furthering the relationship.

He said good night to his mother and retired to his studio. He sat at his desk until ten, making plans for the next day while listening to Mozart, Wagner, and Vivaldi.

He had only seen Patrizia a few times since the Ligato incident. And during those fleeting moments, despite the display of a certain camaraderie, place and time had allowed for only a few perfunctory words. This lack of meaningful communication left him unsatisfied, but rather than making him forget her, it seemed to increase his desire to know her better.

He'd catch himself looking out his window to anticipate her arrival. Or, upon passing her lab door, he instinctively slowed his pace, just to hear her humming a tune or singing a song for a while longer. In the evening, at home, when his work had been lifted from his mind, he found himself thinking about her again. When he sat in the semidarkness of his room, his eyes closed, her sensuous image coming to him on the wings of the musical notes. Slowly invading his mind, his senses, until his desire became intense and a name escaped his lips: "Patrizia."

*****

One sunny day in spring, moments after the siren had sounded the midday break, he noticed Patrizia walking toward the exit rather than toward the bicycle stand as she usually did. She held a small blanket under her arm and a wicker basket with her free hand. She sauntered toward the riverbank, climbed the grassy incline, descended, and disappeared on the other side.

Perhaps this was a good opportunity to meet her. But what if she was meeting someone else? The thought that another man could already be in her life gave him a piercing pain; however, in a paradoxical way, it also gave him the courage to act.

He waited several interminable minutes, until he was sure no one had followed her, and then he took the same route. As the director of the distillery and the person who always strived to be the example of discipline and dedication, he did not want to be perceived as a Don

Giovanni. So, for the next few minutes he walked casually on top of the bank, his hands in his pockets, whistling a tune, pretending to be stretching his legs while his eyes searched below. Failing to see her, he descended to the next terraced bank. He followed the narrow path to its end, noticing traces of footsteps through the tall grass as he continued in that direction. Suddenly, behind a cluster of river cane, at the edge of a sandbank lapped by a swift rivulet of clear water, he saw her white lab coat. His heart jumped with joy. Patrizia was lying on her blanket … alone. Her left forearm was solidly planted on the ground, her right hand was holding a sandwich, and her face was turned directly toward the sun. Her skirt had risen above her knees, and Riccardo couldn't help letting his eyes drift over her shapely legs. Inadvertently, he crushed a small branch that lay across the path.

"Ingegnere!" she exclaimed. "You startled me."

"I'm sorry," he mumbled. "I didn't mean to. I saw you from my window and felt an urge to join you." His face held a shade of hesitation.

"Well, then," she said, "don't just stand there. Come and sit on the blanket beside me. The grass is a bit damp." She moved to one side of the blanket and smoothed a spot for him to sit. "Have you eaten?"

"Yes. Well, not yet," he replied.

"Please take some of this."

"No, no, I don't want to take away your food. I came just for company. Or would you rather be alone?"

"Please take it," she insisted, ignoring his question. "I have enough for both of us. Unless you don't like fresh tomatoes and mozzarella cheese."

"Thank you," he said, taking the sandwich. "Do you come here often?"

"When the weather is nice. It takes me too long to go home. Besides, I feel happy here. The river whispers in my ears as it flows toward the sea," she declaimed theatrically. "The sun caresses my skin as it travels in the sky, and I can rest my soul and dream …"

"You are a romantic creature. What do you dream about?"

"That, I cannot tell you," she said with a mysterious smile. Then she broke into laughter.

It was like adding music to an already pleasant atmosphere. Just being beside her gave him a sense of inexplicable contentment. It felt as though he had known her for a long time.

Riccardo hoped that this episode away from work added something to their rapport, and when it was time to leave he asked, "May I join you some other time? I'll bring the sandwiches next time."

"*Certamente.*"

*****

That evening, as he crossed the bridge over the Arno River on his way home, his mind abandoned the world of furnaces, pipes, and boilers and returned to the river's sandbank and Patrizia. He felt an even stronger desire to be with her again.

A week later, Riccardo told his mother that he had a business meeting and would not be home for lunch. He returned to the riverbank with Patrizia, and they ate the sandwiches he had brought. They talked about their work, their interests, even the state of the country. He joyfully confirmed in his mind that this beautiful lady, in addition to being a competent and conscientious employee, had many of the attributes he had always wanted in a woman: she was a person with principles and courage and was also intelligent—an overall pleasant companion. But a nagging thought seemed to stop Riccardo from a final resolution. *How is it possible,* he wondered, *for a woman like this not to be engaged … or have a romantic relationship with someone? She must have a boyfriend, if not at the distillery, in her town.* The fear of this discovery prevented him from inquiring about her feelings toward him. So, to defer the possibility of rejection and disappointment, he left things as they were and kept enjoying her company.

On sunny days, when the work schedule allowed it, it became customary for them to eat by the river. "Don't prepare lunch for me today," he told his mother one day. "I have lunch with colleagues."

"Like last time?" Luisa commented.

"Yes, Mother, like last time," he answered, deliberately ignoring her teasing tone.

One day, while they sat on the grass after their frugal lunch, he looked at her eyes and lips and felt the impulse to throw his arms around her neck and kiss her. He was about to move forward when she suddenly said, "I feel like wading in the water." She got up and sauntered over the fine sand and up to the water's edge. She slipped out of her cork-soled shoes, tested the temperature with her toes, and then entered the river.

Riccardo stayed where he was, temporarily frozen. His eyes filled with a blurry vision of the young woman moving away through the hazy heat waves that rose from the sand. Her tremulous figure, framed between the golden sandbar and the green blanket of the opposite bank, seemed a reflection over the mirrored veneer of the running river. She moved slowly, holding her skirt above her knees, and suddenly, above the mellow murmur of the flowing waters and the whispered sound of the river cane swaying in the wind, a few melodic notes journeyed over the air. They seemed to come from a house north of the distillery, and they were barely distinguishable. Riccardo held his breath to hear the notes of that lovely melody, and he soon recognized an aria from *Boheme.* Unexpectedly, he felt their impact as he never had before.

For a moment, Patrizia's reflection, the sound of nature, and that of Puccini's lyrical music seemed to come together and blend into a unique, integral whole. He felt drawn into a new emotional awareness. Within it, the image of Patrizia among the shimmering waters became even more appealing, her features more pure, and her sinuous body more sensuous. He began to mouth the words of Puccini's aria as his eyes caressed the feminine figure that seemed to glide over the water's surface. He caressed her and made love to her in his mind, feeling sure that this was the woman with whom he wanted to share his life.

"Ingegnere," she suddenly called, "what time is it?"

It took him a moment to shake off his reverie. When he looked at his watch, he couldn't believe his eyes. It was almost two o'clock!

"I lost track of time," he said. "I'm sorry, but we must go back." He wavered a moment and then added, "By the way, it's also time you call me Riccardo. At least in private."

She smiled and remained silent.

He wondered if she could read on his face the strange yet wondrous something he felt inside. He forced a slight frown, picked up the blanket, and started to move, but he felt on the verge of some action that was not at all in keeping with his normal behavior. Yes, he had felt like kissing a woman before, but never before now had he been almost unable to control his yearning.

Deep in thought, he started to climb the steep incline. Once on top of the ridge, he looked around for anyone in the vicinity. He took her hand, and resisting the strong urge to embrace her, looked in her eyes. "Patrizia," he said, "I know this is not the best time, the best place, or the best way, but if I don't say it now, I will regret it."

She held his stare. Her expressive brown eyes were filled with silent expectation.

What if she has someone? he thought again. *And what if she doesn't? This is the moment of truth. Either way, it may complicate my life, my projects, my future … But what would my future be without her?*

"Patrizia," he finally said, "I think I am falling in love with you."

She did not show any surprise, but she did not answer immediately.

It seemed a long moment indeed before her lips broke into a smile. "Me too," she said.

Riccardo took Patrizia into his arms and kissed her tenderly. For an eternal instant, it was as though the entire world around them had suddenly vanished; below, the river continued its silent voyage toward the sea. Above, the sun shone as bright as before. On top of the riverbank, two human souls seemed suspended above the ground in a timeless moment.

*****

A million thoughts spun inside Riccardo's head. He felt happier than he had ever been, and so full of strength he believed he could overcome whatever obstacle might come his way. He wanted to tell the world about Patrizia, tell his mother that he had finally found the love of his life. However, his reserved nature told him that it was not the right time.

"What is it, Riccardo?" Luisa asked him one evening. "You seem so happy. Pure joy seems to gush out of your every pore."

"What do you mean, Mother? I just had a pleasant conversation with one of my employees, that's all. A nice person … and not a fascist, for a change."

"I see," Luisa said. She used that tone when she doubted what she was told. "It wouldn't be a pretty woman, by any chance?"

"Mother, I would have made the same comment if it were a man."

"Possibly, but I don't think you would have been as radiant."

"Well, whatever you say, Mother." He turned around for fear of betraying himself, adding, "Please call me when supper is ready. I must finish a drawing."

He switched on the small table lamp on the right corner of his desk. He sat with his elbows placed over its top, his hands under his chin, as though he were examining the blueprint in front of him. In reality, his mind was still appraising his mother's words.

Perhaps I should tell her soon, he thought, *but I don't feel the moment is right.* There is some planning to do—practical issues to solve before I can consider getting married.

Married!

The word entailed a host of other things: a family, additional responsibilities, commitments. *Am I ready for marriage?* he wondered.

We may love each other, but is love sufficient for two people to navigate the rough waters of life? Would marriage change our feelings in time?

He thought of his own mother and father and felt reassured. Until his father was taken away by the war, their union seemed to have been a lasting love. Tears came to his eyes when he thought of his mother's pain in leaving her spouse's mortal remains in San Donà. *Soon I will surprise her,* he thought. *I'll tell her that I have saved enough money to move father's remains to the cemetery of Castelvecchio. Then I will talk about my marriage. But where would I live with Patrizia? Our house would be the natural choice. It has sufficient space, and Mother should be quite happy to have some feminine company and some help with house chores. But what about her mother? How could she fend for herself, alone and in poor health? How could I ask Patrizia to leave her behind … to abandon her?*

That was one of the problems he had not yet resolved in his mind.

The next day, Patrizia was parking her bike when he arrived. She turned to face him. "Riccardo," she whispered through a beaming smile, "are you coming to tell me that you changed your mind?"

"No. I came to tell you that I thought of nothing but you last night."

"Me too, Riccardo."

He turned around as several workers arrived.

"Don't worry," she said recognizing his reaction. "In the presence of others, I'll always call you by your title."

"Not always, I hope. But for now, it might be best. I don't want to endanger your position in any way. I could never forgive myself."

*****

By that spring of 1932, Riccardo had no doubt that Patrizia was his perfect match, his soul mate. Life acquired a different fragrance for both of them—like a promising bud that had suddenly blossomed into a full flower, releasing perfume and colors previously imagined but not seen or savored. The time spent together never seemed to be enough. They had so much to discover and learn from one another. Now that he had found her, he couldn't conceive of living without her. He decided it was time to meet her mother and begin to discuss a married life. He finally asked Patrizia about an appropriate time to meet her.

"Unfortunately, she has been taken to the hospital with pneumonia," Patrizia said.

"Why didn't you tell me?" he asked.

"I didn't want to burden your mind with my personal problems or with things you can't do anything about."

"Let me know when she is back. I really would like to meet her."

Two weeks later, on a Saturday morning, he looked for her arrival at the distillery as usual, but did not see her. *I'll meet her during the lunch break,* he thought. About midmorning, as he was sitting at his desk reviewing production schedules, his telephone rang.

"Riccardo," said a voice he could hardly recognize, "it's Patrizia. Would you mind coming to my office? I have something to tell you."

"Good morning, Patrizia. Anything wrong?"

"Please come, and I'll tell you."

The lab was no more than a hundred meters away, but after that phone call, it seemed a much greater distance. Riccardo had to make an effort not to start running. *What could it be?* he thought. Her melodic voice had sounded so flat.

He breathed the fresh morning air, which was mixed with the pungent smell of fermenting *vinaccia*. He walked briskly on the footpath as the river pebbles ground ominously under his feet, sounding like incomprehensible omens.

Something happened to her… She has changed her mind … Perhaps the fascists, maybe in revenge against me …

He knocked and entered her office in a state of apprehension.

"Riccardo," whispered a mournful but tearless Patrizia, "my mother is dead."

"Oh my God."

He was genuinely sad, and he now wished he had made more of an effort to meet her sooner. But at the same time, he was immensely relieved that Patrizia was safe, that nothing seemed changed between them.

"When did it happen?" he asked, hugging her.

"Last night. I only came to finish a few tests so that there will be no disruption. Also, to ask you for a couple of days off. I have many things to attend to …"

"Of course, of course, my dear. Don't worry—I will help you with whatever you need."

"Riccardo, remember our pact," said Patrizia with firmness. "I don't want any special treatment."

"I know that. But my help has nothing to do with the distillery. My time is mine to give."

"All right, then. I wouldn't mind some help with the funeral preparations."

"Of course. When do you think you'll be finished here?"

"By lunchtime, I guess."

"Good. And since it is Saturday, I will have the rest of the day and all day tomorrow to help you. Leave your bike here. We'll go in my car so we can talk."

During the drive to Montepoli, Patrizia told him that after showing a slight improvement, her mother had suddenly passed away.

"I am truly sorry, Patrizia," Riccardo said. He reached over and took her hand.

"I also grieve over the fact that I will never meet her," he said. "Unfortunately, it's too late for idle regrets."

She nodded in silence.

As he slowly drove up the snaking slopes leading to her town, he realized that he had never been at her place, and he had no idea where it was.

"I will need you to give me directions," he said, touching her hand. "I've never been in Montepoli."

"Yes, as we get closer," she replied with a smile. "We rent an apartment near the center from a fine old lady. When her husband died, she had her palace divided into four units to subsidize her income. Since my mother couldn't deal with stairs any longer, we took one on the ground floor. The back, as you'll see, faces a steep ravine with large, mature trees and green slopes. The old lady lives above us. Sometimes I visit and have tea with her. From her back windows, I can see the chimneys of the distillery and the bell tower of Castelvecchio. I stand there for long stretches of time and think of you."

Riccardo felt touched by her remark. He could imagine her with her elbows resting over the windowsill, gazing toward the valley. He was about to make a comment when she spoke again.

"Here we are," she said, pointing to an old palace on their right. "You can stop near that big central door."

*****

The majestic two-story palace had distinctive mid-seventeenth-century construction, with wrought iron terraces and bas-relief work on the stone facing. Made of solid oak, the front door was surmounted by a sculptured family crest—a stylized eagle over an oval shield. Its bronze door knockers were in the shape of lion heads with the knockers hinged into their mouths.

They entered holding hands, Patrizia leading the way in the pitch-black surroundings. After a few steps, she flipped a light switch and a vast entrance hall materialized out of darkness. Its pavement was in a pattern of alternating broad black-and-white marble tiles. Two bearing columns clad in black marble shot from the middle of the floor and held the convex ceiling, giving the appearance of vast umbrellas. Several red clay amphorae housed a host of plants, which helped soften the austere ambiance of the hall. Two doors were situated at the opposing ends of the side walls.

"I live here," Patrizia said, walking to the right.

Her door led directly into a small, carpeted foyer with side closets, a floor coatrack, and an old wooden chest. They left their coats on the bench and went into the living room through the French doors.

Off-white sofas faced a small fireplace framed in Pietra Serena stone. On either side of it, the walls were lined with shelves stocked with a large variety of books: history, chemistry, bibliographies, gardening, and literature and literary novels by Italian, French, German, and Russian authors (in those days, it was neither easy nor wise to be found in possession of English or American books). On the far corner, near a bay window overlooking the ravine, stood a black Steinway piano. Its gleaming surface mirrored the window and a tree branch outside.

"Do you play the piano?" Riccardo asked.

"Sometimes. When I'm happy or sad."

"I'd love to hear you play someday. And I hope it will be a happy occasion."

She nodded and then came close to him, hugging him for a long time. It felt as if she wanted to burrow her body into his or else draw from it all of his strength. He embraced her and caressed her hair, her neck, and her shoulders. They kissed. Tenderly at first, and then more passionately.

It would be so easy to continue, he thought, *to let this instinct sway toward its natural course. So easy and so pleasant, but not proper under the circumstances. We might regret it later.* He gently detached his body from hers.

For one instant, Patrizia clung to his neck. She then seemed to perceive his reason for pulling away, and she promptly loosened her embrace as well. She looked straight into his eyes. "You are right, Riccardo," she said, "and I am grateful to you."

"Thank you, dear," he said. He let his eyes roam about the room, coming to rest on a fresh bunch of wildflowers. "Did you pick them?" he asked, going over to touch them.

"Yes," she said, moving beside him. "There are lots of them in the ravine," she said caressing them. "They were meant for my mother, but …"

"They are beautiful," he said. He was sorry to have involuntarily reminded her of her mother.

"When I leave," he went on, "I'll be able to picture you in every corner of this room," he said looking around. "Dream that I'm still with you." He stopped his eyes in front of a portrait. "Is this your father?" he asked, admiring the oil painting on a narrow wall.

"Yes. A friend of his painted it. It was my mother's favorite. She claimed it revealed his true self, better than any photograph of his."

"Handsome man. I remember your telling me that he died in nineteen seventeen, during the retreat of Caporetto."

"Yes. I have only a vague memory of him. He left for the front in nineteen fifteen; I was only nine years old. And what about your father, Riccardo? You never mentioned him. Is he still alive?"

"No. He died the same year. Our house was near the Piave River, just a few hundred meters from the front lines. It was hit by several shells, and he died under the rubble." He took a few steps. "And what about this painting?" he asked, switching his attention to what appeared to be Tuscan country scene. A flourishing valley took up the foreground, followed by waves of green hills that receded in the distance, growing fainter toward the horizon, finally becoming one with the pale sky.

"My grandfather painted that one," Patrizia said.

"It's a very nice painting."

"Thank you, Riccardo. By the way, you see that light orange spot on the right? The one on the first hilltop?"

"Yes, of course. What about it?"

"It is the only detail that does not exist in reality. My grandfather put it there to please me. It's a facsimile of a castle pictured on a bottle of Tuscan wine—Brunello di Montalcino, I believe. When I was little, I pretended I was a princess and that was my castle. Naturally, one day a handsome prince with blue eyes would appear from the surrounding forest, sweep me off my feet, lift me to his white horse, and we'd gallop far, far away." Her laugh echoed in the silence of the room. "And here you are," she said.

The smile brightening her face faded as she turned to open the drawer of a small walnut desk. "Now, though," she said in a somber voice, "let's forget about dreams and princes … and return to reality. I'm sorry, Riccardo, but I have to jot down a list so I won't forget anything. I must pay my poor mother the respect she deserves."

They worked diligently for a few hours, discussing the necessary steps to be taken the following day. Her voice was calm, her emotions well under control. Riccardo experienced a sense of serenity beside her.

"Thank you, my dear," Patrizia said at the end of their chore. "This helped me a lot. I don't think I would have been able to complete **my** task without you." She touched his hand. "And if you'll return tomorrow, you'll be of great help."

"This sounds like a dismissal," he said, a note of disappointment in his voice. "Would you rather be alone?"

"I'm not alone, Riccardo. My mother's presence is still here with me. Also, I have my piano, my books, and my castle, and now even a face with beautiful blue eyes for my prince charming." It seemed her attempt to make light of a sad moment. "Besides, the nice old lady from upstairs will come in a while to help with the church arrangements. I'm not a very devout person, so she'll deal with the priest and the church functions. My mother wanted it that way."

The last statement seemed to catch him by surprise. Religion was a topic they had never explored.

"All right, then," he said rising from his chair. He looked at the darkness framed by the windows and realized that it was quite late. Time had passed by unnoticed; hours gone by like minutes. He didn't even remember when the electric light had been turned on. He looked at his watch. It was ten after nine. It would be close to ten by the time he got home. His own mother would certainly be a bit apprehensive about his lateness.

"Yes, you are right," he said. "When I am late, my mother always thinks the worst. She worries that I have been beaten by the fascists, or that I had a car accident, or God knows what other mishap. We have no telephone in the house, so I have no way to advise her."

"Neither do I. I made an application and was told that it may take a year before they extend the lines this way. The municipality lacks the money, you know?"

"I know," he replied. "We got the same answer." He picked up his coat and kissed her cheeks, inhaling the scent of her skin. "Good night, my dear," he said. "Oh, one more thing." He hesitated a moment and then blurted out, "Would you mind if I bring my mother to the funeral?"

"Would she want to?" Patrizia asked. "Does she know about me?"

"She probably does, judging from some of her comments. But now I'll make it official."

"That's fine with me, then. Do take her with you; I'd like to meet her. Good night, Riccardo."

"Good night."

*****

"Thank God you're here," said Luisa opening the door. "I was starting to worry. What happened to you?"

"Nothing happened to me, Mother. I'll explain after eating. I'm famished." Riccardo went to place his attaché case on his desk and wash his hands.

I hope it's still nice and hot," said Luisa, placing a plate of stew in front of him a moment later. "I kept it on the corner of the stove. Those briquettes you concocted give double the heat of firewood."

"It smells so good," said Riccardo, inhaling the rising aroma. When he finished eating, he sat back on the chair and closed his eyes, wrestling with a decision. Suddenly, he moved forward and said, "Mother, I'd like you to do me a favor."

"Yes, Riccardo, what is it?"

"The day after tomorrow, I will attend a memorial service. I wish you to come with me."

"Who died? Someone I know?"

"No. It's the mother of one of my employees. Actually, a dear friend, I should say."

"And what's her name, Riccardo?"

"How do you know it's a woman?"

"Come on, son. Just because I didn't ask you," Luisa said with a smile, "it doesn't mean that I haven't noticed."

"Noticed what, Mother?"

"Changes in you. Some subtle and some not so subtle: your dreamy eyes, comments about a certain brave person in the lab, the increased frequency of your 'lunch engagements,' and so on. I was in love too once, you know."

Riccardo felt his blood rise to his cheecks.

"Her name is Patrizia," he said without looking at his mother. "I took her home today and helped her with the funeral planning; that's why I'm late. Now I would like you to meet her. I wanted to tell you for some time now, but I never found the right moment."

"And you think a funeral is the right moment?"

"In a way it is. Later I'll tell you more, but now I wish to know if you will come."

"Are you going to ask her to marry you?"

He was speechless for a moment. He hadn't given his mother sufficient information for her to reach that conclusion. He cleared his throat and said, "Certainly not before you meet her, and not at the funeral."

"Whatever you decide will be fine with me, son. I trust your judgment. You are more serious than your brother in matters of women. I know that if you love her, she is a worthy person. However, you must wait until after the mourning period."

"Of course I will, although her mother's death might hasten matters. Her father died at Caporetto, and she has no close relatives."

"Will she like living here?"

"We haven't talked about it, but I'm sure she'll like the house and your company. Besides, why pay rent if we already have a house?"

Luisa smiled. 'Oh, sweet Jesus,' she whispered, after kissing her son good night, "please let it be true."

"Good night, Mother."

*****

Thank you, God, she said in her mind, walking toward her room. *Just when I was beginning to think that I wouldn't see him settled. And now he'll get married, and if I'm lucky … No, no, sorry, Lord. What I mean is, and if You so wish, I might be lucky enough to see a grandchild.*

She closed her bedroom door and knelt on the small sheepskin stretched beside the bed. She placed her elbows on the bed, joined her hands in prayer, and lifted her eyes to the wooden crucifix hanging on the wall.

"Forgive me, Lord. You can't give me back my Roberto," she whispered with a teary voice, "so I hope You can let me have a grandchild. Anyway, I am already happy just to see my Riccardo settled. The rest I leave up to you."

*****

The religious service was held in the humble little church where Patrizia's mother had attended mass for years. Many people were present at the simple ceremony preceding the burial. Signora Berti was well liked by the people in Montepoli, for, despite her medical condition and modest economic state, she had always been generous and helpful.

During the foot procession to the cemetery, Patrizia noticed that a few people had also come from the distillery, including Antonio Rossi, the chief draftsman, and Signor Ligato, who, regardless of the sad circumstances, would not stop staring at Patrizia's slim figure and beautiful face. Her pallor, heightened by her somber black blouse and dress, made her look like an alabaster statue.

Throughout the brief ritual, Patrizia had not allowed her expression and demeanor to change. Although she dearly loved her mother, she did not want to give a public display of her innermost feelings. She did not like being the object of sympathetic interest.

However, when the coffin was lowered into the grave and the first shovelful of earth clattered over the mahogany lid, she felt an awful wrench inside her heart. She lowered her head and bit her lips to resist crying when she heard the priest pronounce the final words.

"Earth to earth, ashes to ashes, dust to dust," he said, and then intoned the lamentation: "A porta Inferi."

It was the end of the rite, and many people soon came to Patrizia to express their condolences.

First was the priest, who now seemed in a hurry to leave. "Nothing much can be said or done for your dreadful loss," he uttered, forcing his face into a mask of piety, "but it should be of some consolation to you to know that your mother is now in heaven."

"I can't tell you how much we admired your poor mother," said a middle-aged couple she hardly knew.

"I deeply feel for you," said Ligato, bending forward enough to almost touch her chest with his forehead.

"I'm sorry for your loss, Patrizia," said Antonio, simply. "I'll see you soon."

She shook hands and thanked people, while inside, she nurtured her sorrow in the privacy of her heart.

"You are a brave girl, Patrizia," said Luisa. She had been briefly introduced at the beginning, and now she embraced her and kissed her cheeks. "My deep condolences for the loss of your mother. It must have been so difficult for you."

"It was."

Luisa took her hand and said, "Riccardo tells me that you are alone. Would you like to have supper with us tonight?"

"Oh, thank you very much, signora. I would have liked to, but I still have to take care of a few things. I expect some people at the apartment later this evening. Perhaps another time. Besides," she said with a demure voice, "I'd like to linger here a while longer after everyone has gone."

Riccardo nodded in silence and gave her a kiss.

"Not 'perhaps,'" Luisa said vehemently. "Another time for sure. Let me know when you'll be ready. Soon, I hope."

"I will, signora. Thank you."

Luisa smiled, hugged her, and kissed her cheeks again. The gentle, protracted pressure of her lips made the gesture feel even more heartfelt and sincere. Once more, Patrizia had to make an effort not to cry.

The workers filled the grave and placed the flowers over it. Then they took their tools and left.

Finally, everyone was gone.

*****

All around her was silence, except for the odd chirping of birds, and, every now and then, the muffled sound of a vehicle in the distance.

She let her eyes travel over the peaceful landscape adjacent to the cemetery, which lay on the leveled part of the incline. Uphill, the high grounds still held the sunlight, and on her right, the valley and flatland spread widely under the fading evening light. Her gaze glided over the terraced slopes, the way her fingers caressed the piano keyboard, bringing to her heart the same comfort that music did. On her left, the last sliver of sun was just about to set behind the bluish mountain crests. Her eyes returned to the grave.

"We are finally alone, Mother," she said with a sigh. "You know that I don't believe in heaven or hell. But, if by some unfathomable mystery or miracle you can hear me, you know that I loved you, and I always will."

She could say no more. The last word pronounced loosened sobs in her throat, and she began to cry warm tears.

*****

"She is a lovely girl," Luisa said to Riccardo as soon as he started the car.

He did not answer immediately. He was glad for his mother's invitation and gentle insistence with Patrizia, for it meant that she had really liked her.

"And with that figure," Luisa continued in a mocking tone, "she could bear you lots of nice babies."

"Mother," Riccardo exclaimed, "we are not even engaged, and you already talk about babies."

"Well, my dear, I can't wait forever, you know? I am not so young anymore," she added, adjusting her body in her seat. "I've never made any mystery about wishing to nurture my grandchildren and see them grow. Have I?"

"No, you certainly haven't. I'm just surprised that you took a liking to her so quickly. Normally you're more reserved and more … guarded."

"Or protective for my boy, you may say. But I have a good feeling about her. Even from the little you've told me, I surmise that she is good for you. Besides, together you make a beautiful couple, and my grandchildren will be beautiful as well."

"And exactly how many grandchildren would you want?" he was about to ask. But they were in front of the house, and he got out of the car to help his mother out.

"My dear Riccardo," Luisa said, pulling on his arm and caressing his face, "you are an intelligent man, but you still have a lot to learn about women and feelings."

*****

On a warm evening three months after the funeral, just before leaving the distillery, Riccardo asked Patrizia to stop for a moment at a nearby café, in front of the San Romano train station. "I want to talk to you, Patrizia," he said, holding her hand, "and I don't want to do it here. It won't take long."

Riccardo had been to the Café Della Stazione—mostly when he picked up guests or technicians coming by train from other cities. It was a typical small-town café, with an extended bar along one wall, a shiny espresso coffee machine on its top, and dozens of liquor bottles on glass shelving on the mirrored wall. On the opposite side of the bar were several square tables with four bentwood chairs for each table, to accommodate two pairs of card players. Some of the tabletops were inlaid with checker boards.

Riccardo and Patrizia were greeted by the distinctive smell, a blend of espresso coffee and cigarette smoke.

"Good evening, signorina. Good evening, Ingegnere," the barman said. "What can I get you?"

"Just tea for me," said Patrizia, in response to Riccardo's look.

"Espresso for me," said Riccardo.

They sat at the far end of the bar, far from the three old men near the front window.

"Tell me what you wanted to talk to me about, Riccardo," Patrizia said in a cheery tone, stretching her arm across the table to reach his hand. For a man with his directness and experience in business, he seemed absurdly ill at ease. "Well, dear, are you going to speak?"

He waited until the barman had placed the cups on the table and had returned to his other duties.

"You know, Patrizia …," Riccardo began at last.

She nodded and tenderly stroked his hand.

"You know that I love you, and you also know my limitations in expressing sentiment."

"Don't be too modest now," she joked.

"I have been planning to ask you to marry me for a while now. However, knowing the health condition of your mother and the fact that she'd be alone held me back. Now her death, may God rest her soul, has changed the circumstances and so … what do you think?"

"I think you are right," Patrizia chuckled. "Your choice of words, place, and circumstances needs a definite improvement."

Riccardo looked at her in silence. He was unable to determine, from her tone or her words, if her response implied a positive answer or not.

"Don't put on that worried look," she said with another laugh. "After all, I'm only confirming your views. As to whether or not I wish to marry you as soon as possible, if that is what you're asking me, the answer is yes."

The steel in his heart seemed to melt instantly. Then he suddenly turned serious again and blurted out, "I would like to marry in church." Then he added hesitantly, "For my mother, you know …"

"I have no problem with that. I had the same consideration for my mother, didn't I? I am not devout," she said, looking squarely into his eyes, "and I don't think much of the church as an institution. However, I do follow the basic moral principles shared by the church. I am also aware of the social advantages of following society's traditions. After all," she said ironically, "even Mussolini and his cohorts had to come to an arrangement with the Vatican. Anyway, I certainly would not want to offend your mother on matters that are important to her."

"Thank you, Patrizia," said Riccardo, with evident relief. Her views on this matter seemed to be stronger and more definite than he had anticipated. However, it would do for now.

"Oh, I almost forgot," he said, extracting a small velvet box from his pocket and handing it to Patrizia. "It's not that valuable, but it's an old family heirloom, one of the few saved from the ruins of my house in San Donà. I hope you'll wear it."

"Of course I will, my darling. It's from you, and that's what counts."

Patrizia opened the box and tilted it toward the light. A large sapphire ring, mounted on a white gold casing, twinkled from the red velvet interior of the box. She let out a sound of awe. "Riccardo," she said, looking at the iridescent stone, "it's absolutely stunning. Should I put it on now?"

Late 1932

Three months later, Riccardo and Patrizia married in a simple ceremony in the small, secluded chapel of nearby Monte Falco. The witnesses were Riccardo's brother, Lorenzo, who had come from Florence for the occasion, and Meino. Luisa, two of Patrizia's friends from Montepoli, and a dozen other people—including the Lanzis' neighbors—completed the short guest list.

Riccardo and Patrizia had taken a week off work, and they were to travel to Florence and remain there a few days to enjoy the city, as well as visit with Lorenzo.

"And what else?" Meino asked.

"If there is time," Patrizia said, "we'll go to go to Venice. But we shall see."

The married couple arrived in Florence by midafternoon. They took a room at the Hotel Excelsior overlooking the Arno River. From its fourth floor balcony, they could see the Ponte Alle Grazie Bridge, the Ponte Vecchio, a long stretch of the river, and the hills of San Miniato al Monte.

Once refreshed from the short trip, Riccardo called his brother from the hotel. "Hallo, Lorenzo, we're here," he said, "but we wish to rest a while, and then have a quiet supper and go to bed early. Tomorrow we'll spend some time together and do some sightseeing."

A loud laughter was Lorenzo's immediate reply. "Don't worry about me, big brother. I'll be here when you wish to see me. Today you take care of three most essential matters."

"What essential matters are you talking about?" echoed Riccardo.

"Making love, making love, and making love. I didn't think I had to explain it to you."

"All right, clown, I'll call you tomorrow."

Shortly after eating, they retired to their room. Patrizia came out of the bathroom in a silky robe that adhered to her body like a second skin. Her smile was an open invitation for Riccardo, who had patiently waited for this moment for the last several months. He drew the heavy curtains over the window as she walked toward the bed. Then he removed his jacket, unbuckled his belt, and quickly shed his clothes. He was thirty-four, but he had the swift movements of a teenager. Behind him, a light rustling of garments suggested that Patrizia had dropped her robe and entered the bed.

When he turned around, she was already under the blanket, one arm under her head, propping it up from the pillow. Her dark, silken hair spread over it like a cascade. Her eyes unabashedly embraced his nudity, her mouth slightly open with eagerness and desire.

They kissed gently at first—then avidly, denoting months of wait. Their hands journeyed over each other's skin, giving and taking pleasure, their bodies responding to the language of love.

He finally raised his body above hers, entered her, and slowly began to move. His eyes, locked onto hers, revealed the bliss he was experiencing. Shortly, her deliberate movements matched his, until they reached a simultaneous climax that seemed to come from the deepest part of his being and produced an ecstasy that was almost pain. It was close to midnight when finally, fulfilled and exhausted, he switched the light off and let his body fall by her side.

The following evening, Lorenzo joined them for supper. During the conversation, he teased his brother about his excessive seriousness.

"How can you avoid thinking about those matters that are most likely to influence your life?" Riccardo countered.

"Easily," replied Lorenzo. "I know they exist, but I'm going to ignore them as much as possible. What do you think, Patrizia?"

"I think that since we've finished eating and it's a lovely evening," she said diplomatically, "we should go for a short walk along the river."

Both men consulted their watches and agreed that it was a good idea.

They walked along the Lungarno Torrigiani, past the Ponte Vecchio and toward the Santa Trinita' Bridge. Patrizia was in the middle, holding both men by their arms. Below them, the calm river waters flowed silently from bridge to bridge of the city, and then toward the open countryside, along the route to Pisa, and finally, into the embrace of the Thyrrhenian Sea. A thousand lights quivered over its even, dark surface.

They stopped, hypnotized by those flickering lights, which seemed like a heaven turned upside down. They placed their arms over the stone parapet, which still held the warmth of the day's sunshine.

Lorenzo began to hum a well-known tune and then voiced the words of a song, inspired by Florence and the Arno River: "Nell'Arno d'argento, risplende il firmamento, mentre una voce e un canto si perde lontan. Glitters the firmament over the silvery Arno waters, and in the distance echoes the sound of a song ..."

Unexpectedly, Patrizia joined in with a full soprano voice: "Dorme Firenze, sotto I raggi della luna, mentre ad un balcone sta una madonna bruna. Florence sleeps, under the moon's beams, while upon a balcony, a dark-haired maiden dreams."

"My, my," said Lorenzo, marveling at her voice, "I didn't know you could sing like that."

"Neither did I," added a gleeful Riccardo. "Honestly, this girl is full of pleasant surprises." He laughed. "However, we'd better tone it down, or else sleepy Florence will soon be wakened, and the beautiful maiden will douse us from her balcony with a bucket of water."

Their laughter resounded in the quiet night as they continued their sidewalk stroll.

Suddenly, when they were close to Ponte Alla Carraia, the calm atmosphere of the evening was broken by gunshots in the distance. The menacing sounds reverberated under the arched bridge span, traveled to the nearby hills, and bounced back amplified. Behind many windows, lights were turned off, and a siren rang ominously from the city center.

"We'd better go," said Riccardo, grasping Patrizia's hand.

Lorenzo ran back with them until just past the Ponte Vecchio. "This is my turnoff," he said, veering toward Via di Bardi. "I know a shortcut. In twenty minutes, I'll be home. Don't worry about this," he hollered behind them, as Riccardo and Patrizia hurried back toward the hotel. "And have a good night. I'll pick you up in the morning."

In the elevator, Patrizia noticed Riccardo's suddenly sullen mood. "Lorenzo is right. Try not to worry, my dear," she said with a soothing tone. It's probably a fascist crowd fighting with local dissidents. We are secure over here, and in the morning, it will all be gone."

"Yes, except for some innocent who will be dead or wounded, or some blameless bystander who'll get hit by mistake."

She moved closer to him, took his hand affectionately, and kissed him.

"It will be all right," she whispered. "You'll see."

He returned her kiss, and by the time they reached their floor, they were eager to get into their room. A different, more natural urgency had taken over and replaced the fear of a moment ago.

Riccardo opened the door in anticipation. The maid had already pulled back the quilt, and a white linen triangle glowed starkly in the semidarkness. Over the inlaid dresser, she had switched on the small Tiffany lamp. Its multicolor stripes of light, in predominantly orange tones, gave the room a sunset ambiance. The heavy curtains were drawn over the windows.

At the first contact with her skin, every thought or worry magically seemed to disappear from Riccardo's mind. Conflicts, injustice, social problems, and wars suddenly vanished like minuscule specks, swept away by the tide of the immediate pleasure of the senses. His forehead, often showing wrinkles of concern, was now relaxed and smooth. His eyes lost their tense quality; his soul had fallen into a state of absolute serenity. They made love again and again. Then they lay in the dark, their legs entwined, holding hands.

Click-clack, click-clack, click-clack. A solitary horse-driven coach, trotting over the cobblestones of the Lungarno, was the only sound heard from the city below. Somehow, the rhythmic beating of the horse's hooves over the paving was a happy sound. Like a telegraph signal bearing good news, like a metronome beat before the start of music.

Life went on, after all.

A while later, the cadenced clopping receded and was hardly audible. Then it faded away.

"Florence sleeps," said Patrizia, putting her arm across Riccardo's chest.

"I love you," he whispered in reply, and they both fell asleep.

*****

In the morning, Lorenzo took them to the train station and gave them a warm hug. Have a nice stay in Venice. When you come back, I promise to come to Castelvecchio and visit with you and Mother."

"I hope you will," Patrizia said.

"See you soon, then," Riccardo said.

Military personnel patrolled the station, but calm prevailed. The married couple settled in the train compartment with other travelers. All the same, they were able to steal a few kisses when the train entered one of the many dark tunnels through the Appenine Mountains.

Riccardo was familiar with the city, and he had booked a room at a small, charming hotel he remembered, conveniently located across the canal, not far from the train station.

"Do you want to rest awhile?" he asked Patrizia, once they got there and had hung their clothes.

"No, thanks, my dear. I'm not tired. As you know, it's my first time in this beautiful city, and I don't want to waste a moment." Then she looked at him with an amused smile and added, "Or were you asking me something else?"

"No, no," he answered a bit too hastily, adding with a chuckle. "We have all night for that." If he was disappointed, he concealed it well.

She laughed. The happy sound danced through the room like a warm breath of spring air.

"Let's go, then," she said, locking the bedroom door. "Longing for love will make the day go faster."

They dived into the sea of people crowding the bustling Lista di Spagna district. She took his arm as they passed by the yellow sign of Campo di Geremia, went past the first bridge, and continued toward Calle San Leonardo.

"Take me to the Rialto Bridge and Piazza San Marco," she said. "I'd like to see San Marco Square."

"It's a truly beautiful setting," said Riccardo. "The piazza is framed between the Doge's Palace, the Basilica of San Marco, and an edifice shaped like a horseshoe, with arched loggias and elegant shops. It's a delight sitting in one of the many outside cafes, sipping an aperitif as live classical music is played nearby."

"Is the Doge's Palace open to the public?" she asked. "I'd like to visit it."

He noticed her lack of interest toward the Basilica but did not comment.

"Here we are," he said, as they exited a narrow alley. "Our first stop. The Rialto Bridge just ahead of us."

"Was Rialto someone famous?"

"No my dear, just the name of a nearby market."

Patrizia marveled at the view afforded from its summit, her eyes resting over the ancient palaces lined along the rims of the canal. They seemed to flaunt their beauty as naturally as models on stage. When some tourists moved away from the parapet, she took their place, and, her elbows over the banister, she followed, as if in a trance, the passage of motorboats, vaporettos, and gondolas.

"I could stay here all day," she said, with dreamy eyes, "and watch the world go by."

"We can stay if you wish," he said, embracing her, "but we'd miss all the other sights."

"Let's go, then," she said, taking his arm again. Her hold was weight-less and her pace sprightly. He felt as though they were one person. Twenty minutes later, they climbed the steps of the Palazzo Ducale, where they wandered through the magnificent salons and terraced loggias up to the Ponte dei Sospiri—the Bridge of Sighs.

"This was the point of no return," Riccardo commented, "hence the name."

"I know," said Patrizia. "I read that it connects with the old Piombi prisons."

Coming down from the Doge's Palace and onto Piazza San Marco, Riccardo pointed to the majestic façade of the Basilica, its imposing architecture, the solemn statues, the striking golden mosaic. Patrizia, however, did not show any interest in visiting the interior. They sat down outside Henry's Café and consumed an aperitif while the orchestra played Mozart and Chopin and hundred of pigeons flew overhead or ate corn from the hands of tourists. There was a gay bustle; a cheerful, gesticulating crowd; an impression of constant movement against the firmness of centuries-old monuments and palaces.

"Now I know why it's called salotto d'Italia," she said appreciatively. "Despite its size, it does feel as cozy as a living room."

Later, they window-shopped in the contiguous gallery, and Patrizia was astounded at the beauty and variety of the blown-glass vases, sculptures, and accessories. "Are they all made in Murano?" she asked.

"Yes, most of them anyway. The city fathers transferred the furnaces to that island hundreds of years ago, after a terrible fire in the city."

"Can we go there? I'd like to visit some of the studios and maybe see artists at work."

"Yes, we can catch a ferry right around the corner."

*****

"I want to stay outside," said Patrizia, refusing a seat. She walked to the open back of the vaporetto and held onto the metal safety railing, ready to enjoy the view. A moment later, the motorboat left its floating dock, meandering at a measured pace around the canals, which snaked through the city like arteries through a human body. Then, upon reaching the opposite end of the urban area, it gathered speed and nosed straight toward Murano. After a while, Patrizia looked back at the diminishing city outline: a reddish horizontal ribbon of buildings floating between two bands of indigo color. It was so incredible that it seemed unreal. She closed her eyes, and the vision disappeared. And for a brief instant, she felt that upon opening them again, the city would be vanished, and nothing would meet her eyes but the placid loneliness of the lagoon.

"Look, dear," Riccardo called. "There is Murano."

Patrizia turned around and saw the tiny island. It seemed as if it were mysteriously raised from the depth of the lagoon, by the pushing of an electric button or the strike of a magic wand.

Once on the ground, at first they followed the stream of tourists and visited a few studios, including Seguso and Venini, the old glass museum, and several other showrooms.

Afterward, they found themselves on a *calle* lined with quaint artisan shops, and Patrizia was like a child in Toyland. She asked the shopkeepers a million questions, admired and touched all kinds of handcrafted items, tried on multicolored woven scarves and kid leather gloves, and laughed heartily whenever, upon trying on Venetian masks, she saw her disguised image reflected in an antique mirror. They went out again, and coming across a little garden, she picked a daisy and put it in his lapel. She then gathered a bunch of lavender seeds, rubbed them with her hands, and eagerly inhaled the strong fragrance. Later, they entered other shops, where she showed her interest in many other items, yet refused to buy anything. "I prefer to enjoy them without possessing them," she stated.

However, Riccardo, who never ceased looking at her—surprised at her vitality, happiness, and *joi de vivre*—was finally able to buy her a bronze gondola as a memento of their Venetian visit.

Around two o'clock, they finally stopped for lunch in a quaint trattoria with a platform extending over a canal.

It was a bright day, and after placing their order, Patrizia sat quietly, her face typically turned to the sun, her eyes closed, and holding Riccardo's hand. Her skin was radiant, and her hair shone with golden glints of color. Beneath them, the water slapped gently against the pillars of the platform, and in the distance echoed the staccato sound of a diesel engine; a boat plowed through the tranquil waters of the lagoon near the old cemetery. Here and there, the hazy environment was punctured by several medieval bell towers. The sound of bells was heard far away.

"Patrizia," said Riccardo, breaking the silence, "may I ask you a question?"

"Of course, my dear."

"It's rather personal."

She opened her eyes and looked at him with roused interest. "It's all right. You're my husband, and you can ask me personal questions."

"You may wonder why now. Actually, I was thinking about it this morning, and just now the church bells reminded me of it. I'm curious to know what turned you away from religion."

"Oh … that," she said, glancing at the lagoon. "I wondered when you'd ask."

"Well?"

"It was by degrees and for more than one reason, my dear," she said, facing him again. "You see, by nature I'm not inclined to believe in something I don't see or experience personally. Faith eluded me all my life. I never truly understood what it meant, as I did not feel it. Then came the observance of the very people who were supposed to possess it. Like the nuns in my college, who thumbed their rosaries most of the day but would not offer any help or advice when we were in need. Or the priest who, during confession, rather than speaking of the spiritual world, wanted to know in detail if I played with myself. Then came the study of history—and with it the madness of the Crusades; the rapacity of the Vatican State; and, finally, a regrettable school trip to San Giminiano."

"The medieval Tuscan town? What happened there?"

"We went there in a field trip. I remember how happy I was when we arrived. It was a beautiful early summer day. We got off the bus and entered the city through the south gate. I thought I was in a medieval heaven: the scale of the town, the hewn stone and redbrick houses, the towers, the aromas in the food shops … We ventured out in one of the old palaces open to the public whose vestibule had been changed into a winery. While some of my companions were checking the various vintages, I walked farther in and found myself on an open terrace. I had to close my eyes, and I then opened them again to believe the sight was real. I thought I was dreaming in front of a painting: there, right in front of me, rolling hills, vineyards, emerald grass fields, ravines. A countryside that seemed depicted by a master of the Renaissance rather than randomly produced by Mother Nature. It filled my heart with joy." Patrizia paused and closed her eyes again. Her lips curled into a serene smile, as if reviewing the image imprinted in her mind.

"I don't see the connection," said Riccardo.

She looked at him tenderly. "I'm coming to the point. I wanted you to understand my mood before I explained the next episode."

"I'm sorry. Please continue."

"Soon after we walked to the main square, we took some pictures near the olden water well, the towers, and then, since it was still early for lunch, we entered a small museum. I followed my companions, and when I realized its theme, it was too late to go back. My instant scrutiny had already broken the enchantment; my day was ruined."

"Why? What kind of museum was it?"

"It was about ways and instruments of torture used during the Inquisition. There hung the most horrible pictures and description invented by men to torment other human beings. There were gallows, strappado, stakes, and wheels, plus a large exhibition of authentic, smaller metal instruments, which, as the multi-language legend said, were inserted in various orifices and then mechanically expanded until the flesh was torn apart, shattered. Priests were depicted as assisting in these orgies of violence, seated in comfortable armchairs, behind screens or curtains." She rested a moment and took a sip of water. Riccardo listened in silence.

"The graphic representations of unimaginable cruelties," she said, "the actual instruments of torture were such that made me wonder how any human being could do this to another, and in the name of religion. I got out as soon as I could, and when we finally went for lunch, I couldn't eat. I vomited on an empty stomach." Patrizia's voice trailed away; her eyes were downcast.

Riccardo caressed her hand. "Now I'm sorry I asked," he said. "I hope I didn't cause you to lose your appetite again."

"No," she answered. "I'm famished."

"I heard that, madam," said the waiter, who stood a few feet away. "Soup will be served in a moment."

"It's true," said Riccardo, "that mankind caused an awful amount of pain in the name of religion. For me it is different, though. My not caring for the church as an institution doesn't detract from the belief that there must be a Supreme Being."

"If there is, Riccardo, I would need stronger confirmation than that of priests or books written by men like you and me."

"I understand. All the same, I wonder how two persons like us, coming from similarly religious families, could have such a different outlook. Religion can be of help, you know? Take my mother, for instance. During the Great War, only faith and prayer saved her from madness and despair. It gave her the strength to carry on. I too need to know that someone out there listens to my prayers—a creator who guides my existence and the complex universe around us. Do you know what I mean?"

Patrizia nodded in silence and squeezed his hand in understanding.

That evening, they made love again.

Patrizia was right, Riccardo thought, as he lingered in her arms. *The wait made me enjoy the magic of this moment even more.* After a last kiss, he announced, "Tomorrow morning we'll take an early train and go to San Donà."

"I'll finally get to visit your native town," she said enthusiastically. "I've heard so much about it. Now I'll finally see it with my own eyes."

*****

They took the Venice-Trieste train, whose first stop was going to be San Donà. As soon as it left the lagoon behind and made for the open countryside, Riccardo stood up, gazing out of the window with the impatience of a child. After a short while, he said, "Look, Patrizia, we can already see the campanile of San Donà."

Dutifully, she put down the newspaper she was reading and bent her head toward the window, looking in the direction indicated by Riccardo. But from that distance, other than the flat landscape, she could only make out the slim profile of a bell tower and a few red-tiled roofs emerging from the hazy morning air.

What more did I expect? It isn't really unattractive, she thought, *but it lacks the deep green of Tuscan pines and cypress trees; the shimmering silver reflections of our olive trees; and the soft, undulating outline of the Tuscan hills.* She forced a smile, and caressing Riccardo's hand, she said, "Yes. Now I can see it too. How does it feel to you to be back here?"

"I really don't know," he answered. "I'll tell you at the end of our journey."

In San Donà, they took a room at a small new hotel near the train station, and then, since it was too early for lunch, they decided to walk around town. They stopped briefly in front of the old cathedral and then by the monument to fallen soldiers. Upon reading the name of the young soldiers commemorated, Riccardo whispered, "My name could have been there as well."

"No, my dear," Patrizia replied teasingly. "You were condemned to live at least one hundred years."

She put her arm in his and walked, matching his long strides, occasionally feeling contact with his hips. She followed his curious glances until he finally said, "You know what? I'm surprised at how much smaller the town looks compared to my recollection!"

They went through Piazza Indipendenza and were directed to the place where his house had once been—only to find, in its space, a multi-floor edifice that housed a dozen or so apartments. It was similar to many others and was probably erected with government funds for the families who had lost their homes during the Great War. Some of the older houses of the area were hardly recognizable, as they had lost much of their original luster. And others seemed to have been inadequately mended of their war wounds by improvised bricklayers.

*****

Riccardo did not recognize any of the shops, and other than the church, the main square, and the typical local speech inflection of the inhabitants, little remained of what he remembered. "Do you mind if we walk up to the river?" he asked Patrizia. "It's not far from here."

They walked out of town, holding hands tightly, and Riccardo could feel the mounting tension in his chest. Without realizing it, as they came closer to the river, he began to walk faster and faster. In its proximity, he recognized traces of the old trenches, and he pointed to the white signs, with dates and other information, that had been placed where special events or battles had occurred.

Suddenly, he stopped. "This is exactly where I stood," he said, his voice broken by emotion, "on that tragic seventeenth of November, nineteen seventeen." He squinted his eyes, seeming to listen to an arcane, personal message coming through the listless midday air. Contrary to that gloomy, gray day, today the sun shone brightly, and its rays pierced through the foliage of the young, vigorous trees, tracing golden arabesque patterns over the dark ground. A light breeze whispered amidst the higher branches and played nature's peaceful tune. Riccardo, however, in his own mind, heard only the whistling sound of shells, the thunder of explosions, and the cry of wounded men echoing from the distant past.

Soon they left the path, and Riccardo, walking by the riverbank, moved cautiously over the grassy ground, as if afraid to step on the fresh remains of fallen soldiers. Then he glanced below and thought that even the river seemed much smaller than he remembered—too small to have played such an important role during the last phase of the conflict.

Riccardo observed a long moment of silence, as solemn and respectful as a prayer. Then he shook himself and said, "Let's go back and look for a place to eat, Patrizia. All of a sudden, I'm ravenous."

As they reentered the town, she shook his arm. "Why not right here?" she said, pointing to a trattoria on the right side of the street. "I just took a whiff of a delicious smell, and I think it's coming from there."

"You're right," said Riccardo. "It's the enticing smell of roast meat and rosemary. Let's go."

A short while later, they hungrily consumed their meal almost in complete silence.

Patrizia was looking at her husband with such intensity, as though trying to enter his mind and read his thoughts. Riccardo, his eyes lowered to his plate, was wrestling with the countless recollections that thumped at his mind's door unsolicited. Then, as though finally shutting that access and traveling to a conclusion, he let out a deep sigh and said, "Now I have only one more thing to look after. It's something I have been promising myself for a long time. I'm sure you'll understand." He explained what it was, and he was happy when Patrizia agreed wholeheartedly.

Two days later, they took the train back to Venice, and they returned home from there.

*****

Upon arriving at San Romano, Meino, who was waiting outside the train station with his carriage, greeted the couple.

They found Luisa at home, in the front garden, tending her begonias and pulling weeds from the flower beds.

"Hallo, Mother," Riccardo called out.

She stood up slowly, straightened her back, wiped her hands on her apron, and walked toward them. She waved to Meino, who, clearly not wanting to interfere with the family reunion, was already departing.

"Riccardo, Patrizia," she said, "am I ever happy to see you! I didn't know exactly when you would arrive. Are you tired? Are you hungry? I prepared some food."

"We are fine, signora," Patrizia answered, embracing Luisa. "I just need a nice hot bath. The *accellerato* train from Florence was pulled by one of those smoky old locomotives, and I'm afraid I smell of burned coal."

"Riccardo," said Luisa in a mocking stern tone, "haven't you told Patrizia not to call me signora?"

"Yes, of course, Mother, but what can I do?"

"Seriously, Patrizia, I would like you to call me by my name ... or *Mother*, if you prefer. Will you do that for me?"

"If you insist, signora. Mother, I mean."

"That's better. By the way," said Luisa, as they were climbing the front stairs, "the movers delivered your piano and a few cartons from your apartment. We put the piano in the entrance hall. You tell me if you like it there. The boxes are downstairs. Sort them out as you please; they are not in the way."

"Thank you, Mother. It's only my winter clothes, books, a few knickknacks, photographs, and two paintings. Most of the other things I sold or gave away to neighbors and friends."

At supper, they talked about the trip. Patrizia's enthusiasm for Venice, its canals, and the Byzantine style of its buildings was evident.

"It isn't for nothing," said Luisa proudly, "that they call her the Queen of the Adriatic."

"It's beyond belief to think that a small city like that was once a maritime power, more potent and rich than many nations," Patrizia said. "From the balcony of the Palazzo Ducale, I could imagine a doge, his hands resting on the marble balustrade overlooking the Grand Canal, viewing the arrival of the Venetian fleet from the Orient. The unloading of silk, spices, precious stones, and ..."

"And the marble columns of San Marcos, plus the bronze horses of the clock tower, both stolen from Constantinople?" Riccardo added.

"I didn't want to say," Patrizia replied. "I presume, at one time or another, any tribe, city, or nation has been guilty of rape and plunder."

"I suppose," said Luisa, "and some more than others. Too bad you couldn't stay a bit longer."

"At the same time," said Patrizia, "the briefness of the experience gave greater sharpness to the pleasure of the moment. It was long enough this time, and perhaps one day we will go back."

"We were also in San Donà, Mother," said Riccardo.

"I wasn't sure you'd go. Did you show Patrizia where you were born?"

"Among other things."

Luisa gave him an odd look.

"Yes," Riccardo continued with a sober smile, "we also called on the bishop and visited the cemetery."

"The bishop?" Luisa asked, holding a forkful of food suspended in midair. She looked at him earnestly.

"I made arrangements for Papa's remains to be exhumed and brought to Castelvecchio's cemetery."

Luisa's eyes filled with tears. "I'm sorry," she said, resting the fork on her plate and wiping her eyes with the hem of her apron. "Excuse me."

She got up and left the room.

"Perhaps you should have waited 'til after supper, Riccardo," Patrizia said.

"I didn't think she'd take it that way."

"It's an emotional thing for her, you know? She needs time to digest it."

After a while, Luisa returned to the table. "I'm sorry," she said. "I didn't expect it." Then she grabbed Riccardo's hand and shook it gently. "Thank you, Riccardo. I hope it didn't cost you a fortune."

"*I'm* sorry, Mother. I realize that I timed it badly. I wanted to surprise you. As far as the cost is concerned, I know how important this was for you. So it was well worth it. Now please finish your meal."

*****

XI

Late 1932

With Patrizia's arrival, life at the Lanzis' had a new flair. In the evenings, she helped with the housework and enlivened the atmosphere with her conversation. Sometimes she played the piano or sang. Other times, she retired to her room to read or iron her clothing, leaving space and opportunity for Luisa and Riccardo to be alone and converse as they used to.

Luisa continued her usual routines and kept up most of the household chores. One Sunday, as she prepared to go to mass, Luisa thought of asking Patrizia to go with her. "I can wait for you, if you wish," she said, seeing that her daughter-in-law was still in her house clothes.

Patrizia had promised Riccardo not to antagonize his mother on this subject. However, she felt that unless she made a stand now, she'd be embarked on a dangerous pattern of deception or undesired acquiescence. She hesitated and then replied, "Go ahead, Mother. I have a few things to do. If I can, I'll go later." She knew in her heart that it was a lie, but that was all she could think of for now.

At the end of the day, it was evident that the two women were not on the best of terms, and Riccardo asked his wife the reason for the sullen mood.

"It's nothing, Riccardo," she answered, sketching a conciliatory smile. "Women are like this sometimes."

"I wish you would tell me, Patrizia. I would feel uncomfortable sitting at the supper table with this atmosphere."

"All right, my dear. I think it has to do with my not going to church this morning. I don't want to alienate your mother, but I don't want to be a hypocrite either, or be forced into something I don't feel."

For a long instant, Riccardo stood in front of his wife, pondering an answer. Then he took her hand. "I understand, Patrizia. I'll talk to her when I think it opportune. Please act natural at the table. Do it for me."

During the next few days, the atmosphere felt more relaxed, and the two women were able to behave almost as if nothing had happened. However, they knew that the religion was something they could never discuss.

*****

One evening, about three months later, the family had just finished eating. Luisa was about to get up and clear the table when Riccardo said, "So, Patrizia, should I tell Mother, or would you rather do it yourself?"

Patrizia swallowed her last bite and was wiping her mouth, ready to speak, when Luisa openly anticipated her words.

"I think I already know," she said with a broad smile. "But hearing it confirmed will please me even more."

"Yes, Mother," Patrizia said. "I'm going to have a baby."

Luisa got up and embraced her daughter-in-law. "Thank you, my children," she said. "This is one of the happiest moment of my life." She walked toward the sideboard and picked up a bottle of wine. "I was saving this bottle for a special occasion. We must make a toast to the happy arrival of a new Lanzi."

For Luisa, it was the beginning of a new, bright chapter in her life. "Thank you, Lord, for this gift," she said later, kneeling in front of her favorite crucifix. "I'm only sorry that my Roberto won't be here to enjoy the arrival of our first grandchild. I know I've asked you many favors, my Lord. This is the last I will ever request. Please let this baby be healthy and intelligent, and let me live long enough to see him grow into a worthy man."

From that moment, though she had always shown kindness to Patrizia, Luisa became even more concerned with her well-being. She treated her with a tenderness that was truly maternal; her voice had a gentler tone, her eyes a more caressing look. She frequently asked if she'd had enough to eat … if she wanted a rest from her household chores … if she needed anything at all.

For her part, Patrizia appreciated all that attention, but she kept working at the distillery, and she did her share of the housework.

One night, during her eighth month of pregnancy, Riccardo was kept at work quite late, and Patrizia decided to return home by bike.

Rather than the regular route, she took the narrow path that ran along the river, realizing too late that, in certain areas, it was still wet and slippery from the recent rain. She thought of turning back but decided against it. At the next slight turn, her front wheel slipped in a crevice. Taking a bad fall, she rolled over several times and ended up on the side of the street, hugging her now rather portly tummy.

"My baby!" she cried.

After a few moments of sitting on the wet ground and not seeing anyone in sight, she got up and straightened the handlebars. Leaning on the bike, she managed to return home on foot. Her hands and knees, badly scraped from the gravel, bled profusely.

"Gesù mio!" Luisa exclaimed when she saw her. She made her sit, cleaned the wounds with water and vinegar, and then finally expressed her greater concern. "Did you hit your tummy? she asked.

"I'm not sure. I remember trying to protect it as I was falling, but I'm not sure."

"We'd better call the doctor."

"Riccardo will be home soon, Mother. He can get the doctor when he comes. Meanwhile, I'll soak and disinfect these scratches again."

"Except for the superficial cuts and abrasions," said the doctor a short while later, "everything seems all right. But one never knows with these things. You might have an early or sudden delivery. It wouldn't hurt to choose a well-equipped hospital, capable of taking care of a premature or complicated birth."

The local hospital and those of the surrounding towns were rather primitive. After a brief discussion, and consultation with Lorenzo, the family opted for the Santa Maria Nuova Hospital in Florence.

*****

A few days later, Patrizia began to feel sudden pains in her lower abdomen, and she decided to start packing her clothes and go to the hospital. Luisa joined in to help, showing her for the first time the trousseau she had secretly knitted for the newborn.

"It's beautiful!" Patrizia exclaimed. "But it's all in blue, Mother. Are you so sure that it will be a boy?"

"I could bet on it, my dear. I had two boys myself, and you may think it preposterous, but I can tell by the shape of your belly."

"Mother, Mother, you and your unscientific, folksy beliefs," Riccardo said, shaking his head. "I'd better go start the car."

"Drive carefully," Luisa shouted behind him. "Try to avoid the bumps on the road."

Finally, after numerous additional suggestions, admonitions, and blessings, Luisa embraced Patrizia and said, "Take care, my dear. I'll pray every day for you and the child."

"Thank you," Patrizia answered in a neutral voice.

As he drove away, Riccardo could see, in his rearview mirror, his mother in the middle of the road, waving her white apron in a last farewell. After about one kilometer, the road turned slightly north, and she disappeared from his vision. They were completely alone.

"At this pace," he said, after passing the town of Santa Chiara, "it will take us a couple of hours to reach Florence. Are you going to be all right?"

She placed her left hand on his right thigh and stroked him gently. "I hope I will, Riccardo. Thanks for asking."

"How long do you think it will be?"

"For the baby? As the doctor said, it could be anytime now. It does feel as though it could be soon, but being my first, I can't be sure."

"Are you worried?"

"Not for me, Riccardo."

"For the child?"

"A little bit. These pains worry me a bit, and I haven't felt much movement in the last few days."

Riccardo was worried too, but he didn't want to show it. "If it's a boy," he said tentatively, "do you mind if we name him after my father?"

"Roberto," she pronounced slowly. "Roberto Lanzi. No, I don't mind it at all; it has a nice ring to it. And if it's a girl?"

"Then you'll choose the name. I'm sure you'll come up with a nice one."

Near Empoli, where the Arno wandered at a sauntering pace at the footing of pine-covered hills, the road becomes a narrow ribbon squeezed between the river and the ascending slopes. At a certain point, opposite a sharp curve and the left riverbank, a granite boulder as large as a two-story building limits the road to two narrow lanes. Just past the boulder, where the vehicles need to slow down, fascist "Blackshirts" had placed a roadblock, and all traffic came to a stop. Passengers' documents and the contents of cars and trucks were checked. Only half a dozen vehicles were ahead of the Lanzis', but the process seemed rather slow.

"Please be calm, Riccardo," said Patrizia, who clearly sensed his rising irritation.

He did not answer, but after another moment, he engaged the gear and veered sharply to the left, moving up to flank the first vehicle. Two armed men turned toward him. Before they reached the car, Riccardo rolled down the window.

"It's an emergency," he said unapologetically. "My wife is about to give birth. I must hurry to the hospital."

The closest man bent down and looked at Patrizia, who had closed her eyes and placed her hand over her belly. "Show me your documents," he barked.

Riccardo complied.

"Do you have a party card?"

"No, I don't, but I have clearance to travel without restriction. Here," he said pulling another paper from his wallet.

"What do you do?" the man asked suspiciously.

"I am a chemical engineer," he answered icily.

"He is very modest," Patrizia cut in decisively. "He's the director of an important distillery that is very significant for a certain minister in Rome, if you know what I mean."

The fascist caught the cold look in Riccardo's eyes, the calm but slightly strained composure of Patrizia's face, and seemed convinced that she was telling the truth. "So sorry, signora," he said. "We were just doing our duty. Here you are, sir." He returned the papers. He then gestured for the gate bar to be raised, waving good-bye to them.

"Stupid bastards," said Riccardo through his teeth. "What on earth are they trying to find?"

Patrizia's laughter turned into a grimace of pain, unseen by Riccardo.

"Why are you laughing?"

"Because you're funny. No, perhaps funny is the wrong term, but I am somewhat amused to see that you're so entrapped by your pride and principles that you forget your child. To me, the child is my priority, and if I have to cook up an excuse to protect him, I'll do it."

Riccardo was about to reply, but he thought better of it. After all, he recognized that he was no longer accountable to himself alone. In the future, it would be wise for him to modify his behavior to reflect his new responsibilities. He drove in silence for some time, pondering the new condition that marriage and fatherhood would necessarily bring about. Would he be able to alter his nature for the sake of his child? he wondered.

When they entered Florence, the sun was about to set, and the surrounding hills encircled the city in a warm embrace, while the pale-yellow façades of numerous Renaissance villas emerged from the thick woodland's green. All around them, tall cypress trees pierced the air with their dark spears. The last rays of the sun seemed to linger a while longer over the glowing cupola of Santa Maria Del Fiore and the upper segment of Giotto's bell tower. Below, the city was already immersed in the twilight atmosphere of the fading day. Soon the city lights would come on.

"Will we go by Lorenzo's?" Patrizia asked.

"Yes, my dear. He spoke to the head physician at the hospital, and he should come with us for the introduction."

"Stop at the next dark place, then. I want to kiss you."

He pulled over near the sidewalk, under a large canopy of a horse chestnut tree. Patrizia turned slightly toward Riccardo and gently pulled his head toward her. She kissed him eagerly. "This will have to last you for a while, you know that."

"Not too long, I hope."

"All right," she then said in a whisper, "let's go and have this child."

*****

Riccardo left the hospital more worried than he had wanted to appear to Patrizia and Lorenzo. He hoped that both mother and child would be fine, but a doubt lingered in his mind. He started on his way home, leaving the city lights behind, but as soon as he entered the countryside, he was overcome by a sense of loneliness. He had barely left his wife, and he already missed her more than he could have imagined. *For the next few days,* he thought, *I'll immerse myself in my work and pretend that she is still in the lab, only a block away from me.*

He drove slowly down the narrow road, which looked eerie in its emptiness. The pale-orange lights of the car barely pierced the density of the dark night curtain. He drove with the blind confidence that after the fifty or so meters of visible roadway, another fifty would follow, and another fifty after that, and then fifty more. *Just like one's life journey,* he thought. One can barely see the present … and perhaps have a vague vision of tomorrow, but beyond that, it's pure conjecture, hope, a figment of the imagination.

"Roberto Lanzi, my son," he then said aloud. A quiver of fear crossed his mind; it didn't seem possible that he'd soon be a father.

When he got home, his mother asked a thousand questions: *Is Patrizia still okay? Did the doctor say anything new? Was Lorenzo told to call you at the distillery the moment Patrizia's in labor? Is the baby going to be called Roberto?*

"Only if he is a boy, Mother," said Riccardo in jest.

"Well," Luisa retorted, "if she is a girl, we'll call her Roberta."

*****

"Good morning, sir," said Antonio Rossi, as he walked through the door of Riccardo's office. "You sent for me?"

Antonio was one of four full-time draftsmen who worked at the San Romano distillery. He had been employed there since its opening, and he was confident of his professional capabilities.

"Good morning, Antonio," said Riccardo with a pleasant smile. "Dispense with the 'sir'; it reminds me of military days. You may call me Riccardo … or Ingegnere, if you prefer. Please sit down."

Antonio pulled a chair closer to the desk and breathed out a sigh of relief.

"I have been following your work for a while," said Riccardo, rolling his chair away from the desk and assuming a more relaxed position, "and I must tell you that I am quite satisfied with your performance."

"Thank you."

"What I like most, in addition to your work ethic, is your attention to detail." He paused for a moment and then added, "I would like to make you my special assistant."

Antonio nearly jumped from his chair, as though he couldn't have dreamed of a better offer. "Ingegnere!" he exclaimed.

"Before you say anything," Riccardo interjected, "I must tell you that in exchange for considerably much more work, I can only offer you a nominal raise."

It was no secret that Antonio was one of the people who had appreciated Riccardo's directorship from the time of his initial speech. Contrary to his predecessor, Ingegnere Lanzi brought to the job outstanding technical abilities and a clear vision. The draftsman had grinned during the opening remarks, when Riccardo declared: "Please don't waste your time and mine in useless recommendations ..." He had laughed when he heard of the reversal of the Salani gradation. The man in front of him had made it clear that he would never demand from others what he himself could not do. He led by example and was not a bloody fascist to boot.

"I appreciate that," he said, "and I am thankful for the opportunity to work with you and learn more. As for the money, I don't have a family to support, so I can manage."

"Good." Riccardo smiled with satisfaction. "I must remind you, though, that I will be even more demanding than I've been so far."

"No problem, Ingegnere. I don't mind working hard."

With the completion of his first unsupervised assignments, Antonio clearly showed the particular technical talent and devotion to his job that Riccardo demanded. Soon it became evident that he also shared with him another distinguishing attribute. One day, upon returning a blueprint to Riccardo, he looked around and said, "I find your office inspiring, Ingegnere."

"And why is that?"

"Well," he continued hesitantly, "I like your choice of wall decorations." "You like blueprints of copper pipes, boilers, check and relief valves, and other gadgets, do you?" Riccardo said, a tinge of mockery in his voice.

"Well, not exactly, but I certainly prefer them to the usual pictures of self-decorated buffoons hanging from the walls of most offices nowadays."

Riccardo frowned and said, "Close the door, please." He then waited until the draftsman returned to stand in front of his desk. "Sit down, Antonio," he said in a low, even tone. "I appreciate the fact that you feel your confidence is safe with me. But … at work, I don't tolerate political statements of any kind. Be they pro or against the regime."

Antonio seemed confused. His eyes darted toward the walls and then to the folded newspaper on a corner of the desk. Riccardo had underlined some of the bold letter titles with a red pencil. *This is no good!* he had also written on the white margins. The stories related to Hitler's recent ascent to the Chancellorship of Germany, and to the Japanese withdrawal from the League of Nations.

"I'm sorry, sir, but I thought …"

"Please let me finish," said Riccardo. Then he shifted comfortably to the back of his chair and looked straight at his younger colleague, the hint of a smile beginning to grow at the corner of his eyes. "I was going to conclude that those particular statements and ideas can be exchanged after work." He winked knowingly and said in a softer tone,

"If we have more in common than technical interests, it will come out in time, perhaps during a stroll along the riverbanks or during a private after-supper chat. But I warn you, don't follow my example too closely; it could be dangerous to your health."

Antonio looked at Riccardo questioningly.

"This morning I overheard a conversation," Riccardo said, nodding toward Ligato's office. "People boasting of a fascist bravado last night. Four or five half-drunk Blackshirts forcefully 'purged' a poor devil, just because he had not raised his glass when they toasted Al Duce. They held him, beat him, and then forced a full liter of linseed oil down his throat."

Antonio made a sound of revulsion. "Such heroism," he said. "It's one of their usual punishments. The poor man will shit his eyeballs and be sick for two weeks." As he spoke, he twisted his mouth as if tasting the repugnant potion himself.

"Exactly, and that is not all. Bands of Blackshirts in Santa Chiara have joined those of other towns to harass and beat people, burn co-ops, and commit other felonies against antifascists."

"I understand," said Antonio.

Riccardo knew he had made his point. He tapped his hand over his desk. "Now, please go and bring me the modified sketches of the new boiler as soon as possible."

Antonio sprang up from his chair, a wide smile on his face, "Yes, Ingegnere. Thank you."

As he closed the door, Riccardo's thoughts went to his child soon to be born. He was going to arrive in a world of violence and hatred. How would he cope with all that?

- XII -

"*Pronto … Pronto.* Hallo, Riccardo, it's me, Lorenzo. Can you hear me?"

"Yes, I can hear you. Anything wrong?"

The Line went dead, and for the next few minutes, Riccardo's mind was in turmoil. *Did something bad happen?* he thought. He tried to be calm and resist the thought. Finally, the telephone rang again.

"Nothing wrong, big brother, but I wanted to notify you that my official status has changed."

"What official status?" said Riccardo. "Did you get married?"

"No, my dear brother. But I'm now a very proud Uncle Lorenzo."

It was ten in the morning on June 13, 1933.

"Did everything go well?" he asked, with relief in his voice. "How's Patrizia? How is the baby? Is it a boy or a girl?"

"Everyone is fine, Riccardo. It is a handsome boy. Too soon to say whom he resembles, but from the stern look on his face, I think he'll grow to be a meditative, uncompromising bastard like you." He laughed loudly and then said, "But why do we waste time talking? Step on it and come to the hospital; I'll wait for you there."

*****

One week later, Patrizia and little Roberto were discharged, and they returned to Castelvecchio.

Luisa had invited the neighbors and prepared a table with sweets and a bottle of *vinsanto*. Erina Giani came with her six-month-old daughter, Lucia. "Let's rejoice in the arrival of these two children," said Luisa, including Lucia in the celebration. "Let this be one of the happiest days of our lives." She could hardly contain her joy, and she took the warm bundle from Patrizia's arms and held it against her bosom, "Roberto *mio*," she said, alternating laughs and tears of joy. "Roberto *mio*."

"Mother," said Riccardo after a while, "don't you think you should let Patrizia hold the baby now?"

"It's all right, Mother," said Patrizia, observing Luisa's happiness. "You can keep him for a while."

A few weeks went by, and all seemed normal with Roberto, until Luisa realized that the baby was not gaining weight. Further examination revealed that Patrizia, despite her generous bosom, did not have sufficient milk. The doctor confirmed this fact and suggested other alternatives. The baby, however, stubbornly refused the new food.

Following the customs of the time, the doctor told the Lanzis to search for a wet nurse to care for him. They pursued several leads and interviewed half a dozen women. Finally, they settled for Amelia, a robust compatriot and Meino's distant relative, who had just given birth to a baby girl of her own.

Amelia lived on a remote farm with her husband and their three children, several hours from Castelvecchio. Although the house had no running water or electricity, upon visiting it, the Lanzis found it clean, well kept, and containing plentiful food.

In modern terms, the distance from Castelvecchio was not great. However, the means of transportation were limited, particularly in the smaller centers far from railway lines. The country roads leading to the town where Amelia lived were so narrow, bumpy, and slow that it took the better part of a day for a round trip by car. Furthermore, by now, Riccardo was often away, and consequently, despite Luisa's and Patrizia's displeasure, visits to the newborn were rather infrequent.

Luisa was particularly vocal on this matter. "Why?" she wondered aloud. "Why has God granted his birth … only to take him away?"

"Mother," Patrizia said after the ninth complaint, "it might be better neither to credit God for Roberto's birth, nor blame Him for his temporary absence. Given the state of our world, I think God has more serious things to worry about."

Mindful of their previous quarrel, Luisa did not reply but continued to knit furiously what must have been the tenth jumpsuit for the baby.

"I miss him too, Mother," Patrizia added, placing her hand over Luisa's shoulder. "During the day, my job helps me keep my mind busy, but at night I miss him so. When Riccardo returns from Rome, we will go visit him and tell you all about it."

"How is he?" Luisa asked after one of their rare visits. "Is he growing well? Who does he resemble?" She had attempted to go with them, but long car rides over winding roads made her dreadfully carsick, and she regretfully had to give up the visits.

So it was that Roberto was raised as one of Amelia's, in the same manner she'd raised Rosina, who was only two months older than he, and her two boys, Franco and Armando, respectively thirteen and nine years old.

In August 1934, the fourteen-month-old child started to eat solid food, and it was finally time to bring him home. Everyone was euphoric, and Luisa, who had spent the last several months knitting woolen garments for him, anticipated his homecoming with joy. She was going to watch over him, teach him all she knew, cook her best recipes.

Patrizia seemed glad to leave certain concerns to her mother-in-law. After all, she had enough to do at the distillery, and Luisa was the one with the most time and most expertise. The baby would be safe in her capable hands, and Patrizia would have plenty of time with him at night and on Sundays, as well as holidays.

"I've already raised two children," Luisa reassured Patrizia and Riccardo, "and in worse times than these. Don't worry; I'll look after the little one."

A few weeks later, the family was in the kitchen. The cook stove generated sufficient heat to make it the warmest room in the house. Patrizia was setting the table for supper, and Luisa sat on a rocking chair, feeding little Roberto, who sat quietly on her lap, directing his alert eyes toward whomever was talking at the time. The dry logs splitting open in the flames sent out intermittent crackling noises. The air was lightly spiced with the smell of garlic and rosemary coming from the saucepan placed on the stove.

"It makes my mouth water," Patrizia said.

Riccardo sat in a corner, reading the daily paper. He had removed his denim jacket and was wearing a light green cardigan and his brown house slippers. Since he had become a father, the political news appeared to affect him more negatively than ever before. The world seemed to have gone insane, and his son would have to grow up in the middle of that mess.

"What's happening in Germany," he suddenly said, "is going to affect us all."

"Who do you mean by *us all?*" Patrizia asked.

"Italy, Europe … maybe even the rest of the world. Look at the facts: in nineteen thirty, Hitler's National Socialist Party gained one hundred and seven seats in the Reichstag and became the second largest party in the country. By nineteen thirty-two, it had the backing of some four hundred thousand storm troopers. *Plus,*" he emphasized, "a superbly trained elite group called Schutz Staffeln, or SS, as personal body guards, under the direct command of Heinrich Himmler." He slapped the daily with the back of his hand and kept reading. Now, 'President Von Hindenburg, unable to arrive at any alternative solution and fearing civil war, has appointed Hitler as chancellor …' I wouldn't be surprised," he said, frowning, "if in less than a year, that madman doesn't dispose of all other parties in the Reichstag—and we see the birth of yet another dictatorship."

"You are such a pessimist."

"Yes, Patrizia, people call me that when I make certain predictions. Then, when they do occur, they conveniently forget I made them."

"Cuckolded and beaten," she replied, laughing, "like Calandrino in Boccaccio's novel."

"How do you know he is a madman, Riccardo?" Luisa asked, without taking her eyes from her grandson.

"I've read his *bible*," he answered. *"Mein Kampf* says it all."

*****

"What's the matter, Mother?" Patrizia asked a week later, finding Luisa coiled in an armchair in the dark, tightly rapped in a heavy blanket.

"I don't know what's wrong with me. I've been shivering all day. And half an hour ago, I tried to get up and prepare supper, but I almost collapsed."

"Did you check your temperature?" said Patrizia, placing her hand over Luisa's forehead, "You feel very hot."

"Yes, I did, just after putting Roberto to bed, but there must be something wrong with the thermometer. It shows forty-two."

Patrizia fed Roberto, and as soon as Riccardo came home, she told him to go get the doctor. "Be quick, Riccardo. Meanwhile, I'll help mother into her bed."

"I have bad news," said the doctor awhile later, in answer to Patrizia's worried look. "The town has been hit by a serious strain of typhoid, and from the symptoms described by your husband, Signora Luisa might have caught it too."

"How serious is it?"

"We don't know for sure, but some of them, especially young children and older people, may die from it."

"How come we haven't heard about it?" Patrizia said. "Shouldn't there have been an alert?" She opened Luisa's bedroom door, and the doctor went to pick up Luisa's wrist.

"*Signora,*" he answered, "we are still discussing whether an alert would benefit people … or create undue fear. Anyway, from what I can see, I must confirm what I was saying."

"What about the baby?" said Patrizia with a tone of dismay.

"You must keep him away," the doctor responded.

"But where?"

"Away," he repeated, "to the countryside. To his wet nurse if you can, and as soon as possible."

"Why, my Lord," Luisa cried, "why are You giving me this grief? I hate to part from him again. He'll forget all the things I taught him, poor darling. Yesterday he learned the days of the week, and I was halfway through teaching him the months of the year."

"Don't worry, Mother," Patrizia tried. "He'll be back soon."

"And what will he learn on a farm?" Luisa insisted. "It'd be a waste of time for such a bright child."

"Mother, he'll be far from our care and affection for a short time," Patrizia said, "but also far from this nasty outbreak."

"Indeed, Mother. Patrizia is right," Riccardo said. "It is safer to take the child to Amelia's farm until the outbreak is controlled. He'll catch up with your teaching when he returns."

"Don't worry about what she's saying," the doctor whispered. "It's the high fever. Here, give her these pills, two every hour on the hour. Sorry, but I must run now; I still have many people to visit."

"Here, Doctor," said Patrizia, handing him a clean linen towel. "You can wash your hands in that bathroom."

"It would be advisable," said the doctor before leaving, "not to visit the baby while the virus is still around. You may be unaffected but still be the carriers."

"Mother," Patrizia said gently, "it's the best for Roberto. Stay calm now; this will pass." "I know, I know," she moaned. Then she turned her head toward the wall and cried.

- XIII -

1935

The next day, Riccardo and Patrizia brought Roberto back to the farm. He only cried the first day. He mentioned his parents and his *nonna*, or grandmother, for a week or so, but then, distracted by the care and attention of the other children, he soon adjusted again to the farm environment.

Everyone there was proud of "the little one," as they affectionately called him. At night, when the chores of the day were done, the family gathered in the vast kitchen. Amelia's husband, Nello, started a fire in the open pit, and the bright flames bounced on the shiny copper kitchenware before shooting up the black chimney. Amelia took the incandescent embers and cooked on the side spits while singing old folk songs.

Months later, Roberto began to kneel on a chair to follow some of what Amelia's son Armando, then just over thirteen, read for his home assignment. He looked at the book of illustrations and asked questions. He read some of the easy words and showed interest and understanding far beyond his age. One evening, Armando was reviewing a chapter of Roman history, reading aloud as usual, about the events surrounding one of Julius Caesar's battles in Gallia. Roberto, kneeling on a straw chair, his little body propped up against the heavy kitchen table, his hand under his chin, suddenly interrupted Rino's reading and asked, "Why didn't Caesar use the *leophants,* like the other general?"

Armando seemed surprised by the question. He had read chapters on the Punic War several days earlier. He did not expect the little boy to have learned and retained the information.

"Which other general?" he asked, just to test him further.

"You know, Armando. You read it that other day."

"I know I read it, Roberto, but do you remember his name or not?"

"Of course I do; it was Hannibal."

Armando smacked the little boy jokingly. "Bravo. That was good." *And rather unusual for a three-and-a-half-year-old,* he was surely thinking. "Rosina is the very same age," he mused aloud, "but not nearly as smart. For that matter, nor is Franco."

*****

At long last, after many months delay, the work at the house started after Luisa's sickness was finally completed. The new boiler, the heating coils, and all the pipes were properly installed and the system checked. All the rooms in the house would now be comfortably warm even in winter. The Lanzis were anxious to take Roberto home.

"I will come too," Luisa said.

"Mother, you know car rides upset you," Riccardo said. "You'd be sick for days."

"I'll ask Meino to take me with his horse-drawn carriage. I'm all right in the open air."

"Even if you were crazy enough to do that, what about the little one? It'd be a five-hour ride each way."

"Riccardo is right, Mother," Patrizia interjected. "Wait here, and we'll leave in the morning; we'll be back by early afternoon."

A few days later, Amelia received a letter from the Lanzis, stating that they would soon come by car and take Roberto home. Amelia and the rest of the family were saddened by the news. Although they knew this had been a temporary situation, everyone felt attached to the child and now considered him a member of the family.

That evening, she told the boy, but the news of his parents coming made no impression on him. His mind had only retained the image of two well-dressed people he was supposed to call Mother and Father.

They had come once before the gathering of grapes, he thought. And another time when Franco gave him piggyback rides, chased him, and then rolled him over the freshly cut hay. And the last time was before the start of spring, when the leaves still slept inside the branches, as Nello said, and the fruit trees, after the long winter rest, were ready to give birth to their beautiful crops.

Roberto knew the fruit trees well, for he had seen them in nature and in some of Armando's schoolbooks: green apples, red succulent cherries, gold-yellow and blood red plums, velvety peaches, apricots, figs, and many other delights.

The whole family was in the field near the house, picking ripe tomatoes, and he and Rosina were given their own basket to fill. Suddenly, the unusual buzz of an engine broke into the pastoral silence of the countryside. Everyone looked up.

"Look, a black Fiat," Nello said. He pointed his finger toward the cloud of dust rising from the gravel road. Then he turned toward the boy. "It must be your parents coming to take you home," he said sadly, "I thought it was tomorrow."

Everyone walked back through the field and reached the yard just as the black car swung around and came to a stop. Both passengers got out of the car, and Nello, lifting his straw hat deferentially said, "Good day, Signor and Signora Lanzi."

"Signora," said Amelia apologetically, twisting her hands in discomfort. "We didn't expect you until the morrow. We didn't prepare *il signorino.*"

"*Buon giorno,* Amelia. Don't worry; it is our fault. There was no time to advise you of our change of plans." Then she looked at her son, who was standing at some distance, uncertain as to what was expected of him, and said, "All the same, I wouldn't want his grandmother to see him in this condition."

Roberto was wondering what condition she meant when she continued, saying, "Let's give him a bit of a scrub and change him. We brought some new clothes. I hope I got the right size; he has grown so much ..."

"Right away, signora." Then, looking at her husband, Amelia said, "Nello, don't stand there like a post. Hurry up and warm some water."

He rushed inside the house.

Finally, Patrizia turned toward the boy, who hadn't moved. "Come here, *cucciolo.*" *Puppy.* "Give your mother a big kiss." She bent down gracefully and placed a kiss on each of his cheeks. "He has grown a lot since we saw him last," she said to Riccardo, "and look how dark his complexion has turned."

"You're right," echoed Riccardo, who was a few paces behind. "But he still does look like a puppy." He affectionately ruffled Roberto's sun-bleached hair and kissed him on the forehead.

They seemed a bit apprehensive of what the boy's reaction would be. It was a sudden departure from the only home and people he had known for a long while. His mother was fidgeting at first, and then smiling without any apparent reason.

"We missed you very much, you know," she said, as he stared at her. It sounded like an attempt at answering his questioning look. Or perhaps it was a reflection of her inner insecurity.

The boy did not know what to respond, and he just looked at her in silence, clearly making her feel even more uncomfortable.

His parents were both elegant, and Roberto thought they had a pleasant smell. His mother's scent was like freshly cut lavender and wild flowers; father's was more like sweet tobacco mixed with something else. But if they were his mother and father, why didn't they hug him or squeeze him or lift him over their heads, as Amelia or Nello did? What was he supposed to do?

After the bath, Roberto's head was still buzzing with the echo of those words that seemed so important to everyone else, but had little meaning to him: *home, voyage, grandmother.* The only home he'd known for some time was the farmhouse. Voyages were the short trips, on foot or ox-driven cart, to the fields and back. And Grandmother, or Nonna, was what Franco and Armando called the old black-dressed woman whose face was covered by a netlike patch of wrinkles, and whose mouth often dripped with bubbly saliva. Her withered body trembled like a tree leaf in the breeze, and her bony hands had bulbous joints and twisted fingers that could not hold on to anything. When someone talked to her, she uttered incomprehensible, babbling sounds, making strange gestures that no one seemed to understand. She never got up from her chair with wheels.

He didn't remember what his other nonna looked like.

He also felt uncomfortable in his new clothes, and he kept pulling down the collar of his shirt, which they had insisted on buttoning completely. He looked down at his high socks and tight, shiny shoes, and he stomped his feet on the floor like a young colt.

When it was time to leave, the children stood by looking at him as if it were the first time they'd set eyes on him. Nello blew his nose with his yellowing handkerchief, and Amelia kept on sniffling as if she had a cold. Finally, she stepped forward, scooped him effortlessly from the ground, and pressed him tightly against her generous bosom. "Give me a big kiss, Roberto, and come and see us soon. We're gonna miss you a lot, you know. 'Specially Rosina."

The boy kissed everyone and then hugged Rosina for a long moment. He gave her a little package his mother had brought for her. They unloaded from the trunk other boxes with clothes, books, and toys for the rest of the family. Patrizia gave Amelia some money and thanked her for the care she had given Roberto.

"We are grateful to you Amelia," she said, hugging the woman. "You've done a great job with our little boy."

"He is like my own," said Amelia with a choked voice.

Riccardo was already at the wheel, and Patrizia took Roberto by the hand and walked toward the car.

"Come, cucciolo."

"Don't forget the guy with the elephants," Armando called from behind him.

Roberto turned around and gave him a cheerless smile. "I won't," he whispered. There didn't seem much to say or do, and the short, silent pause that followed verged on embarrassment.

"We will bring him back sometimes," said Patrizia, breaking the silence. "Good-bye for now."

"Good-bye, signora."

As the vehicle began to move, everyone waved. Amelia rubbed her eyes with a corner of her apron.

What did it all mean? Where exactly were they going? How soon would he come back? What did his "other" home look like? Were there children there? Would Rosina, Franco, and Armando come see him? It didn't seem to matter to anyone else that he didn't quite understand, and it all seemed too difficult to ask.

Roberto sat silently for a short while, feeling like crying but not daring to. Armando always told him that crying was for babies, and he certainly wasn't one. He tried to make sense of this new situation, but he felt confused. He liked the new smell of the car, though: a mixture of perfume, pipe tobacco, and an odor similar to when they poured fuel into the old tractor. He recognized the three distinct smells coming, respectively, from his new mother, his father, and from the car itself. He liked how they blended together.

He knelt on the back seat and faced the rear window. His eyes were glued to the countryside, which seemed to run away from him, and to the farmhouse that, up to this moment, had been his home. It was now barely visible in the cloud of dust that formed behind the car, and for a moment longer, he thought he could still see tiny human figures waving their arms in the air. Instinctively, he raised his arm in a salute, and then he dropped it again. At the end of a long, straight road, the car turned, and the house disappeared forever. His eyes filled with warm tears that began to fall down his cheeks. A choked sob escaped from his mouth, and his mother swung on her seat and looked at him.

Probably not wanting to make things worse, she said with a calm voice, "What is it, dear?"

"Nothing," he said, without turning. He dried his cheeks and his eyes with his hands. A few moments ago, the entire matter of leaving the farm to join his "real" parents had seemed of little relevance, like a scene witnessed from the outside. Suddenly, with the disappearance of all the people he knew and loved, it had become real, and he, Roberto, was at the center of it.

Patrizia pushed her hand toward Riccardo and squeezed his arm. He nodded in silence. She let a long sigh and said, "Don't worry; you are going to like your home. We are your real mother and father. We and your nonna will be there for you."

"Are Rosina and Rino coming too?"

"We shall see, my darling. But don't be concerned. Your nonna will play with you and cuddle you to no end. Do you remember your nonna?"

"No," he answered, a bit too decisively.

Patrizia studied her husband. They had discussed the prolonged absence of the child, wondering how long it would take him to adjust to his normal reality. Would there be any permanent trace of this unfortunate episode?

Soon the road widened, and the gravel was replaced by a smoother, darker surface. The dust vanished from the air. There was more countryside to see, and towns were somewhat alike—houses crowded against each other, with churches and redbrick bell towers. Sometimes, when the road cut through one of these towns, he saw people on foot or bikes, as well as town squares with fountains and statues in the middle of them.

Along the way, some of the houses aligned with the street had wide white bands painted in front, with large black letters over them. Roberto could only make out a few words. "What does it mean?" he asked, pointing his little finger.

"*Vincere o morir!* Win or die," answered his father.

"And that one?" Roberto asked, pointing at another one.

"*Viva Il Duce.* Hurrah for the Duce."

"Who is the Duce?"

"He is the maniac …" Riccardo's words died in his mouth as Patrizia pinched his arm.

"He is the present chief of state," she said instead. "The boss of Italy, our country. His real name is Mussolini. Benito Mussolini."

"Oh, I know him!" exclaimed the little boy. "But … I *thought* his first name was *Delcazzo.*

When the burst of laughter finally subsided, and his parents recovered from their son's use of the word *prick,* Riccardo asked, "And who made you think that was his name, darling?"

"Nello." Roberto answered matter-of-factly. "He always called him that when he got some bill. He'd throw them bills over the table and shout *Mussolini Delcazzo.*"

The laughter resumed until Patrizia, with tears in her eyes, said, "His name is definitely Benito, my dear, but people call him Il Duce. It is like calling someone chief, commandant, or boss ..."

"Like Julius Caesar," Roberto stated assertively.

Openly surprised, his parents looked at each other. They smiled, and then his father asked, "And do you know who Julius Caesar was?"

"Yes. It's the guy who fought without the *leophants.*"

"Oh, the elephants. Very good," said Patrizia. "And who taught you that?"

"Armando did. He read it from his book."

"You see?" Riccardo whispered to his wife, "and you were afraid he would learn only about beans and tomatoes at the farm."

"I know about those too," said Roberto, and then asked, "Who wrote those words on them houses?"

"*Those* houses, darling," Patrizia corrected. "People. Just people." Then, as if realizing her answer had been rather abrupt, she added, "*Cucciolo cheri,* we don't know the persons who actually wrote those words. But why do you want to know?"

"I like to know things. That's why."

Patrizia raised her eyebrows and looked at Riccardo, who exclaimed, "What an inquisitive little darling!"

"What's *inkisitive*?"

Both parents burst into laughter, and Roberto, unsure of the reason for that reaction, dropped his inquiries.

They drove in silence for a while. Then, his mother, perhaps wondering why the boy had suddenly fallen silent, turned around and asked, "Are you hungry, darling?"

He shook his head.

"Roberto," she said, giving him a stern look, "only donkeys shake their heads. People talk. You should answer, *No, thank you, Mother*."

Roberto looked at his mother fixedly. "No, thank you, Mother … is what I should answer." He also mimicked her tone.

She laughed again, and although he didn't understand the reason, it pleased him. Her laugh uncovered a beautiful set of white teeth that stood in positive contrast to Amelia's.

After another long while, his father slowed the car. "Roberto, look in that direction." He eased the car to the curb and came to a stop. They got out of the car and walked a few steps toward a terraced clearing on the woody hilltop.

"You see down there?" his father asked, lifting the boy over the parapet. "Down in the valley? That town is called Castelvecchio. Our home is there."

Roberto's eager eyes swept down the slope, across the quilted flat of the valley, and kept running down the straight country road leading southward to the even landscape. There, his gaze rested on the opposite wave of hills, a great distance away, between the quilted land and the blue sky. From where they stood, those hills resembled tall waves of varying shades of gray, their motion frozen in a static pose.

The boy retraced his visual journey to the dense patch of reddish roofs floating on a sea of green. "Castelvecchio," he repeated, with the perfect enunciation of every single letter.

"Bravo!" his mother exclaimed.

There were green fields, and yellow squares of wheat, and then, sparsely scattered and contained within smaller plots of brown soil, the more familiar shapes of farmhouses. There were sheds nearby, like at Amelia's, where farm tools and other equipment were stored. At the edges of the yards were the yellow cones of straw stacks, his favorite hiding place when they where playing hide-and-seek.

The dense fluffs of green were big trees. *Walnut trees,* he thought, *like those Nello used to club with a long cane to knock down the shelled fruits.* He noticed a narrow silvery line snaking through the green, just beyond the peachy town. "A creek," he said, pointing his little finger.

"No, Roberto, that is the Arno River. A river is bigger than a creek," answered his father. "And you see there? A bit to the left, where the smoke is rising toward the sky? Those are the chimneys of the distillery, where your mother and I work."

"What is a chimney? What is a *distelery?*"

"Distillery," Patrizia corrected.

"What is a distillery?" Roberto asked again, this time pronouncing the word correctly.

"One of these days I will take you there," he said. "It will be much easier for you to understand if you see it with your own eyes. Now let's get back into the car." He lowered the boy to the ground. "Your nonna is waiting for you."

The car moved forward, and Roberto's attention was soon taken by the interesting descent. The road cut through a densely wooded area with large pine trees. They had copper-colored trunks and umbrella-shaped tops, and at their feet, a thick bed of brown needles and many pinecones. The air was pleasantly spiced with their scent.

At the bottom, the car sped across the flat countryside, and soon the boy was distracted again by the view of the nearing town of Castelvecchio. From that angle, the town appeared squeezed upward by the tight embrace of its medieval walls, with the cupola of a church near the center and a tall quadrangular bell tower well to the left. Pigeons were flying to and from its numerous recesses. There were redbrick tenements with numerous narrow windows and wrought iron balconies, some with vases of red geraniums, others with clotheslines and garments hanging to dry.

Roberto stood up, looking forward, holding onto the back of the seats. Before reaching the archway that entered the town, they turned left, following the circular embrace of the old defensive walls. When the car turned left again, he looked back and saw the massive structure of the bell tower and, under it, its high vaulted gateway. Beneath it, the asphalt road ended and gave way to a stone paved street that led toward the town center.

The right-hand side was lined with open fields intersecting with the road at almost right angles. On the left rose small villas with flourishing gardens, surrounded by peripheral walls or shrubs, perfectly parallel to the road.

"Voilà," said Patrizia, as the car came to a stop.

"Here we are," echoed Riccardo, blowing the horn twice. "And there is your nonna."

Roberto looked across the street at the pretty villa with green Persian shutters and palm leaf decorations beneath the windows. Now he thought he remembered. Through the foliage of fruit trees, he saw an older woman, with silvery hair and a broad smile. She was coming down from the short stairway that connected the front terrace to the house. A little girl with golden hair, of about his age, was following her closely. When she came near, he saw that her eyes were the color of the sky.

"Roberto," Luisa called from across the way.

He was pleased to see that this nonna was different from the one he knew at the farm.

Nonna Luisa had completely recovered. She was now fifty-two, and considering her age and turbulent past, she was in good physical shape. It was common knowledge that she was mortified that her untimely sickness and the house renovations had delayed the return of little Roberto. Now it was clear that she intended to regain the time lost. She came down more swiftly than one would have thought possible, waving her arms and calling to him.

"Roberto, Roberto! You have grown so much since I saw you last," said Luisa, picking him up impetuously. She held him tightly to her chest for a long moment, as Amelia always did. "You are so huggable, my little darling. I missed you so much," she added with enthusiasm, and then she kissed him repeatedly on his cheeks. She nodded to the little girl "This is Lucia. She lives in the house next to ours. She'll come and play with you sometimes."

He began to cry. Silently. And then an impulse drove him to put his arms around his nonna's neck and return the embrace and the kisses.

She did not wear perfume, but her skin had a pleasant scent of lavender. He felt secure in her arms, and he could feel sincerity through the strength and effusion in her embrace. He liked this nonna and her pleasant flowery smell. She seemed to love him more than the others did, and maybe soon she'd help him return to the farm.

- XIV -

1936

Days, weeks, and months withered away, but every now and then, the young boy would mention the members of his previous family and ask when he would see them again. Sometimes, after his nonna had put him to bed, he would even cry, silently, and call their names: "Rino, Rosina, Amelia, Nello …'"

Little by little, however, the bond between him and Nonna Luisa began to grow, and he didn't notice the absence of his previous family as much. When Lucia came to visit with him, they played house and other games.

With his mother, it was a different story. When Patrizia returned home from work, it was time for Roberto to go to bed, so their time together was limited. On Sundays and holidays, she tried to be closer to him. However, if she was too persistent, the boy turned to his nonna who was, perhaps unwittingly, always too ready to shelter him. She just had to open her arms, and he nestled up to her like a hatchling to the hen. When he went to bed, his hugs and kisses didn't have the same warmth and sincerity of those reserved for Nonna Luisa.

*****

In time, Patrizia somewhat adjusted to Roberto's apparent preference, and she suffered in silence. *After all,* she thought, *given the amount of time he spends with his nonna and her absolute dedication to him, how could it be otherwise?* But when she played the piano or sang, he would slowly approach her and stand nearby, a pleased look on his face, as if to say, *I approve. You're good at this.* Then he would return his attention to his grandmother once again.

Sometimes Patrizia had the wild impulse to seize the little boy by the shoulders, give him a gentle shake, and say, *Don't you know that I am your mother? That I conceived you out of love and harbored and nurtured you inside my body for months? Save some of your love for me as well, will you?* But when she attempted a firmer approach, he seemed to erect a barrier and retreat to a distant, unreachable level.

In the meantime, Riccardo was busy with all his responsibilities and seemed satisfied to enjoy the progress of his son from a distance. Under his competent direction, the distillery of San Romano achieved several of his objectives on schedule. The extraction and yield of pure alcohol increased, the seeds were successfully separated from the residue of the grapes, and the first grape seed oil was produced. The final dregs were further ground and compressed into small cylindrical shapes and used in cooking and heating stoves in lieu of wood. The distillery had begun to earn good money.

Happy for the results obtained and keeping good the original promise, the powers that be in Rome finally commissioned Riccardo to build the "model" distillery. As anticipated, it was to be situated at the outskirts of the capital, in a place called Ciampino. The news did not seem to excite him as much as Patrizia expected.

"What is the matter, Riccardo?" she asked him one day, as they drove home from work. "Aren't you satisfied with your success?"

"Up to a point," he answered dryly. "My personal success is one thing, but the rest …"

"What rest?"

"Now I know for sure that the powers that be are not interested in procuring jobs for the people, or letting farmers gain more from their hard work, or producing useful commodities."

"What do they want, then?"

"Everyone a different thing, my dear. It depends on their agenda. One wants to show off the regime's newest complex; another wants to prove to the Germans that, at least in one technological field—albeit a modest one—we are keeping up with them. Then there are the ones who want to make money by getting kickbacks from the contractors. Finally, there are those who are in this for the thrill of a compliment or a medal—deserved or not—from their beloved *duce*."

"I understand," Patrizia said. She arched her left arm over his shoulder and began to rub his neck.

"I suppose I shouldn't complain," he said after a moment. "After all, I got what I wanted."

Patrizia had learned to read him well, and she sensed a hidden undertow in his mood. "What else worries you, Riccardo?"

"Being away from you so much in such difficult times. Among other things, your closeness also has a calming effect on me. When I'm far from you, I worry constantly."

"But why?" she asked gently, now stroking his knee.

"You know … my usual concerns. The world seems determined to descend toward chaos, and having a family worries me. Germany has denunciated the disarmament clauses of Versailles. Italy has invaded Ethiopia. The League of Nations, which was supposed to solve these problems, has responded inanely."

"Why inanely?"

"They have imposed sanctions on imports of irrelevant commodities, without obstructing the import of steel, coal, and other strategic materials necessary to the war apparatus … What else can I tell you?"

"You should tell me that you love me, that things will get better, and that our son will be a genius like you—but hopefully with a more optimistic outlook."

He turned his face toward her and kissed her. "I'm glad you are not an ordinary woman."

*****

Nonna Luisa was Roberto's surrogate mother, his tutor, and his mentor. Under her care, his days were quite different from those he had known at the farm. Time was no longer measured by words such as sunrise, noon, sundown, supper, and bedtime. His every activity now went by shorter, more precise spans of time, regulated by the house clock or the tolling of bells from Castelvecchio's tower, or the beginning of the next lesson.

Arithmetic and reading were the first subjects patiently administered by Nonna Luisa. Her passion for numbers was soon passed to Roberto, even while performing her daily chores, like weighing the ingredients of a new cake or adding the time necessary to prepare it, or in the garden, measuring the space available for a given number of plants or flowers. She involved the young boy in those calculations, and to her surprise, he responded beyond expectation.

Everything became a playful exercise, a game, a challenge that soon engaged Roberto's mind and interest. She taught him to use an abacus, occupying him in difficult calculations, which he often completed mentally, to her amazement and satisfaction. He now asked her all the questions that, at the farm, he had reserved for Armando.

His nonna seemed to know much more, and she could talk for hours about so many subjects, including the place up north where she was born, or episodes and battles of the Great War, which she had seen at close range, along the famous Piave River battlefront. He had an insatiable interest in these war tales, and he'd even memorized a wartime song that his nonna sang:

Muti passavan quella notte I fanti,
tacere bisognava andare avanti,
... come un presagio dolce e lusinghiero,
il Piave mormoro', non passa lo straniero; boom, boom.

Tacit our soldiers marched that night,
silently needing to go forth all right.
But like an omen sweet and promising
the Piave River was heard murmuring,
the enemy shall not pass; boom, boom!

Under her supervision, his reading soon became fluent, and when he told her that he had little interest for children's books and children's subjects, she did not hesitate to feed him more mature material. De Amicis's book *Cuore* became one of his favorites, and in particular, three episodes where the young protagonists behaved heroically. The first was about a twelve-year-old Florentine boy who, unknown to the family, got up silently every night and spent hours in the study, duplicating by hand some of his father's work, in order to increase the family's inadequate income.

The second had a patriotic flavor. It was about a poor, young immigrant, alone on a boat to America. Several adult fellow passengers, moved to pity, gave him a few coins, which he threw back in their faces without hesitation when he heard them belittling his native country.

The third story was about a teenager gone bad, who, in a moment of redemption, saved his grandmother by thrusting his body between her and the knife of an assailant. The boy, lying in his grandmother's arms, asked her forgiveness moments before dying.

Roberto admired equally the diverse qualities of these young heroes, but he could hardly keep from crying when reading the episode about the grandmother. It went right to the core of his relationship with his *nonna* and his love for her.

His vocabulary, though vast for his age, was occasionally tainted by the poor grammar and colloquialisms used at the farm. "I should have went downtown with you, nonna," he said once.

"I should have *gone*," Luisa promptly corrected him. "You must learn how to decline your verbs properly, Roberto; otherwise you will not learn how to speak the way you should."

Sensitive to the comments his grandmother made about some of his expressions, Roberto imitated her speech and seldom made the same error twice. He even memorized written sentences, and in a brief time, he improved almost to excess and spoke in a manner that was formal in style and well beyond his years of age; he was barely four.

One afternoon, Luisa was knitting a new sweater for her grandson. The rhythmic clicking of the metal needles mixed with the hushed cantilena sound of her afternoon prayer and the soft rustle of pages being turned. She was sitting near the large western window for better lighting. Every now and then, she turned her head and glanced at her grandson, who knelt on a kitchen chair, his forearms resting on the kitchen table. He had placed a thick book in front of him, and he flipped the pages after long, attentive scrutiny.

"Nonna," he suddenly called, "would it be appropriate if I spoke like Dante?"

She slowed her mechanical movements; her forehead acquired deeper wrinkles. "Dante who?" she asked, looking at Roberto from above her horn-rimmed glasses.

"Dante Alighieri. You know, the Florentine man who perfected the Italian language."

"Yes, of course I know of Dante Alighieri."

"Look, Nonna, here is his picture," said Roberto, lifting the book toward her. "I recognized him because of his big nose and laurel leaves around his head."

"Of course, my dear," she said, smiling. "It would be wonderful if you did, taking or leaving a few words that have changed in the last six hundred years."

Encouraged by the praise he received for the new way of expressing himself, it soon became the norm. Then came reading history books and young adult books, as well as the memorization of poems.

*****

The many daily activities scheduled by his nonna left Roberto little free time. That, he spent mostly in the garden, following Grandmother's chores, chasing after imaginary foes or watching hired hands clipping the fruit trees. How did they know what to cut? What if they hurt the little fruits hiding inside the naked branches, waiting there for spring?

Occasionally, the Gianis' daughter, Lucia, of approximately his age, and some other children in the neighborhood joined him. Most of the time, however, he was by himself, and in those moments, he felt lonely. He wasn't quite sure about this new life. At times, he thought that his new parents loved him too, although differently from Amelia and Nello. He also appreciated some of the comforts his new place offered, like having his own bedroom or having a bath in a large white enamel tub, held by pewter-colored panther legs and filled to the rim with steaming hot water. But he yearned for Rino's and Rosina's company and missed the freedom he had before. It was all so confusing.

Here, it was a much smaller world to roam and discover, a world with exact borders and limitations and many dos and don'ts: *Do check with me before you pick a fruit. Don't go outside the gate. Do ask permission before entering the neighbors' property. Don't get all dirty with mud!* Sometimes he did wander farther away, crossing the shallow ditches that separated the neighbors' properties, to explore his surroundings. He liked to stray into the Barsottis' because they had an apricot tree, and Marina, the owner, was kind and gave him some fruit. But then, mindful of his nonna's recommendation, he would quickly return to his garden.

He thought with longing about the random symmetry and spontaneity of the farm, the open spaces, the long grassy fields, and the greater freedom they allowed. Now he could no longer run barefooted, and his shoes had the bad habit of getting dirty or the laces coming undone. He wasn't allowed to taste or eat unripe fruit. Or to go to bed without saying those prayers and invocations his grandmother taught him, and which he must recite before getting under the blankets.

Of all the subjects that his nonna taught him, religion was the only one that failed to make a positive impression on the young boy. He tried to imagine these all-powerful yet invisible gods and angels but despite his sincere efforts, he could not bring to mind any image or picture with which to compare to the concrete world he knew.

At the farm, they never thanked God for the food they grew and cooked. Nor did they kneel on the floor to recite prayers with seemingly meaningless words. With Rino, he had learned many things, but not about religion. But now he learned prayers like he learned poems, and he recited them at bedtime, kneeling on the cold marble floor in front of a large oval picture hanging over his bed.

Every evening, he stared at that Madonna holding a chubby child Jesus on her lap, surrounded by a peaceful garden with large trees and cooing pigeons. The trees and pigeons reminded him of Amelia and the kids at the farm. He thought with nostalgia about the large fireplace, where, before going to bed, rather than washing and praying, he watched the wooden logs burn in the spit and stared at the flames changing into different shapes and colors, and the sparks shooting against the blackened wall. He listened, in his memory, to the hissing sounds damp logs expelled from their wooden bodies, as their vapor, or the soul of the trees, as Nello called it, rose slowly through the chimney toward the sky.

So Roberto recited his prayers with his mouth to please his nonna, while his mind, unintentionally, wandered away.

*****

Nonna Luisa seemed to be in charge of everything. In addition to tutoring and caring for Roberto, and with little outside help, she cooked the meals, washed the dishes, looked after the garden, directed the work in the orchard, and sewed or knitted sweaters and socks.

There seemed to be no end to her energy.

On Sundays, she would get up early and attend the first mass so that the time spent in church would not deprive the family of her presence. Sometimes, when she went to a late function, she took Roberto with her. Despite the fact that this was obviously related to "religion," he didn't mind. In fact, the outing afforded him the enjoyable opportunity of escaping his confinement and seeing new places. While the others prayed, he observed the people around him, surveyed paintings and bas-relief on the walls, and assessed new experiences.

On one of these outings, an old woman stopped once to chat with his grandmother. She started speaking to him as if to any child his age. She seemed surprised at his serious and coherent answers. Then, as if it was a question related to the previous ones, she asked him, "Who do you love best in the family?"

What a silly question, he thought. He hardly saw his mother and father. And when he did, it was for a quick salute before bedtime, or to ask him the progress of his French, mathematics, or piano lesson. *Up to which page did you read today? It's getting late; you should be in bed.*

His nonna was always there for him. He looked up at the woman.

"The person I love best," he answered without hesitation, "is my nonna."

Both women burst into laughter.

He did not understand their hilarity.

⸻ XV ⸻

May 5, 1936

Riccardo leaned forward to hear the radio announcement.

"*Camicie Nere della rivoluzione*—Blackshirts of the revolution—men and women of Italy, Italians and friends of Italy, beyond the mountains and the seas, listen … Benito Mussolini is announcing that Addis Ababa, the capital of Ethiopia has been conquered. The region is now under Italian control; the colonial war has finally ended!

A thunderclap of applause interrupted the broadcast. Riccardo and Antonio, who were listening to the broadcast in Riccardo's office, looked at each other.

"Italy has its own empire," Il Duce continued. "A fascist empire. Empire of peace, of humanity and civility …"

More applause burst through he airwaves.

"After fifteen centuries, the soldiers of the fascist revolution salute the return of the empire to the sacred Roman Hills …!"

"I could throw up," Riccardo said to Antonio.

In the adjoining office, Mr. Ligato listened to the same broadcast. He was elated by the announcement. His clapping was heard through the walls. The fascist committee at the distillery decreed that all workers take the rest of the day off and join the festivities downtown. Antonio, Riccardo, and Patrizia remained at their posts and left work at their usual time.

At home, they found Luisa in front of the stove, preparing a stew. The dining room table was already set for supper.

"Did you hear the news?" Luisa asked.

"Yes, Mother," Riccardo replied. "We have heard that we conquered a fragment of wasteland and called it our empire!"

Four-year-old Roberto came through the door, "Good evening, Mother; good evening, Father." He ran toward them to kiss and be kissed. "What's an empire, Father?"

"Won't you even give us time to settle in?" his mother asked.

"It's all right," said Riccardo, lifting the boy. "When a nation acquires territories beyond its own borders and has dominance over other countries, their people, and their resources, it is called an empire. Do you understand, Roberto?"

"Yes, of course, Father. Like the old Egyptian Empire, the Roman Empire, or the British … I just wanted to hear it from you."

"Very well, Roberto, and do you know where Ethiopia is?"

"Yes, Nonna showed me in the atlas. It's in Africa, near Somalia. She also called it the Horn of Africa, and you just called it wasteland."

"Very, very good, Roberto. I don't know whether to congratulate you or your nonna. Both of you, I suppose."

"It was easy," said Luisa. "This kid has the memory of an elephant." She paused for an instant and then added, "We'd better watch what we say in front of him, though. He'll remember it … and he might repeat it at the most inopportune time. You know what I mean?"

"When is it opportune to repeat it, Nonna?"

"Go wash your hands, cucciolo," Patrizia intervened, laughing. "It's almost dinnertime."

*****

The Zinis, neighbors to the north, celebrated the event with other fascist sympathizers. Days later, Pia Zini received a letter from her son Giuliano, Blackshirt of the "First Hour" and volunteer of the Ethiopian campaign since 1935. He had written home in glowing terms even more bombastic than Mussolini's, and Pia needed to share her enthusiasm with whoever was available at the moment. From her window, she saw Luisa in the garden, bent over a green patch of romaine lettuce, collecting some fresh leaves for their meal. Pia was soon walking behind her, holding a sheet of paper, her reading glasses down on her nose. She wanted to relate her son's thoughts to Luisa, despite the latter's known lack of enthusiasm for the fascist regime.

"I'm so excited," she said, without any preamble.

"And good evening to you too," said Luisa, continuing to pick lettuce leaves.

"Listen to what Giuliano wrote me," Pia said. 'We are only a brief episode on earth. What really counts is the greatness of Italy!' Aren't they beautiful words? He says that in his battalion, they have absolute faith in Il Duce, that they always believed in the final victory … that they will continue to chase every enemy, including the British, all the way down to Kenya, or India, or wherever they will try to escape."

"My dear Pia," Luisa replied, as she raised herself from her kneeling position, "I wouldn't be so sure. It has taken our troops over three years to conquer a patch of sand at the expense of poor African tribes. I doubt very much that we will prevail over the British …"

"Obviously you haven't heard about the new Rome-Berlin pact and the other with Japan. The 'Axis'—what a good name for this new alliance—will prevail, you'll see. And with the help of God …"

"Pia," Luisa interrupted, "we have so far prevailed because we have not been taken seriously, and no one else is foolish enough to fight and die for a patch of sand. As for 'the help of God,' I'm sure that, as Patrizia would say, He has better things to consider than Mussolini's sandbox."

"I wouldn't talk like that if I were you. People would think that you don't care for the motherland."

"On the contrary. It is because I do care that I speak as I do. And not even Mussolini shall stop me from saying what I think."

"Well, Luisa, one of these days … maybe you'll …"

"I'll what?"

"Oh nothing. We'd better change the topic."

"Yes, we'd better. I've got to go and cook supper anyway."

Patrizia had heard part of the conversation between the two older women. "You should be more careful of what you say, and to whom, Mother," she told her gently. "You know the consequences …"

"I can't bear to hear that type of nonsense," Luisa snapped back.

*****

Riccardo looked at them and appeared to be on the verge of making a comment. He remained silent. After all, his antipathy for political arguments was well known, and his respect for his mother prevented him from stating it once more. Besides, he did not want to interfere between the two women.

Despite these differences with the Zinis, though, as in many other cases between neighbors, the two families continued to have what could be described as a reasonable rapport. At least publicly. Luisa and Pia often attended the same church functions and returned home together. Or they gathered with other neighbors near the artesian well, at the edge of the Lanzis' property, to knit while chitchatting or reciting prayers. Privately, though, it was a different matter, and both indulged in condemnations of each other's position and predictions of defeat for the opposite camp.

*****

By June, work at the distillery of Ciampino was well under way. Riccardo traveled there, assisting architects, project managers, and technicians with the choice and placement of equipment and with the introductions of his latest innovations.

Being a project of some importance, it had the special "blessing" of Il Duce. Hence, the fascist apparatus encouraged visits by technicians of other countries—and particularly Germany—as well as by politi-cians and military attaché stationed in nearby Rome.

Usually, Riccardo shunned contact with these men and preferred people with similar professional interests as his. One such a person was Franz Rheinhold, a young German engineer who approached Riccardo—or *Herr Rickard,* as he called him—and expressed surprise and admiration for the Italian, especially when the latter spoke to him in German.

"When I was told of this project," Franz said, "knowing the Italian tendency to exaggerate, I was skeptical. Now, however, I must confess that it measures up to what it claims to be. Your depurative process means we can potentially extract more oil from seeds and kernels than from olives. The transformation of the dregs eliminates the costs of discarding the residues. It's a genuine advancement in the field."

"Thank you," said Riccardo.

The mutual scientific interests, the unusually gregarious tempera-ment of the German, and Riccardo's sense of hospitality helped gener-ate a sense of friendship between the two men.

Riccardo used some of his limited spare time to acquaint Franz with the historical sites of Imperial Rome. Together, they visited such places as Nero's Baths, the Caracalla Spa, the Coliseum, and *I Fori Imperiali*—The Forum of the Empire.

"I read that this area was once a swamp," said Franz at the Forum, "and that it was drained through ingenious aqueducts and underground channels."

"Yes, although that was not a native Roman talent," said Riccardo.

"Etruscan engineers provided that and other skills to the Romans. The latter were more inclined to build roads, bridges, and other devices."

"Not a bad trait when you want to maximize the movements of troops and facilitate conquests of other lands."

"Exactly."

Whenever possible, Riccardo took the opportunity to refresh his German, and Franz, encouraged by Riccardo, tried some Italian. Eventually, they came to trust each other enough to cautiously venture even into political territory.

The Berlin Olympic Games were on at the time, and Jessie Owens, a black sharecropper's son from Alabama, had just won his fourth gold medal. The matter had more than just the normal significance related to sports. In fact, it challenged the Nazi theory of racial superiority. One evening, over a plate of pasta and a glass of red wine, Riccardo looked at his new friend squarely and asked, "How did the Germans take Owens's victories?"

"Well," Franz replied after a moment of hesitation, "I must admit that it was a bit of a shock."

"A rather clear contradiction to Hitler's master race theory, I would say."

"I suppose," Franz admitted reluctantly. "You must acknowledge, though," he said after a moment, "that having already earned almost double the medals than the United States does prove something for Germany."

"Prove what? Medals in sports mainly reflect a nation's effort and expenses to promote those disciplines. Look at Italy, Franz; it is presently fourth in the medals count, a good six spots higher than Great

Britain. Do you think that this is really representative of our place in the world?"

The German seemed puzzled as he tried to evaluate the last observation.

"Don't mind my comment, my friend," Riccardo added, noticing Franz's discomfort. "I am not trying to provoke or offend you. I am just as hard on Italians. At least those who claim superiority because of medals or the large number of artists and scholars we had during the Renaissance. Or even worse, on account of the latest victory of a football game!"

Upon leaving Italy, Franz said, "Herr Rickard, I am glad that we met and became friends." Then, as they shook hands vigorously, he added, "Given your interest in chemical engineering and other technical matters, you should come to Germany one of these days. Come see for yourself how much we have progressed since your years at Koblenz University."

"If there is an opportunity, I will be glad to come. Let's keep in touch."

- XVI -

1937

It was April 27, 1937, and Riccardo read aloud from the newspapers that the day before, the town of Guernica, in Spain, which was in Republican hands, had been bombed by Franco's Loyalists and his Nazi allies. "An estimated sixteen hundred people, mostly civilians, have perished and, at the time this article was written, what remains of the town is still being devoured by the flames."

"Oh my God!" Luisa exclaimed, turning toward him. "What is the human race up to? Civil wars seem to be as bad or worse than wars with other countries."

Riccardo lowered the newspaper to his knees, looked at his mother—who was busy at the stove—and said, "Can you just imagine all those poor people? Women, children ... Hitler must be pleased about the effectiveness of his *Luftwaffe*." His facial expression turned more solemn. "It's the first time in history that airplanes have been massively used as killing machines. With this, we have reached a new low in the conduct of warfare. I am afraid that the bombing of cities and towns and the indiscriminate killing of civilian population will now become part of war. Mark my words!" His voice was laden with emotion.

"It's a catastrophe," Patrizia echoed. She had entered the room in time to hear the last comment.

"No one thinks of the poor Spanish people," Riccardo said. "Their ideals, their suffering. Hitler is there to try the effectiveness of his new weapons, Mussolini to secure the minerals and ores necessary for Italy. On the other side, the Russians are trying to convert Spain to their communist model."

"And what about Britain, France, the United States of America?" Patrizia asked. "What are they doing about all this?"

"Besides their usual claims of neutrality, and the covert, token help to the Republicans, our so-called democracies are looking the other way."

"What a shameful irony!" Patrizia cried out.

*****

Roberto, who had listened in silence, now approached his father and looked at the newspaper still resting on his knees. Beside the article on Spain was a picture of a Republican soldier, caught the very moment a bullet snatched his life. His knees bent under the weight of his body, which was falling backward, his arms outstretched, a rifle still held in his right hand, his face tilted toward the sky. Roberto stared at that picture and held his breath. He was almost expecting to witness the completion of the movement, to hear the cry and the crash of the body over the parched-looking soil. The words under the photo simply read, HOW THEY FELL, by Robert Capa.

The boy did not say a word, but as he ate his meal, the picture reappeared in his mind repeatedly. How awful! He had not felt disturbed when his father had read that sixteen hundred people had perished in Guernica, when he predicted that thousands of children and women would die. Yet his heart ached for a single fighter, a man caught by a photographer the very moment his life was abruptly snatched from him.

*****

A few days later, the women had just returned from shopping for groceries and were preparing supper. Riccardo was in his studio, bent over his desk, one hand pressed hard over a drawing to prevent its movement. The other hand held a sharp pencil that moved effortlessly over the white surface, tracing lines and symbols. He stopped a moment to contemplate his work; the task was nearly finished.

In the kitchen, Roberto had finished reading a chapter of history; he closed his book and walked to the studio. He stopped at the door and observed his father's face hidden by the lamp shade; the lower part of his body was concealed by the desk. Under the semicircular beam of the desk light, he noticed the strong fingers of his veined hands, the well-trimmed nails, and his shiny wedding bend. The radio played a classical piece that he liked but did not recognize. He waited until it was finished and then said, "Hallo, Father."

"Oh, hallo, Roberto. I didn't hear you coming. Have you finished your assignment?"

"Yes, Father." He was on the verge of asking a question, but he hesitated.

"Yes, Roberto. What is it?"

"May I ask you a question?"

"Of course you can. What is it?" Riccardo pushed away from the desk and invited the boy to sit on his lap.

"It's about Guernica, Father. Maybe it's a stupid question."

"No, Roberto. It would be sillier not to ask. What bothers you about Guernica?"

"You said that sixteen hundred people died in the bombing."

"Yes."

"Well, I don't seem to care about them as much as I do for the soldier I saw in the newspaper. I don't know why, and I don't know if that is bad."

Riccardo smiled and gently stroked Roberto's hair. "No, son, it's not bad. It's natural. As to the *why*, it is a more complicated matter to explain. Would you like me to try?"

"Please, Father."

Riccardo switched off the radio, and Roberto changed position on his father's leg. He was ready to listen.

"The human mind has a limited capacity, Roberto. We can look at the universe, but can only understand its smallest details. We can look at a battlefield with thousand of dead men, but cannot quantify or understand the cumulative pain of thousands of mothers, sisters, spouses, and children related to those deaths. Likewise, the sixteen hundred victims of Guernica are a number too large for us to comprehend, and therefore it becomes an abstraction. Whereas the picture of a single man caught at the moment of death is not an abstraction. It is a single moment of reality that synthesizes death. One has no problem in imagining his crying mother, his wife, his sister."

"His children," Roberto added.

"Exactly, my dear. One can easily identify with a single person caught by a camera at the moment of death—can imagine his history, his belief, his pain. In other words, Roberto, that picture triggers thoughts and feelings derived by one's personal experience, whereas the deaths of thousands of people, horrible as that is, remains an incomprehensible generality. Are you getting the sense of what I'm saying, Roberto?"

"I think so, Father. I felt something like that, but I couldn't explain it. Also, I thought it was bad to feel for one person more than for so many."

"Believe me, Roberto," said Riccardo, affectionately embracing his son, "not only are your feelings normal, but you are showing great thoughtfulness by even thinking of a matter like that. Especially at your age."

*****

That September, the Ciampino distillery was completed. The regime, with the usual press and fanfare reserved for major events, used the inauguration of this project to disseminate the standard propaganda of self-aggrandizement.

Riccardo was invited to participate in his capacity of technical director. He was to have personal contact with il Duce and was "duly advised" to wear his military uniform and war decorations.

"I don't think I can do it," he confessed to, Patrizia before departing for Rome. "Every donkey subservient to the regime will wear his ceremonial uniform and kilos of decorations, whether earned or not. I can't lower myself to their level!"

"Be careful, Riccardo," implored Patrizia. "Think about the family, your son ..." She kissed him. "Don't keep us in suspense. Let us know the outcome as soon as possible."

He returned her kiss, gave her a reassuring smile, and left.

On the morning of the inauguration day, Riccardo was having breakfast at a table at the Grand Hotel Minerva. He was wearing a conventional gray suit with a light blue shirt and a tie with burgundy and navy blue diagonal stripes. A small group of fascist hierarchs, including the minister who had offered Riccardo his job and had ensured deliveries of materials in short supply, walked the marbled hall adjacent to the breakfast area. He spotted Riccardo at a table and departed from his escort.

"It has been a long time, Ingegnere," he said, stopping near the table. "Al Duce."

Riccardo looked at the arm stiffly raised in the Roman salute, "Good morning, sir," he answered, rising to his feet. "Yes, it has been several months. Since my last request for help for the delivery of copper sheets, I believe."

"For certain things you seem to have a good memory. For others, however ..."

"I don't understand."

"You were advised, I believe, to wear your high uniform for this important event. May I strongly suggest that you cut short your breakfast and present yourself with attire suited for the occasion? After all, as the engineer of the complex, you'll be required to meet our Duce; it's about time you give something in return." He raised his arm again and said, "Al Duce." Then he swung around on his heels and disappeared among the crowd.

"Damn it all," Riccardo uttered.

He looked down at his unfinished breakfast. His stomach was suddenly in knots, and he had lost his appetite. *What on earth am I to do?* He pondered pushing away even the coffee cup. *Would they truly take my job away? Hurt my family? Why is my everyday life always filled with these predicaments? Why do my principles clash with what most people would consider simple and practical aspects of life? Perhaps Patrizia is right; I'm too idealistic too …*

"Ah, damn it all!" he exclaimed again, getting up and leaving the buffet area.

*****

A few days later, the national newspapers, magazines, and news-reels showed pictures of the inauguration, with row upon row of high-ranking fascist officials dressed in black uniforms decorated with medals, ribbons, sashes. They were shown marching through the streets of Ciampino, directed toward the new distillery, with Il Duce, General Starace, and other fascist leaders in the front row. They were parading through the provincial town among the exultant crowd of civilians that lined the streets—a crowd composed mostly of women and school-age children, mobilized by the party for the occasion and placed strategically to act as a fitting frame for the main picture.

Inside the distillery, in front of intricate machinery and a forest of copper pipes, several photos showcased the hefty profile of Mussolini in attentive stance. Beside him was the slim figure of a man in civilian clothes, who appeared to be explaining the function of the equipment to the Italian dictator; it was Riccardo Lanzi. The miniscule multicolor ribbon pinned to the front pocket of his denim jacket was the sole sign of his military past. He had been incapable of obeying orders, and now wondered if his action was worth the punishment he was certainly going to incur.

When they saw the pictures, Patrizia and Luisa Lanzi looked at each other in astonishment.

"Such a stubborn man," Luisa uttered. The harsh words could not hide the tone of pride she felt for her son.

"Sometimes too stubborn," Patrizia said. "What would it have cost him to wear his military uniform? After all, he *is* a reserve officer."

Luisa shook her head. "You don't understand him," she said. "For someone else, it might have seemed like just a simple change of clothes, but not for him. It's not the changing of a shirt; it's what it implies!"

"And what about his family? His son? What about those implications? Or does he care only about his pride, his ideals?" Her tone and words had been rather provocative, and Luisa's reaction came immediately.

"What would you know about ideals? Your concerns are always practical and mundane, but without people with faith and principles, the world would be a mess."

"What on earth are you talking about, Luisa?" It was the first time that Patrizia had addressed her mother-in-law by name. "Are you suggesting that because I encourage caution, I lack moral rectitude? Or perhaps that not sharing your religious beliefs makes me less deserving?" she continued, anger in her voice. "As to the state of the world. I'm not so sure it is that good, or that we can rely on pious people to put it on a better frame."

"There you are again, taking a stand against the church."

As the discussion was about to take a turn for the worse, a noise came from the other room, and light steps echoed beyond the kitchen door.

"I'm sorry, Luisa," said Patrizia, lowering her tone. "Roberto is coming; I don't want him to hear our dissensions."

Roberto opened the door, and Patrizia left the room.

"Were you fighting?" he asked his grandmother.

"No. Not really, Roberto. We were just discussing matters."

"Was it about the church? I heard the word …"

"Don't worry, Roberto. It isn't anything serious. Go out and play for a while. I'll call you when it's time to eat."

Two days later, the family received a concise telegram that simply stated, *Received compliments from our Duce.*

The Lanzis understood the message and felt relieved. At least for now, the dangers seemed past. Luisa and Patrizia had slowly begun to talk again, at least in front of Roberto, and all seemed normal.

Upon his return, Riccardo told them that the word "our" was not part of his original message, and it had been forcefully inserted in the telegram by the zealous civil servant at the Ciampino post office.

*****

That evening, Roberto received the news of Uncle Lorenzo's visit with eager anticipation, for he was secretly fascinated with his uncle. In his eyes, thirty-two-year-old Lorenzo was as handsome and clever as his father was. According to family talk, he had fewer academic credits to his name. This, however, was not due to lesser intellect, but rather to his entirely dissimilar personality, perceptions, and priorities.

After leaving the university, Lorenzo had remained in Florence, the city he had loved since his first visit. He still rented a small apartment not far from the Ponte Vecchio. He was a "confirmed bachelor," as his mother would say, and he worked in an import/export office as a temporary clerk and translator, often meeting interesting people.

After supper that night, Uncle Lorenzo and Riccardo retired to the studio, and Roberto heard them talk in hushed tones.

"Where did you hear that?" Riccardo asked.

Lorenzo tilted his body forward as if shortening the space between himself and his brother lessened the chances of being unwelcome ears overhearing.

Roberto, playing in close proximity, noticed the gesture but pretended to be oblivious to the conversation.

"An acquaintance of mine, Riccardo. A Mata Hari of sorts, she goes around social gatherings, mingles with politicians, and collects delicate information."

"On whose account?"

"That, I'm yet to find out. However, I can assure you that all I ever heard from her lips has always proved true. And now," Lorenzo added, almost whispering, "she told me that our so-called allies of the East ..."

"The Japanese?"

"Yes, the Japanese. In a week of uncontrolled rampage in Nankin, they slaughtered over three hundred thousand people and raped tens of thousand of women."

Roberto looked sideway at the expression of the two adults. They stared silently into each other's faces.

"Are you sure, Lorenzo?" Riccardo finally asked. "I know they have been fighting in China for quite some time, but information from that theater is so sparse. It seems so … so incredible. I know they are a bellicose race, but … three hundred thousand people?"

"Yes. And apparently not only soldiers, but civilians as well: old people, women, children."

"Have the Japanese confirmed this?"

"Come on, Riccardo, did General Franco assume the responsibility for Guernica?"

"What are they saying, then?"

"They gave the standard response of people in denial. They said that the pictures were staged. That thousands of bodies were placed in the streets, in front of a camera, to fabricate a photographic corroboration of something that did not happened. Alternatively, that it was in fact General Chiang Kai-shek who ordered the shooting of thousands of deserters among his own troop."

"And what about the women and children?"

"They were added, of course, or so the Japanese said, to create a particularly gruesome sight and rally more foreign support for the Chinese."

"What's this world coming to?" questioned Riccardo. "How can human beings be so cruel? Not even wild beasts behave like that toward their own."

Roberto had followed the conversation and tried to quantify what three hundred thousand people would look like. Would it be a long column of humans stretching from Castelvecchio to Pisa? Or maybe even to Florence? He couldn't decide. He finally looked toward the two adults.

"Uncle Lorenzo," he called, "what is rape?"

- XVII -

1937

Toward the end of May, Riccardo received a letter from Franz Reinhold, the young German technician he had befriended a few months earlier. In it, Franz expressed the appreciation and gratitude for "Herr Rickard's" kindness during his Italian visit. The envelope also contained an invitation, a return train ticket, and his expressed desire to reciprocate during the upcoming conference in Coblenz and a tour of industrial complexes to be held in Nuremberg.

"Only if you promise to let me practice my German," replied Riccardo jokingly.

Two weeks later, upon leaving for the train station, Riccardo said good-bye to his mother and kissed his wife. "I'll see you in a few days," he said reassuringly. "If you are good," he then said to Roberto, hugging him and kissing his forehead, "I'll bring you a nice new toy from Nuremberg. The city is famous for its mechanical models."

"A tank or an airplane," the boy said.

"Or a more peaceful object—perhaps an electric train."

*****

It took Riccardo only a couple of days to realize the amazing progress the German manufacturing sector had made since his university days. Every place he went, he sensed a feverish, almost fanatic fervor driving everyone, from the industrial baron to the common worker. The infrastructure and equipment were new and technologically advanced; the pace rapid and constant; the output, as compared to that of Italy, simply immense.

During the visit to a chemical complex, the tour was suddenly interrupted by the metallic voice of a loudspeaker: *"Achtung, achtung … Alle arbeiter und Gaste mussen dem berichten."*

"All personnel, including visitors, should immediately gather in the auditorium for a special presentation," Franz translated.

In German, Riccardo asked, "We too?"

"Sorry, I'm afraid so," his friend returned in kind.

Everyone went to the auditorium as instructed, and as soon as it was filled, the lights were turned off. A special presentation began.

A Nazi troop parade filled the gigantic screen. Soldiers, modern weapons in hand, singing and lifting their legs as if by mechanical means, marched toward the Wilhelm Platz, which was packed to capacity. Suddenly, upon a sharp command, they were still and silent like granite sculptures, a static mass inserted as an essential element of Albert Speer's architecture of the square. In this context, they seemed to have lost their individuality and become an abstract and integral part of the spectacle.

In a flash of premonition, Riccardo felt a shiver cross his body. A sudden realization burst into his mind: *This army is not for parades*, he thought. *It's for war!*

The perfect order of the masses, the narrow passageways used by the echelon to ascend to the elevated stage, the monochrome colors of the standards, and the exact graphic nature of symbols and uniforms formed a coherent architecture that evoked ancient rituals and warrior spirit. The music and oaths reminded him of a Wagnerian opera, of Sigfried's oath, of the mythological feminine figures called Valkyries, which accompanied the dead heroes to their Valhalla. From that day forward, Riccardo would think of the German dictator as the "Rider of the Valkyries."

During supper that evening, Franz noticed Riccardo's pensive mood. "Why such a … solemn look, Rickard?" he asked.

After a slight hesitation, Riccardo said, "Frankly, Franz, I am rather uneasy about what I saw today. I think the direction of the new chancellor to be dangerous for Germany, for Europe."

"But you see, Rickard," Franz replied in a conciliatory tone, "since Hitler came to power, Germany has regained its place in the world. Our industries have strengthened, our economy is growing at a fast pace, our people are proud again. How can we not be on his side? Besides, while it's true we lost the 1915–1918 war, it's also true that we were treated unfairly at Versailles. How can we accept those conditions?"

A middle-aged waiter came to the table, gave them the menus, and poured mineral water in their glasses.

"And so were we, for that matter, Franz. But—"

"But what, dear Rickard?" Franz interrupted. "*Varum?* Why was it so? Why were the Germans humiliated? Our territory mutilated? The reparations set at such an absurd level, so obviously beyond Germany's ability to repay? We were reduced to a state of permanent economic serfdom, for God's sake! What were the British and the French thinking?"

"My dear Franz, as I was trying to say earlier, Italy wasn't treated much better," said Riccardo, with a sad smile. "But just the same, those are not easy questions to answer. We are all guilty of certain actions, and we all end up paying for them."

"I do not follow you, Rickard. What exactly do you mean?"

Riccardo sighed, took a sip of water, and then said, "In the course of any war, or even during the preparations for one, to boost the morale of one's citizens or to convince them that one is fighting a just or necessary war, governments engage in propaganda—any government, Franz, in any country. Their mantra states over and over the same things: *We* are justified in our endeavour; *we* fight with clean hands, for the sake of higher justice, for higher moral principles, and for the preservation of 'our' civilization. Whatever it is that 'we' mean by that."

Franz looked at his friend with some perplexity.

"The enemy," Riccardo continued, "has always been depicted by its adversary as uncivilized barbarians, brutal, even subhuman, and as such, deserving of the utmost loathing and denunciations."

"I'll have the Wiener schnitzel with vegetables," said Riccardo to the waiter, who stood by to take the orders.

"Make it two." Franz handed his menu back to the waiter and bring us also two glasses of red wine."

"Think of the Hittites, the Persians, the Huns, the Arabs, and many others. When the people of any nation are fed this type of propagandistic diet for a long time, there are certain psychological difficulties in implementing 'fair' and equitable peace treaties. No person or society, after being subjected to the propaganda and the suffering of war is well disposed toward these barbarians … toward those who started the fight and are perceived as being the most responsible for inflicting pain and damages. Unfortunately, because of this, at Versailles, the focus was not on how to propose conditions that could foster a permanent or durable peace, but how to make Germany pay for its culpability."

"But, Rickard, this is hypocritical. We were all guilty of something or other. And let's even forget Germany for a moment. What about all the senseless promises made by France and England to dozens of lesser powers for self-serving reasons? The Slavic lines of Austria and Yugoslavia, the new Polish corridor—cutting out Eastern Prussia and disrupting the integrity of our territory—the promise to the Zionists of a 'national' home in Palestine, while the Arabs have been told that Palestine would be theirs, the slices taken out of Turkey and many other unwise actions like these. And, as you mentioned yourself, the treatment of Italy, which, though on the side of the winners in the battlefield, was a loser at Versailles.

"Tell me, Rickard, don't you think that the treaty was too harsh and prejudicial to Germany? Don't you think that it hurt the stability of our Republican regime, which should have been the aim of the Allies to help? That all these territorial adjustments, dislocation of people, hardships, and injustices will create problems in the future?"

Several more people had come into the bistro and were now taking their seats at nearby tables. Many of them were young, like the ones Riccardo had seen in military uniforms during the afternoon's newsreel. They looked well bred, well behaved, and since most of them carried books, they were most likely well educated. They all displayed party badges. It was therefore safe to assume they participated in parades, listened to and applauded Goeble's long tirades, and abdicated their own judgment. In Riccardo's opinion, contrary to many young Italians who had joined the fascists on the threat of Bolshevism or in response to other events, the Germans had thoroughly assimilated the Nazi propaganda. They appeared to have fallen prey to the sinister political apparatus that might take them to another war.

"No doubt they will create problems," Riccardo finally answered. "And they have already. But, Franz, throwing fuel into the fire does not help extinguish it. We ought to choke it before it devours us all. That's my point. After all, in the last few years, Germany has retaken most of its lost territories—"

"And now that we have," Franz interrupted, "we will smother the flames, as you put it. Do not despair, Rickard. We will. Remember that in nineteen thirty-two, there were over six million unemployed in Germany. Also, dictatorships have been established not only in this country, but in Italy, Poland, Yugoslavia, Hungary, Spain, and Russia as well. Why, then, do people around the world only look at us? We are not much worse than others; we too want peace."

Riccardo took his time, chewing slowly on a piece of bread.

He almost answered that the fear caused by what was happening in Germany was proportionate to the number of times that country had initiated aggression against other nations, to the growing size of its military apparatus, to its own belligerent propaganda. Then he thought better of it, swallowed the food, took another sip of water, and said, "I truly hope so, Franz. For our children. For all of us!" He lifted his wineglass. "To peace, my friend. Prosit!"

- XVIII -

1938

As Riccardo had anticipated, the following months saw Hitler—who, having realized the weakness of those countries and leaders whom he made demands against—continue a policy of expansion. Britain and France, guarantors of the status quo for the smaller powers, seemed unwilling to oppose him militarily.

Austria was annexed to the German territory in March 1938.

Then came demands for the Sudeten land of Czechoslovakia, where many German-speaking citizens lived.

Initially, the British—who were the lead negotiators for the "great" powers— responded positively to this new demand. British Prime Minister Chamberlain, as well as most of his cabinet, agreed that, according to the principle of self-determination, the Germans had a rightful claim to this territory.

However, on September 22, 1938, in a news conference with Prime Minister Chamberlain, held at Godesberg, emboldened by the recent concessions, Hitler increased his demands, and Chamberlain refused. The clouds of war became darker than ever over the skies of Europe.

In an attempt to defuse the looming crisis, United States President Roosevelt appealed to Hitler to call another conference and try to solve the dispute by peaceful means.

Unfortunately, the United States had abstained from membership in the League of Nations, fearing it would dilute its own sovereignty—and, in particular, that it would sponsor the doctrine of self-determination for its Native Americans and African Americans. Therefore, America was perceived as having withdrawn into a state of isolation, from which its moral power of persuasion was greatly diminished.

Chamberlain requested that the Italian dictator Mussolini use his influence with Hitler, and another meeting was held.

The news media characterized the event as follows:

On September 29, 1938, Hitler, Mussolini, Chamberlain, and Prime Minister Deladier of France met in Munich and adopted a draft agreement, which, though presented by Mussolini, was in fact drafted by the Germans. All of Hitler's demands were accepted. The Czech—though declaring their willingness to fight to maintain the integrity of their country—undermined and deprived of the help of their major allies, acquiesced to the inevitable.

In different degrees, three of the four participants returned home convinced that they had, once again, avoided war.

His French citizens applauded Deladier.

Upon his return to Britain, Chamberlain declared he had "achieved peace for our time." He was received by an equally exultant crowd chanting "For he's a jolly good fellow ... "

Of the three, Mussolini seemed the least convinced. Though glad to have played an important diplomatic role, he did not believe this to be the end of German demands. He was envious of the great power his ally continued to gather. He was also worried, wondering if he would soon be dragged into a war for which Italy was not prepared, and which the Italian people, despite eighteen years of fascist indoctrination, seemed to wish to avoid at all costs.

In confirming this fact, the Italian newspapers wrote:

Along the train line which brought Il Duce back to Rome, Italians of all ages and social backgrounds, crowded the areas adjacent to the railroad line. Women knelt and raised their hands in thanks toward the speeding train, thanking their "savior" for the peace achieved.

In certain circles, it was reported that the Italian dictator was said to be angered by this open display of pacifism, for it clearly indicated the failure and rejection of almost twenty years of fascist pro-war doctrine.

Rumors had it that at the sight of those people along the train lines, Mussolini exclaimed in disgust, "Are these the people with whom I shall make new conquests?"

"Up to now," said Riccardo to Antonio at the distillery, "events have moved in Hitler's favor. I hope he doesn't believe this will go on forever. His next move could be one too many. After the failure of diplomacy, the talking will be done with cannons."

"But who will stop him?"

Riccardo pondered the question. Then, his unseeing eyes fixed in space, he answered slowly, "The democracies will. The same little people who have done it since the beginning of time. When tired of abuse and oppression, they will rise from their dormant state and muster the will to defeat the enemies of freedom and justice. Sometimes it takes a long time. Too long, it seems, but trust me, Antonio, ultimately the time always comes."

*****

In Castelvecchio, life went on, with ever-increasing disquietude and worry about the economy, as well as the rumors of possible armed conflicts in other parts of Europe.

Luisa had gone to church as usual one morning, and Meino greeted her as she exited after the service. "Good morning, Luisa. Did you see the Blackshirts parade in the Piazza Dei Caduti?"

"They'd better add more memorial plates to the monument," said Luisa. "I'm afraid that soon there will be more names to add."

As the cabbie had told Luisa upon her first arrival in Castelvecchio, the Piazza Dei Caduti, just outside the south side of town, was built after the Great War. The immense gray monument—of a seated, crying mother holding her lifeless son—rested on a large white Carrara marble base. On the sides of this base were bolted two bronze plates with the names of the local soldiers killed during the conflict.

"You're right," Meino said. "Our soldiers are on their way to Spain. They are singing now, but they'll soon realize that war is not a parade!"

"I pray to God that this madness will soon end … I'll see you, my friend. I'm rushing home to prepare breakfast for Roberto."

"Pardon?" Meino repeated, turning his better ear toward Luisa.

She repeated what she'd said.

"Oh, yes," said Meino. "By the way, how old is he now? I haven't seen him in a while."

"He is six, but quite mature and articulate for his age."

"With all the geniuses in the house, what did you expect? Anyway," he added, "I must be going too. I'll see you next Sunday."

Luisa left, a smile still lingering on her lips. Speaking about her grandson always produced that effect.

*****

For Patrizia, it was a different story. She yearned to establish a closer relationship with her son. She had tried. But additional attention, show of affection, or other means hadn't worked so far in her favor. She did not want to insert herself in any of the activities he performed with his nonna, so, as a last resort, on Sundays, she began to give him French and piano lessons. Roberto, however, did not seem to enjoy the process, and he did not respond beyond the strict adherence of her instructions. During these sessions, his vigilant green eyes scanned her face with perplexing attentiveness, giving her long, unembarrassed looks of appraisal. It was as though he couldn't hear her voice. His attention seemingly diverted to a strange search, as if questioning whether beyond their appearances, her obvious efforts had other aims.

Patrizia found his behavior disconcerting. After a while, it was decided that both French and piano lessons would be continued at a local institute run by a particular order of nuns. The place specialized in early education for advanced children, some kind of monastic Montessori, as Patrizia called it. After an extensive exam that confirmed his advanced educational status, and thanks to Luisa's generosity toward the nuns, he was allowed to enter grade three. His mathematical and language skills exceeded those of students several years older, and he was always promoted to the top of his class.

Later that year, though, a new nun was appointed to teach religion to his class. Her name was Sister Cesaria, and Roberto took a strong dislike to her and her teaching methods. So much so that after reciting the memorized prayer and sitting down, instead of listening to her lesson, he usually began to wander into his inner world or draw pictures in his notebook.

One particular morning, realizing that he was not paying attention, Sister Cesaria asked Roberto to repeat her last sentence.

He stood up, as he was supposed to when addressed by his teachers, and frankly admitted that he couldn't answer.

"Why not?" she asked.

"Because it doesn't interest me."

Sister Cesaria became incensed and immediately swung into action with her standard punishment. No matter what kind of infraction, the student was chastised by having to stand in front of the teacher's desk, facing the class and holding his chair upside down over his head.

The punished youngster was only allowed to use his hands to hold the back portion of the chair, not to reduce the pressure on his head, but to keep it from falling. The oak chair was heavy and hard on the skull. In addition, the grid effect of the back spindles—positioned right in front of one's eyes—added a psychological effect of enforced submission. Behind those wooden bars, the sense of shame, coupled with the derisive stares of the other students, combined to create a dreaded feeling of captivity. On this occasion, in addition to the punishment, Roberto was subjected to a public tongue-lashing.

"Regardless of your intelligence, which of course is entirely a gift from God, unless you promptly redeem yourself," sister Cesaria predicted, "you will follow the path of Lucifer, straight into hell!"

Roberto had difficulty repenting for something he did not consider a serious infraction, and he maintained a bold expression. He had learned how to evade unpleasant realities by concentrating on more pleasant matters. Rash predictions did not affect him, particularly when prophesized by people he did not like or trust. In the case of Sister Cesaria, not only did he not trust her, but he couldn't stand the sight of her. Nor, for that matter, could he stand looking at the faces of his classmates, staring at him with strange grins. Even those he considered his friends gave him the distinct impression they were enjoying his punishment.

So, instead of succumbing to the negative aspects of the situation, he entered into his own dream world. His gaze transfixed on the large yellow and blue world map hanging on the far wall. Roberto fantasized about the great men his nonna spoke of or made him read about.

There, he was free to be whoever and go wherever he wanted: with Caesar's Tenth Legion at the conquest of an empire, with the Vikings to their discovery of distant lands, with Columbus to the beaches of the New World.

His arms were numb, his skull aching, his leg muscles in pain from the prolonged stationary position. Yet he was happy, in his own world, and almost invulnerable to the outside.

Every now and then, Sister Cesaria looked at him with curiosity. Roberto felt that she was searching for the signs of fear, resignation, remorse, or pain that other students usually showed in similar circumstances. *But,* he stubbornly decided, *she is not going to detect any of those responses in me.*

He stood there, seemingly impervious to the punishment. He did not appear shameful or guilty. He carried this cumbersome weight as if it were the national flag, the insignia of a Roman Legion or any other precious object entrusted to his personal care. With his legs slightly apart for better balance, his limpid green eyes gazed straight into the distance at a world of his own. His lips curled with just a trace of defiance, as though he was the offended party and not the offender.

He knew that Sister Cesaria would have liked to detect at least a hint of hostility, hate even, for his indifference seemed to suggest that, but in Roberto's eyes, she didn't even deserve his animosity.

Yes, he was tired, but admitting it would not have made it any better. He was hurt by what he considered an undeserved punishment, but knew that showing it meant surrender. While he did not like the sly smiles on the faces of his companions, maintaining his indifference lessened their sadistic enjoyment.

He recalled the lesson contained in a story his grandmother had once read to him: Returning from his training camp, a young Spartan was questioned by his father, but he refused to list the things he had learned. The angered father, taking this as disobedience, beat the youth, who stood his ground without protecting himself or even crying. Finally, the father—exhausted and surprised at the stoicism of his son—ceased his beating. The young man then calmly stated, "Father, this is but one of the many things I have learned!"

That, Roberto thought, *must be the stuff of great men!* Oh, how he wished to be like those men of history who defied adversities, defeated enemies, conquered lands, tamed wild beasts.

How could the weight of an ordinary chair overwhelm him? How could he let the stares of peers bother him? How could Sister Cesaria intimidate him?

The bell rang, announcing the end of the lesson and time for the children to go home. The class was dismissed. The students started to leave, their routine farewells echoing throughout the room: *Good-bye, Sister Cesarlia. See you tomorrow, Sister Cesaria.*

Roberto remained standing where he was. He did not plead to leave.

Left alone with the boy, the nun finally snapped, "You too, Lanzi."

"Fine!" he answered, but the tone sounded more like *Go to hell!*

When Roberto stepped out of the school compound, the sun was shining at its peak. A light breeze of the seasonal *Maestrale* wind blew from the northwest. Instantly, he felt happy. He took a deep breath and began to run toward home. He felt the wind enveloping his chest through his open shirt, his feet pounding the dusty, cobbled surface of the road, his heart pumping at a faster rhythm.

He was a galloping stallion breaking away from confinement. Then, as he crossed the bell tower gate, he was a prisoner escaping captivity, running faster and faster toward the open countryside, toward freedom, unrestrained by the will of others or by ropes or bondage. He was flying toward freedom and glory.

He was soon in front of his house, and he slowed to a brisk walk. He buttoned his shirt again and finger-combed his hair. An appetizing smell, accompanied by a crackling sound in the frying pan, greeted him upstairs. In the kitchen, Nonna Luisa was facing the woodstove, her white and red apron tight around her waist, a light scarf gathering her silver-gray hair, and her face purple from the heat.

"There's my big boy." She also greeted him with a broad smile and an embrace. "How was school?"

"Good," he replied, with a tinge of contrition.

He preferred to be truthful to his nonna, but he knew she would not have shared his opinion about the morning's events.

– XIX –

1938

"Tonight," said Patrizia to her son, "Uncle Lorenzo is coming for supper."

"Good!" Roberto exclaimed. "Maybe he'll give me a ride in his fast car."

Every now and then, Lorenzo made an unexpected appearance in Castelvecchio, the screeching tires of his sports car—which he had bought on credit, to his mother's displeasure—audible in the distance long before his actual arrival. His dramatic appearances were always a welcome surprise for Roberto.

The athletic, handsome man stepped out of the car the moment it came to a halt, hugging and kissing everyone in a manner not common in the Lanzi household, hugging and tossing Roberto up in the air while complimenting him on his growth and good looks. When the initial commotion subsided, everyone's attention turned toward Lorenzo's—more often than not—new female companion.

"Oh. Excuse my manners," he would utter. "This is Diana" (or "Monica" or "Maria.").

This night he appeared with a stunning brunette. "Anita," he simply said, "is my business associate in a new venture."

"A new adventure, you mean," retorted Luisa. "That, I do believe."

"And why not?" was Lorenzo's unflinching comeback. "I came for one of your fabulous dinners, Mother," he said. "I told Anita what a wonderful cook you are."

"Go on, you big ruffian," Luisa answered, in mocking indignation. Then she turned toward Anita and said, "You see, signorina, if you want to catch a man, don't bother with his brains; they are too shrewd. Nor with his heart; his is more conniving. Just go for his stomach; it is his Achilles' heel!"

"I could suggest another anatomical region, Mother, but …" He couldn't finish the sentence, for Luisa smacked him.

"Don't talk like that in front of Roberto."

"Speaking of Roberto, I also came to see this nephew of mine," Lorenzo said, lifting the boy with ease above his own head. "Look at him growing. Look at those stunning green eyes. Do you have a girl-friend yet?"

"No, Uncle. I am too young. I'm only six."

"What's the problem? Are all the girls in this town completely blind?"

Roberto did not seem to know what to say.

"Quit teasing him, you rascal," said Patrizia. "Just because you're a Don Giovanni …"

"Patrizia *cara*, as you know, I don't need any advertising. I am doing just fine as it is." He laughed and removed his jacket. From one of the pockets protruded a folded daily newspaper. One of the titles was clearly visible and attracted Roberto's attention. He bent his head sideways and read it aloud: "Germany annexes Austria! *Annettere,*" he said, trying to trace in his mind the exact suffix of that verb. "Is it more like attach, or appropriate?" he asked no one in particular.

"Appropriate, I am afraid," his uncle replied, but don't you worry about the difference, young man. The result may be the same."

"Why did they do that, Uncle?" Roberto insisted.

"It's a long story, cucciolo," Patrizia interrupted. "One of these days, Uncle Lorenzo will tell you, but now go wash your hands. Dinner is ready."

They sat around the supper table. The men poured the wine and commented on the good smell of the food, the clemency of the weather, and other ordinary subjects. Then Lorenzo, as if still thinking of Roberto's remark, slipped in a short reference to the German annexation of Austria, which was followed with comments by Riccardo about self-determination and other matters related to the Treaty of Versailles.

If I let them go on, Patrizia thought, *they will talk of nothing but politics. I am in no mood to listen to this subject tonight. It will invariably be followed by prognostication of war and other calamities. No, tonight there will be none of that!*

"Tell us Lorenzo," she interrupted with a smile, "what are you up to these days? Any significant undertaking on your horizon?"

After a moment of hesitation, he said, "I invested a little money in real estate, and I sold my first building. Times are tough, but I made some profit. Next week, I may sell another one. Who knows? I have also started to trade in some commodities. There is a scarcity of raw materials in Italy. So I search and discover which country exports them, and I make deals."

"You speak with the inexhaustible enthusiasm of a missionary haranguing an audience of potential converts," Riccardo interjected.

"But I am not converting you, right?"

"No, Lorenzo. You are not converting me." He took a sip of wine and then continued. "If you just stopped playing at these dreams and focused your energies on a steady job, you would achieve professional status and security in no time at all."

"Security? Who has security in this day and age—with wars and revolutions brewing everywhere? With a world inclined toward madness? Besides, who wants security? To you, it may be heaven, Riccardo; to me, it's purgatory at best. I want some excitement from life, not security."

"You talk like this because you are still young. What will you say and do later in life? Or when you have a family?"

"A family?" Anita interjected. "But Lorenzo doesn't want a family. At least not one of his own."

"Look," Lorenzo said, "I know who I am and what I want. I know that if I had a desk job, I would die of boredom in no time at all. I like traveling abroad, new challenges, and even the uncertain nature of my business. I enjoy what I do, and I am sure one day I will succeed even more so than most so-called professionals."

"It depends on what you consider 'success.' Your chosen perambulating activities will never give you the respect of a community that a person like you ought to have."

"Listen, Riccardo." Lorenzo set his fork down, looking straight into his brother's eyes. "Although I never aspired to being one, I confess that at one time, I too regarded lawyers, doctors, dentists, and engineers as the pinnacles of society."

"Let's return to less contentious topics," Luisa said.

"Sorry, Mother. I won't take long, but you must let me finish, please." He turned again toward Riccardo. "Even I know that government officials such as the podesta, along with the priest, the *Carabinieri's* marshal, your doctors, etcetera, are still viewed by townsfolk as the symbols of knowledge and power—a sort of modern aristocracy. But you know what? I no longer think this way. I have argued too many cases far better than many muddling lawyers I know of to be impressed by them. My body has healed itself just as frequently as it has been when attended to by a human 'plumber.' My spiritual needs are satisfied without the presence of the high priest."

"What is this?" Riccardo asked calmly. "The glorification of ignorance?"

"No, my dear brother. It's the praise of education and the knowledge gained through reading, observing, traveling, practical experience, or research, albeit without the sanction of the establishment. It's my telling you that you can administer all the distilleries existing in Italy, but you will not earn one penny more than someone else will allow you to. Someone most likely with far less intelligence and integrity than you have. And even your so-called 'security' will one day depend on just such a person. So, why bother?" The statement ended with a louder and somewhat bitter edge to it.

Roberto looked at his father, who had just wiped his mouth and was ready to reply when Patrizia took her husband's hand. "Enough now, Riccardo," she said with a smile. Then she turned to Lorenzo and added, "And you should be ashamed of yourself, inviting this pleasant young lady for supper and then starting a family squabble." Her wink and smile softened her mild reproach.

"Let's eat in peace," added Luisa.

"All right," Riccardo conceded.

"This risotto is good, as always, Mom," said Lorenzo, indicating his willingness to begin the truce. "And these zucchini *trifolati are* even better.*"

"Thank you, Lorenzo. You need good food, with all your activities!"

"Don't worry, Mom. I look after myself."

"No, you don't!" insisted Luisa. "You need a good woman to look after you. You are thirty-two and still running around. You should get married, start a family."

"With war looming, dear Mother, I am not really inclined to start a family. Besides, didn't you just say we should eat? Well, let's, then." He raised his glass, while his face delivered a mollifying smile and jokingly recited, "I, for one, hereby solemnly promise not to discuss war, job security, or any other controversial topics at this table … tonight. *Salute!*" He toasted everyone and then took a sip of wine.

"*Salute!*" everyone responded, doing likewise.

Roberto had followed the conversation with interest. He understood that there were two distinct points of view between his father and his uncle, but he couldn't decide which was better. He had heard that there were different ways to earn a living, but he couldn't understand Uncle Lorenzo's.

The way of his own future was still a remote decision for six-and-a-half-year-old Roberto. Unconsciously, though, he felt an emerging desire, a curiosity to understand those choices that one day would help him become a grown-up in the image of either his father or his uncle.

Two words had remained with him and seemed to stand out in his mind: "excitement" and "security." He did not know exactly why this was so, but so many differing viewpoints and perspectives seemed enclosed in those two terms.

To him, *excitement* meant voyages to unknown cities, traveling in fast cars or trains, visiting beautiful places. Money was good too; sometimes he overheard his parents and Nonna Luisa discuss its necessity.

Security, on the other hand, was a warm house, his nonna and parents nearby, and the comforting, muffled bustle within the kitchen when he was in his bed, underneath warm blankets. *But why couldn't I have both?* No one had talked about that possibility. It was good that it was still a long time off before he had to decide which road to follow!

"Roberto," Patrizia said, "finish your pudding, brush your teeth, and go to bed. It's way past your bedtime. You can skip your reading for tonight."

"Oh, Mother, can't I stay a bit longer? Uncle Lorenzo is here ..."

"By all means, let him, Patrizia," roared the complacent voice of Lorenzo. "He is a big boy now."

"Don't you know better than to interfere?" Luisa chided him. "I didn't realize the time," she then said to Patrizia. "You are right; he is never up so late. He'll have to skip his reading tonight!"

A few minutes later, after he'd kissed everyone and bid them all good night, Nonna took Roberto to bed. "Remember to say your prayers," she reminded him.

In the short time before falling asleep, several thoughts intruded into his mind. First was the pleasant impression Anita's perfume and soft skin left behind from when she hugged him and kissed him good night.

Second was the annoyance of having to recite prayers and thank the Lord, even for what he didn't like to eat—like tonight's zucchini à la *whatever*.

Perhaps more persistent than the others was the thought related to those two words: security and excitement. He kept wondering what they really meant for him, and which one he might one day choose to pursue.

One last word, as he tossed and turned in his bed, seemed to be caught in the web of his thoughts: war! He was now hearing it with more frequency, with more concern on the part of the adults, and he found this rather disturbing. The only wars he knew were those chronicled in history books, some mythical, some real, but so distant in place and time from his reality. A closer one of course, was the one where his namesake grandfather had died, and where his father had actually fought. But though his nonna related how it had affected the family, it did not seem to impact him directly. He turned in his bed as he imagined himself as a youth, fighting an illusory enemy beside his own father, charging the enemy lines.

It was during one of these visionary charges that he suddenly fell asleep.

- XX -

Several weeks later, Lorenzo came alone.

"What is it, Lorenzo?" Luisa asked during supper. "You look a bit strange today."

"Oh, it's nothing, Mother, just a bit of nostalgia. Sometime I miss all of you. I would like to come more often, but nowadays, with the price of gas and all the other problems …"

"What problems are you referring to?" Patrizia asked.

"Unrest, roadblocks, lengthy identity controls … you know. Every day something new and annoying. Traveling has become a real chore."

"I know," Patrizia interrupted. "Now there's even a milizia patrol at the San Romano bridge. Anyway, if you come next Sunday, nonna promised Roberto a supper on the beach at the river. It would be a nice family outing."

"You're joking!" Lorenzo said toward his mother. "How did you convince Riccardo not to work on Sunday?"

"Easily," Luisa said in jest. "I told him it was either that or no supper at all. Roberto has been waiting for this jaunt for a long time. It had been months since we had the last *scampagnata,* or picnic supper, as he called it."

"I'll try," Lorenzo said.

For the next few days, Roberto relished the thought of the *scampagnata*. Even Mother relaxed her table manners at the beach, and he could run barefoot on the fine sand, throw stones in the water, and try to catch the fish trapped in shallow ponds.

On Sunday afternoon, they readied the food; took a checkered tablecloth, two blankets, and a folding stool; and started toward the Arno River on foot. Riccardo and Patrizia shared the burden of the heavier basket with food and drinks. Across Riccardo's shoulder was a tube with drawings that he said would only take minutes to review. Luisa and Roberto carried the bundle with blankets, table linens, and a couple of towels.

On the way, they exchanged greetings with passersby. The Lanzis answered politely to the greetings they received. Roberto knew very few of those townspeople, but he took notice of two factors: first, most people addressed his father and grandmother with the utmost respect; second, most people—men in particular—looked at his mother first, but few of them addressed her directly. Tall, beautiful, dignified, her demeanor seemed to underline the distance between her and them. He noticed that, but he could not explain the reason.

Midway to the river, they met Ferruccio the baker and Meino the cabman who, fishing gear in hand, were walking toward the *pescaia.*

"What about that fish you've been promising me?" Luisa called to Meino.

"You're right!" he yelled back. "Today I feel lucky; I might have some for you."

"I'll watch you from the beach," she said.

They crossed the bridge, and as soon as they arrived at the opposite riverbank, Roberto asked permission to remove his shoes. He took one of the blankets and ran ahead of the family, kicking clouds of dust on his way down. He placed the blanket on a slightly elevated spot, not too far from the water, where the sand was dry and fine. Then he looked back at the oncoming trio and felt fortunate that fate had granted him such good-looking and distinguished parents and grandmother.

He played near the water for a while, and when he returned to the sandbar, his mother and his nonna were finishing setting the eating area. Patrizia checked her watch and said, "It's all right, cucciolo. We'll call you when we're ready to eat."

Roberto looked across the river and saw Meino cast his line. He followed the cork floating unhurriedly over the current. It danced over the ripples and then stopped, held by the tensed line. He was about to return to his games when he noticed his father bent over a blueprint. He did not understand what all those lines represented, but their faultless symmetry and precision made a powerful impression on him.

"Father," he asked, "could you spare a sheet of paper and a pencil? I'd like to draw something too."

"And what would you like to draw? A boiler? A distillery?

"No, no. I don't like those things. I like the river, the old mill, and the weir."

"All right," said Riccardo, handing him a sheet and a pencil. "Show me what you can do."

The boy placed the paper over the folding stool, knelt in front of it, and then, pencil in hand, fixed his eyes in concentration over the subjects he was going to draw. He stayed like that for a long time. The immediate world around him began to fade away, his concentration swinging between the actual structures in front of him, and the simplified, imaginary picture he felt developing inside his head. Then, having mentally removed those details he considered inessential, he bent over the paper and began to draw with sharp, precise strokes. He heard the voice of the river whispering nearby, a truck thundering far over the bridge, the prolonged whistle of a train in the distance … but nothing seemed to distract him.

Luisa raised her eyes from her book and saw Riccardo, now resting on one elbow, his face in the sun, his eyes closed, relishing a moment of rest. Roberto, close by his father, was completely absorbed in his effort. Diagonal sunbeams stroked him from behind, adding gold and luminosity to his soft hair.

"Look at them," Luisa whispered, touching Patrizia's elbow. "Genius at work."

Patrizia looked their way. "Which one?" she asked mischievously. Then she looked again at her watch. "It's time to eat."

"Let's see your sketch, Roberto," Luisa said. "Then it's time to eat."

The boy handed the sketch to his nonna and waited for her comment.

"It's beautiful!" she exclaimed convincingly.

"It is," Patrizia echoed from behind, "but things are not where they should be. You put the mill on the right rather than the left of the *pescaia,* and you left out many details."

"Yes, Mother," Roberto said, "because that's where the mill should be. It looks better that way. Also, I didn't worry about the likeness; I only used what looked good to me."

Riccardo took the sheet from Patrizia's hand and studied the drawing. Then he looked at the mill, and at the drawing again. "You know what?" he said. "You are right, Roberto. Your perspective and composition are more pleasing than the real thing." He sat down on the picnic blanket. "A true artist should not be happy with mere reality; he must build his own. His greatness and happiness is not in trying to reproduce what's already there, but in the freedom to express his own creativity."

"Thank you for your professional critique, Riccardo," said Luisa, "but … could you not keep it simpler?"

"For you or for Roberto?"

Both women burst into laughter.

"Does it mean you like it, Father?" Roberto asked, ignoring the previous exchange.

"More than that, my child," said Riccardo convincingly. "I love it."

Roberto's face lit up with satisfaction. "Look, look," he then cried. The boy had given a last look at the mill and noticed Meino's fishing rod bent suddenly under the tug of a large fish. "He's caught a big one."

Everyone turned around. The old coachman had caught the rod with both hands and was now reeling in his prey. They followed the patient struggle for a while, and at long last, a long, silvery eel came out of the water, twisting violently at the end of the line, glistening in the afternoon sun. Ferruccio, who was fishing a few meters away, planted his rod on the ground, fetched his net, and in a matter of seconds, took hold of the eel, hurled the net over his shoulders, and let it drop with a thump on a sandy patch.

"That was a good one!" Luisa shouted across the water.

Ferruccio bent forward, apparently to convey the message to Meino, and the latter yelled back, "I told you I felt lucky!"

The family finished eating as the sun descended near the summit of Monte Serra. The voice of the river seemed suddenly hushed to a murmur. Under the bridge, the current swirled silently around the huge Medici pylons, which now projected long, dark shadows over the beige sand. Flocks of bats and sparrows whirled in the serene blue sky, hunting insects or chasing each other, tracing tortuous paths in the evening air.

"It's getting cool," Luisa said, reaching for her shawl and wrapping it around her shoulders. "We should be going soon."

"It was an ideal day," commented Patrizia.

"Yes," Roberto said, "and it would have been perfect if Uncle Lorenzo had come. I hope he'll make it next time."

The women began to pack. "I'll carry that with Roberto," said Riccardo, pointing to the large basket.

They started back, father and son ahead, the women behind.

Roberto liked to walk beside his father. He tried to match his long strides and straight posture, his almost military demeanor. He wished they could come more often to the river, be all together like that.

From the height of the riverbank, Roberto took a look around. He saw Meino, Ferruccio, and other fishermen on their way home. In the fields below, a farmer guided two Chianina cows to his stable, and a few women hurried home to prepare supper. Soon Venus would shine in the western sky. The evening light was withdrawing from the valley, so gradually that it seemed unwilling to leave and let the night slowly set in.

"Father," Roberto suddenly said, "do you really like my drawing?"

"Yes, Roberto, I do."

"Then I'll sign it like real artists do and give it to you."

"Thank you, Roberto. You are a generous boy. You know what? I'll take it with me to the distillery and keep it with mine."

- XXI -

1939

The weekly publication read:

> *January saw the capture of Barcelona by General Franco's troops. In March, the city of Madrid, last bastion of resistance of the Republicans, at the end of its resources, surrenders, signaling the end of the Spanish war and the beginning of yet another rightist regime in Europe. Generalissimo Francisco Franco has become the absolute ruler of Spain.*

"As if there weren't enough fascists and dictators," Luisa exclaimed, upon reading the news.

It was just the beginning.

During the following months, the Lanzis followed with apprehension the increase of sinister events on the European stage. At the end of March, pursuing the ongoing tension between Germany and Poland, they read that England and France pledged their help to Poland in case of war. In response to this, toward the end of May, there was news that Hitler and Mussolini had forged a "formal" military alliance.

In August, while waiting for their meal to be served, Riccardo heard about the crisis over the border city of Danzig, between Germany and Poland.

"Here we go again," Riccardo said loudly, as if speaking to an audience. He had just switched off the radio and walked into the kitchen, where Luisa and Patrizia were preparing dinner. "Who will say that I was too pessimistic now?" he said indignantly. "I'm telling you, it will be total war!"

It was September 1, 1939, and the BBC station, which he was listening to despite the prohibition by the fascist regime, had just announced the German invasion of Poland. It also said that France and Britain had honored their commitment by declaring war on Germany.

"It doesn't mean that it will be war for us …," said Patrizia. It wasn't clear by her tone if this was a statement or a question.

"What do you think, Riccardo?" Luisa asked. "Will we be dragged into this mess?"

There was a moment of silence. "Perhaps not immediately; later, though, it may be difficult to avoid it."

"But why?" Luisa asked.

"Why? Because the fascist regime is still firmly in power, and Il Duce is still promising to enlarge his empire, Mother. Because most Italians, either by force or by conviction, conform to the outward precepts of the system like a bunch of puppets; they raise their arm in 'Roman' salute, wear the mandatory black shirt at official gatherings, applaud Mussolini's rhetorical speeches, chant party slogans, and march to parades. That's why, mother. And one of these days, the parade will end in a battlefield, and everyone will wonder how we got there."

At the kitchen table, Roberto was dismantling and then reassembling the toy train that his father had brought from Nuremberg, and he took in the conversation. His father's past forecasts and his unusual angry tone conveyed the gravity of the topic being discussed. He watched him pause for a moment and then speak in a softer voice.

"Since he is unable to improve the country's economy or reduce the growing number of unemployed, il Duce enrolls tens of thousands of men into the armed forces and delivers tirades on the past glory of Italy, soon to be regained. Soon he will announce that he has joined the crazy man of the North in a damned war."

"Riccardo!" Patrizia admonished him. "Watch your mouth. Nowadays, even the walls have ears. And the little one has ears too, as you know, and a rather fast mouth ..."

As if on cue, Roberto raised his head from the instruction book of his train. "Father," he called, "who is the crazy man of the North?"

Patrizia emitted a sound of repressed laughter, and everyone turned toward the boy, who, up to that moment, had seemed oblivious to the conversation and absorbed in his game.

"I am just referring to the crazy Rider of the Valkyries," said Riccardo. "It's something I borrowed from German mythology."

Roberto looked at his mother questioningly.

"Don't worry, cucciolo," she said to her child, while looking at her husband slyly. "It is a mystery for me as well. Let's leave it at that."

*****

Signor Baroni, the board director of the distillery, with whom Riccardo shared his passion for Wagner's opera, had been invited for supper with his wife.

Roberto was always excited at these rare opportunities, for he was allowed to stay up later than usual, and sometimes to even skip his reading. Besides, the issues often ensuing from these conversations seemed to offer more than the guarded monologues of tutors, the rehearsed lectures of teachers, the recited litanies of priests. And his father, it seemed to him, was an effective orator who held unusual views that no one appeared able to challenge.

Roberto usually sat quietly and listened to the unguarded views of the people around the supper table. Aspects of the mysterious world of the adults were thus sometimes unknowingly disclosed to the attentive mind of the young boy.

Tonight his mother had changed into a loose silk dress, and from the top of her high cork platform shoes, she towered over the approaching guests. She also wore some makeup, and in his eyes, she looked as beautiful as some of Uncle Lorenzo's companions.

Mrs. Baroni wore an elegant black dress that seemed barely capable of containing the overabundance of her bosom. A coral necklace hung perilously in the deep crevice of her cleavage; her round face was devoid of any expression. Her husband, Luigi, had donned a dark striped suit and a green bow tie. A conspicuous gold chain swung from a buttonhole of his vest and ended in a small pocket that held a large pocket watch. He had a prompt smile that, coupled with his portly figure, gave an impression of joviality.

Father stood in stark contrast in a gray suit that was slightly worn at the elbows but freshly pressed. His face was closely shaven and youthful, his body erect—yet without strain or tension. Nonna Luisa had changed into her somber dark blue dress with white lace collar, which was her attire for Sunday mass.

"Dinner is ready," she chanted from the kitchen door.

Roberto observed with curiosity the people coming to the dining room. At the beginning of the evening, he'd heard the two men in the studio talking, in low, guarded tones, about the troubled economy, the invasion of Poland, and the dangers it may pose for the rest of Europe.

In the dining room, the conversation moved to subjects of lesser risk.

"Surely, Riccardo," Mr. Baroni said jovially, "you shouldn't be unnecessarily modest with your talent. Soon you could probably buy a full-fledged villa. Why not provide evidence of the rightful fruits intelligence can provide?"

Roberto studied the faces of his mother and grandmother to assess their reaction. They seemed suddenly overly concerned with the food in front of them, keeping their eyes down. Mrs. Baroni nodded forcefully, indicating her support for her husband's views. Father's face did not betray any emotion except for the strange, ironic smile held at the corner of his deep blue eyes.

"My dear, Luigi," he finally answered, "since your view may be held by many people, I cannot say that I'm surprised by your statement. There is nothing intrinsically wrong, I suppose, in showing one's talent. Too often, though, talent is measured only by the size of one's bank account; productivity gauged only by the sweat one sheds; sanctity established by the correctness of one's kneeling posture."

"See what you started, Luigi," Patrizia interjected with a smile. "Now we are in for the usual lecture!"

"Come on, my friend," Mr. Baroni exclaimed. "Lighten up a bit."

"Are there not more fortunes made by cheaters than by talented people?" Riccardo continued. "More millionaires made by profiting from the misfortunes of others rather than from their own efforts? Why should I find it rewarding to exhibit my talent by the brick and mortar it could buy me?"

"I don't disagree with you, Riccardo, but you are too pessimistic."

"No. Just realistic. Look around you, if you please: Fellows with big muscles and large sweat glands, kicking a ball around a field, or knocking another man down in a cordoned ring, make more money than professors or engineers. Juveniles who invent a three-note-song become the overnight idols of the common folk. Make money—in whatever way you can—and the world will bestow upon you more virtues than even your mother knew you had. And all this while, the country is on the verge of a disastrous war. Yet you call me pessimistic and think I should find value in a larger amount of bricks and mortar ..."

"Well, well," said Mr. Baroni with a knowing smile, "I agree that our ancient fathers had a point when they said 'Homo doctus in se semper divitias habet'—a wise man's wealth is inside himself. But not all news is bad news, Riccardo. I, for instance, have good news for you, my friend."

There was so much cheerfulness in his voice that everyone looked at him with curiosity.

"The budget you requested for the new equipment at the distillery," he said, "has been approved." He raised his glass and invited the others to join him. "Here is to Riccardo, the idealist and master technician."

"*Salute,*" everyone replied.

*****

Another time, Signor Antonio supplied the theme of the conversation. He had come to the house of his own initiative to deliver an urgently needed drawing, and Riccardo, conscious of the extra effort, invited him for dinner. It was an informal, improvised occasion, and they were all wearing their everyday clothes.

They had already consumed the vegetable soup that Luisa had prepared, and as they waited for seconds to be served, the draftsman asked, "Tell me, Riccardo, if, as you say, our army and the country are so weak, why does Hitler covet us so much as an ally?"

"It's a good question, Antonio. My guess is that no one, not even Germany, can afford to be completely alone. It is a psychological boost to have someone else beside you. Moreover, were we not on their side, it would be a return to the alignment of the Great War, with the blockades and the virtual isolation of Germany."

"I can see that from Hitler's point of view. But Mussolini ... what does he get out of it? Why does he encourage our shifting toward the German's orbit?"

Riccardo nodded and pondered the question for a few moments. "Inertia," he finally said. "We have been sliding down that incline for so long that we have gained too much momentum. It might already be too late to turn back!"

"What do you mean?"

"We have become too dependent on the Germans. Without their coal, steel, copper, and other strategic materials, we would be at the level of third-world countries. Our industries, meager as they are, would be starved in no time at all."

"But we also buy some of those materials from the British."

"Yes, but in diminishing quantities and with lots of strings attached. Besides, their recent stoppage and inspection of our merchant ships on the high seas have damaged the image of il Duce. Self-conscious as he is, that will push him toward Hitler even more."

"You are probably right," Antonio said. "I read of the incident concerning our transatlantic ship *Augustus*. It was kept at Gibraltar for over a week … but then," he uttered, as if hit by a new realization, "what are we saying? Are the Brits too stupid to understand that? Or do they consider us so … inconsequential as an ally for Germany that they purposely push us in Hitler's direction?"

"Neither of the two, I would say. In my opinion, all it means is that the British, come what may, continue to pursue the maritime policy that has given them dominion of the seas for centuries. The very policy that contributed to their victory over Germany in nineteen eighteen. No, Antonio, no one at this point, not even the British, can foresee if we will be a help or hindrance to Hitler's grand plan. In the meantime, they shape their destiny, while we let others shape ours!"

"So, Riccardo, if I hear you correctly, you don't believe that our … temporary state of being nonbelligerent will remain such for long?"

"No, unfortunately, I don't."

"But why?"

"After so much hype and talk about past greatness, empires,

vindication of the injustices of the Versailles agreement, etcetera, etcetera, our glorious leaders will be forced to act. Just like two little kids who begin to shove each other in front of an audience and then end up fighting because neither of the two wants to lose face."

"Just as simple as that?"

"I am afraid so. Actually, it's even worse. Little kids end up doing their own fighting. These 'heroes' of ours will have us do it, and we are so unprepared, so unaware …"

Riccardo seemed to be following an inner thought, but after a moment, he said, "Our schools teach a lot about the dead empires of the past, and there is merit in that. However, they should also teach about the contemporary industrial empires, draw some comparison and the appropriate conclusions."

"But, Riccardo, why do you always imply that we are so utterly unprepared? Our air force seems to be on a par with or even better than others. Look at how many international speed records we have won in the last few years. We have one airplane that can fly at seven hundred kilometers an hour, and … Why do you laugh, Riccardo?"

"Antonio, my friend, no one can deny the ability and entrepreneurial spirit of the Italians. We always had it, we probably always will. But wars are not won by a few artisans, artists, or engineers. They are won by countries with deep pockets—by industries with money for research, money for production, discipline, and great manufacturing capacity. Granted, we have some of the most advanced prototypes in the world. However, as soon as they are short of parts or shot down, our real state of debility will show for what it is. War, my friend, is not a short sport competition; it is, at best, a long, grinding struggle that pounds, smashes, and pulverizes men and equipment." He paused for a moment and then added, "Believe me, I've seen it firsthand."

"I certainly believe you, but Fiat, Macchi, Piaggio, and Isotta Fraschini are reasonably large industries, and they produce good motors."

"In our national context, they are. However, in comparison with the resources and capability of Rolls Royce, Daimler-Benz, BMW, Pratt-Whitney, and other industrial giants, they are insignificant."

Antonio was now listening even more intently, his mouth half-open, his eyes still holding an expression of disbelief. "But …," he proffered.

"*But* nothing, my dear friend. So far, we have only talked about the air force. Do you know that the armament of our army is virtually that of nineteen fifteen? That the firepower of one of our divisions is approximately one-fourth of that of a French equivalent? One-ninth of a German one? As if that wasn't enough, Lorenzo, doing maneuvers with the Julia Division, tells me that all military maneuvers he has participated in were completely rigged."

"What do you mean?"

"The 'Blue Team' invariably wins over the 'Red Team.' But not thanks to its superior strategy or firepower. It's only because, through disclosure and other artifices, results are made to match the intentions. Inexistent air groups are suddenly appearing from other locations. The Red are told to offer little resistance, and the officers of the Blue Team are informed in advance of the predetermined movements of their adversaries. But in real war, my dear Antonio, the Blue Team will not benefit from these tricks; it will be on its own!"

Riccardo looked at his friend and then said in a lower voice, "Lorenzo sounded absolutely disgusted! 'A farce,' he said in his letter. 'A fabrication.' And 'at the end of the exercise', he wrote, 'we all marched in a triumphal parade in front of the grandstands, where a crowd of black-shirted acolytes congratulated each other on the pre-cooked results.'

"And that's what armament like the 1881 rifles and the Skoda cannons—captured from the Austrians in nineteen eighteen—is barely good for: parades! Barely suitable to delude ignorant people, but certainly not experts, or to win wars."

*****

For the next year or so, many similar dinner conversations with the family were dominated by those events that were turning the continent of Europe into a battlefield.

Initially, the military success of the Germans seemed to contradict Riccardo's earlier predictions. The quickness of the conquest in Poland, the lightning occupation of Norway, the significant victory over the French army, and the bottling of the British forces at Dunkirk convinced most people that the German blitzkrieg was actually close to producing "final victory." Newspapers all over the world seemed to confirm this belief.

The German advance against enemy forces seems unstoppable, read a weekly magazine.

The French army has been destroyed and the British badly beaten, echoed another.

The word *blitzkrieg* recently appeared in print, became a common word.

"What does it mean, Father?" Roberto asked.

"It denotes the lightning speed of the German advances. Their novel, combined use of air attack, coordinated with ground armored forces, makes the Allies' old schemes of static defense outmoded and ineffectual."

The Panzer Divisions smashed through the combined French-British defenses and pinned their entire army on the beaches of the French town of Dunkirk.

It was a serious blow, but not a mortal one, as Hitler inexplicably ordered the German advance stopped, therefore allowing the evacuation and escape of the British Army. Some newspapers alluded to the "almost miraculous escape," due partly to the bad weather that grounded the *Luftwaffe,* and even more so to the largest and most oddly assorted flotillas in history, which shuttled the stranded Allied combatants across the channel. Although the armament was lost, by the end of May, over three hundred thousand men were evacuated.

"What a silly blunder," Riccardo commented. "Those men will rearm and eventually fight the Germans again."

"Shouldn't we be glad about it?" Patrizia asked.

"Of course we should. I was only commenting that, from a strategic point of view, it was a gigantic error."

Despite the missed exploitation of this opportunity, everyone was by now convinced of the invincibility of the German army.

"'*Marshal Herman Goering, chief of the Luftwaffe,*' read Patrizia aloud, "*is said to be about to begin the bombing campaign of England.*' More death and destruction is on the way," she concluded.

Roberto had been silent for the last little while. He was thinking of the town bombed by the Germans during the Spanish Civil War. How many more towns and cities were going to suffer the same fate? How many more people were going to die?

Would Castelvecchio suffer the same fate?

- XXII -

1940

"*Autarchia!* Autarchy!" declaimed Riccardo that Sunday, as he read the section of the morning paper that dealt with national matters. He shook his head. "As if we didn't have sufficient bad news …"

Luisa, who was stirring a pot over the stove, looked in his direction but did not comment.

"The etymology of the word," he continued, "suggests the literary translation of 'auto-sufficiency.' The problem is, this is not literature, and in its customary political terms, it should be honestly called … self-made insufficiency."

With the beginning of hostilities, the doors of the Mediterranean were shut by the British fleet, operating from its Egyptian ports—Gibraltar, the islands of Malta and Cyprus. Supplies from many continental countries to Italy were stopped or drastically reduced, and food, like many other strategic commodities, needed to be rationed.

"The state declares," Riccardo read aloud, "that for the public benefit, wheat, corn, sugar beets, coffee, olive oil, oatmeal, rye, oats, red meat, and a host of other commodities are now severely rationed." He lifted his eyes from the paper. "The list would be considerably shorter had they stated what is not rationed. Can you imagine a kilogram of coffee costing one thousand lire? That's about a month's wage for a skilled worker. And listen to what they quote for other commodities," he said derisively. "Eggs, six lire a dozen; oil, fifteen lire a liter; butter, twenty-eight a kilo; and bread, two sixty."

"Rubbish," said Luisa. "Those are the published prices for purchases with the *tessera*—card. The truth is, those commodities have disappeared from the open market, and your only chance is to get them in the *mercato nero*. And their eggs are ninety lire a dozen; oil is one hundred and twenty; butter, if one can find it, is one hundred and fifty; and bread, with God knows what mixture of ingredients in it, is twenty-three. Believe me, I know. I shop and struggle every day."

"I know, Mother," said Riccardo, discarding the newspaper. "It's the usual propaganda. The regime is starting to feel the air of opposition to its policies, and it feeds us this rubbish with the connivance of the press."

In larger metropolitan areas, prices had risen even more, and many necessities were now beyond affordability. People were beginning to suffer a serious shortage of basic food. In smaller towns, where many people had relatives or friends with farmland, the hardship was not yet felt to the same degree, but even here one began to fear for the future.

Luisa was more provident than most. Having lived under similar circumstances during the Great War, she had been gathering a supply of olive oil, sugar, and other important food staples. She had bartered some of her provisions with local farmers. She also spent countless evenings and nights preparing dozens upon dozens of different jams, preserves, and pickled vegetables. She sealed them in sterilized glass jars to last a long time. She raised more chickens and rabbits than ever before. Roberto witnessed her fervent activity, helping her during preliminary work. Like drying to perfection—as Nonna demanded—the insides of cans and containers destined for preserves.

"Your hands are smaller and more agile, Roberto," Luisa would say. "Make sure you clean and dry completely even the far corners; otherwise, mold may result, and all our work will be for naught."

Neighbors calling on Luisa sometimes found her at the stove, her face red with heat, the little boy at the kitchen table lining up dozens of glass containers waiting to be filled. "Luisa," they would mock her, "are you trying to feed an army?" Or they shook their heads and said something like, "There are only three adults and a child in the family. Aren't you overdoing it?"

She seldom gave explanations, but at times, as these visitors left the house, Roberto would hear her mutter, "We shall see. I've already experienced one damned war. He who laughs last, laughs best."

The troubles, however, were just beginning.

"Listen to this," said Riccardo one evening, while the two women were clearing the table. "I was perusing the editorials section and found this excerpt. It's from a recent interview from our great Il Duce:

> It is humiliating to be sitting on our arses while others are making history. To make a great people, one must take matters to the battlefield. If necessary, even with kicks in their asses. Why keep six hundred thousand tons of battleships if we don't want to compete

with those of France or England? We might as well have a few yachts to take our signorine sailing around the Mediterranean Sea.

"Spell it out for me, Riccardo," Luisa said.

"I'm saying that the press, spurred by Mussolini, has intensified the frequency and tone of the articles designed to prepare us for war. The enthusiasm for the German successes and the fear of exclusion from a favorable peace treaty, are making Italians shift their opinion in favor of intervention."

Riccardo placed the newspaper on the table and remained silent for a moment. "What worries me most," he then added with unusual emphasis, "is that the majority of people—in their deep ignorance— whether fired by false patriotic ardor or misplaced hopes of grandeur, are falling for this degrading home-spun rationale."

"War," Patrizia said. "But why and with whom?"

"You already know the answer to the *why,* my dear. We have discussed it many times before. As to 'with whom,' I wouldn't speculate. However, knowing our great leaders, they'll pick on some country perceived as being weaker than we are."

"At least this time it will be far away from us," said Luisa.

"And Riccardo," added Patrizia, "will hopefully be considered too old or too important to the economy to serve."

Riccardo's sudden silence did not give a clue as to his opinion on either of those matters. However, he had begun to mull over the eventuality, and even the mere consideration of this remote occurrence caused him inner turmoil. He hoped to avoid the conflict that his decision would necessarily create for him and for the family.

By now, however, most people thought it was only a matter of time.

*****

Finally, on June 10, 1940, Mussolini, anxious to be included in what he expected to be the imminent peace negotiations and to reap personal glory and territorial gains for Italy, declared war on France and Britain.

Foreign Minister Galeazzo Ciano summoned the French Ambassador Poncet and the British Sir Percy Lorrain to announce Italy's declaration of war against their respective countries.

It was June 11, 1940.

The radio and the party organizers exhorted the Italian people to assemble on the public squares at 10:00 AM to hear a 'special' broadcast.

In Rome, Piazza Venezia was packed with a huge crowd that instigated frequent bursts into a crescendo of shouts and acclamations. Finally, the glass door to the balcony opened. Mussolini, in full military uniform, received by thunderous applause, began his usual staccato announcement.

It was replayed on the hour, and Riccardo heard it at midday when he went home for lunch with his brother, Lorenzo, who was visiting the family.

The women set the table and prepared the food, while the men retired to the studio, which had closed windows and shutters, since Riccardo often listened to clandestine stations. Shortly, there was a knock at the studio door, and Roberto, just back from school, rushed in to greet his father and uncle.

"Hallo, Uncle," he said cheerfully giving him a hug.

Lorenzo grabbed Roberto by his arms and pretended to be unable to lift him. "My God, you're growing fast. How old are you now?"

"Just over seven, Uncle, but I am already in grade four."

"Amazing! If you continue like this, you'll be taller than I am ... and be an engineer by age twenty. You'll beat your father by one year."

"But Nonna said that he lost time because of the Great War," Roberto answered. "Besides, I don't want to be a chemical engineer like father. Just pipes and boilers. It's too boring."

Lorenzo burst into laughter.

"You'll have plenty of time to decide what you want to be, Roberto," Riccardo said in a hushed voice. "Come here, my son. The announcement is about to start; we'll listen to it together." He kissed his son's forehead, made space beside him, and put his arm over the boy's shoulders. Roberto sat quietly near the edge of the armchair, his head resting against his father's chest. Lorenzo closed the door again, and the bustle from the kitchen became barely audible. Now there were only glimmers of light in the room: those of the radio dial and a small reading lamp in the far corner of Riccardo's desk.

Moments later, the historical announcement began:

> *Fighters of the land, sea, and air ... Blackshirts of the legion and the revolution ... men and women of Italy ... of the empire and of the Albanian Kingdom ... listen to my words.*
> *The hour ... marked by destiny, strikes in the skies of our motherland; it is the hour of irrevocable decisions!*
> *The declaration of war has been given to the ambassadors of France and Great Britain. We are taking to the battlefield against the plutocratic democracies of the West, which, since time immemorial, have obstructed the progress ...*

And we will persevere until final victory!

Thunderous applause burst through the speakers. Lorenzo switched off the radio, and as its light dimmed, the numbers of the dial panel disappeared into darkness. The room seemed still saturated with the sounds of Mussolini's usual staccato phrases and the subsequent cries of the crowd gathered in front of the fifteenth-century Palazzo Venezia.

Roberto felt the arm over his shoulder become more rigid and heavier. It was no longer an embrace. New tension seemed to vibrate through his father's body. The boy was aware that he had witnessed something very dramatic. The war his father had predicted for such a long time was suddenly here—but what did it really mean to him? To his family?

The hushed atmosphere, the forward, static posture the two grown-ups had taken in their respective chairs, and their solemn expressions made his heartbeat quicken as he thought about the war. Not the one he read about in books and fantasized about; not that of the Greeks against Troy, Rome's against the Gauls, nor even Napoleon's wars. But the one his father never talked about. The one his nonna always described with dramatic words and eyes wet with tears: the Great War. The war fought in the trenches; in the mountains; across riverbanks of the Tagliamento, the Isonzo, and the Piave rivers, with devastating weapons and poison gas and airplanes. The one where millions of people, including his grandfather, had died, killed by bombs, machine guns, bayonets. The one where countless men were wounded and maimed, or had their legs amputated because their feet were frozen or infected by gangrene. Even in Castelvecchio, he had seen veterans who walked with crutches or were wheeled around by others, as their legs had been severed above their thighs.

He remembered the picture his history professor had shown to the class, secretly, as it was considered "enemy's propaganda" by the regime. An artist called Picasso had painted it, and it was called *Guernica.* As the teacher revealed, it commemorated and symbolized the destruction of the Spanish city with that name. Those strange human figures and animal forms had made some of the children laugh. They were not used to extreme stylized renderings of artists like Picasso. At the time, Roberto hadn't understood them either. But now, at this very moment, thinking of the horrors of war, he could. He heard the screaming people, the howling cows … saw the segmented limbs and horribly contorted human faces. Now the picture made sense, and it embodied the feeling of the room.

He remembered the words pronounced by his father at the time the town had been destroyed by air bombardments: "I am afraid that now the bombing of cities and towns and the indiscriminate killing of civilian population will become part of war."

"Is this bad, Father?" Roberto asked, breaking the uneasy silence.

"I am afraid so, my son. Wars are always bad." His voice was colored by an unusual tone of apprehension. "This one might be one of the worst."

All over the squares of Italy, masses of people had fallen into silence. Here and there, party organizers tried to foment a bellicose enthusiasm among the crowds. But the short *Hurrahs!* and *Viva Il Duce!* were soon suffocated by the ensuing silence.

For some Italians, now that it was here, the romantic illusion of a "regenerating war" was soon washed away by the tide of recollections of the deaths, wounds, and sufferings of the Great War. Being one of those who had fully experienced its ravages, Riccardo shook his head in dismay. "What final victory?" he exclaimed with rage. "Poor deluded imbeciles, wait and see when the bombs begin to fall over your heads, and death and destruction replace the silly parades, when the Americans will throw in their full support to the British and French …"

"The Americans?" Lorenzo repeated. "Why? Do you think they will take part in this?"

"I'm sure they will, dear brother—one way or another. You don't think they'll just stand there and watch as Hitler and Mussolini defeat the democracies and subvert the world …"

"But they have declared neutrality."

"They can declare whatever they want, yet they are not neutral. They are already helping Britain with war vessels and other armament through the Lend-Lease agreement, which is nothing but an obvious way to circumvent their so-called neutrality. Yes, Lorenzo, they will wait, get ready, and eventually intervene and play the saviors."

"I didn't consider that possibility," said Lorenzo, as if to himself. Then, looking at his brother, he continued in a somber tone. "You have already served in a war, Riccardo. Your age and position should spare you this time. I, on the other hand …" It was no secret that Lorenzo felt a rebellious attitude toward a destiny that, already twice during his short life span, had placed him in the war arena. He hated to join the army. To kill or be killed. Serve under an incompetent class of officers whose mission seemed—from the many examples he had heard or seen—to stay clear of danger while ordering other people to their deaths.

"Yes," Riccardo confirmed unhurriedly. "Now the relatively safe distraction of parades and make-believe has become a matter of dangerous consequences. Italy will soon show itself for what it really is: weak and ill prepared."

For him, it was a simple deduction: the present had been irreversibly shaped by the actions of the past, resulting in Italy at war. It was now too late to change course. Nothing could be done, except wait for the future to unfold.

- XXIII -

"What do you think, Riccardo?" Antonio asked. "Now that France has capitulated, and the African front is temporarily at an impasse. Will peace have a chance?"

"I doubt it, Antonio. Our cowardly attack on France, and our miserable military performance after the Germans had already won that conflict, won't satisfy our leader. No, my friend, I'm afraid not."

It was a beautiful, sunny day, and the two men had taken a breather from their work. The walked up and down the ridge of the riverbank, away from indiscreet ears, each of them smoking a cigarette. On one side stood the gray concrete buildings of the distillery, dominated by the tall, redbrick silhouette of two chimneys exhaling a whitish smoke from their subterranean lungs. High dark dunes of pressed dregs rose from the vast yard. The prolonged hissing of relief valves and the loud mechanical clatter of the machinery pierced the air.

The other side was a picture of pastoral serenity; the Arno journeyed silently toward the sea, and the river cane swayed under the gentle breeze. Then distant hills, the Appenine Mountains, and the blue canopy of the sky.

"But why couldn't we have peace?" Antonio insisted.

"Because Mussolini has been humiliated in the eyes of the crazy man of the North, and in the eyes of the whole world. Hence, I am convinced that he'll try again."

"Why did we perform so badly?"

"For all the reasons I already told you," said Riccardo, shaking his head. "And listen to this as well: An old comrade of mine—from the old days on the Piave Line—writes me every now and then. He is a regular army officer and was with the troops against the French on the Monte Bianco attack. He told me stories of our customary lack of preparation, lack of ammunitions, and incompetence of our higher ranks." Riccardo blew a puff of gray smoke upward. "After thirty-six hours of uninterrupted travel, his company arrived at the front, ahead of their heavy equipment. All the same, they received the order to attack. 'Where?' they asked. 'Wherever you can,' they were answered. 'With what?' 'With what you've got.'"

"Oh my," Antonio drawled. "Now I understand why we couldn't even dent their lines, despite our numerical advantage."

"Yes, Antonio. Nothing has changed, and the submissive press is already minimizing the event, covering our failures with lies. Therefore, I am afraid to say, we'll be in for more at the first opportunity. Knowing the character of our leaders, they'll pick on a country perceived as being easy prey. Although if they misjudge it as they did France, we're in for more trouble. As to when, it's hard to predict with certainty, but my guess would be very soon."

*****

They were prophetic words. Only weeks later, Mussolini and his militaries decided to attack Greece.

Riccardo was more somber than usual.

Antonio appeared briefly in his doorway, but seeing him busy with drawings, he saluted and left.

Though apparently occupied with a set of blueprints on his desk, he was unable to concentrate on his work. He knew this further adventure would spell trouble for the country. It would surely affect Lorenzo, who would probably be called to arms. Perhaps even himself.

He couldn't conceive the idea of his young brother in a military uniform, following the orders of some inept career officer, mired in the muck of a trench in a foreign land. For what? For whom?

And what about me? he thought. *How would I respond if called?*

Suddenly, his mind reeled back to the trenches north of San Donà, the many bloody battles … the deaths. He remembered that seventeenth of November when, through his field glasses, he saw his town shelled, blown to pieces. He'd seen the bombs explode near his house and feared the worse. *Everyone is dead,* he'd thought, as dark clouds of smoke rose quickly toward the sky. He had felt the urge to run there, under the raining shells—like some of the local soldiers had done—to see if his mother, father, and younger brother were dead. He had not. The death of the battalion commander had left him in charge of the situation. Abandoning his post at that crucial moment would have been disastrous. Though his heart wept tears of blood, he held firm. He stopped the other men who were about to run away, with his own example, with shouts of encouragement, even with threats.

The morning after, a soldier from his brigade returned from San Donà after a short defection. Riccardo, who had been without food, sleep, or communication from the rear lines for over twenty-four hours, stopped the man.

"Soldier," he called, "has the Piave Line been breached in any place?"

The man stood to attention, petrified. He looked at the officer, at the Beretta pistol he held in his hand. "Please, sir," he begged, "I came back as soon as I could. Don't kill me. I have a family."

Riccardo did not intend to kill one of his men. In fact, he had even forgotten that he was holding a pistol.

"I have a family …," the man lamented.

A family, Riccardo thought. He suddenly remembered that someone had told him his own father had been killed in the shelling, and that his mother and brother were sheltered with a multitude of people in the basement of the courthouse or the church.

"I have a family," the soldier implored again.

"We all do, soldier," said Riccardo, placing his pistol in its holster, "and that's why we must hold the line. Go now. Return to your unit and give them hell."

Riccardo realized that "family" had a new meaning now for him. And another war was knocking at the door. *Roberto,* he muttered in his mind. *Patrizia.* He shuddered at the thought they might be involved in circumstances similar to those he experienced during the Great War and, given the technological advance of weapons, perhaps even worse.

A light knock at the door interrupted his thoughts.

He cleared his throat. "Come in," he said.

Patrizia entered the office, closing the door behind her. "Hallo, my dear," she said with a forced nonchalant demeanor. "Antonio gave me the bad news. I think he wanted to ask you something personal. Will you talk to him later?"

"Hallo, Patrizia." The way he said her name made it sound as if he had said *my love,* but he never allowed himself to say that at work. "I gathered that, but I am not at my best. Perhaps later …"

"All right, Riccardo. When will we be going home? I don't have my bike."

"I won't be long, half an hour maybe. I'll call you when I'm ready."

*****

"Look," said Patrizia, spotting Lorenzo's car in front of the house, "your brother is here. Roberto will be delighted."

"Yes," Riccardo replied. He fervently hoped his conjecture for his brother's presence was wrong.

Supper that evening was a rather quiet affair, with verbal exchanges between Roberto and Lorenzo, and frequent silent looks between the two brothers traded over the dishes and flatware.

"So, Uncle, when are you taking me to Florence? You promised me last time."

"One of these days I will, I'm sure."

"Uncle, can you please mark 'one of these days' in nonna's calendar?"

Everybody laughed.

It was finally the end of the meal. Luisa took Roberto to bed.

Lorenzo, draining the last bit of wine from his glass, said, "You have guessed, Riccardo, haven't you?"

"When?" Riccardo simply said.

"A couple of weeks, three at most. I've been attached to the Julia Division because I was born in San Donà. I'll be sent to the Greek front."

"Does Mother know?"

"No, not yet. I'll tell her now."

"Do you want me to leave?" Patrizia said.

"No, Patrizia. You are family."

Luisa returned to the kitchen, saying, "Coffee, anyone?" Then she glanced at them and said, "Listen boys, I've been around too long, and I know you too well not to feel that there is something you are not telling me."

"I know, Mother," said Lorenzo. "I just wanted Roberto in bed and all of us here, close to each other, before I told you."

"What is it, son? Don't tell me you've been drafted."

"That's right, Mother. I'll be going to the Greek front with the Julia. But not right away. First we'll assemble and equip near Bari. Then from there to Albania, and then … but don't fret. Everyone agrees it'll be a piece of cake."

"And that's what worries me," Riccardo said. "Underestimating your enemy is always a grave mistake. I'm glad they attached you to the Julia Division; it's mostly made of northerners. It has a tradition of good soldiers and officers."

Luisa dropped onto her chair as if suddenly her weight were too much for her legs to bear, but she found the courage to raise her glass and say, "This is for your safe return, my son. *Salute,* and may God protect you."

Everyone made a toast and wished Lorenzo a speedy, safe return. Luisa tried to smile and disguise the pain. *God, give me the strength required*, she prayed in her heart, *to see yet another son sucked into a war. And a completely unnecessary one at that.*

"I'll be back to see you before I leave," Lorenzo said. "I have several more days, and I'd like to say good-bye personally to my nephew. Tonight I didn't have the heart to do it."

"We'll be waiting for you," Patrizia said.

*****

Lorenzo made good his promise and returned to say good-bye to Roberto. By then, the entire family had planned to appear as normal as possible in front of the young boy, and the emphasis was on a prompt return rather than the immediate departure. Roberto, however, focused his interest on the heroic role he hoped his uncle would play. "Will you be decorated like father was?" he asked. "Will you command a battalion? Will you kill many enemies?"

"Don't fire so many questions at once, Roberto," Riccardo reproached, "and please do not talk about killing. It's not a nice word in anyone's mouth, least of all that of a child."

But everybody knows that killing is what war is about, Roberto thought in puzzlement, *and if you kill enough, you may even become a general.*

During the following days, Roberto mentioned his uncle a few times. But he was already used to his long absences, and in the family, they did their best to avoid mentioning the war, which Patrizia had already baptized "déjà vu."

The Italian military attaché and the ambassador in Athens tried their utmost to deny rumors that pro-fascist elements in the Greek government were ready for a coup d'état—that the country would be delivered to the Italians, perhaps even without a fight. However, neither Mussolini nor Foreign Minister Galeazzo Ciano were inclined to believe the truth. And, again, they embarked in a war without suitable preparation and with all the top generals believing—in their unjustified optimism—that the Greek invasion would be an easy affair.

Lorenzo's first letter from Bari soon gave an idea of the situation. He wrote of the exaggerated, unfounded confidence, the inadequate equipment, the under-strength condition of his division, the disjointed relation between army and navy. The letter was written in a mocking tone:

> *Roberto would be unhappy to find out that in our headquarters,*
> *we can't even find a map of the terrain we are supposed to "conquer,"*
> *nor Nonna's calendar to mark the day of embarkation.*
> *By the way, Riccardo, I forgot to tell you that the master sergeant in*
> *our company is an old guy (oops, he is about your age) who claims to*
> *know you. A certain Livio Piccinin, who apparently was under your*
> *command on the Piave Line. "Goddamn it, sir," he said when he*
> *heard I am your brother, "I hope you're not as tough as he was, or else*

I'll ask to be transferred." He was joking, of course, and told me to say hallo.

In a matter of days, reality overtook pretense, and the Italians soon realized that the Greek soldiers intended to defend their land and fight.

- XXIV -

Contrary to his previous posturing, Mussolini had finally entered the war. General Graziani, commander of the First Italian Army, attacked the British in northern Africa. By February 1941, however, the British had chased the Italians out of Cyrenaica.

As Riccardo Lanzi had predicted, the poorly armed and insufficiently supplied Italian army, left leaderless by a largely inept class of officers, was on the verge of giving up the fight. In fact, thousands of its soldiers had already begun to do so.

At this turn of events, and in order to save himself from the embarrassment of a total failure, Mussolini asked Hitler for help. Fearing the consequences that might befall his old ally, Hitler agreed to send three German divisions to Libya. An essential condition for this concession was that the Italians resolve to defend the Tripolitanian territory.

Once agreement was reached, General Erwin Rommel and three well-equipped German divisions—two motorized and one panzer—were dispatched to the African front.

The Italian high command could only respond and reciprocate by drafting additional soldiers to replenish the thoroughly demoralized Ariete and Pavia divisions already depleted by casualties and defections.

*****

That afternoon, Roberto was returning from school, running toward his house, pretending to be a horse-mounted knight approaching his castle.

It hadn't rained for weeks, and the grass at the edge of the road was coated with dust. Roberto deliberately thumped on it and observed the powder clouds his horse left behind. When his mind reeled back to reality, he anticipated the pleasure of telling the family of the good marks received, and he could already savour Grandmother's food.

As he walked into the kitchen, he immediately sensed that something was wrong.

Though only nine years old, he was able to predict troubles from the nuances of family members, just as his beloved nonna was able to forecast rain by the change of winds or the shapes of the clouds over Monte Serra.

His feelings were confirmed as he noticed his grandmother's solemn expression, father's deeply pensive mood, and mother's reddened eyes.

No one had welcomed his arrival from school as they usually did. Was it something he had done? He briefly examined his conscience, but could not come up with anything. He hadn't missed school, his marks were better than good, and he had scrupulously carried out all the chores assigned to him. What was it, then?

As he'd entered, he'd thought his mother had uttered the word *war*, and her tone seemed rather troubled. His father, however, noticing his arrival, had quickly hushed her. Was war their concern, then? Had something happened to Uncle Lorenzo? The uncertainty caused him a great deal of discomfort, but he didn't dare ask.

Until that moment, war had always been an abstract event—something he read in history books or heard on the radio or at supper, when the family discussed the events of the day. Something happening to other people in other countries or in the distant past. Sitting on his father's lap, he had often looked at colored maps, learning to locate different countries, familiarizing himself with the ones invaded by Germany: Poland, Belgium, France, Czechoslovakia. And the two where Italians were fighting: Greece and North Africa.

With such a strong ally as Germany, suggested the papers, those fights were virtually already won.

During 1940, the Germans had seemed unstoppable. Poland was conquered; Belgium and France had capitulated; Britain, after the reversal of Dunkirk, had retreated to its island. So why worry?

Sure enough, he had heard his father's cautionary words. "This is only the beginning," he had said. "It's only a question of time before the Americans will join the fray. You wait and see; they'll play neutrality until they are ready, and meanwhile, they'll make money with their Lend-Lease agreement with the British. Then, at the first opportunity, they'll jump in with both feet and tilt the scale. Just like they did in nineteen eighteen."

Was this perhaps what had happened? Roberto asked himself.

Supper that night was unusually meager, as if more important things had interfered with its preparation. For some reason, rather than in the kitchen, it was consumed in the formal dining room. Tonight, however, the somber grace of the cherry-wood furniture, the classic elegance of the *Ginori* porcelain dishware, and the pleasant smell of home-cooked food were insufficient to overcome the mournful silence. The few words exchanged were awkward, toneless, and perfunctory.

"Would you like more soup, Riccardo?"

"No, thanks, Mother. I had plenty."

"Would you please pass the water, Patrizia?"

And so on …

When the meal was finally over, his mother said, "Read a few pages from your book, Roberto, and then go to bed, *mon chou.*"

He began to read aloud, as he routinely did after supper, but he could not concentrate. His thoughts were still lingering on the awkward silence and sullen mood of the family. He purposely skipped a few lines, and as he anticipated, no one noticed. He finished the chapter and said good night to everyone. When he kissed his mother, she responded without meeting his eyes. His father, however, held him a bit longer than usual and hugged him more tightly. His return good night was uttered in a voice that seemed choked with emotion.

Even his nonna, when she came to his room to tuck him in and remind him to say his prayers, behaved strangely. He wanted to question her, but her uncharacteristically withdrawn mood stopped him. She did not chat or joke with him after the prayers. She did not ask him about school. She just bent over him and kissed his forehead, made the sign of the cross over him while mumbling some prayer, and then she turned off the lights and left.

As soon as his eyes adjusted to the darkness, Roberto got up and opened the bedroom door slightly. When he returned to bed, he could now hear the movements and conversation of the family.

Someone was putting the dishes into the sink. "Don't worry, Mother," he heard his own mother say. "I'll look after these."

"*Va bene,* I'm rather tired tonight," he heard his nonna reply. "I think I will go to bed. Good night to everyone."

Roberto found it strange. She was always the last one to retire. The kitchen door opened and closed, and a sliver of light intruded briefly in his room. After a few muffled steps, another door opened and closed. For a few moments, there was absolute silence, and Roberto waited with anticipation and concern.

Then he heard his mother say, "So you have decided. No matter what your poor mother or I think of it. No matter how our child will feel …" She spoke in a low, restrained tone, as if picking up an interrupted conversation.

"Please, Patrizia, don't make it harder than it is already." Father's voice sounded unusually weary. "I've already explained my reasons to you."

"And so you have. But honestly, my dear, I don't understand them! Your brother has already been drafted. You have already fought one war, lost your father, umpteen relatives, your home … What else can this family give to the country?"

"It's not a matter of giv—"

"What is it, then? You know as well as I do that your age and position would allow you to refute the call."

"Please! Don't insist." His voice sounded calm but resolute. "You know I'd never use my position and connections in Rome to be exempted from what I consider my duty."

"Your duty? But if you hate fascism with all your heart … You laughed at them when they bragged about having eight million bayonets. You said that bayonets, contrary to party propaganda, won't stop tanks and airplanes. You said we're doomed. If you are convinced of such an outcome, why on earth would you want to risk your life, our future? Why, why, why?"

That morning, Riccardo had received a registered letter from Rome. Imagining its content, he read it in private and discovered that, as a reserve artillery officer of the Pavia Division, unless he could produce evidence of physical infirmity or other serious impediments, he was to join his unit in a matter of days. Roberto was just discovering this, following the aftermath of his father telling his wife and his mother.

He is really going to war, Roberto thought. Those three words, "risk your life," struck a sensitive cord in his heart. It never occurred to him before that any member of his family would be at risk. In that moment, the towering figure of his father seemed irreplaceable. If he went to war, two women and a child would be left on their own. *It seems so …* He couldn't even finish the thought inside his head!

"Shhh. Please calm down, Patrizia. We don't want to wake Roberto. My answer is the same as before. Whatever I think of the regime doesn't relieve me from my responsibility."

"Many so-called patriots, Blackshirts, and fascist sympathizers do," said Patrizia in a pleading softer tone. "They try to escape this …

calamity, or 'duty,' as you call it, with whatever means they can—faking sickness, disabilities, or deformities. Even with bribery and desertion."

"Patrizia, you know I don't look to others. I do what I do because I am what I am. Because this is the only country I have, and I will not dishonor it just because others do."

"And what about the anguish you are going to cause your family? Does that not count for anything?"

There was a moment of silence, and Roberto held his breath, afraid to miss any part of the conversation.

"Yes, it does … and quite a lot! It hasn't been an easy decision. I am not even sure what urges me to go. All I know is that only by sharing the burden of war would I remain the same man of principle you love. If I stay, I would betray myself. I wouldn't be able to sit at this table and look at you, at my child, or my mother if I were to forgo my principles because of the danger involved."

"But Riccardo …"

"Darling, you are a person of courage and principles yourself. You have shown it at the distillery. You ought to understand. I want you to be as proud of me as I am of you."

"This war doesn't make any sense. It's all for nothing. You said it yourself …"

"Please don't fail me now. You have always understood my feelings, my ideas, my very being. Can't you understand now? Now that I need you more than ever? I am not the invincible man you all think I am. I need to see you strong because that is the image I want to carry with me. I want to think that you'll be able to overcome the inevitable hardship as I prepare to face mine. And if I should not return …"

"Don't say that, Riccardo! Please don't say that!"

There was silence.

Both of them knew what he was asking. It was not only their personal relationship and mutual support that was being discussed. For in a country, in a culture, in a time where traditionally each and every member of a family and of a community had a clearly understood role to play, women—even those of Patrizia's caliber and resourcefulness—were expected to play a supporting role for their menfolk.

A movement of chairs and a brief shuffling of feet broke the silence. Roberto thought he heard sighs, kisses … perhaps crying. He imagined his father and mother embracing, tears falling on each other's shoulders.

Overwhelmed by what he'd just heard, Roberto got up and closed the door, placing his full weight against it. As if that simple act would shut out the world and make the conversation he'd just heard disappear.

That night, he couldn't sleep at all. Fear of the unknown overwhelmed him, but most of all, the fear of losing his father, the person who was the pillar of the family.

He tossed and turned and found the bed covers too hot, too rough, too binding. He discarded them, and then, feeling his body shiver as if with a winter chill, he pulled them up again. Toward morning, he slipped onto a state of drowsiness where words and images resonated in his consciousness, where fantasy was no longer discernible from reality.

- XXV -

1941

The following days, Riccardo and Patrizia continued to go to work, and Luisa attended to the household chores. Roberto went to school in the mornings and took French or piano lessons in the afternoons.

At supper, Riccardo now talked more about what was accomplished or unfinished at the distillery. He mentioned the people he had entrusted with specific technical responsibilities. Often, the conversation was a continuation of matters already partially discussed with Patrizia.

"Don't forget what I told you about the disposition of movable assets. I already spoke to Mr. Baroni and the other shareholders, so you won't have any problems. There are also provisions for the workers."

"But what about Ligato?" Patrizia asked. "Will he permit—"

"Remember," Riccardo interrupted her, "that as far as Rome is concerned, although temporarily absent, I am still the director. I will entrust you, in writing, with the implementation of certain matters.

Certainly those matters concerning the lab, but also others, which I will specify later."

"I understand," she said, nodding.

"If needed," he concluded, "you know where to find the drawings of the new boiler and other documents. Antonio, whom I trust, can give you a hand."

At times, he was so focused on reviewing all he wanted done that he seemed impervious to the world around him.

Roberto understood the situation, felt the additional sense of sobriety of the family, and tried not to make requests of his father that would add to his apparent anxiety. Outside of his own feelings, which he tried to conceal, and outside the family, the other changes for Roberto were the increased interruption of his classes by party representatives. A militiaman in a black shirt frequently appeared unannounced at the door of the class, pushed the classroom door wide open, and barked out the order, "Everybody out."

The entire class gathered in the street, soon joined by all other classes, which then marched to the main square. Sometimes after a long wait, the loudspeakers would come on and play martial music, quickly followed by thundering applause. It was the prelude of Mussolini's appearance on the balcony of Palazzo Venezia in Rome, and the delivery of his usual harangue to the Italian people. It was thought to be the necessary ingredient to foment the Italians' scarce combative spirit.

One day, at the conclusion of one such theatrical speech, during which il Duce had spoken until past lunchtime, the children were dismissed right on the square and told to go home.

"Nonna Luisa, I'm home!" Roberto chanted, as he passed through the iron gate and entered the garden. He had run all the way from the main square, as he usually did after leaving school, letting the breeze go through his shirt and blow away the stale classroom air. He was imitating a horse's gallop, pretending as usual to be a brave warrior returning from a victorious battle or executing a brilliant escape from vastly superior enemy forces.

His head still full of dreams and sunshine, he slowed his pace as he arrived safely at his personal sanctuary.

He jumped over a flower bed and dashed toward the side stairs that led to the kitchen. "Nonna, I'm here," he repeated, expecting to find her preparing his midday meal.

Surprisingly, his father loomed in the doorway, dressed in a military uniform. It was khaki in color, with a brown leather belt and matching boots. On the right flank, a holster housed a Beretta pistol. The upper left side of his jacket was decorated with the colorful ribbons of his Great War campaigns, and his epaulettes bore the bands and ornaments pertaining to his rank.

Roberto stopped in shock as the nighttime conversation of a week before echoed in his mind. *He is really going, then,* he thought.

"Hallo," he whispered, taking a step forward and staring at his father, who appeared so strange to him, so different and unfamiliar.

No one seemed to have noticed the boy's arrival.

"Hallo," he repeated, with a somewhat firmer voice, while advancing another step or two into the kitchen.

Finally, the adults turned toward him. The suddenness of their smiles was not convincing enough to conceal from the young boy that the matter they were discussing must have been serious.

In those few instants, when everyone was making the best effort to show calm, normal behavior, he read, in the poorly hidden trepidation of the adults, an ominous premonition.

His eyes journeyed eagerly over the faces of his mother, father, and grandmother, who stood mute in front of him. Under his scrutiny, they seemed to draw closer to each other, as if to better preserve a secret they dared not reveal. He did not know exactly why, but he felt that this moment would have an important impact on the rest of his life.

The next morning, Luisa woke Roberto. "Get up, darling," she said with a joyless voice. "Come and say good-bye to your father." Her eyes were red.

As Roberto dressed, the stimulating aroma of freshly made coffee and toasted bread wafted from the kitchen, just like any other day. As soon as he opened the kitchen door, he saw his mother and father bound in a tight embrace. He had rarely seen them in such an open display of affection.

"Good morning," he said.

"Hallo, cucciolo," his mother replied. Although she turned quickly toward the stove, he still noticed her furtive gesture as she wiped her eyes.

Finally, his father looked at him. "Roberto," he said, flashing a forced smile. "I am leaving on the early train, and I wanted to kiss you good-bye."

He picked his son up, and for a long moment, he held his face against his boy's. Roberto put his arms around his father's neck. He could smell the fresh fragrance of his aftershave, and he felt the unusual bump of the epaulettes under his forearms.

"I will be gone for a while," he said to the boy. "I'm going to the African front. Remember when I showed you the map?"

The young boy nodded. Then, remembering his mother's comment when he did not properly voice his answer, he said, "Yes, Father, I do."

"You are the man of the house now," Riccardo continued. "I am counting on you to look after your mother and your nonna." He kissed him on the cheek, and after another hug, he put him down. "Thanks for this, Patrizia," he said, collecting a leather-bound diary from the kitchen table. "I'll keep a journal and think of you." He turned and, without a backward glance, headed for the door.

Roberto stood there, motionless, in the middle of the kitchen, until a gentle push from his mother nudged him forward.

Silently, he followed his father until he walked through the garden gate. Then he stood there, at the side of the road, for a long time, uncertain whether to go farther or return to the house.

His brain felt numbed by the many questions that suddenly swarmed his mind. *Why is he going? When will he be back? Will it be as bad as Mother said …? What will become of us without him? He said I'm the man of the house now, but what can I do?*

There had been many other good-byes. The boy was used to his father's departures and absences, but this was different. Father was not leaving on a business trip. He was now going to war!

War was a dangerous affair. People got wounded, even killed! Death was something he rarely thought about. It seemed to occur mainly when people were very old or sick. His nonna had often told him stories from the Great War. Despite her serious tone, though, and the tales of suffering, mutilations, death, and the importance she attached to each detail, that's what he had taken them for: old stories.

He knew that.

He also knew that this situation was serious enough, for both his mother and grandmother had cried at his father's departure.

He had never seen them cry before.

Roberto's eyes remained fixed on that figure in the khaki uniform. The soldier who had just told him that he was now "the man of the house." His father!

At the curve in the road, as though sensing his son's stare burning into his skin, Riccardo turned around and, without breaking his stride, waved a final time.

Roberto waved back and saw his father fade away from view, walking into the unknown.

"Good-bye, Father," he said silently.

- XXVI-

1941

The next several days were characterized by an unusual silence at the dinner table. Roberto's eyes would often rest on Father's vacant chair, and he would feel a sense of emptiness. He wondered where he was, when he might return. He looked silently at his mother and grandmother and tried to imagine what their thoughts were.

Just to make conversation, he sometimes tried to talk about school. "Today the teacher said …," he'd begin. His phrases, however, sounded as hollow and meaningless as the clinking of knives and forks over the plates. Their echo still lingered in the air as everyone quickly retreated to the confines of his or her own thoughts.

The only question on everyone's mind was, *When are we going to have news?* Time and events were now measured with adverbs such as *before* or *after* his departure, and that date became a milestone in the Lanzis' life.

Finally, almost two weeks after his departure, the postman rang the bell and delivered Riccardo's first letter:

April 24, 1941
Just south of Naples

My dear Patrizia,

I take the opportunity of a moment of tranquility to write you a few lines.

After a terrible train voyage to Rome (and even a worse one to Naples), I was taken by truck to the little village of S, where I am to wait for my company to assemble before shipping out to the North African front.

I am temporarily lodged in a small apartment near the harbor. The place is small, dirty, and rather depressing, but it offers a decent view of the bay. At any rate, after viewing the lodging where the common soldiers have been … "billeted," I have little reason to complain. Poor bastards—even animals should aspire to better lodgings than theirs; not a very good springboard from which to "reconquer an empire!"

There are all kinds of people here, from almost any walk of life and from any latitude. Quite honestly, though, in my eyes, the "quality" that permeates this environment is the total incompetence and inappropriate preparation for whatever it is that we are about to do.

There are regular soldiers whose main occupation is to avoid their duties; young volunteers who truly believe that they are patriots going to reestablish the old Roman Empire; officers who spend their time in the town taverns or in search of amorous adventures; leaders who are not even familiar with the terrain, the climate, or any other characteristic of the war theater!

Most of the common soldiers are from the South—destitute devils who have joined this adventure to escape poverty, a condition that has been their inseparable companion for many generations. A good portion of them believes in Mussolini, albeit without understanding that rhetoric and enthusiasm don't constitute solid reasons for embarking in foolish adventures. Others, unlike the patriotic spirit and faith that animated the volunteers of the Great War, couldn't even say why they are here.

Unfortunately, Macchiavelli's conclusion seems as valid today— some four hundred years later—as it was then: "We have soldiers, but we don't have an army."

Jumping to less … political topics, I miss you very much. I thank you for being so strong. For an instant, at the moment of departure, I was afraid I would break down. As I walked away, I felt Roberto's eyes burning in my back all the way to the curve. Then I turned and saw him standing there, in front of our garden, his gaze directed at me … I almost turned around, just to give him another hug.

Now I am regretful that I did not dedicate more of my time to you and to our puppy, or "cucciolo," as you call him. But time is like the arrow that, once it darts off the bow, can never be recalled.

What else can I tell you? I do love you, and I will write you again soon and send you my address as soon as I know how long we will stay here, or when we are told of our next destination.

My love and warm embrace to all of you,
Riccardo

Written words were not a valid substitute for his presence, but the letter was a welcome relief. Everyone in the family read it over and over, hoping to discover nuances that were missed the first time. Now they would wait for the next one and hopefully for an address to which to reply.

*****

Despite the poor performance of the Italians in Northern Africa, the early months of 1941 were favorable to the three nations known as the Axis powers—Germany, Italy, and Japan—who had forged a pact, or alliance, on September 27, 1940.

280

The months of April and May, radio and newspapers reported the German occupation of Athens and Crete and the counterattack of the Italo-German forces in Northern Africa under General Rommel. General Graziani, who, despite the temporary numerical advantage of his troops, had been badly defeated by the British, and he returned to Italy.

Riccardo entered the following notes in his journal:

April 1941

At my arrival in Africa, I was told that Rommel, already apprised of the dismal situation of the Italian troops, ordered immediate countermeasures. The German Air Force was to intervene en mass and stop the British advance.

As soon as the first armored German division landed in Africa, Rommel ordered the attack. It worked. The British are now retreating toward Bengasi.

April 1941

We have taken Bengasi.

The British continue to retreat, and they will soon be out of Cirenaica. Either they overrate our strength or they are confounded by Rommel's strategy and swift decisions.

We still advance, with a minimum of escort and materials, short of fuel and ammunitions, dragged forward by the momentum of the Deutsche Afrika Korps.

Unfortunately, for reasons I do not understand, our navy keeps unloading our supplies in Tripoli rather than Bengasi; from Tripoli to our front lines there are almost 1,700 km!

In June, although the British continued to retreat under the constant German offensives, Riccardo's letters started to acquire a different tone. As several disastrous decisions made by Axis leaders vastly increased the number and power of their enemies in the field, he began to witness the results he had feared.

On the third week of June, Riccardo tersely recorded the following event in his diary:

June 22, 1941

Hitler repudiated his "Non- Aggression Pact" with Stalin, and his armies invaded Russia.
The lesson of Napoleon has been obviously overlooked.

*****

As Riccardo had feared, the spiral toward total war continued. On December 7, 1941, Japan made the next and gravest mistake and attacked the American navy base of Pearl Harbor.

On December 8, the United States declared war on Japan, and the following day, Germany and Italy honored their pact with Japan and declared war on the United States.

Now, more people in Italy began to recognize that these absurd actions would eventually bring about predictable, dire consequences.

In fact, despite the successes of the Germans and Japanese in early 1942, as the voracity of the war devoured more and more men and materials, the tide began to turn. The American industrial output, the stubborn defense of the British in the air, and the valiant effort of the Russian armies on the ground soon became a combination too powerful to overcome.

By mid-1942, the Americans counterattacked in the Pacific, while the Russians made a heroic stand at Stalingrad. And just as Riccardo had predicted, the British were chasing the German and Italian troops across Egypt and Libya.

In June, another letter was received from Riccardo. Month and locations had been blacked out. Obviously, the censor considered them inappropriate.

My dearest Patrizia:

In my previous letter, I promised I would write you. Well, I am finally keeping my promise.

We are temporarily billeted in wooden huts, planted in the middle of nowhere. All around us, for as far as the eyes can see, is an immense plateau of crimson sand. We are in a place called XXXX, a few kilometers from XXXX.

At times, the Ghibli wind lifts clouds of sand that obliterate the view and bury roadways, equipment, and men. It feels like being under a gigantic sieve while invisible blowers blast away and push the sand toward us. Even the shortest walk from one barrack to the next requires effort and preparation beyond belief. We wear goggles and hats and place handkerchiefs over our mouths. The pullover jackets are all buttoned up and held against one's chest for better protection. Still, when we undress, the finest sand has managed to penetrate the several layers of clothes, and our skin is coated with red powder.

Yet … aggravating as it is, the Ghibli also impedes war actions, and even its constant, monotonous beating is preferable to that of enemy shelling, air bombardment, and the deadly rattling of machine guns.

It gives us a respite from the madness of war and the temporary illusion that nature will eventually prevail over the folly and violence of man.

Speaking of folly, Patrizia, it would be foolish for me to tell you now that I am sorry and that I wished I had never left you. For I know—as you do—that under the same circumstances, I undoubtedly would reach the same decision again.

I love you and wish I were near you. When I now think of all the travel, the days and weeks that I was away when I could have been near you …

Do not despair, my dear, for one day I'll make it up to you. I know you must worry about the situation here. I shall survive for you and our son. I would like to say more, but then again, you may want to have mother read my letter as well. Give her and our son a big hug for me and tell them not to worry. I will write again as soon as possible.

Forever,
Riccardo

"He seems all right," Luisa commented, "but he never gives us any details regarding the campaign. Does he think they can resist? Will they look for a cessation of fighting, an armistice?"

"Perhaps he can't say, Mother, you know? They censor the soldiers' letters."

Silently, Roberto held the image of his father in his mind, dressed in his khaki uniform, sitting at a makeshift desk, writing his letter, while the Ghibly whistled outside and the desert sand enveloped the armed camp.

"Father," he whispered. He felt a knot in his throat and lowered his head. He had never thought that he would miss him so much. Before, even when he traveled to other distilleries, it had been for short periods, and Roberto had always felt his reassuring presence near him. Why did he take for granted his nearness, his affection? Now he longed to sit on his lap again, look at maps, and listen to his soothing voice as he read from *The Iliad*, *Les Miserables*, or *Dante's Inferno*—even though he often had to wait for Father's explanations of Dante's allegories to make sense of what was read. He thought with nostalgia of those rare Saturday outings when the sun had begun to descend toward Monte

Serra and the family went to the Arno River to have supper on the sand, near the water's edge, while the river streamed silently toward the sea, the very sea that now stood between him and his father.

"I'm going to the bath," he said suddenly. He closed the kitchen door behind him and ran to his father's studio, tears streaming copiously down his cheeks. *They mustn't see me cry,* he thought. *I'm the man of the house.* He sat on the floor, behind his father's desk.

"Please," he said, touching the seat of his father's chair, "please, please come back."

*****

That evening, as soon as the chores were completed, while Luisa put away the dishes and Roberto attended to his evening reading, Patrizia went to her room as she usually did when she received his letters. She took Riccardo's letter from her pocket and raised it toward her face. She inhaled the paper as if hoping that some residue of his scent would still be trapped on its invisible grain. She pressed it over her heart and then she read it again.

She sat on the very armchair where they had sat together a few days before his departure.

"Come here near me, my love," he had whispered, patting the wide chair arm. She had sat there, his left arm embracing her slim waist while his palm rested gently over her abdomen. His blue gaze had stroked her lowered face, his look intimate yet penetrating. No words were necessary.

They must have been like that for longer than she realized, as the late afternoon glow had suddenly dimmed into a paler crepuscular blush. Then she gently took his arm down, placed a kiss on his temple, and got up to shut the window before the dimming framed image turned into threatening night blackness.

Afterward, they had made love. Passionately, and with the same hunger of the very first time. Silently, almost as if to tell each other with the tactile language of the body all the things that weighed on their minds and were impossible to translate in conventional, meaningful sounds. Their eyes, locked on each other's, read those unexpressed thoughts—reflecting the fear, the love, and the pleasure received by the other being. A being who, in the moment of fulfillment, had become almost undistinguishable from the self.

Later, they lay on the bed in complete stillness, holding hands, as if through that bodily link, they could continue the spiritual and physical communion they had experienced. A long time later, Patrizia felt a light squeeze of her hand as Riccardo whispered, "Good night, my love."

This evening, as night fell, she did not get up, but stared into the darkness. And suddenly, something from that black, empty space, seemed to stare blindly back at her. Like a presentiment, a silent premonition. She felt her hand tremble, and a quiver traveled the length of her body.

She missed him so much! How could she even fathom an endless future without him?

She thought of the countless nights yet to come, of the lonely hours she would have to spend in the rational, lonely confines of her own mind. Hours without pleasure, devoid of excitement, devoted only to the basic duties of the family and the continuation of her now barren existence.

Damned war! Damned Mussolini!

Then her thoughts shifted to her son. She felt a tinge of remorse. "Cucciolo," she uttered under her breath. She remembered having scolded him earlier, for something unimportant. Probably she had been unfair. Yet he had listened to her silently, without complaint. He had not even defended himself. He had just stood there, in front of her, looking straight into her eyes, betraying only a slight tinge of resignation. Or had it just been forced deference?

So much of his father in that cold, green stare!

He must miss him too, the poor darling, Patrizia thought. *Strange, though, why did he hardly speak of his father, then? Surely he must miss him, and yet he hardly mentions him at all, and when he does … Perhaps he has taken too seriously his father's departing statement: "You are the man of the house now." Perhaps the child, in his own way, is trying to live up to his father's expectations. But why doesn't he confide his feelings to anyone? Not even to his beloved* nonna?

There was a knock at her door, and Roberto came in to kiss her good night. She looked at him with tenderness, noticed that he had red eyes. She was about to ask him if he had been crying, but thought better of it and just stroked his hair with her hand. She would have liked to be more affectionate with him, but his salutation, though dutiful, was rather quick, and in a way unmindful.

Perhaps she felt too tired and spiritually exhausted to react suitably.

Shortly afterward, she said good night to Luisa, who was also going to bed. As Patrizia returned to her room, her eyes darted toward Riccardo's picture. It was the enlargement of the one taken for his military identity card; he looked so good in that freshly pressed uniform.

She sat down at the edge of the bed, indulging for another moment in the luxury of many cherished memories. Here, she could rest her eyes over space and objects that echoed the words, the laughs, and even the eloquent silences of the past—treasured images, suspended in the dimension of time and space of her mind, like fresh linen stretched under the sun of May. In this room, they kissed and embraced, they made love, they talked. She remembered their whispered conversation, their exact words, and even the words that had remained unsaid. Everything, even those things that had not really happened, but which she now wished they had.

She breathed out a long sigh and began undressing. *Tomorrow I'll write you, my love*, she thought, and started mentally to compose her reply: *My dearest Riccardo ... My dearest ...*

These were the only words she repeated just before falling asleep.

In the morning, she awakened with a new determination dawning in her mind. She had to be strong for herself, for her son, for Luisa. She could not be weakened by Riccardo's absence, but summon strength from his reliance in her. Yes, this was her new resolution. She would be strong, protect her child, and help Luisa who, with both of her sons away, must have suffered more than anyone in the family. In her room, at night, she could reminisce and even cry, if tears would care to flow. But now, in the daytime, no one should see her sadness, least of all Roberto. She sat on her bed briefly, and then she pushed her feet out and resolutely walked to the window. She unlatched the shutters and pushed them wide open. The sunlight poured in unimpeded, and she had to half close her eyes. Riccardo's letter and her thoughts were still fresh in her mind, but were now purged of the negative emotional intensity of the night before.

She inhaled greedily and then exhaled. The poisonous feelings were blown out of her body, out of her mind. She began to straighten her bed blankets, humming one of her favorite tunes:

> *Vivere finché c'è gioventù. Perchè la vita è bella e la voglio vivere sempre più.*

> *Live, while youth is here,*
> *Because life is beautiful and I want to live it more and more …*

Today was indeed another day.

- XXVII -

1942

One day, toward the end of October, Patrizia heard a knock at her office door. She opened it and was surprised by the presence of a man in military uniform. She did not immediately identify him.

"Antonio," she then exclaimed, recognizing Riccardo's draftsman, "what are you doing here? You've grown a beard. So nice to see you."

"I'm on a short leave," he said, "and I thought I'd pay you a visit."

"It's a great pleasure, Antonio. How are you?" He seemed to have aged ten years. He was pale and had lost some weight. His eyes, usually alert and darting, were veiled with sadness.

"Antonio." Patrizia hugged him. "Is it really you?" She pushed aside a few glass vessels toward the center of her white-tiled analysis bench. "Let's sit on these stools," she said. "I don't charge extra for the privilege."

Antonio attempted a weak smile. "Have you heard from Riccardo?" he asked.

She told him of his last letters and shared some of the information. Then she fell silent.

Finally, he pulled a brown envelope from his pocket. "It's from him," he said. "I got it just before I left for the front and never had the chance to show you. It's three months old, but I thought you might want to read it anyway."

She extracted the letter from the envelope with great trepidation and began to read.

Dear Antonio:

I am sorry to hear that you have been called as well. Greece won't be an easy front either. As you know, Lorenzo is there with the Julia Division, and from what I hear, it's not uplifting.
If you have an opportunity go see my family before your departure, I beg you to give them my love.
Meanwhile, give my warmest regards to your parents. I wish you heartfelt good luck for your next assignment.
Let's try to keep in touch.

Un abbraccio,
Riccardo

Patrizia held it awhile longer, staring at that signature, and the image of her last night with Riccardo flooded her mind. How long would it be before she saw him again? How long before she could feel his strong arms around her body … his gentle kisses on her lips?

"It doesn't sound too good, does it?" Antonio said. "Especially now that the Germans have taken on Russia as well."

Patrizia did not answer. She could not clear her mind of Riccardo's vivid image.

"Mind you," Antonio said, "they seem to be pretty well invincible at this moment ..."

"And you?" Patrizia finally uttered. "How is the Greek front? Will you be going back soon?"

Antonio looked at her in bafflement. They were perfectly plausible questions, yet he seemed unable to answer them. She realized that and pushed the lab door shut. "What is it, Antonio?"

"I'm sorry, but I'd rather not say now, Patrizia. It's so difficult to explain ... and there are people around. Ligato saw me as I came in. He asked me why I was here, if I had registered my presence at the presidio, how long a furlough I had. I mustn't stay long Patrizia; it could be dangerous for both of us."

"But I don't understand ..."

"Perhaps if I could visit you at home ... I could explain."

"We'll be glad to see you. It has been a while. Even Roberto was asking about you the other day."

"How's the little guy?"

"He is well, but he misses his father."

"I will try to come, Patrizia. We'll make an evening out of it. Like old times." He turned away quickly, and Patrizia wondered what significant thing he wanted to unburden, and why it couldn't be now.

Several days went by, and then Patrizia heard from a colleague that Antonio had been seen at the San Romano train station, with uniform and backpack, obviously returning to his unit. She wondered why their planned encounter had not taken place. She had sensed that he wanted to say something important, and now she wondered what that might have been.

*****

The postman stopped his bike at the Lanzis' and delivered another letter from Riccardo, addressed to Luisa.

Roberto answered the bell.

"Here you are, kid," said the postman, handing him the brown envelope with several stamps with the effigy of Mussolini and the king. "I hope your father is all right; it's not so good over there!"

Perhaps the postman meant well, but Roberto didn't like his tone, nor his air of contrived compassion.

"Thank you," he answered coolly. "I am sure my father is well."

He ran upstairs and handed the envelope to his nonna.

" Thanks to God!" she exclaimed. "I have been praying for this." Then, not finding her reading glasses, she gave the letter back to Roberto. "Here, you read it to me."

"This letter is five months old," Roberto commented, reading the date.

"Go on, darling," Luisa urged as he opened the envelope.

"There's black ink where the name of the location should be," he said, unfolding the letter.

"I understand, darling. Go on anyway."

Giancarlo Gabbrielli

Carissimi …

Finally a moment … of peace, to write you these few lines. As you can see, I am still alive, and under the circumstances, this is already an amazing thing.

I am sure that by now, the seriousness of our situation has been divulged even in the homeland. Therefore, I will not indulge in useless details that probably would not pass the censors anyway.

All I can say is that I pledged to do my duty to the end … but never imagined that my main purpose would become that of saving as many as possible of the young men under my command. They have no one else to look up to, and some of them think of me as their father! Such is destiny!

But enough of me.

I hope life is not too hard on you. It has been a while since I have received any news, but given the fast pace at which we are advancing backward and things are happening, it would be rather amazing if I did.

The last letter I received (and which I always keep in my front pocket and read again when I need cheering) is the one from you, Patrizia, written back in September. In it, you tell me that Roberto is progressing well in school and is becoming quite an industrious young man.

I also read with great joy the page he wrote himself; quite thoughtful and factual. I miss you too, Roberto, and hope that one day soon, God willing, I will be back and will have the pleasure to watch you grow by my side.

In your note, you mention episodes that I had almost forgotten (like the morning you came into my bed and I read you a chapter of The Iliad … 'cantami o Diva del Pelide Achille …' It is nice to see that you have such a good memory. It will serve you well in school and throughout life.

I too have fond recollections of our brief moments together. Like the last time we went to the Arno River, and you drew a beautiful picture of the old mill. Or the time I had you on the handlebars of my bike and we fell in a shallow ditch. "Are you hurt, Father?" you asked. You worried about me, while you were the one with most of the scratches. Your selfless concern was of great solace to me. I love you, Roberto.

As for you, Mother, what can I say? I hope you are well. Your prayers must be good for something if I am still in one piece. Thank you for all your recommendations regarding my health. I don't honestly know how many of them I can keep. I am dreaming of one of your special suppers—chicken alla carbonara, for instance, or chicken cacciatore. You must promise to indulge me upon my return.

I miss you all. Kisses and hugs. Patrizia, I will write you soon.

Un abbraccio,
Riccardo

P.S. Thanks also for the information about Lorenzo. I am relieved to know he is well.

When he finished reading, Roberto held the letter in his hands; looking at the familiar, regular writing, slightly inclined to the right; searching between its lines as if for hidden messages that had escaped his first reading. He was trying to imagine the mood and feeling of his father, seeing him bent over a field desk, with his green fountain pen, thinking about the family, his mind echoing with the words "You are the man of the house."

"Thank God he is alive," his nonna whispered, reclaiming the letter. "Now, if only we had news from Lorenzo …"

The last news they had received from him was from the port of Brindisi, on the southeast coast of Italy, where he was about to embark for the Greek front.

Roberto was about to comment that Father's five-month-old letter was not exactly proof of his being alive and well. But when he looked at his nonna and saw her clutching that letter as if it were a holy relic, he did not have the heart to contradict her conclusion. Five months was a long time, especially in war. Who knew where his father would be by now. He could even be … He did not allow his mind to pronounce the ominous word.

- XXVIII -

1943

It was the second day of intense air bombardment by the Allies. Streaks of dust and smoke swirled all around, almost simultaneously with the deafening explosions. The air smelled of cordite and burnt vehicles. Amidst that hellish sight stood the figure of a tall, sunburned officer, his upper body protruding from the sandbag parapet protection of the antiaircraft batteries.

Colonel Lanzi would have been difficult to recognize as the person who had landed in Africa two years before. He had lost a lot of weight; his face was tight and drawn; and his mouth held what seemed to be a permanent sneer. Only his eyes, despite all they had seen, retained their original spark.

He was calculating the adjustment of the cannons' elevation and appeared unperturbed in spite of the closeness of the explosions and besieging danger. His apparent calm demeanor was the best ingredient to keep his men from panicking and his antiaircraft batteries shooting.

He had always seemed that way, from his youthful days on the Piave Line right up to this moment. Dangerous situations seemed to add steadfastness and confidence, conferring on him the unchallenged authority of a natural leader. His almost miraculous survival under numerous perilous circumstances had instilled in his men a trust that, at times, seemed almost to assume a mystic quality. Some of them were heard saying that the bullet with his name on it hadn't yet been made.

In reality, though, Riccardo feared bombs and dangers as much as any other normal being. He was just able to control his reactions and assume a demeanor that seemed fearless and inspired his soldiers.

"Give me a report on casualties and ammunition," he coolly said to a subordinate as the raid passed overhead. "Then try to have a bite … while they'll let us."

"Yes, sir. I'll check immediately."

"Sir," shouted a subordinate officer from a foxhole nearby, "I think they hit your barracks! I can see smoke."

Riccardo looked at the barracks and then at the blue sky. The airplane formation was now disappearing toward the horizon. He removed his binoculars from around his neck. "Stay on the lookout," he ordered his subaltern, "and call me if the airplanes return for another strike."

"Yes, sir."

He ran toward the barracks. His main concern, now that the raid had passed, was for the few personal things of value left in his possession: the letters from home, the pictures of his family, the leather-bound journal Patrizia had given him at his departure.

"Here," she had said, "log your days and nights away from me. They're only white pages, but I kissed every one of them. All my love is there for you."

He pulled his scarf over his mouth and entered the wooden shack that had been his quarters for the last few weeks, fighting the thick, acrid smoke that filled the air. The blast had torn the door from its hinges. The windows were shattered, and shafts of dusty sunlight poured through the walls from numerous shrapnel holes. Through the glaze of his watery eyes, he saw that many of his books had fallen from their wooden shelf and were now smoldering on the ground. He promptly recovered the unburned letters and the photos. His journal was damaged. Its remaining unspoiled pages were scattered all over the room from the blast.

He opened the windows, tossing out the items beyond repair and some of the still-burning books. He stepped on the remaining flames until they were completely extinguished. As the cross-ventilation cleared the smoke, he began to retrieve and remove the dust and ashes from the journal pages snatched from the fire. When he finished, he guessed that only about one-fifth of them had been salvageable.

Pulling down his scarf, he sat on the sandy, grimy floor, the caustic taste of smoke sour in his parched mouth. He spread the white sheets within his reach, beginning to place them in chronological order.

In most cases, he didn't even have to look at the dates. The names of the locations alone, indelibly etched in his memory, were sufficient to suggest the progression of his African journey: *Tripoli, Buerat, Benghasi, Derna, Tobruk, Sidi Barrani, Fuka, Mersa Matruh, El Alamein!*

And, after that, a two-thousand-kilometer flight—a sequence that echoed in his mind like the monotonous train station calls during a return voyage: *Fuka, Mersa Matruh, Sidi Barrani, Tobruk, Derna, Benghasi, Buerat, Tripoli.*

This time, though, pushed by the British forces always in pursuit, the train continued farther west. It entered Tunisia and marched toward the American lines, who were waiting for the depleted Italo-German army from their entrenchments of their Algerian border.

When he finished reassembling the book, he stared at it miserably; his precious bundle had shrunk to one-fifth its original size. The rest was irreparably burned.

Over two long years—fraught with danger, extraordinary incidents, and unspeakable life experiences—were now reduced to a measly five millimeters of smoky paper.

Remembering Patrizia's words, he also picked up many unwritten pages from the floor, blew the dust off, and put them back into the folder. *Your kisses,* he said in his mind, *will not be lost.*

He held his precious bundle in his hands, as gently as if clutching a tangible, mutilated part of his own body. Then he began to read.

Tripoli

April 10, 1941

Here "we" are, surrounded by an assemblage of humanity that looks more like an encampment of gypsies than a disciplined army.
We are waiting! Waiting for the "armament" to arrive, for the "plans" to be conceived, for "destiny" to unfold.
Our convoy arrived a few days ago, well under capacity—as if our navy had vessels to spare—for no reason other than that our

Stato Maggiore (supreme command!!!) is unable to coordinate even the simplest logistic movement! (Can you imagine if they weren't "supreme"?) And the "real" war has not even started!

I hope that things will remain bearable on the home front, but I am not too optimistic for the future. My only hope is for a quick conclusion for this recurring human madness called war, and for the return to some kind of normality.

April 11, 1941

We have taken Beda Fomm and Bengazi. We are now approaching the line from where the British launched their attack four months ago.

Tobruk is too well defended and well supplied from the sea. Despite pressure from the higher-ups, the field commanders have wisely decided to bypass it for now. The human cost would be too great. We continue our advance eastward toward Egypt.

So far, we have been reasonably successful; we have conquered kilometers of sand with "relatively" few casualties. That's what war does to you—you measure the degree of your achievements in terms of territory gained, enemies killed or made prisoner, equipment gained or lost, casualties suffered … Statistics!

April 15, 1941

Yesterday I returned to Benghazi with a few other officers to celebrate the holiday of the "Statuto."

There were many generals and high-ranking party officers, including Italo Balbo. After the ritual speeches, our soldiers marched in a parade (which is what they do best). Indigenous troops, wearing colorful caftans and mounted on their camels, completed the … "choreography."

Riccardo remembered erasing the word "charade" and substituting it with "choreography." He was still being cautious in those days.

The best thing about the event is that we remained for supper and, given the presence of so many XXXX and "luminaries," it was the best meal we have had in several weeks. We returned to XXXX toward evening as the last rays of the sun played over the humps of the far mountains and colored them with a violet hue. Then, suddenly, over the endless ocean of sand, darkness fell with a dense blue mantle. At first, it was mysteriously and uniformly dark. Then, slowly, progressively, bright stars canopied it.

(An odd thought occurred to me: I imagined someone looking on us from above, in the absolute silence and beauty of the heavens. How absurd must it be from there, to see these insignificant little creatures on earth fighting and killing each other for no apparent reason. How beautiful it'd be, if everyone were suddenly infused with this vision and simultaneously dropped his weapons, shook hands, and laughed at our common temporary insanity! But we won't, and the stars remain cold and far away).

"Far" ... "away" ... I feel forlorn and irrelevant in this extraordinary universe. It is your distance that ...

After the word "that," the paper was partially burned and impossible to read. He could not remember what he had written.

April 18, 1941

'Fortunately, math and science are my favorite subjects. For here in Africa, in the desolate and sometimes featureless immensity of the desert, one must navigate with instruments: maps and compass during the day, stars by night. Distance and fuel consumption must be calculated with extreme precision. Not always can this be done. Due to weather conditions, our vehicles are sometimes forced to advance blindly in clouds of sand. The fine grains flow down from our windshield like rain in a downpour. We try to follow the tracks of the vehicle ahead, hoping it is one of ours!

April 20, 1941

The German armored divisions are driving the British back toward Egypt. What our General Graziani could not do with two hundred thousand men, General Rommel is doing with seventy thousand. Better equipment, better prepared, and more disciplined men, I suppose. He is an exceptional leader and a brave man. I've seen him with my own eyes, leading his armored units into combat, his head sticking out of the turret of a tank, ready to jump into the thick of battle.

Most of our own generals keep kilometers away from the front lines.

May, 1941

How strange life is! Today, during a short refueling stop near XXXX. I learned that in 1917, Rommel commanded a battalion on the Piave Line. Who knows? Maybe we faced each other there; maybe he ordered the bombing of San Donà and was responsible for my father's death. We were enemies then, and now, twenty-odd years later, circumstances have made us allies, and we fight side by side. Sometimes life is stranger than fiction!

Talking of fiction, that's what my past life now seems. I think of the distillery as if it only existed in my dreams.

Even my family does not seem a reality.

June 25, 1941

A few days ago, our communication center picked up the news that, under the code name of Barbarossa, Germany invaded Russia and opened another front. It seems to have caught everyone by surprise. Miles of territory have been already conquered, and tens of thousands of Russians either killed or made prisoner.
The initial invasion seems quite successful—but then, so was Napoleon's.

August 10, 1941

We have entered a period that one could describe as a temporary stalemate. Neither the British nor we seem to have sufficient strength to attack. We are beginning to be overstretched. The British Navy or Air Force often sends our scarce supplies to the bottom of the Mediterranean Sea. Trucks and tanks don't move on unfulfilled promises or enthusiasm alone.

Now that we have a rest from combat, we can concentrate our fury against the other enemy—the infamous desert fleas. We've tried all kinds of remedies, even spreading fuel residues over our bodies, but nothing seems to work.

We can't sleep; if it isn't the air raids, it's the darn fleas.

September 20, 1941

Our numerical forces have increased, but the armament is poor, and we lack the vehicles to move the troops. The Germans, with less than one-third of our forces (but better equipped and with a clearer vision), have taken the initiative (as they ought to) and are now in total command; we have no other option but to follow.

Some of our generals bicker, but then they must adapt to reality.

December 8, 1941

Late November, the British began their attack. It was a large movement hinging toward Tobruk. Neither side had sufficient strength to prevail, and the efforts ended up in a stalemate. Sometimes, it would seem that neither opposing commander could resist conquering a few square kilometers of sand, regardless of cost.

However, all efforts are secondary now, compared to the latest extraordinary event—yesterday the Japanese bombed Pearl Harbor, and America has entered the war. From the reaction of our generals, I doubt they understand the gravity of this occurrence. Perhaps they don't remember the impact of the American intervention during the Great War.

December 25, 1941

Christmas!

Home sweet home! At this time, more than any other, all of us feel a deep nostalgia and think of our families: wife, children, parents.

Counting those of the Great War, this is my fourth Christmas away from home. Roberto was nine when I left; he'll be almost ten now. Among other things, war seems to have changed even the laws of physics; it has lengthened the time and stretched the distance between us.

I feel the strain caused by the remoteness of loved ones. But as an officer with thousands of men under my command, I can ill afford to let my emotions show.

Last night, I shared my supper with a group of officers in my battalion. We ate the tender meat of a gazelle killed by one of our men two days ago. After supper, drinking sour wine—stolen from who knows where—one of the soldiers began to play his harmonica. Soon another one started singing a Neapolitan song.

It was a beautiful, heartrending song. Images of home, of love and loved ones seemed to surge from the music and flow right into our hearts. Many eyes shone with tears, and many battle-hardened men fell gloomily silent.

There were a few private soldiers as well, some enlisted but mostly volunteers. Simple people, mostly from the poorest regions of Italy: Basilicata, Calabria, Sicilia … Peasants who joined the army because they had no other alternative. People who speak with candor: "I had no money, no work, four kids to feed, my old mother and father. What could I have done? Now the army gives me a little money. I send it all home to my family."

Tears often went together with their words.

Were it not for my position and the regard my men hold for me, I would have cried as well.

May 1942

It is our turn to attack. Why now?

Two theories prevail: Either Rommel is convinced that his military genius will be sufficient to succeed, or—and this is what I tend to believe—he deems that past this point in time, the productive war machine of the Allies will make it impossible for us to prevail. Their 'Grant' tanks, armed with 75 mm cannons, have already appeared in battle. Our M13, suitably named the "rolling coffins" by our troops, can't stand up to the comparison, in speed, power, or armament.

June 10, 1942

This morning, assault groups of the DAK (Deutsche Afrika Korps) have entered the oasis of Bir Hacheim. Though there was great risk taken, the battle is won. Now Rommel, despite the recalcitrance of our generals, again turns his attention toward Tobruk.

Everything is too fast, even for the British. Their defense is broken. This time we may take it.

June 21, 1942

Tobruk has fallen. Dragged by and sandwiched between German units, our troops have behaved well but are exhausted. Even the Germans have sustained heavy losses. Despite the shortcomings, we experience a moment of euphoria; victory is a powerful narcotic.

August 15, 1942

Today is Ferragosto—Feriae Augusti, as the early Romans called it. I don't remember if it was in honor of Emperor Augustus, or if it preceded him.

It was a pagan mid-August holiday that remained under a different name.

On this day two years ago, I was still a civilian at the distillery. Patrizia and I distributed 'comfort packages' to the workers, shook their hands, and wished them a good holiday.

Only two years, and already it seems like a lifetime ago.

August 25, 1942

The news we receive from our information services is not good. We know that the Allies are getting stronger every day, while we are immobilized on a static, frontal line—approximately fifty kilometers long—hopelessly waiting to be resupplied. Our supply lines now extend over 1,700 km of desert; too little, too late is what we get. Our diminishing forces are stretched from the Mediterranean Sea (far from being a mare nostrum now that it is dominated by the British fleet) to a southern location called Himmeimat. Sidi Rahman is just behind us, and a place called El Alamain lies eastward, not far off.

The fortunate successes of the last few months have nourished the illusions of our politicians; they still believe in a forthcoming victory. From the safety of their headquarters, they look at a North African map and notice how close we now are to Egypt, the Suez Canal, Alexandria. They think these objectives can be reached as easily as the stretching of their fingers over the chart, and are dreaming of an imminent triumphal parade. They discount the thousands of enemy cannons and armored vehicles positioned a few kilometers ahead. They don't think of the Allied Air Force plowing the skies almost unopposed and constantly dropping bombs over our positions. They don't think of the exhaustion that has now settled on our poor abandoned soldiers. Nor of the deficiency in fuel. They only dream of themselves, imagining a laurel branch around their heads, riding a white horse, trotting toward an "Arc De Triumph."

October 23, 1942

The battle of El Alamain has begun.
Never before have I been under such concentrated artillery fire. People are dying all around me. The younger soldiers call my name; some of them even call me Father. I am in a daze as I keep on moving among my troops, somehow immune to this hellish fire.
Perhaps my day has not yet come.
The communication lines among our troops have been devastated by the bombardment. Therefore, as coordinated actions are impossible, each sector responds on its own—reacting to the needs of the moment without reference to plans or logic other than that of survival. The

soldiers in the advanced positions are isolated; they fight to the last bullet. Then they surrender or fall where they stand, mowed down by the enemy fire.

October 29, 1942

Many localized battles are decimating us.

The enemy is testing different targets to discover the weakest point of our line. It's usually a position held by our poorly armed Italian units. By the time the German armor rushes in to plug the gap and counterattack, the British disengage. They now have time and strength on their side. They can afford this strategy, which seems based on the seemingly infinite amount of shells at their disposal, abundance of tanks and armored cars, and their superb preparation.

In our position, we can't even afford to chase them, to take advantage of the few opportunities they offer. We can't risk losing any of our scarce armored vehicles over the minefields, and we must preserve every drop of fuel for the next inevitable retreat.

Somehow, it reminds me of some of the static battles of the Great War.

However, the larger or final attack that we expected has fortunately not materialized.

Yet!

The Allies must be reorganizing.

Riccardo flipped through the rest of the journal. He ascertained that the entries for the next several months were in chronological sequence. Then he read again his last entry, written only a few days earlier:

May 10, 1943

We have received news that the 15th German Division has been totally destroyed. Our flank is now completely open, and nothing is left between us and the advancing Allied troops.

I am sure the end is near.

It is sad to think of all the youth needlessly sacrificed over the sandy shores of Africa.

Even sadder, in this fatal hour, to hear our "leaders" shout over the airwaves (from the safety of their shelters), "Resist! Resist! Resist!"

He remembered all too well that tragic day.

Before Cabalero's departure, there was one last conference with field commanders. It was "conveniently" held far from the front lines. Riccardo and General Baldi, commander of the Folgore Division, braved the British Air patrols and after a drive of several hours arrived at the convened location near Bizerte as a Caproni-Campini biplane was being readied on the airstrip.

In the tent that served as headquarters, General Cabalero, already wearing his traveling gear, placed his gloved hands over the top of the provisional table. He looked around at the dozen or so officers who sat around it and then stopped his eyes over Riccardo's face and addressed him.

"Colonel Lanzi, you are deemed to be a man who speaks his mind. Since I will soon meet our Duce, I'd like you to suggest what our men would want from Rome."

Riccardo felt the weight of several pairs of eyes aimed at him. As he got up slowly, his forehead acquired additional deep lines. His attention seemed to be focused on forlorn thoughts.

General Baldi—his immediate superior and a veteran of the African campaign—had given him a friendly hint prior to the conference. "Colonel," he had told him, placing his hand on his shoulder, "I know what you think of our situation and its causes. Quite honestly, I can't disagree with you. However, your future could depend on your conduct at the pending conference."

"I don't understand, sir."

"What I mean is," said General Baldi, "if you ingratiate yourself to General Cabalero, he might recommend you for immediate repatriation. After all, he would need someone trustworthy when he talks to Il Duce, someone with your standing and experience."

When Riccardo's delayed his reply, the general added, "Your records show that you already met Mussolini once, at the inauguration of the Ciampino distillery. That adds to your credibility …"

"Sir," said Riccardo, ignoring the last detail, "are you suggesting that I should lie and suck up to Cabalero so that I might be among the ruffi—"

"When did you pick up the jargon of common soldiers?" the general interrupted. "I'm only suggesting that, if questioned, you should ponder your words carefully. Many officers would love to be in Cabalero's airplane when he leaves. As much as I would hate to see you go, no one else deserves it as much as you. How long is it since you've seen your family?"

"What would you recommend, Colonel?" repeated General Cabalero now, tapping impatiently over the table.

For an instant longer, Riccardo considered his choices. He looked up at the man who was going to decide his destiny. He noticed Cabalero's wrinkled brow, his eyes filled with dark impatience and anger. This was the moment General Boldi had warned him about. He could still seize the opportunity, give an answer blurred enough to satisfy appearances and sway the outcome in his favor.

Moments of his joyful past flashed through his mind: Patrizia resting on a sandy shore, their first kiss, caressing her nakedness, making love to her; Roberto returning from school, his tender embrace; his loving mother, Luisa. He heard the subtle voice of the Arno River running toward the sea, saw the green Tuscan hills, the mountains peaks in their shimmering winter vest; heaven.

And then he saw the hell of the battlefield, young men being blown to pieces. He heard their cries, imagined their tearful consorts, their heartbroken mothers. He heard generals who, from their safe havens, continued to shout, *Resist ... fight ... die!*

In the space of few seconds, heaven and hell repeatedly appeared and disappeared within his troubled mind. Riccardo's heart leaped in his chest.

"General," he heard his voice spurt from deep inside his bowels, "we need better weapons, more equipment, adequate fuel supply, food. We need timely decisions from the leadership. In short, sir, the things our men always needed and never received."

General Cabalero became visibly flustered. He straightened his posture; his face hardened. He placed his hands behind his back and launched a threatening look at the men around the table. Many of them, whether or not in agreement with Riccardo, looked down or away and did not hold the stare.

He finally returned his attention to Riccardo and snapped, "I didn't ask you about the past. I cannot alter the consequences of three years of war. No one can. All I want to know is what we should do at this moment."

"Sir, forgive my audacity. ," Riccardo's eyes shone with a mixture of pity and contempt, "You asked me to be frank, and frankness is all I can offer. The outcome can only be affected by the immediate delivery of vehicles and fuel to move our foot soldiers out of harm's way. And even this, at this point in time, will not reverse the end result, but it will certainly prevent a pointless waste of additional lives."

After the conference, General Baldi shook hands with Riccardo before returning to his post. The general had a dejected air about him. "Colonel," he said, "General Cabalero intended to decorate you and take you to Rome. However, after your reply I'm afraid our airplane just ran out of seats. Now you're stuck in the sand."

"I know, sir. It was beyond my power to answer otherwise."

After saying good-bye to his immediate superior, Riccardo told his attendant that he was tired from the trip and would skip supper in favor of some rest. "I'll try to take a nap before the 'the music' starts, he told him.

"Yes, sir. I hope there won't be an air raid tonight."

*****

Riccardo entered the temporary quarters assigned to him for the night. After he removed his jacket and his desert boots, he turned off the acetylane lamp, let his body fall on his cot, and covered his face with his hands.

"Why? Why? Why?" he cried, as if listening to the distant echo of Patrizia's words before his departure. "Why?"

Why could I not listen to the voice of reason? Why didn't I make up a reply acceptable to that bastard? Why didn't I think of my family first?

I am a damned foolish idealist! he concluded. *Why else would I risk everything I hold dear just to preserve my integrity? For whom? For what? Is this the only thing that matters to me? What about my wife? My son? My mother? I could be in Italy in a few hours, and with my family in a matter of days. Am I so conceited to think that I'm the only person suited to save my men? What difference do I make in the larger scope of things?*

My brother was right, he thought. *I will always serve the interest of people, perhaps not even as good or clever, but unscrupulous enough to use my principles against me.*

"It's all for nothing!" he suddenly cried out. He was surprised by the unexpected thought that perhaps it was all an illusion. All the things he had believed during the terrible days of the Piave Line, during his entire life. Duty, responsibility, courage, fame! What did they all mean? Why had they abruptly lost all their significance?

"Oh dear Lord," he whispered, "what am I to believe in now? Are these my only choices? To be disloyal to my principles or betray my family?"

"Forgive me, Patrizia," he whispered through his closed hands. "I know I failed you again." He finally let his body fall flat on the cot, closed his eyes, and after a few moments, he was overcome by sleep.

At first, he heard the distant crash of waves, the cry of dead soldiers, Roberto's laughter. And then he heard a female voice, seductive and far away: "Why are you sleeping, Riccardo?" she said. "Wake up and listen. What do you hear? Go out and see … now!"

Riccardo woke up at once, became disoriented, and bolted upright. "Patrizia!" he cried out. He sat on his cot, held his breath, and listened. Who had spoken to him? There was no one around, and the room was in complete darkness. He was sure it was Patrizia's voice. He rubbed his eyes and noticed a sliver of moonlight filtering from under the door. He slipped his feet into his boots, walked across the room, and got out in the open.

The desert was bathed in the moonlight and appeared unreal. It had the same chiaroscuro effect of a charcoal drawing, with barracks and vehicles barely sketched in. It was all quiet, as if frozen in the stillness of the night. Suddenly, the silence was torn by the prolonged wail of a jackal.

Riccardo was about to go back to his cot, but he remembered the voice telling him to "go out and see," and he hadn't seen anything yet.

He heard the jackal howl again and walked in the direction of the sound, away from the barracks. Finally, he saw it, standing at the top of a dune, its neck and face tensed toward the mysterious white disk hanging overhead.

"It's just the moon, you fool!" he shouted to the beast.

He then stopped, as another noise had intervened; it was the rumble of approaching aircrafts. He saw a few soldiers scatter out of the barracks, run in different directions, and disappear into invisible holes as if swallowed by the earth. Unfamiliar with the layout of this provisional camp, he decided to stay where he was.

He heard the whistle of falling bombs and threw himself down. His hands slithered under the sand and felt the day's warmth still trapped beneath the surface.

The airplanes made a single pass over the encampment, and several explosions deafened Riccardo. One of them was close enough to send a shock wave through his body.

Riccardo got up to return to his lodgings, and he was stunned by what he saw. A deep hole stood where his barracks had been.

A shiver ran through him. "And I don't believe in miracles?" he said. "Perhaps I should no longer ask *why*. There must be a purpose.

"Thank you, Patrizia."

*****

"Colonel sir," said a voice from behind Riccardo. "Do you need anything from me?"

Riccardo had returned to his camp with his superior and was trying to forget the events of the last twenty-four hours.

"No, thanks, Sergeant." He said absentmindedly. The man remained standing at attention. "What else?"

"General Baldi will be leaving at three hundred hours. If you have a letter or something to send to your family, he said he'd take it to Italy and forward it for you from there. He'll be flying with the last plane out of Bizerte."

"Thank you, Sergeant."

Riccardo sat on a metal folding chair in front of an improvised desk consisting of a wide wooden plank over two wooden sawhorses. He noticed that on the plank, someone had carved several designs with a knife: a naked woman, a palm tree, a heart with the name "Karla" carved in the center. Had it been done by a German soldier? Was he still alive? Who was Karla? His girlfriend? His wife? His daughter? Some rubble had been swept to one corner, and beside it, there was a rusting metal closet whose doors had been torn open.

Riccardo let out a deep sigh and then raised the flame of the oil lamp, opened the journal again, and stared for a moment at those remaining blank pages. They appeared too thin and delicate to hold the weight of the feeling now caged in his heart … and the words wrestling in his mind.

He stopped again, wondering if he was in the best mental state to write a letter.

Italy, he thought. *My family!*

"Patrizia," he then uttered. The sound of that name was as pleasant as a drop of honey on his lips. He let his mind linger over the sweetest memories. He thought of the distillery, the first time he heard her voice, and her honest, straightforward reply to his question: "Aren't we all?" Her delightful silhouette as she walked in the shallow water of the Arno River; the first time they made love; the last time. Oh, how he wished to rest his weary head on the hollow of her neck and inhale the alluring scent of her skin.

A sudden languor overtook him. "Patrizia," he whispered again. "Roberto. Mother."

Roberto would be almost eleven now. He tried to imagine him, with his spirited green eyes, his sudden smile, the keen questions for which he sometimes already knew the answer: "What's an empire, Father?" And after his father's answer, "Yes, I know. Nonna told me." "Is war really bad, Father?"

He missed holding his hand as they walked down the street, his son trying to match his step. He missed feeling his strong embrace as he greeted him on his return from a business trip. The touch of his soft, naked skin as he held him in the swift, clear current of the Arno River. Feeling his look of admiration as he spoke to friends and acquaintances during supper.

"Can we go fishing with Meino one of these days?" Roberto had asked him once. He had promised they would, but never had. Always too busy or far away, and now … "Yes, my son," he said with a voice choked by emotions. "We will go fishing when I return. I promise."

Suddenly, he pulled away from his memories and glanced at his watch. Only ten minutes had elapsed since the sergeant's call; it seemed like hours to him.

He had time.

He took his pen and began to write again. *My dear Patrizia …*

At the end, he wrote Patrizia's complete address in large capital letters and put down the pen. He placed the pages at the beginning of the journal. "I'm sending you back to her," he said, holding the folder tightly against his chest. He got a large envelope from his attendant and delivered it himself to General Boldi, who was about to leave.

"It has been an honour to serve under you, General. Farewell."

"Good-bye, my friend. I'll make sure this envelope will reach your family. I hope I'll see you again under better circumstances." He paused. "Riccardo," he then said almost affectionately, "tell me one thing. If a friend told you to abandon ship, would you be able to do it?"

Riccardo reflected for a moment, not for his answer, but for what had prompted the question. "No, sir," he finally said. "I don't think I could." He looked the general straight in the eyes. "That's why destiny has given me the easier task: if it comes to that, I'll go down with the ship."

"I thought so," said the general. He raised his hand to the rim of his cap and saluted. "Good luck, my friend. Farewell."

A few minutes later, the airplane rolled over the sandy runway, and Riccardo watched it take off and disappear into the night. At least his message of love was flying back to his family.

*****

Riccardo walked along the runway for a long time. Even after he knew it to be impossible, the sound of the airplane was still in his ears. He looked at the starry sky and pretended to follow the vanished airplane all the way to Italy. He didn't feel able to sleep. So he kept on walking until the sound of waves breaking onto the shore and the saline scent of the sea shook him from his trance. He took a deep breath and sat on the sand. The sea was so calm that it resembled a lagoon. *Venice,* he thought. *Patrizia. How long was it since they had met? Twelve years, thirteen years?* He closed his eyes and bid his mind to abandon all other thoughts but those of her.

*****

On May 1943, barely six months after the American forces had landed in Northwest Africa, the Italo-German forces were compelled to cease operations in that theater. The Italians, worn out, ill equipped, leaderless, and further deprived of their already scarce transport vehicles by the Germans, could do nothing else but surrender.

The end of the war in Africa was announced to the Italian people on May 13, 1943: *As of this morning, the First Army has ceased to resist, by order of Il Duce.*

Some of the German troops were able to save themselves. They were transported to Italy, soon ready to fight other battles. The Italian propaganda called it a "strategic retreat." A truer, more objective definition would have been a "rout."

The Lanzis listened to the doctored news on the radio and began to hope that Riccardo, from whom they had not heard in a long time, would be among those few who had been able to escape. Or, at worst, that he'd be in one of the internment prison camps they heard about.

Weeks went by, and then months, and the original hope and unfounded optimism was slowly stifled by the lack of information. Every now and then, they heard of someone who, after long and perilous travel, had finally returned home. They heard of others who were confirmed dead or prisoners, but try that they might, they heard nothing about Riccardo.

- XXIX -

July 5, 1943

In Castelvecchio, life continued with ever-growing difficulties and increased anxiety. For many people in town, food supplies were running out. That very morning, the local bakery had run out of bread minutes after its door opened.

"I couldn't even get a goddamned crust of bread for my babies," a frustrated mother cried to the gathering crowd. She held a three-year-old girl against her bosom, and another one, perhaps five or six, stood by her side, clutching the side of her skirt. "What am I to do?"

A chorus of angry voices joined her shout, and the carabinieri had to intervene to prevent a riot.

No one knew yet that at the extreme southern part of the country, other dramatic events were about to unfold.

In fact, on that day, the U.S. Seventh Army under General Patton embarked from the Northwestern African ports of Orano, Algiers, and Bizerte. Concurrently, the British Eighth Army under General Montgomery, the ordained victor of El Alamain, sailed from Tripoli, Benghazi, Alexandria, and other African ports.

The time had come for British Prime Minister Churchill to fulfill his promise to Joseph Stalin that the Anglo-Americans, in order to relieve some German pressure from Russia, would finally open a "second front" in Europe during 1943.

"Why Sicily?" many people asked. It appeared that, among the several possible destinations initially considered by the Allied High Command—Greece, Southern France, Sardinia—they had finally chosen what Churchill described as "the soft underbelly" of the Italo-Germanic alliance: the island of Sicily, to be followed by an invasion of the Italian mainland.

"Operation Husky" was now under way!

A few days later, on her way back from an evening church function, Luisa saw Meino and a couple of other men huddled close in conversation in a dark corner near the bell tower. She nodded a hasty greeting and went on her way, thinking they did not want to be disturbed. One of the men, however, turned around and called her by name. "Luisa," he said, "it's me, Giacomo ..."

"Hallo, Giacomo," she said, recognizing her southern neighbor. "I don't want to intrude." She also had a quick look at the third man. She did not recognize him, but she noticed that he could have been in his middle thirties. He was fit, and his body stance suggested—but it was only an impression—that despite his civilian clothes, he might be a military man.

"It's no intrusion," Giacomo said when she was close to them. "We know where you stand. We're talking about the landing. By the way, this is—"

"Let's skip introductions," the third man firmly cut in. "Their word is good enough for me." He offered a polite smile and raised his cap in greeting. "As I was saying, gaining southern Italy's port facilities and airfields would give the Allies bases from which to reach and bomb whichever corner of *Festung Europa* they chose."

"Fortress Europa is no more," Meino said. "Where are they now?" He turned his head slightly, to hear the answer better. "Montgomery and his British Eighth Army have landed in the Gulf of Noto and Cassibile; and Patton, with his American Seventh Army, in the Gulf of Gela."

"How is it going so far?" Giacomo asked.

"The start seems propitious. As the invasion begins to take hold, many Italian units offer little resistance. Our soldiers see no value in this futile war, and they surrender by the thousands."

"But the papers say that most of our military continues to fight," said Giacomo.

"The usual exaggerations," said Meino. "By now, only a few remain faithful to Il Duce."

"Not so loudly," said Giacomo toward Meino.

The four people suddenly fell silent. Merely mentioning that name seemed to have the power to threaten their lives. They looked around to ensure they had remained undetected, and they instinctively huddled together.

"True," Giacomo whispered. "Not many people still believe that

Mussolini is such a great man, or that his eight million bayonets can regain an empire."

"Unfortunately, there are exceptions," Luisa added. "Young men who only know and believe what they read in school books sanctioned by the state, or what they hear from fascist propaganda. Unfortunately, these poor souls don't know any other 'truth' than the one invented by the regime."

"You are right, Luisa, if I may call you by your first name," said the unknown man. "But eight million bayonets should never have impressed anyone. Whether by ignorance or self-deception, how can one ignore the existence of modern weapons? Or that of countries eight to ten times the population of Italy, and an even greater ratio of industrial production?"

"That's what my son always repeated," Luisa replied. "But as I was saying earlier, a mélange of ignorance, myth, and fascist propaganda. Plus the illusion attached to our glorious past."

"At least our glorious past," said Giacomo passionately, "is not one of Mussolini's inventions. It did exist, and it stretched across many centuries, including the Etruscans, the Romans, and the giants of the Renaissance …"

"Giacomo," barged in the unknown man, "I am as proud of our heritage as anyone here. But let's forget the past now and focus on the pres—"

"Shhh …," Meino interrupted. "I think I see a patrol. He looked up at the bell tower's clock. "It's almost six. Nearly curfew time. We'd better go."

The small group dispersed and disappeared in the darkness. In the distance, they heard the bell toll six times, followed by the salvo of the guns announcing the start of the curfew.

The clandestine news confirmed that many Italian soldiers were indeed surrendering. It also reported, however, that the *Wehrmacht* soldiers—many of them hardened veterans who had fought in the Russian and African fronts—executed a skillful defensive battle and, with the aid of the difficult rocky terrain, inflicted heavy casualties on the Allies.

Rumors that were later confirmed had it that the Americans, in order to facilitate the invasion and save some of their own lives, had armed a local criminal organization called Mafia.

Some people thought this to be a myopic, short-gain scheme.

"There might be some small advantage now," said one such person, "but both Italy and America will pay dearly for it in the future; once a criminal, always a criminal!"

*****

On August 18, the Corriere della Sera newspaper reported the following:

> *A month and a half after the landing, the Allies have taken Messina, on the northeastern part of Sicily. However, a great portion of the German army was able to cross the straight to the mainland, and soon they will be ready for yet another battle …*

In Tuscany, as in the rest of the country, the Italian newspapers and the local propaganda tried to minimize the event. After all, they claimed, Sicily is only an irrelevant island, a piece of land physically detached from the mainland. The attack of the peninsula, if any, will be a different story. Or so the fascists said.

However, listening to clandestine stations and BBC brought the realization of a different, more factual reality. The magnitude of the Italian failure to defend the island became known—as did the inexorable if slow advance of the Allies and their apparent determination to occupy the entire peninsula.

Together with the occupation of a part of the national territory—far and half-forgotten though it be—the conquest of Sicily by allied forces achieved a collateral objective; it caused the thin, illusory fabric woven by twenty-odd years of fascism to disintegrate quickly.

On July 26, 1943, Luisa read in the papers:

> *Two days ago, the Grand Council of Fascism deposed Benito Mussolini. Yesterday, he was arrested in the name of the king and the monarchic wing of the party. His majesty the king has entrusted the reins of the government to Maresciallo Pietro Badoglio.*

Luisa experienced a moment of satisfaction. "Finally, the brutal dictator is out of our life," she said with pleasure. "He no longer is the idol of the crowds, the builder of a 'new Roman Empire.' Now he'll be known as the villain responsible for all the events that have befallen our country."

History does repeat itself. She thought. *He will be another Cola Di Rienzo! He too owed much of his success to his big mouth. He too attempted to revive the glory of the old Roman Empire with the help of foreign powers. I hope that, like Cola di Rienzo, Mussolini will end up being killed by the very crowds who had acclaimed him.*

No one was yet aware that Il Duce was later secretly moved to

Ponza, and from there, to an isolated hotel situated on top of the Gran Sasso, the highest peak of the Apennines, guarded by Badoglio's men.

On September 8, 1943, shortly before the invasion of the Italian mainland, Marshal Badoglio, caretaker of the crumbling Italian state, surrendered unconditionally to the Allies. The added proviso stipulated that Italy was to receive a generous treatment commensurate with the amount of help its remaining army would give the Allies in fighting the Germans.

That day, at eighteen hundred hours, in the hushed silence of the darkened family room, Luisa, Patrizia, and Roberto listened to the clandestine radio broadcasting as they always had before Riccardo's departure. They were astonished to hear American president Franklin D. Roosevelt and British prime minister Winston Churchill issue an appeal to Marshal Badoglio and the Italian people, urging them to take decisive steps to rid Italy of the German oppressors. Informing them that the Allied forces had gained a beachhead in several parts of southern Italy, and that the Germans would soon be driven out.

They also reminded them that in Africa, in order to cover their own retreat and save their own lives, the Germans had commandeered all vehicles, abandoning the Italian troops on the battlefield.

"Bastards," Patrizia exclaimed, hearing the last detail.

Roberto looked up at his mother, whose face was barely visible in the dim light coming from behind the radio dial. He noticed her jaw tighten as if clamping on any word or feelings that otherwise would spew from her mouth. "Do you think Father might have escaped?" he asked his mother.

Noticing his nonna making the sign of the cross and moving her lips, he concluded that she was reciting a prayer.

"I certainly hope so, cucciolo," Patrizia whispered, hugging him.

Roberto didn't know whether it was to show her affection or to hide the tears he saw welling in her eyes. He just knew that she did not sound particularly convincing, and her comment, rather than alleviate his fears, added to them.

Afterward, the two women discussed the unexpected news, but neither of them knew what to conclude. They were glad that one sad episode of the war seemed obviously ended. The near future, however, with the German army on Italian soil, appeared to be fraught with dangers.

Finally, at twenty hundred hours, Pietro Badoglio and King Emanuele III, who had meanwhile escaped Rome and found temporary refuge in the southern town of Brindisi, went on air with their own broadcast.

They asked the Italian people not to resist the Allied forces. They also announced that the Germans, Italians' allies until recently, had now occupied Italian ports and other strategic precincts and were carrying out acts of aggression against the population.

"The moment is grave," they said from their safe place of concealment. "Only acts of virile decision will save Italy …"

"From whom?" Patrizia commented on hearing those words. "And what do those eunuchs know about virility?"

Roberto heard the broadcast and then his mother's comments. "Mother, then it's true, the war is over. Or is it?"

"I don't know, cucciolo. In a literal sense it is, but I am afraid the Germans will not let us off the hook so easily."

Peculiarly, the Roosevelt-Churchill broadcast had preceded the Italian one by almost two hours, and, purposely or not, it favored and alerted the more vigilant Germans who, by now, monitored all communications.

Luisa went downtown after the first transmission. She traveled from store to store, trying to get a loaf of bread, half a kilogram of beans, or any other bit of nourishment she could find. She heard chants and indistinct shouts of the crowd while negotiating for the last piece of stale bread, which she was going to use to create some sort of meal, meager as it might be. She walked to the door and peeked outside.

People seemed to have gone crazy. Large groups flocked into the main square from all side streets, yelling and singing. She stopped one of the closest pedestrians and asked if there had been additional news.

"Yes, the king and Marshal Badoglio have confirmed it!" he shouted with joy. "The war is over!"

If that was verified in an official broadcast, then she would feel justified in allowing herself more than a shred of hope. She grabbed her scant bag of groceries and speedily returned home to share her news with the family.

"Some of the townsfolk," she told Patrizia, "have gone to the church and asked the bishop to celebrate a Te Deum to thank God for the end of the hostilities. Likewise, in many cities, they say, people have poured into the streets and main squares. In Rome, they marched along the Campidoglio, the Fori Imperiali, Piazza di Spagna, and St. Peter's square, singing and chanting slogans. In Milan, similar scenes are said to be going on in Piazza del Duomo and other major sites ..."

"I am sorry, Mother," Patrizia interrupted. "I don't want to sound like a Cassandra. In my opinion, though, this celebration is premature. I don't think it's going to be as easy as that!"

*****

The German High Command, or OKW, already suspicious of the Italians, who were said to be plotting behind their backs, had a contingency plan. They had placed spies and "technical" advisors throughout the peninsula to monitor all communications.

Hitler kept abreast of the progress of the talks between Badoglio and Eisenhower and dispatched several crack units to Mashal Kesselring, the commander of the German troops in Italy, with the express directive to disarm the Italians.

As soon as they heard the first broadcast, the *Wehrmacht* was ready to act. The final code message was issued: *Ernte Einbringen. Bring in the harvest.*

"My usual contact," Meino said to Luisa a few days later, "told me that in the critical hours preceding and following the broadcast, most of the Italian garrisons were completely left to themselves. What could the poor soldiers do? They were confused, to say the least. They were completely isolated by the sudden disappearance of all commanders. Some of the junior officers who remained at their posts discovered the news of the Italian capitulation via the Germans who came to demand their surrender. Imagine that!"

"So what's the situation now?" Luisa asked.

Meino made a derisive sound. "In many cases, our soldiers dropped their weapons, changed into civilian clothes, and vanished into the hills. That's what the situation is, my dear Luisa." He paused, and then, not receiving any comment from her, he continued. "Others tried to reach the higher ranks by telephone or other means. A few resisted and were quickly wiped out. In other words, we are in the hands of the Germans."

"Oh my God!"

"What do you expect, Luisa?" said Meino, opening his arms in exasperation. The Germans are better informed and better armed. Our poor bastards never had a chance."

In Roberto's school, the old history teacher, his reading glasses midway down his large red nose, was bent over the morning paper. Some of the students, likely out of both curiosity and in order to delay the regular lesson, said they wished to know his opinion about the situation. He looked at them unseeingly and remained silent. Roberto raised his hand, and the teacher, after staring at him for a long instant, finally nodded his consent.

"Sir," the boy began, "what do you think will now happen to us? As a country, I mean … as a people?"

The teacher lowered his head, looked at him above his glasses, and sighed. "*Acerba fata Romanus agunt*, he gravely pronounced in a cheerless voice. "It means that, as of now, as in many other times through our sad history, the Italians are virtual prisoners in their own land. From this moment on, only survival will count."

Roberto wondered why the teacher had said "the Italians," rather than "we," and what survival as "prisoners" might entail. His mind traveled to the examples of the Great War, when many northern people had resisted the Austrian occupation. Heroes such as Cesare Battisti, Fabio Filzi, and Nazzario Sauro had preferred to die rather than betray the motherland or cooperate with the enemies.

What would Father do in similar circumstances? Why had they not heard from him for such a long time? His mother continued to write letters. Nonna Luisa had even gone to see the archbishop and asked to inquire through the Vatican, but nothing had come of it. If he had fallen prisoner, shouldn't they know by now? They had heard that a soldier who had fought in Africa was seen back in the nearby town of Santa Chiara, and two were seen in San Romano.

Why couldn't they have been my father and Uncle Lorenzo? thought Roberto, lying in bed that night.

After a few hours of sleep, he awoke with a jolt, drenched in sweat. He had just experienced his recurring nightmare: a scorching sun, dunes that rose like waves over a vast sea of sand, a man in uniform running away from him. It was his father, he knew, but though running as fast as he could, he was unable to catch up to him. He called, but his voice remained in his throat. The hot sun shone over the desert, bleaching the bare bones of animals and humans abandoned on the ocean of sand. Through renewed effort, he almost caught up to him, but as he tried to reach his arm, he fell down.

The jolt woke him up.

He opened his eyes in the dark and felt the bed blankets and sheets around his legs. The memory and emotion of his chase were still fresh and real in his mind. He felt tears popping in his eyes and crushed them angrily with his eyelids. Then, unable to stop them, he wept quietly so that he would not be heard.

*****

A few days later as Luisa went to church, the grounds were still covered by leaflets and other sheets of papers printed covertly. They contained details of the armistice and the end of the war.

Near the bell tower, she met her neighbor Erina Giani, who was returning from downtown. "Good morning, Luisa," she said. "If you are going shopping, forget it. There is nothing to be found this morning. Anything that even resembles food has suddenly disappeared from the shelves."

"And we're running short too. Did they tell you when they expect some food?"

"Tomorrow, they said. Always tomorrow. So you go home, you pull another notch on your belt, and hope."

"Well," said Luisa, "since I'm out, I'll go ask the bishop if there is any news from Rome about the prisoners of war."

The two women were almost under the bell tower. A gust of air swept several leaflets almost to their feet. The word ARMISTICE was stamped all over them.

"What do you think of this, Luisa?" Nina asked, picking one up and reading its contents: "'Are we any better off today than yesterday?'"

At that exact moment, a small convoy of German trucks went by, leaving a scattering of white papers in their wake. They were filled with troops armed to their teeth. Their dour faces and demeanor did not allow for a very optimistic prognosis.

"It doesn't appear so," said Luisa shaking her head. "I wouldn't be surprised if things get much worse before they get better."

Several days later, in church, Luisa noticed a middle-aged couple she had never seen before. She heard the man as he spoke to the bishop after mass.

"I come from a village south of Naples. I escaped with my family when all hell broke loose over there," he said. "Most villages near the coast were bombed from the sea and from the air. We lost everything: the house, a brother, my folks, friends and relatives, a real hell."

"What's the name of the village?" the bishop asked.

"Vietri. Vietri Sul Mare, just a few kilometers from Salerno."

"And from Paestum," the bishop added with nostalgia. "It seems only yesterday that I visited the ancient temples of the area. In my mind's eyes, I can still see the Doric columns, the statue of Poseidon … I wonder if those relics of past civilizations will survive the ravages of modern war this time …"

The words died on his lips as he noticed the look of disbelief on the faces of the people assembled around him. They looked as if their worries were more urgent and personal than those concerning antiquities.

September 12, 1943

In the days immediately following the armistice declaration, news of festivities and confusion, followed by that of the Germans' disarmament of Italian soldiers, prevailed. In the North, few people were aware that under the code name "Avalanche," a large Allied expeditionary force under General Clark had landed on the beaches of Salerno.

As the mysterious man who talked with Meino had predicted, the main objective of the invasion was to capture the neighboring airfields and secure the city of Naples and its port.

That early Sunday morning, Castelvecchio, some six hundred kilometers north of the beaches of Salerno, was waking up to beautiful sunshine. The church bells had called the faithful to mass, and Luisa briskly walked the short distance, arriving just as the bishop approached the main altar. She nodded to a couple of acquaintances and took her usual place at the kneeling stool slightly left of the preacher's wooden pulpit. Some moments she tuned in to the Latin cantilena of the officiating priest, while at other times, her mind wandered amidst its own thoughts.

At the end of mass, as the small crowd shuffled toward the exit, Luisa walked in the opposite direction, toward a smaller chapel situated to the right of the main altar. She knelt on the cold marble step and made the sign of the cross. Hung above the altar was a larger- than-life fourteenth-century wooden crucifix, with blood dripping from his head, chest, and limbs. His head tilted to the right, His glossy eyes seemingly looked down sadly toward her.

Of all the statues and images in the church, she felt a particular relationship with this suffering Christ, who seemed to be in the throes of death, and it was here, in the semidarkness of this minor chapel, that she came to pray when in need of special comfort.

"I pray for the safety of my sons, my Lord," she whispered, as if to a confessor, "and for a quick end of the hostilities. Please guard over them and let me hear from them soon. I also pray for that innocent soul of my grandson, Roberto. And finally, for Patrizia, to be instilled with faith in You. I can't understand how a good person like her could be so devoid of devotion toward You and Your Heavenly Father. Please, Jesus, listen to my prayers and help us all."

She remained in her kneeling position for a while longer, reciting prayers, her head bowed and her hands partially covering her face. When she finally left the church, the sunshine was bathing the main square, and small groups of people lingered around speculating about the latest rumors concerning the war.

Meino, who spotted her in the square, left his group and walked toward her. "Luisa," he called, "I was just talking to someone who told me of terrible German reprisals against our troops. He told me that because of lack of communications and the betrayal in the upper echelons"—he paused and looked around suspiciously—"hundreds of thousands of Italian soldiers have been rounded up and sent to Germany."

"To do what?" Luisa inquired.

"They'll be sent to labor camps, and they won't even have the benefit of prisoners of war status."

"What does it mean?"

"It means that the poor bastards will be under the harshest conditions. It also means that the Geneva Convention won't be of any help to them. In the Balkans," Meino continued, "a few divisions saved themselves and joined Tito to fight the Germans as partisans."

Another man approached them, and Meino fell suddenly silent.

"The Americans have established a good hold in Salerno," he whispered.

"Are you sure?" she asked. "Yesterday the news was not so good."

"I heard it from a man who's supposed to know these things …"

"I hope you're right, but Salerno is south of Naples," Luisa uttered, "still a long way from here. It will take a long time before we are liberated."

"By the way," said Meino, "do you have any news about your sons?"

"No, Meino, nothing at all. It's all in His hands now," she said, pointing to the heavens.

*****

Luisa was sitting on her favorite straw-seat chair, reading the newspaper in a corner of the kitchen. The glow of the setting sun was coming through the two long glass panes of the west window. Her reading glasses were midway down her nose. Her nervous, veined hands held the rim of the paper as if wanting to tear its content.

"What now, Mother?" said Patrizia, hearing the old woman mumble.

"You won't believe this," she said, looking up from the paper. "Mussolini has been freed by the Germans." She read aloud:

> *Il Duce, who had been recently moved from his Ponza prison to a high mountain site in the Abruzzi region, has been freed. Last night, the extraordinary SS commando leader Colonel Otto Skorzeny, under direct orders from the führer, liberated our beloved leader. Skorzeny and his commandos landed with glider airplanes on the narrow plateau fronting the Campo Imperiale Hotel, where Mussolini was being held by order of Badoglio, and overran the scant garrison. Il Duce, who is pictured below, among his liberators, was then taken to a light airplane and flown to secure grounds in the north part of the country. As of now, he resumes the supreme direction of fascism.*

"I hope he won't instigate a civil war," Patrizia said.

A day later, there was another astounding news item in the press. It was the first official report of a landing by the Allies in the Salerno area.

"How much of this can we believe, Patrizia?" Luisa asked. "It's all over the front page. This particular headline reads, THE GERMANS SMASH THE ALLIES' BRIDGEHEAD AT SALERNO."

Patrizia, who was folding clothes on the kitchen table, said, "I don't know anymore what we can believe, Mother. I hope it's the usual party line."

"So do I, Patrizia, or else we'll never see the end of this darn war. Some of the refugees from that area, though, did confirm that things are not going so well for the Allies." She rested the paper on her lap, and after a moment, she continued. "As I was coming home from mass, I saw that fat ass of the podesta. He was wearing his black uniform and waving the morning paper. Obviously, he thought it was true, because he yelled to passersby, 'You see? Mussolini was right; we'll throw the Americans back into the sea!'"

"I hope you didn't make any comments," said Patrizia. Then, not hearing an answer to her explicit statement, she turned toward Luisa and said, "Well, Mother, did you?"

"I couldn't resist it," Luisa said unapologetically. "I looked him straight in the eyes and said, 'Provided it isn't the usual propaganda, it seems to me the Germans, not 'we', are throwing the Americans into the sea.'"

"Oh, Mother ... And what did he say to you?"

"Nothing. Absolutely nothing. But I did notice a few people quickly turn their heads away when I voiced my comment."

"I think I've heard enough, Mother. I finished my ironing. Do you have anything you want me to do?"

"No, dear, we are in good shape. I'll do the rest tomorrow."

"All right, then. I'll fold this shirt and go to bed and read for a while."

It had been a long day, and now Patrizia could relax in the privacy of her room and think of Riccardo. For her, it was the best time of the day, and the worst. His clothes, his chair, his books, his cologne brought back cherished memories of him. The empty spot on his side of the bed, however, sadly underlined his absence and made her even more aware of her solitude, of her skin missing his caresses, her lips missing his kisses. In their room, they were free to be themselves. Depending on their mood, they would listen to the soothing music of Chopin, in silence, while resting on each other's arms; make love; or engage in small talk or in serious reflections regarding the future of the family, the outlook of the country.

She felt exhausted. She couldn't even read tonight. She looked gladly forward to the few hours of sleep, without worries and pain.

She shifted her head on the pillow, searching for a cooler spot.

"Good night, Riccardo," she whispered, turning on her side. She switched off the light and let her tired body drift into sleep.

*****

One evening, as the family was finishing supper, Roberto placed his index finger over his mouth to signal silence. He hushed his mother and grandmother and whispered, "There is someone outside."

They looked at each other and gestured, indicating that they had heard nothing. Just then, there was a light knock at the door. The two women looked astonished. Another light knock and Patrizia got up and opened the inner door, "Who is it?" she asked in a whisper.

"It's me, Patrizia," said a voice she didn't immediately recognize.

Patrizia unlocked the outside Persian shutters, and Antonio squeezed in through the opening.

"Antonio!" Patrizia exclaimed, "I thought you had returned to your—"

"Sorry to come unannounced. I'll explain." Then, noticing the other two people in the room, he said, "Good evening, Signora Luisa. Hallo, Roberto. How are you, young man?"

"I'm well. Thank you, sir."

"He is actually quite tired," Patrizia said. "He'll be going to bed soon …"

"I'm not tired," Roberto protested.

"All the same," Luisa cut in, "it's your bedtime. Brush your teeth properly and then go to bed. I'll join you shortly to tuck you in."

It was an uneven battle, but he tried his last weapon. "But I haven't even read my book tonight."

"You'll catch up tomorrow, cucciolo. Now please obey and go to bed."

No sooner had Luisa left his bedroom than he swiftly got up and carefully opened his door. The conversation in the kitchen had resumed.

*****

"Have a glass of wine, Antonio," Luisa said. Roberto heard the noise of a glass making contact with the marble surface of the table.

"Just a drop, though. I still have a long night in front of me."

"What's going on, Antonio?" Patrizia asked. "I have been thinking about you since you came to my office with Riccardo's letter … and then I heard you had left."

"Yes … well, I had to pretend I was returning to my unit."

"Pretend? I don't understand."

"I had come to a decision, a tough one, Patrizia, and I needed to tell you myself. I didn't want you to wonder why and to think less of me."

"Please go on, Antonio. I'm listening."

"A few weeks back, I received my new assignment. I was supposed to return to the Greek front." The pause and the noise of the glass suggested that he had taken a long sip of wine, as if he had to swallow a large mouthful of food. "I thought about it," he said. "I thought of the many conversations I had with Riccardo. I am now convinced that sooner or later, this mess will end up the way he predicted, and I see no good in answering the call."

"What will you do then?" Patrizia asked.

"I can't stay around here, that's for sure. I'd be found and imprisoned in no time at all."

Two pairs of eyes stared at him with anticipation.

"I'll join a group in the Monte Amiata Mountains," he added.

"A group?"

"Yes, Patrizia. One of the many that will fight to free Italy from fascism and the German occupation … I could be more specific, but it's better for me and for you if I'm not."

"But why tell us even this much, Antonio?"

"Because of Riccardo and because I know the person you are. Italy is a divided country now. Many Italians are fighting on one side or the other, some out of their convictions, others out of convenience. I have the luxury to choose according to my personal belief, and that belief tells me that I cannot answer the call of the regime."

"I understand what you're saying Antonio," Patrizia said at last. "I don't think less of you for this decision."

"My Riccardo would understand too," Luisa added after a moment. "Who knows? By now, he might have done the same …" Her tone did not sound convincing, but Antonio looked grateful nonetheless.

"Thank you," he said getting up, "I promise that I'll try to be in touch. I hope next time I come, you have news of your sons, signora." He then turned to Patrizia, saying, "Don't say a word about this, please. There are still too many deluded people around." He hugged the two women.

Luisa made the sign of the cross over his head and said, "May God be with you."

*****

For the next several days, broadcasts from the clandestine radio confirmed that the outcome of the battle near Salerno hung in suspense, with attacks and counterattacks from both sides.

It was a confusing battle, lacking precise boundaries, geometric alignment of troops or trenches. The rugged terrain, the scattered hills, the strategically located towns, rivers, ravines, and other accidents of nature determined, more than anything else, the direction of the advance or the amount of progress. For days on end, towns, hilltops, and roads were taken, lost, and regained by either side, with great loss of men and materials. However, by this time, the Americans were able to land additional rein-forcement and loads of materiel, while the Germans were getting short on fuel and ammunition. At this point, Kesselring, preoccupied with the orderly withdrawal of his German divisions to safer lines of defense, issued a directive of disengagement. The 10th Panzer Division began to fall back, and the 11th Battalion Panzergrenadiers were ordered to leave the key area of Altavilla, which they had just reconquered, and head north. Just as the Germans moved out of the area, the Allies launched a massive shelling of the town itself. Later, it was discovered that only scores of Italian civilians and no Germans had been killed during that bombardment.

It was reported that even General Walker, commander of the 36th Texas Army, upon visiting the devastated town, stated that its bombardment had been "brutal and to no purpose." Unfortunately, war being what it is, it was not to be the last time that such a destructive and futile event would occur.

*****

"What's new, Meino?" Luisa asked.

To exchange whatever bit of information was available, they met more frequently now, usually in a dark corner of the church, after mass or other services. This way, they avoided being suspected of wrong-ful assembly and seditious activity. This morning, they stood behind the baptismal fountain, the large marble basin concealing them from people who might walk by. A beam of light filtered from the green panel of stained glass window up high, making Meino look as though his blood had been drained from his veins. He wore his usual brown leather jacket and held his hat in his hand.

"I hear they have been fighting in the Salerno area for several weeks now," he answered, "but on the twenty-third of September, Montgomery has been reported to have reached the town."

"Who's he?"

"He's the one who beat us at El Alamein, and even if his troops are overextended, his mere presence will be a boost for the Americans and a blow for the Germans."

"Are the Germans retreating yet?"

"What?"

Luisa got even closer to him and repeated the question.

"Yes, but not as quickly as you and I would like to see them leave. They continue to oppose resistance and slow the pace of the Allies. Then they stop and fight in easily defendable areas. Meanwhile, their demolition squads blow up roads and bridges, lay mines, and blast cliff-side hills so that tons of rubble falls into the gorges below and obstructs the narrow passages. My source tells me that there might be another Allied offensive soon. I'll let you know when I know something more."

"Thank you, Meino. Watch yourself."

In the North, the newspapers now reported some of the fighting, and the Lanzis avidly read the news, hoping for a quick victory by the Allies.

It was easy to presume that these were mainly guarded reports filtered through German propaganda offices in Rome. It was more difficult to know how much to believe. Sometimes there would be side stories or hearsay, allegedly from refugees from southern towns affected by the fighting. However, unless heard from these people directly, one could not rely on them either.

Toward the end of September, the press began to report that the battle for the conquest of the city of Naples had begun. It could then be assumed that the Salerno landing, as costly as it had been, had succeeded. Although the amount of devastation and number of casualties were not yet clear, summing up all that had been heard made it obvious it must have been catastrophic.

In Castelvecchio, after Sunday mass, it was now common practice for people to stop in the sacristy and question the bishop about the latest news. Luisa was often among these people. She inquired about known casualties, prisoners of war, the status of the front line, and the most recent accounts from this town or that. Somehow, either through the influence of the Vatican or the relationship with the local authorities, or even via the confessional, the bishop seemed always to know more than any other person in town.

After these encounters, she would return home and relate the information to Patrizia. They would speculate for a while on Riccardo and Lorenzo's fate. Sometimes, if Roberto heard them, he went quietly to his room, took the atlas his father had given him, and searched for those towns and places his mother and grandmother had mentioned. Salerno, Altavilla, Eboli, and farther north … Cassino!

He pondered the height of each hill and mountain peak shown on the map and noticed that the few narrow paths were often crossed or flanked by rivers. He remembered that one of his previous history teachers had once told his class that Rome had never been conquered from the south. "Well, almost never," the professor had said. "The only time had been during the Justinian reign when, after tremendous efforts, two of his generals, Flavius Belisarius and Nantes, had somehow succeeded."

Roberto wondered if the diversity in weapons and technology would make it any easier today.

If his father were here, they could have talked about these things. Or he could have just listened as his father spoke to other adults. He hoped he was still alive, but if he was a prisoner of war, it was unlikely that he would make it back until the war front was north of Tuscany, or at least north of the Arno River. Would the Arno become a front line of sorts, as the Piave had been during the Great War? he wondered. What if his house was going to be bombed like Nonna Luisa's? At this rate, it was going to be a long time yet, but it was something to think about. And what about Uncle Lorenzo? He too might be a prisoner, or even dead. He hoped that both his father and uncle would return unharmed. He felt a bit guilty thinking that if destiny allowed only one, he wished it to be his father.

One late evening, early in October, their neighbor Giacomo, after listening to a clandestine radio transmission, visited the Lanzis. "I can only be a moment," he said, squeezing through the half-opened door. "I just heard that the city of Naples has been liberated by the Allies."

The spontaneous rejoicing of Luisa and Patrizia was short-lived. With a voice choked with emotion, Giacomo went on to tell them of the disastrous conditions of the city, the number of dead people, and the subhuman conditions prevailing at the arrival of the American troops.

Both women were speechless.

"I'm on my way to my hiding place," he then said. "Please switch off the light as I exit."

It was confirmed that on October 1, 1943, the Allies had finally entered the rubble that had been the city of Naples.

The following Sunday, the bishop made this particular event the theme of his sermon.

"You must have noticed some new people in town," he said, resting his hands on the balustrade. "People from the south, from the city of Naples. The allied air bombing has obliterated the industrial area. The retreating Germans have blown up the port facilities and completely destroyed the electrical, water, and sewer systems. Anything that might have been of any use or value has been looted or destroyed." He paused and let his eyes measure the effect of his words and quivering voice upon the sparse crowd of faithful.

"When the houses of these poor creatures of God were bombed and food ran completely out, they came north hoping to find refuge," he continued. "Others remained to fight for days, in the streets of their city, the retreating Germans. They were starved, brutalized, and hysterical. Anything remotely edible had already been consumed. People tried to scrape any kind of subsistence whatever way possible." He opened his arms and turned his eyes toward the heavens.

"I am told, by those who braved the front and crossed the lines," he said with a new, more dramatic tone of voice, "that the fallen city has now been turned into the black market and the brothel capital of the world. May God forgive us. No item, person, or commodity, it seems, is too small, too large, or too sacred; sisters, daughters, and wives are offered in exchange for food, money, blankets, and even cigarettes. Neapolitan children, many of them orphaned by the war, are selling to each other the clothing and shoes of drunken American soldiers who have been stripped and left naked on the crumbled sidewalks of the city. Military cars are stolen or left without the wheels, and the gas is sucked out of their tanks. Sodom and Gomorra did not experience anything worse than that.

"Even boats at anchor in the harbor have vanished from their moorings as if swallowed by the night!" he shouted.

As he fell silent, murmurs were heard from amidst the multitude, and people looked at each other incredulously, for not even in their most extreme imaginations could they have conjured up conditions such as those described by the priest.

"The basket below the altar is for the benefit of those poor souls who have traveled this far and are knocking at our door."

The Bishop concluded, "Pray, my brethren, that we may be spared these dreadful things. Be generous with your brothers, for tomorrow, God forbid, we may be in the same situation."

The response was not as good as hoped for. After all, refugees or not, they were from the South, with strange incomprehensible dialects, bad manners, and long, dirty fingernails. Besides, someone had already heard the rumors that things went missing after "some of those Neapolitans" had been near.

"So much for brotherly love," said Luisa, making her contribution.

*****

Patrizia had picked up the newspaper, while Roberto drew pictures for his art class, and Luisa stirred a pot on the stove. Patrizia read aloud:

From Italian sources active in the city, it has been reported that many Allied soldiers were dismayed by the appalling conditions they found. Others, though, just shrugged and took advantage of the situation, and even began to trade goods stolen from their military depots—and not always for money! Meanwhile, advance troops of the 5th American Army moved north and crossed the Volturno River.

"It's where Garibaldi won an important battle against the Bourbons in eighteen sixty," Roberto interrupted, upon hearing the name of the river. His mother looked at him blankly, and he said unapologetically, "I studied it in school."

Luisa, still facing the woodstove and intent on finishing her task, said, "And what's the name of the town where Garibaldi met with King Vittorio Emanuele II, agreeing to relinquish his fight against the Bourbons and leaving the initiative with the king?" she asked.

Patrizia had stopped reading, and she stood with one hand resting on her hip, the other holding the newspaper along her side.

Roberto smiled. He could describe in detail the illustrations found in history books: the protagonists on horseback on a dusty country road; the king riding a white horse; and Garibaldi, his traditional red scarf blowing in the wind, riding a brown one. Several cavalry officers stood a short distance away, and the typical hills of the region filled the distant background. Roberto had often looked at that picture, thought of the moment. Had he been in Garibaldi's shoes, he would not have obeyed the king! Garibaldi, a leader of men, freedom fighter of two continents, hence named "The Hero of Two Worlds." Why should he relinquish his command to this Emanuele the Second? What had the king accomplished in his life? Sure, he was a king, but as his father said,

"It's a much greater achievement to get things on your own merit than by heredity." Why should being born of certain parents entitle anyone to high positions?

"So?" Luisa said, "Do you know it or not?

"Teano," Roberto blurted out. "The meeting took place near the Town of Teano."

"Well said, my boy, but do you know the exact date?"

"Yes, Nonna. It was the twenty-sixth of October ... eighteen sixty."

"Very good, my little genius."

"Come on, Mother," Patrizia said, "don't exaggerate with your praise; at that age everyone has a great memory."

"I disagree, my dear," said Luisa emphatically. "Personally, I don't know many children with a memory like that, or that kind of interest in history."

"Don't say those things in front of the child."

"Everyone needs praise sometimes," Luisa concluded, with a wink and a smile for her grandson. When she turned back to the stove, there was a sound like a slap. She swiftly swung around to find Roberto holding his hand over his face.

"Did she smack you?" she asked him.

"No, Nonna," he answered hesitantly.

Luisa didn't seem convinced, and she looked at Patrizia, who remained unperturbed.

"What was that sound, then?"

"Nothing, really," Roberto said.

Two of the pots had started to boil, and Luisa had to return to her task to avoid spoiling the meal.

****

When Luisa winked, Roberto had looked at his mother with a mocking smile. She had had a tough day and reacted by reflex, hitting him with the back of her hand. Not for the lack of respect of the moment. But for the years and hundreds of times she had witnessed the empathy between him and Luisa, while she had been pushed aside by both. For the pain she had felt for days, without being able to receive comfort from anyone. For many other reasons that she could not even remember. She was sorry now, and glad that Roberto's white lie saved her from a sure fight with the older woman.

****

Roberto, however, had not understood the cause of the punishment. This undeserved slap would be remembered and held against his mother for a long, long time.

*****

A week later, the two women were in the kitchen. Luisa faced the stove, and Patrizia was setting the table for supper. Roberto was in his room, completing his homework. A mild aroma of garlic and rosemary rose from the pan and stirred up the appetite.

"Who told you that, Mother?" Patrizia asked.

"Meino told me," Luisa replied. "I met him in church again. You know what? I think his contact is that fellow I told you about. The one I met that evening with Meino and Giacomo, who seems to have all the information. Perhaps the bishop is in on this too; they must have a radio receiver somewhere," Luisa said.

"And what did he tell you, exactly?"

"He said that the American general in charge of the invasion, now that the Port of Naples has been captured, is expected to forge ahead for Rome."

"Rome? What for? There are nothing but priests and nuns in Rome. Oh, yes, and armchair admirals and whores. Why don't they bypass that darn place and head north instead?"

"My dear Patrizia, even generals play little games. This Clark apparently wants to be there ahead of his ally and competitor Montgomery—the general of El Alamein."

"Why?"

"As Meino's friend explained," said Luisa, "compared to the relative importance of barren land in southern Italy, the occupation of Rome would carry a large amount of prestige. It will have useful propaganda value."

"Maybe he is planning a triumphal parade through the Fori Imperiali, like Giulio Caesare or Mussolini," said Patrizia.

"I wouldn't be surprised."

"Every man, whether renowned or not, seems to have the need of widespread admiration. In fact, it seems to me the more insignificant they are, the louder they want to yell *Mission accomplished!* And the poor bastards who do the fighting for them think they do it for their country, for liberty, for humanity. Poor innocent, delusional beings."

"The conquest of Rome," said Giacomo Giani that evening, "is not going to be as quick as the Allies hoped. The generals have one agenda; the weather, however, has a different one."

"What are you saying, Giacomo?" said Luisa.

"I'm told it's been raining more than usual in the region."

"But surely they won't stop fighting because of the rain."

"Well, it appears that it has caused many rivers, which run almost perpendicular to the sea, to be swollen and impossible to cross due to the destruction of the bridges by the retreating Germans. For good measure, they have also blown up some dams. And now the flat areas have become lakes of mud that hinder the passage of tanks and other heavy equipment."

"So, in addition to everything else, now even the bloody weather is against us. What's going to be next?"

*****

Operation "Orkan"

Kesselring took full advantage of the delay. He ordered the creation of a temporary line of defense, called the Winter Line, and gained sufficient time to reinforce his main fortifications on the Gustav Line.

The Germans occupied the high ground around the hills of Montecassino. Their 88 mm cannons and high-caliber mortars blew up the allied armor, while "nebelwerfer"—dubbed "screaming meemies" by American soldiers— blasted the infantry.

Facing this difficult situation, the Allies tried to outflank the German defenses by sea. On January 22, 1944, they mounted an amphibious opera-

tion and landed two divisions on the beaches of the resort town of Anzio, situated approximately fifty kilometers south of Rome.

The initial surprise landing was promising, but the opportunity was not exploited. It was reported that the American VI Corps wasted too much time trying to consolidate its positions, hence allowing the Germans time to rush troops in from the quieter sectors of the Gustav Line and reach the Anzio area. To add insult to injury, the German reinforcements came from the very roads and bridges long thought rendered unusable by Allies' bombing.

The eventual German counterattack came close to wiping out the Allies' beachhead, which remained pinned down for months and sustained heavy casualties.

In Castelvecchio, as in other places north of the Gustav Line, news of the battle was anxiously followed in whatever manner possible: newspapers, clandestine radios, listening to the refugees from the South, and even by talking to some rare approachable German. One of these soldiers, a survivor of the Russian front, had fought in two of the battles of Cassino before his division was sent north. He described the fighting and conditions there as just as hard and ferocious as experienced at Stalingrad. He was a young officer in the First Paratroops Division, a fervent Catholic who was frequently seen speaking to the archbishop in church.

One Sunday morning, Luisa and Roberto, among others, were present during one of these conversations in the church sacristy.

"He speaks Italian," said Luisa to her grandson. "Let's hear what he is saying."

"Yes, thank you, Reverend," the German was saying in slightly accented Italian. "I am better now." He raised his arms and stretched his open hands in front. "You see? No more trembling."

"Kurt was under constant bombardment for months," the bishop explained to the people who had gathered around. "There is only so much a man can take. Then, sooner or later, his nerves give up."

"Yes," the soldier confirmed, "it was like living in hell. The shuddering of the explosions, the raining debris, the cracking of splintered granite rock, the howling echo flung back from the hills, and the whining scream of oncoming shells … Such a pandemonium, it felt like hell."

Roberto remembered his father's evening readings and wondered if that wouldn't really qualify for yet another stage of *Dante's Inferno*.

"You know," Kurt continued, "even in the deepest hole, trench, or cave, you would feel the earth quake and shudder under your body as you tried to hold and hug it, while rubble and dust covered your entire body. The air was filled with deafening blasting sounds and saturated with the acrid smell of cordite …" His voice lowered to an almost inaudible level when he said, "and the smell of rotting bodies."

Luisa pitied that poor soldier, for under that frightening uniform, he was but a young man. But then, he was a German, one of those who had started the darn war. Or was he? He seemed so young and innocent.

Give or take a couple of years, he must be about the age of my Lorenzo, she thought.

"Why does he speak such good Italian?" she asked one of the listeners.

The old man beside her gestured that he didn't know, but another man who heard Luisa's question turned toward her. "He is from just north of Bolzano," he whispered. "He comes from the Austrian area given to Italy after the Great War. He speaks German and Italian."

Luisa's feelings were now even more confused. On the one hand, she saw the uniform of a despised enemy, and on the other, a vulnerable young man who perhaps, not unlike her Lorenzo, was accidentally caught in the clogs of war.

The sounds echoing in the sacristy suddenly did not seem to make any sense. War did not make any sense. *Why is God allowing this mess to go on?* she caught herself wondering.

February 1944

"Today," said the history professor, "we cannot conduct our normal lesson." One of the teachers had fallen sick, and he had taken in two classes with students of different ages and grades.

"Instead," he said, "we will take the opportunity to examine some of our history and some geography. This will hurt a bit," he said with a smirk, "but we'd better get used to pain."

He went to the large map of Italy that hung at the far wall of the classroom, and forty bodies and forty pair of eyes shifted toward it.

"If we had to give a title to this lesson, we could call it 'A disaster of historical proportions.'

The students looked at each other.

He raised his long, wooden pointer to a costal area just south of Rome. "The Allies' failure at Anzio," he said, placing the point of his pole on the black circle indicating the position of the town, "has dashed their hopes and ours for a quick run north and the occupation of Rome. It has also thrown the weight of the campaign back on Kesselring's Gustav Line, which includes the Montecassino massif, the neighboring hills, and stretches along the Liri and Garigliano rivers."

"Lanzi, come here, please," the teacher said, sitting down on the top of a desk.

Roberto advanced at a swift pace. He was used to being called to answer questions other students did not know. It did not make him popular with some of his classmates, but at this stage, he'd rather have the approval of his teacher than the endorsement of his companions.

The teacher handed his pointer to the boy. "Show us, please," he said.

Roberto promptly moved the pointer to the inside of the Italian Peninsula and traced the narrow winding lines of the two rivers.

"The Allied command, we are told," the teacher continued, "suspected the high location of the medieval Abbey of Montecassino, which is considered the stronghold and hinge of the line, to be used by German spotters and artillery fire directors."

The pointer moved slightly north to the mountainous central region and then to Montecassino itself.

"Allies' prisoners and people from the area confirmed that New Zelanders, Polish, French, Indians, British, Algerians, Moroccans, Americans—and other armies of different nationalities—have tried unsuccessfully to force the line at an extreme cost of lives. Three of the bloodiest battles of the campaign were fought on those hills. Hence, the abbey itself became like a scourge in the mind of all Allied soldiers and their commanders."

The teacher noticed that Roberto's arm was starting to tremble. "You can put the pole down, Lanzi, and rest your arm."

Roberto lowered the pole to the floor but held it upright as if it were a rifle. As the teacher spoke, he had been dreaming of the battle over the hills: Calvary Point, Caira, Castle Hill, Cassino. He saw himself in a tent, just below the Ridge of Death, less than a kilometer from the front line, planning a new assault.

The teacher began to read from a newspaper clip dug out of his pocket:

> *Lacking other immediate alternatives, it was finally proposed that in order to eliminate this physical and by now psychological obstacle, and soften the German defenses, the abbey and the town should be bombed. Some discussion ensued. Some Allied commanders, including General Clark, remembered that as recently as December, Eisenhower himself had stated that Italy was a country that, with its monuments and art treasures, had contributed immensely to furthering the development of civilization common to the Western world. Therefore, he warned his commanders that all efforts should be made to preserve buildings and places of international importance from the ravages of war.*

That sounded decent and appropriate, but how many people in the past had ignored such realities? Roberto thought of the Romans destroying Carthage; the Huns ravaging Samarqand, Aquileia, and dozens of other places; the Vandals devastating Rome. And more recently, many other cities had been utterly obliterated: Nankin, Coventry, Essen, Stalingrad … These cities, too, in addition to being home to countless human beings, possessed art and architecture important to the rest of mankind.

The teacher placed the article on the desk. "My guess is that other generals, and particularly those in charge of the troops who had failed the assault on Cassino, chose to remember Eisenhower's concluding words, which stated"—he picked up the article again—"'nevertheless, should we have to choose between destroying famous buildings and saving our men, nothing must stand in the way of military necessity!'"

"It is our understanding," said the teacher, "that General Alexander reinforced this directive by adding, 'When men are fighting for a "just cause," bricks and mortar, no matter how venerable, cannot be allowed to weigh against human life.'

"Thank you, Lanzi," the teacher said. "You can return to your place."

Roberto did not move at first. His mind had stopped at the assessment of that last phrase: *bricks and mortar ... cannot be allowed to weigh against human life.* That sounded right too. Was there no choice, then?

"Lanzi," the teacher called again, "have you fallen asleep?"

"Sorry, sir, I was just thinking."

"Unbelievable as it might seem," said the teacher, when Roberto was again at his desk, "it was a short step between watering down Eisenhower's original statement of intent, to finding Allied field commanders who would jump to a horrible conclusion. In fact, having utterly failed to solve the Cassino riddle by means of suicidal frontal attacks, they quickly fabricated 'irrefutable proof' that the Germans were using the monastery as an observation post." His voice acquired a momentous pitch.

"It thus followed that the ancient monastery—with all its history and art treasures—should be bombed. The Allied commanders were also aware that the monastery sheltered hundreds of civilian refugees. One general in particular, we are told, based more on expediency and practical considerations than on ethical or moral grounds, presented some strong objections to the bombing. During one last meeting, he reminded the other officers that the almost total destruction of a certain Russian city, far from hindering its defenders, had instead helped them."

The students seemed rather uninterested.

"Which city am I talking about?" he barked.

Roberto raised his hand.

"Yes, Lanzi?"

"Stalingrad, sir. Destroyed by the Germans in nineteen forty-two."

"Is anybody else following this lesson?" said the teacher, annoyance in his voice.

"Yes," voiced a few students. Others repeated the assertion, and several looked at Roberto with evident displeasure. *If it weren't for you,* said their expressions, *we wouldn't look so bad in the eyes of the teacher.*

Roberto looked down at his book, pretending to be reading. What was he supposed to do? Pretend that he didn't know it?

"Nonetheless," the teacher said, after a contemptuous look at the class, "the comments of this general were disregarded, and the bombing was authorized by the High Command. As we all know, on February fourteenth, nineteen forty-four, with air raids conducted by an armada of 254 American airplanes, the old abbey was bombed and completely destroyed.

"The subterranean tomb of St. Benedict—sixth-century Abbey founder—remained intact. As, fortunately, did tens of thousands of invaluable books and ancient manuscripts and other valuable cultural articles which, with the help of the Germans, had been moved to Rome only days before the attack."

*****

In the following days, eyewitnesses and refugees who had been evacuated prior to the bombing corroborated the German version that not a single German soldier was inside the monastery. The Allie's *irrefutable evidence* was disproved immediately, but the ancient sanctuary with its remaining treasures was now gone forever.

Some of the people from the area escaped, and several went as far north as Tuscany.

In Castelvecchio, a small group of these refugees, who had gathered near the church in search of food and shelter, recounted to the bemused townsfolk converged in the square the destruction they had witnessed.

Luisa and Roberto approached the group and listened.

"It served no purpose," said an older man who, despite the heat, seemed to shiver under his torn winter jacket. "Especially since no German was there!"

"Not only did it serve no purpose," confirmed another refugee, who still wore the upper half of a disheveled Italian army uniform, "but if anything, it achieved the opposite result."

In fact, it soon became evident that, together with the complete destruction of the sixth-century monastery, the bombing of this structure eliminated the reason for its being considered a neutral area by the Germans. No sooner had the air raid finished than the *Wehrmacht* occupied the place and set up impregnable positions behind the massive masonry ruins.

The young man who had spoken last smiled sadly and, as if at the end of an inner thought, he concluded, "Now it will be even harder to dislodge them from their entrenched positions and, consequently, break through that line."

"What about the town of Montecassino?" asked one of the bystanders. It's far from the top of the mountain. Did it get hit too?"

"Wiped out. The town doesn't exist anymore," replied a woman with tears in her eyes. "All the houses and buildings have been destroyed. Hundreds of innocent civilians have been killed. We lost everything." She looked at her small crowd of refugees. "But we consider ourselves lucky. We are among those who chose to believe in the warning leaflets dropped by the Americans, and we're still alive."

"What leaflets?"

"A few days before the bombing, an airplane dropped thousands of flyers. Most of them were taken by the wind and fell far away. A few were retrieved and read. They advised the population to move away from the vicinity of the abbey and the town, as bombing would be intensified."

An old man dug out a folded piece of paper and showed it to no one in particular. "I don't know how to read," he confessed, "but I saved this anyway …"

A younger man took it from his hands and read it aloud: "Against our will we are now obliged to direct our weapons against the monastery itself. We are warning you so that you may now save yourselves. Leave the monastery and its vicinity at once. It's signed 'The Allied Command Italy.'

"So why didn't everyone move?" someone asked.

"Not everyone read them. Not everyone believed them, and many people didn't have the courage to abandon their only possessions or leave behind those who were too old or too sick to be moved."

The destruction of the ancient monastery, with its physical and spiritual treasures, and the news of other senseless bombardments and loss of lives, clearly caused bewilderment in the minds and hearts of the Italians.

"Is this what will happen to us?" someone whispered.

Luisa let go Roberto's hand and took a handkerchief from her pocket. "Such a devastation!" she said, wiping her tears. "Such a waste of lives. At this pace, we'll be liberated through death."

"So, if the Germans won't kill us, the Americans will," Giacomo's wife, Erina, said to Luisa as they walked home from church. "At the end of the day, there isn't much difference between one kind of death or another."

"In a way, there is," Luisa replied. "Death at the hands of the Germans not only is more terrifying, but it also requires a more cruel temperament on their part. It is often administered within hearing and sight of their screaming victims. For the Americans, it is impersonal, managed from a distance by a gloved hand, with the casual remote opening of a hatch in an airplane. By the time the deadly cargo explodes over towns or cities, the airplanes are over the horizon. No cries are heard; no blood is seen."

"And yet, as I was saying, you're still dead."

"I was being sarcastic, Erina. I wasn't really thinking of the victims … but the executioners. Wondering if at the end of it all, one is much better than the other."

- XXXII -

May 1944

At about ten o'clock at night, there was a light knock at the Lanzis' door. Roberto was in bed, and his mother and grandmother were still in the kitchen, tidying up after supper. Patrizia opened the inner door.

"Who is it?" Patrizia asked.

"It's me, Antonio."

She opened the Persian shutter.

"I told you I'd keep in touch," he whispered, slipping through the partially open door.

"Good evening, Signora Luisa. Don't worry, nobody saw me," he said to Patrizia, who was still near the door, listening to see if she could hear anything outside.

"Antonio," she then said, hugging him. "How are you?"

"Tired. Very tired, but I'm not here to talk about me. I was sent to brief certain people, and since I was close, I came to pay a visit."

"Would you like some food?" Luisa asked. "It's just leftovers, but nowadays …"

"I don't mind if I do," he said, taking the chair that Patrizia had pulled from the table. "I'm rather hungry."

Luisa started to set the tablecloth. "No, no," Antonio interjected, "thanks, but I have no time for niceties. Just give me a plate, please."

Luisa picked up a plate and scooped some of the stew left in the earthenware pan. "It's mostly vegetables with a few scraps of meat. We gave most of the little meat there was to Roberto. He needs it more than us. He's a growing boy."

Patrizia gave him some bread and a glass of wine. "What can you tell us, Antonio? What is going on?"

Antonio swallowed a mouthful of food, sipped a bit of wine, and said, "If I say the word *partisan*, do you know what I mean?"

Patrizia and Luisa looked at each other. "We've heard of some groups who fight the Germans. Is that what you mean?"

"Precisely, Patrizia. As the Allies advance north of the peninsula, more and more groups will begin to operate behind the German lines."

"But are they communists?" said Luisa.

"Not necessarily, signora. There are some communists, but there are just as many Catholics, liberals, or even apolitical people; all nationalists I suppose. They're all united to liberate Italy from Fascism and the yoke of German oppression. They are all part of what is known as the *resistenza*."

"But how did it start?" Patrizia asked. "Is it similar to the French Resistance?"

"Yes, it did start in France, and initially it was just passive struggle against the German occupation. The Italian Resistance began after the armistice, with the sporadic armed opposition of military units that refused to be disarmed by the *Wehrmacht*."

"And now?" Luisa asked.

"It has grown. Now there are civilians who oppose German excesses and brutality, and others who wanted to escape Nazi labor camps. Recently, we've also been joined by prisoners of war—English, Americans, Russians, Greeks—escaped from prison camps or liberated by the Italians in the days following the armistice."

"What do you …? Sorry," Patrizia said. "I meant, what do they do?"

"It's not a secret. The primary objective is the harassment of the retreating German army; the killing of fascist diehards; the disruption of communication lines in German-occupied Italian territory; the defense and safeguarding of strategic places—like bridges, harbors, airports, and major manufacturing plants—from programmed destruction. As time goes by and they become better armed, they will also confront and engage smaller German units."

"Oh my God!" Luisa exclaimed. "What are you saying Antonio? Was it the partisans, then, who killed those Germans in Rome and caused the death of over three hundred Italians?"

She was referring to March 23, 1944, when a group named

GAP—*Gruppi di Azione Patriottica,* or Patriotic Action Groups—exploded a bomb in Rome's Via Rasella as a German platoon passed by, killing 35 soldiers. SS Lieutenant Colonel Herbert Kappler reacted immediately with the execution of 335 Italians—10 Italians for every German. They were mostly political prisoners taken from the Reginae Coeli prisons. The location and method of execution were initially undisclosed. Soon, however, the full extent of the tragedy became known, much to the horror of the population.

"Yes, signora. Unfortunately, German retaliation has to be expected, but *we* cannot abandon fighting them."

"You said *we,* Antonio," Patrizia said. It was the first clear admission that he was a *partigiano.*

"Yes," he whispered.

There was silence in the room. The three people looked at each other across the table. Everyone seemed to assess the possible consequences of that admission, the danger that Antonio's presence brought to the household.

"I have a young son …," Patrizia said, voicing her concern.

"And a neighbor who would probably enjoy telling the fascists of your visit," said Luisa.

"I'm sorry; I wanted to see you people so badly that I didn't think of the danger."

"No, Antonio. We are sorry," said Patrizia emphatically. "We're just two women and a child, but if you need a place to rest, or a bite to eat, don't hesitate. We want to carry our weight as well."

"She's right," Luisa said. "We are all Italians."

"Thanks to both of you. I'll have to leave in a minute," he said, checking his watch, "but please tell me, have you heard from Riccardo?"

"Not in a long time, Antonio," said Patrizia. "I've sent dozens of letters all over the place: War Department, embassies, Red Cross, even the Vatican. I have talked to many, many people, but so far …" She shook her head as if, under the strain, her vocal cords had suddenly failed.

"Let's keep up hope," said Antonio.

"And pray," added Luisa.

Antonio's assertions added a new dimension to the anxiety of the two women. After his departure, they sat quietly for some time, each occupied with her own thoughts, trying to assess the new risks.

"I'm going to make some tea," Patrizia said. "Would you like some, Mother?"

"Yes, dear, there is a can of camomile flowers in the right-hand cupboard."

Patrizia boiled some water in a copper pan, added some camomile, put a pellet of saccharine into the infusion, and suddenly announced, "I'm going to read in bed for a while. Good night."

Before retiring to her room, she walked by Roberto's room, opened his door, and listened. His regular breathing was interrupted by the odd sigh. He turned restlessly, as if having nightmarish dreams. *Poor child,* she thought. She blew a soundless kiss in his direction. "Good night, cucciolo," she said, closing the door.

- XXXIII -

June 4, 1944

General Clark entered Rome among cheering crowds. Two days later, on what became known as D-Day, a formidable invasion force finally began "Operation Overlord" and landed in Normandy.

Meanwhile, Central and Northern Italy were still under complete German control.

Luisa was attending to household chores when Erina came running to the house. Her neighbor must have been cooking, because she held a fork in her right hand, and she was still wearing a white apron.

"Some quick news," she said, almost out of breath. "I got it from our usual source. The Americans have entered Rome. The Germans left without fighting."

"That's great news!" Luisa exclaimed. "They probably made a deal with the Vatican."

Erina began rubbing her fork on her apron. She lowered her voice and said, "There is bad news too. The fascists are in the streets of Castelvecchio, 'collecting' again in the name of the motherland, so hide what you can."

Already short of raw materials at the beginning of the conflict, the country was now almost depleted of everything, and metals in particular. A special appeal had been issued by the government a month before for the people of Italy to donate some of their personal belongings for the greater benefit of the motherland.

At the time, some of the items contributed were woolen blankets, scarves, and heavy boots, supposedly to be sent to the Italian soldiers still trapped at the eastern front. This time, the request was for copper vessels—common utensils in Italian households—which were to be melted and made into bullets.

In Castelvecchio, as in many other places, rumor had it that the fascist elements entrusted with the requisition were actually keeping some of the best items for themselves, or selling them to collectors and speculators.

Two militiamen in black shirts were canvassing Via Francesca, and Luisa, in order to minimize her contact with them, had already prepared her contribution. When they arrived at her door, she handed over two of her pitchers without returning their ritual fascist salute, and swiftly turned away.

"Just a minute, lady ...," called one of the two. "We hear you have another one. The country needs it too." He spoke in a scornful tone.

"Why? The country is already getting two of mine, while many people, I am told, have given none."

"Well, lady, not everyone is as lucky as you are."

"Luck has little to do with it, dear fellow. We worked very hard for what we have!"

"That doesn't mean a thing to us! You still must give all the copper you have. Some people have gone to jail for contravening il Duce's request."

For a moment, anger seemed to take over Luisa. Despite her dislike for the fascists and the knowledge that donations often fell into the hands of thieves and speculators, she had always given generously. For she thought that if even the smallest portion trickled down to the soldiers at the front—her sons—her sacrifice was worthwhile. The last pitcher, though, was a family heirloom, passed on from generation to generation, and one of the few items she had saved from the ruins of her demolished house in 1917. Besides, its aesthetic value made it highly unlikely that it be given to the "Country." *Who could have told these bastards of its existence?* she wondered. Then she remembered that just a few days before, Pia Zini had come to the house with the excuse of borrowing some sugar. As Luisa was fetching it, Pia had looked around the room and commented on the beautiful hand-wrought designs of the copper pitcher. It had been a bit strange, particularly because, upon taking leave, Pia had forgotten to pick up the sugar. Now the reason for her visit was clear. *Judas in woman's clothes,* Luisa fumed internally. *Damned fascist!*

They had done their homework and sent in their own spy. It was useless to argue or lie. Luisa fought back her rising anger and said to the militiamen, "I already gave you two *brocche*. The last one has been in the family for over two centuries; it has deep sentimental value for me. I'd like to keep it."

The older soldier said, "The … *motherland* wants it more than you do. It's needed to make bullets."

Luisa swallowed the lump in her throat and said, "You wait right here. I'll go fetch the pitcher I'll make sure it will go to the motherland, all right."

The two looked at each other and exchanged a subtle nod of satisfaction.

A moment later, a loud, ringing clunk resonated behind them. They turned toward the noise in time to see, a few feet away, the smashed copper vessel on the stone path of the garden, and several brass ornamental rings, separated on impact from the pitcher, rolling toward the nearest flower bed. Instinctively, they turned their heads upward and saw Luisa's head protruding from a small window.

"It was in the attic," she said with a baffling smile. "I thought I'd spare the effort of carrying it down. As you said, it will be melted for bullets, so il Duce won't mind that it got smashed."

She withdrew from the window and slammed the shutter.

- XXXIV -

July 1944

That afternoon, while twelve-year-old Roberto was in the garden, a couple of old men were sitting on the stony ridge of the artesian well, smoking and talking about the war. On the street beyond, a small column of German trucks and soldiers passed by now and then.

Though the scene was a common one by now, Roberto looked at their uniforms and weaponry with anxiety. He remembered his father's warning about the possibility of an Arno Line, his nonna telling him about the terrible days on the Piave, the bombardments of San Donà, the death of his grandfather. Perhaps that moment was near; what would happen to them?

The two old men paused only to draw hard on their worn pipes as the acrid smell of cheap tobacco spiced the air around them.

"Those Germans will fight to the last man," speculated the elder, his voice betraying a mixture of fear and admiration for that Teutonic trait.

"I saw them fight in nineteen fifteen. They are a disciplined bunch."

"Never mind nineteen fifteen. What about Salerno, Anzio, Cassino?"

There was a moment of silence. These recent battles, often illustrated by the many refugees who had fled those unfortunate places and stopped in Castelvecchio, had supplied strong evidence of German discipline and determination.

"You are right, and the Americans don't seem in no hurry," finally replied the other, spitting his dark saliva just past the narrow patch of parsley. "They'll just stand back and let us be killed by the Germans, or starve."

"Or bomb us into oblivion themselves from a safe distance."

They expressed irony and frustration at risking death now, at the moment the final result of the conflict was evident to one and all and, according to some, almost in sight.

Roberto continued to listen intently to the conversation. Ever since he could remember, adults had spoken about the war in disturbing terms. "Bomb us into oblivion," however, was a new expression. Not even his father had ever used it. He was trying to translate those obscure, abstract words into concrete, significant images when his nonna called.

"Roberto, where are you?"

He had seen her go by awhile earlier to join several women who sat on straw-bottomed chairs in a shady spot of the garden. Roberto could hear them chatter—*gossip,* as Father would have said—or mumble prayers while knitting woolen socks, scarves, and pullovers to prepare for the coming winter.

The boy peeked through the thick laurel hedge to detect, unseen, the urgency on his grandmother's face.

"Roberto," she called again. This time louder and in a higher pitch. "I must measure this sleeve on you," she shouted upon seeing movement behind the bush. "Come here this moment."

Her tone demanded immediate obedience.

He sighed, placed his book on the ground, and advanced reluctantly toward the old woman. He stopped in front of her, and she pulled him closer. He offered his arm and prepared to withstand the itchy texture of the virgin wool against his bare arm. Why would she force him to wear that itchy sleeve on a hot summer day like this? He couldn't even stand it in wintertime, let alone summer. In fact, the last time he had worn a pullover of that same material, his bare skin had broken into boils where the wool touched it.

"Don't move now," she said impatiently. "I have to count the stitches. I'll be but a moment."

He stiffened his arm, slowly turned his face away, and closed his eyes.

It'll soon pass, he thought, *like most other unpleasant things, like the punishments of the nuns, like medicines, and long church functions.* The thought of church and Nonna's knitting needles sticking from his chest reminded him of a particular fresco above the main altar. It depicted a saint standing in a wooded area, surrounded by soldiers.

A dozen arrows pierced his body as he gazed toward the sky. An old, bearded Jehovah, who appeared to be floating above the clouds, looked benevolently upon him. Roberto opened his eyes as if to cancel that unpleasant vision.

His previous thoughts were dispelled by the vista before his eyes. He felt embraced by the brilliance of the sun, the blue depth of the sky, the color of ripe plums on a tree nearby, the green of the garden. Many different elements mingled mysteriously in his mind, composing a single, auspicious feeling that filled his heart with happiness.

"All done." Luisa drew the sleeve back, and he started to pull away and return to his games.

Suddenly, his movement froze in midair as the earth shook violently and a prolonged rumbling, similar to a clap of thunder, obliterated the chatter of voices and all other sounds.

This was followed by a sinister silence that hung in the still summer air. Anxious eyes aimed at the sky in search of a plausible answer. Then the rumbling grew in intensity and became more distinct.

Finally, a man spoke faintly, as if afraid the sound of his words would verify the reality just perceived. He pointed his arm westward. "Pisa," he said. "They are bombing Pisa." And then added with a thin thread of voice, "We will be next!"

"Oh my God," said Luisa, dropping a couple of stitches.

Roberto heard that cry and searched the faces around him for reassurance. He saw one of the old men expel more saliva, and the spit fell on his shoes. The eyes of the adults seemed the mirror images of terror. He was speechless, petrified, prey to a primordial instinct that fear had suddenly unleashed and that now gnawed at the depth of his stomach.

Roberto was shaken. Even the adults seemed unable of thinking in this moment of need; perhaps that's what "oblivion" meant.

Now he began to understand fear! What was he supposed to do if even adults were lost?

Luisa must have realized that, for she regained her composure and said, "Don't worry, my darling, your nonna is here."

Roberto looked up at her and finally asked, "Will they bomb us too?"

"I don't think so, darling." They stood there for a while, speculating as to the exact place and nature of that bombing. Then, seeing a small group of people assembling in the street, Luisa said, "Let's see what those people say." They crossed the garden, opened the gate, and walked toward them.

"I only know that there was lots of death," said a middle-aged man with no hair. He worked at the *Poste & Telegrafi* office and was often a good source of information, which came to him through the wires from colleagues and friends.

"Did you say Pisa's train station?" Luisa asked.

"Si, signora, but lots of buildings nearby were damaged as well. Many people died."

*****

That evening, Patrizia checked to make sure all shutters were shut before putting a match to the acetylene lamp that was the only source of light ever since the destruction of the electric power plant. Blackouts were strictly enforced, as lit windows were said to attract enemy fire.

But the people they called "enemy" were also those they anxiously waited for, to be liberated; it didn't seem to make sense.

The family ate a frugal meal, and then Patrizia extinguished the lights and carefully opened the kitchen door. In complete darkness, they moved to the terrace.

"There," she said, holding Roberto's hand while he stood on the wide stone parapet, following the direction of her outstretched arm. Toward the western horizon, narrow beams of light moved from a common ground vertex, piercing the dark ceiling of the earth.

"Searchlights … looking for airplanes," whispered Patrizia, as if in danger of being heard by an enemy.

Every now and then, sudden flashes resembling lightening brightened the leaden sky. Thunder followed soon after, reverberating in the empty space of the night like a dreadful premonition.

"They are over Pisa again," uttered Luisa. "I hope your cousin Assunta moved to the countryside."

"Never mind Assunta, Mother. It will soon be our turn. We'd better find a safer place. Remember Riccardo's advice?"

*****

Before leaving for the African front, Riccardo had predicted with astonishing accuracy the probable phases of the conflict. "Be ready," he said, "because, unless there is a miracle, Africa will be lost in a short time. Then it might be Italy's turn. They will probably come from somewhere south of here, and although Castelvecchio has no strategic importance, the Arno River does. Chances are that the river, with its high banks and the hills behind, will become a front line, like the

Piave was during the Great War. The bridges will also become prime targets…"

At that point, he stopped. "Sorry," he said with a softer voice, "it must sound as if I were conducting an assessment of the battlefield with my military staff. I just hope this family will never experience what I did twenty-odd years ago, on the banks of the Piave River."

No one spoke, and he continued.

"Our house is too close to the San Romano bridge; it will be too dangerous to remain here. If what I'm saying comes to pass, you will have to find another place, a farmhouse in the countryside—but not too close to the hills, as they will be dangerous too."

He didn't have to say anymore. Everyone in the family knew the story of his house in San Doná, destroyed by mortar shells, killing his father.

Those were ominous words, made even more believable by the fact that lately events were occurring with an incredible resemblance to his earlier predictions.

The African campaign had ended in a disaster for the Italians and their German allies, and the Italians' attempt to negotiate a separate armistice with the Anglo-American forces had backfired. And now, in mid-1944, after fierce battles in Salerno, Anzio, and Cassino, the Allied forces had barely managed to cross the flatland of Lazio in pursuit of the retreating German army. With the approach of the hilly terrain of the Tuscan region, the process of "liberation" suffered another perilous slowdown. Central and Northern Italians still remained under the heavy yoke of German occupation forces—threatened on the ground by the ruthlessness of the former allies and from the sky by the often-erratic bombing of the Americans.

"For months now, the fighting is around the high grounds, south of Volterra," said a man who had come from the South, ahead of the front. He was a friendly man who rode an old bicycle on his way to work in Santa Chiara. If he saw Luisa in the garden, he stopped near the gate and engaged in small talk. Sometimes another passerby stopped as well, and full conversations ensued.

"The Americans advance a bit," he said that evening, "and then the Germans push them back. The Americans counterattack, and then they are pushed back again. The Germans are well placed on Monte Amiata, and with their cannons, they target anything that moves in the valley, just like they did at Monte Cassino."

"So what is going to happen?" Luisa asked.

"Who knows? In Montecassino, the Americans have lost a lot of what is known as their color troop infantry," replied the same man. "Perhaps they are waiting for more cannon fodder before trying another forward move."

"But I heard from a refugee of that area," replied another, "that Cassino was finally taken by Polish, French, and Canadian troops."

"Whatever. Still cannon fodder to them."

Every day, there were new rumors: the Allies had taken Volterra … The Germans had retaken it … The harbor of Leghorn had been obliterated … The Americans would advance soon …

"Not soon enough!" Patrizia uttered when hearing the latest. "You hear everyone's propaganda, and you don't know whom or what to believe."

The truth was that nothing was certain. The people of Castelvecchio, like those of any other place under fascist or German rule, could not trust the propaganda of the regime.

The complete lack of electricity now made it impossible for common folk to listen to the radio. So, people continued to be fed by rumors and hope.

And, as someone had voiced, it did look as if the next leap forward by the Americans was predicated more by the Germans' determination to stand, or retreat behind a new defensible line, rather than to the American ability or desire to advance.

And would that next line really be on the Arno River, as Riccardo had predicted? And how long would the Germans hold that line? These were the frightening questions in the Lanzis' minds as the hot summer of 1944 continued.

*****

The day after the bombing of Pisa, news confirmed that the railroad station was completely destroyed. The invisible force of the explosions flattened the adjacent area for many blocks, eradicating large trees from the ground like weeds, flinging cars and heavy equipment in the air like toys. Many people died, all of them innocent civilians.

That evening, Roberto listened as the adults discussed the news. Nonna Luisa made the sign of the cross. "*Gesù mio, misericordia,*" she said, her face a reflection of deep emotion. "It's nineteen seventeen all over again."

"This too will pass, Mother," Patrizia whispered. "In the meantime, we have more immediate problems to worry about."

"What problems?" Luisa asked.

"Today Ligato called us and said that in a matter of weeks the distillery will be closed."

"I was expecting this, but not so soon."

"Actually, Mother, it's not soon enough. As someone told me, either the Americans will bomb it from the sky, or the Germans will blow it up before the Americans arrive. Anything of industrial importance on the south side of the river will end up that way."

"You sound so sure of that. How do you …"

"I am."

Luisa gave her an inquiring look, but Patrizia nodded toward Roberto, and she understood. "Will everybody leave now?" Luisa asked.

"Being a slow period, temporary personnel were laid off in April. But yes, now everyone else will leave."

"Will you receive some compensation?"

"Yes, although I don't know if Ligato will play fair. It would appear that Riccardo, before leaving, was able to have it entrenched into the workers' agreement."

"May God bless him!" Luisa exclaimed. "He'd be so sad if he knew the distillery will be destroyed."

"He probably envisioned that too, Mother."

After that exchange, Luisa remained silent for a long time, thinking of her two sons in harm's way. They had not heard from them for months now. The only thing she could do was plead with all her heart that they safely returned, and hope that God listened to her prayers.

In Castelvecchio, except for short-lived moments of calm, life had become almost a constant worry. Worry about the increased fascist skittishness, which betrayed their insecurity, making them more prone to react and punish the general population. Worry about the bombing … and about the scarcity of food.

Luisa had to become ever more inventive; a couple of eggs and some vegetables would be stretched into a tasty frittata. A few slices of hard bread would be soaked in cold water, sprinkled with olive oil, covered with fresh tomato slices and basil leaves, and brought to the table as if it were a gourmet dish. There were days, though, that even these meager provisions were scarce or not available, and Luisa pretended not to be hungry and gave all the food to Roberto and Patrizia. For many other families without a garden, a few chickens, or any means to barter, even these frugal dishes were often beyond their reach.

During the following days and weeks, people began to look with increased anxiety at American airplanes—their white stars sometimes visible to the naked eye—flying overhead in close formations. They worried until they saw them return, the lighter hum of their engines indicating their deadly cargo had been unloaded on someone else's head this time.

Another "mission" had been accomplished.

"They got Bologna this time," someone commented, or Modena, or Genoa. The immediate danger seemed to affect others, so far away.

Hearing all this, Roberto marveled at the ability of these people to determine the targets of those airplanes just from their unmarked path on the immense sky. For him, they were just coming from beyond the horizon or going behind the tall mountains way north of the house. He could see these mountains from his northern bathroom window, and when the sun shone upon their snowy peaks in winter, they seemed to touch the sky.

- XXXV -

Patrizia arrived at her usual time and dashed to her office. She busied herself all day, putting her records and laboratory in order. It seemed so utterly futile; it was her last day at the distillery.

Why am I doing this? she thought, storing glass vessels on the shelves, filing out her paperwork. *What's the point if the entire place will go up in smoke?*

All the same, she continued as if it were an ordinary day, even finding the strength to hum the odd song.

In the middle of the afternoon, there was a knock at the door, and Mr. Ligato entered the room before she could even answer. "Good afternoon, Patrizia," he said. "If Mohamed doesn't go to the mountain, the mountain will go to Mohamed." His tone was scornful. "Since you didn't come to my office, I came to say good-bye to you."

"Thank you, Signor Ligato. I was busy with my things ..."

"Well, Patrizia, it's a pity that we couldn't have been better associates, especially now that our great director is away. Who knows, you could have found it rewarding."

"My work is rewarding enough for me, Signor Ligato," she said, ignoring the insinuation, "but thanks anyway."

"Well, don't thank me yet. I haven't done anything for you, but perhaps one of these days …" He got closer as if to hug or kiss her. Patrizia held her position and pushed her arm forward.

He took her hand and shook it briefly. "Good-bye then. But one of these days …," he repeated upon leaving.

That day will never come, she said in her mind.

Toward quitting time, after collecting her paycheck and saying good-bye to her colleagues, she went to Riccardo's office. It had remained unoccupied. Despite having its key in her drawer, and walking by it several times a week, it was only the third time she crossed the threshold since his departure. That way, she was able to pretend that he was still at his desk, bent over his drawings or studying a new process.

She walked the short distance from her lab with the same eagerness as if he were there waiting for her. She opened the door cautiously, as if afraid something inside the room would escape. Her eyes darted toward his chair and desk, as if the miracle of her love had the power to bring him back.

"Ciao, Riccardo," she said. "Sorry to disturb you. Are you ready to go home?"

She stopped in the middle of the room and stood there for a moment, prey of her emotions. Swallowing the knot that gripped her throat, she moved around the desk. She removed the family photos from the corner. She opened the drawers and took just the items of personal nature: his fountain pen, the silver letter opener with his initials—her last birthday present to him, his old diary … She wiped the dust off the cover and placed it near the pictures.

She opened the top drawer and moved away some items of no personal value. Then, looking toward the back of the drawer, she saw a rolled sheet of paper. It was Roberto's drawing of the old mill. She smiled at the sight of the stylized initials of his signature. Evidently, he had tried to emulate his father's handwriting. She placed the drawing on the desk and opened the last drawer. Under a filing folder, she saw the large glass paperweight that normally Riccardo kept on the top of his desk. She lifted the weight and noticed that it concealed a carefully folded paper.

She looked at it briefly, perturbed by this unexpected find. She did not know what to expect: a secret, perhaps?

She sat on Riccardo's chair, listening to the accelerated beats of her heart, lifted the folded page, and started to unwrap it. Her heart beat faster as her curiosity battled with the fear of unveiling something Riccardo did not wish revealed.

Two objects fell onto the desk, and a wave of emotion rose inside her. One was the first photograph she had ever given him. The other was the multicolored hand-drawn bookmarker Roberto had created for his father two years before. It read, *To my dear daddy with love, Jan. 31, 1940.*

In the last fold of the paper, in Riccardo's unmistakable handwriting, a short phrase in blue ink jumped from the white sheet: *My treasures,* it read, *wait for me!*

For a moment, Patrizia had the illusion that he was really there;

she felt his presence right beside her. Motionless, she willfully inhaled the air of the office where she had first met him, remembering the interview.

"Ah," he had said, "I get to meet my first ally in this company. At least I hope that we shall be allies."

She heard someone talking outside. For a moment, it had sounded like his voice. No. It was a small group of workers passing by the window on their way out. "Who knows if we'll ever be back," she heard one of them say.

That simple reality shook her from her fantasy and threw her back into her loneliness. She got up and placed the small collection of Riccardo's personal items and Roberto's drawing in her bag. She let her hand slip over the back of his chair, a gentle caress. "Good-bye, my dear," she whispered. She stopped at the door, as she had done that first time. She wiped her eyes and left.

At the gate, she picked up her bike and shook hands with the guardian. "Good-bye for now, Ovidio," she said.

"Good-bye, signora," he answered. "I hope I'll see you and your husband soon." The echo of his words was still lingering in the air when the heavy gate closed behind her with an ominous clank.

She took the narrow path that ran over the riverbank. She could not resist looking toward the grassy mound below, thinking of the many happy times spent there with Riccardo and the first time he had so impulsively declared his love for her.

She kept pedaling, moving in the same direction of the river below, leaving the distillery behind, farther and farther away with every turn of the wheel. She passed the spot where, during her eighth month of pregnancy, she had fallen and feared to have lost her child. The straight outline of the bridge loomed in front against the sunset. Sustained by the massive brick pylons planted in the ground, it seemed to arch in an extreme effort to hold together the two opposite banks.

At least symbolically it was, Patrizia thought. Tonight she was going to cross it, not knowing if or when she would do so again.

She climbed the short ascent toward the bridge and noticed that now soldiers were stationed on both sides. A machine gun nest had been installed on this side. Partially camouflaged with tree branches and netting, a large tank was parked below a chestnut tree.

"Halt!" shouted one of the soldiers. "What are you carrying in your bag?"

She stopped and looked at that young soldier. Then she turned her eyes toward the gentle spiral curve of the river, toward San Romano. Beyond it, she saw in her mind's eye the grassy spot and the sandbar where she had spent happy moments with Riccardo for a last time.

"I asked you what's in your bag," the soldier repeated.

"Nothing that should concern you," she said, opening it. "Only memories."

He glanced inside. "Where are you going?" he asked.

"Home."

"Where are you coming from?"

"See those chimneys?" She pointed toward them. The two tall structures rose proudly toward the gray sky while a soft plume of smoke climbed lazily in the evening air—like the last breath of a dying person. "It's a distillery," she said tonessly. "Until half an hour ago I was working there. Now it's closed, and I'm going home."

"The bridge will be blocked early tomorrow."

Patrizia did not reply. She had lived most of her life on the left side of the river. That was the place of her youth, her occupation, where she had met Riccardo, where she had fallen in love. Until now, there had been no distinction; her life and memories had always been one unbroken line. Now, though, with the closure of the bridge, the link was broken, and one side of her life cut away.

"Only military personnel with special permits will be able to pass," the guard continued.

"Amen," she replied, and rode off on her bike.

- XXXVI -

July 1944

Days and weeks went by. The flow of news of destruction of cities and towns and the increasingly horrifying reports from the south were now constant. However, neither that nor the now frequent air raid alarms had so far wiped out the illusion people nurtured about the safety of their town.

"They bombed Pisa and Bologna because they are important railway junctions," people rationalized. "They bombed Livorno and Genoa because of the port facilities. Why on earth should they waste bombs on Castelvecchio?"

But despite the assertions of the most optimistic, by now, even in the small town, life could not return to any semblance of normality. No one could claim that war was just a distant affair that eventually would disappear on its own.

Few people now had jobs to go to. Farmers attended the land, fearing their dwindling crops would be raided by starving people or garnered by some state agency. Feeding and caring for the domestic animals, they wondered if it was all for nothing. Those remaining shopkeepers who still opened their doors had fewer and fewer goods to sell. Everybody's most immediate concern was the procurement of food.

Thanks to Luisa's foresight, the Lanzis had plenty of vegetables, jam, jelly, and other preserves. However, commodities such as sugar, coffee, oil, bread, and red meat were scarce indeed and required "connections" and high costs; some of these staples were not to be found anywhere.

Patrizia, now out of work, helped Luisa with the chores and continued to write letters to government organizations, to the Red Cross, to the Vatican—in the hope of receiving news of her husband, without any results so far.

Despite the end of the regular school year and his much-desired holidays, Roberto kept receiving tutoring lessons two days a week. Friday mornings were dedicated to piano lessons. His teacher, Mrs. Virna Parini, either by conviction or necessity, had expressed what even Roberto thought to be exaggerated compliments on his musical abilities.

"Yes, Mrs. Lanzi," he heard her say to his grandmother, "we must keep the lessons going through the summer; with his memory and talent, who knows what he can achieve." Nonna Luisa smiled with pride.

Patrizia, though acknowledging her son's numerous talents, was not convinced that music was one of them. "But," she said to Luisa, "it will keep him occupied."

The lessons continued.

Roberto did not share his grandmother's enthusiasm either. He knew he was no Mozart. One day he saw his nonna slip several extra bank notes into her eager hands, and he understood why his teacher praised him so lavishly.

Even grown-ups, he deduced, and intelligent ones at that, could be deceived by their own wishful thinking into believing whatever they wanted to believe, regardless of evidence to the contrary.

He would have been happier to reduce the number of lessons, which seemed projected toward this distant objective called "future," for a "present" with more free time of his own. All the same, perhaps aided by the frequent family comments, he came to think that this must be the price to pay in order to maintain a certain position in society—whatever that was—and he derived some pleasure from their approval, and especially that of his grandmother.

One Friday morning, he left the house to attend the piano lesson at Mrs. Parini's third-floor apartment in the older part of town. Nonna Luisa walked by his side, generous as usual with her last-minute recommendations.

"If the air-raid sirens go off," she said, "run home at once."

Roberto could not suppress a smile, as he invariably heard and saw the airplanes much sooner than the alarm would start its whining call.

"Yes, nonna," he said, nodding.

"Don't get distracted during your lesson."

He nodded again.

"Remember what your mother would say of nodding."

"Only donkeys nod," he recited. "People voice their reply." It had become a family joke, often repeated to reinforce what was perceived as proper behavior.

"Come home immediately after the piano lesson."

They were now approaching the northern gate, where the street cut under the archway of the bell tower. Roberto took a last look at the open fields and the distant hump of Monte Serra, which, through the strange optical effect produced by the morning haze, appeared to have moved closer to the town.

"I will, Nonna," he said, in answer to her shaking his arm for a prompt, verbal acknowledgement.

Once below the tower, she remembered her informal, domestic attire: kitchen apron, open garden shoes, and worn-out scarf. She stopped, faced the boy, and then, as if to entrust him to the care of God, she made the sign of the cross over his head. "Go now," she said, kissing his forehead as if they were separating for a long time, "and don't stop anywhere."

He turned away and began walking at a brisk pace, feeling her intense stare. As soon as he knew that she could no longer see him, he began running toward the main square. He dashed by the butcher shop on the west side, where many women were standing in line in the vain hope of receiving their scant weekly ration of meat. Farther along, others held their limited provisions of bread and produce in small brown bags. Crossing to the opposite side of the street, he ran under the vaulted ceiling of the town hall, exaggerating the impact of his feet on the paved walkway, producing an echo that, to him, resembled a cavalry charge. He noticed that now a German flag with a large central swastika hung beside the tricolor Italian flag. *Strange,* he thought. *It wasn't there last week.*

Every once in a while, he jumped up in the air to reach the heavy hand-forged rings spiked onto the green *Serena* stone of the façade. He had heard Meino tell his nonna that they were used for horse tethers. "Cavalry officers did that during the Great War," he'd said. He added that a long time ago, when the Arno River overflowed its banks and flooded the countryside, those rings served as anchors for barges and rafts that brought food and relief to the submerged town.

Roberto kept running. All the hours and days of stillness and confinement seemed to find release in that effortless run. So effortless, in fact, that at times he thought he was just lifting his legs and the land was rolling under his feet.

He dashed by the cathedral. The smell of burned candles and incense reminded him of the sadness and boredom of burial ceremonies, of church functions, of forced attendance. *Another activity aimed at an even more remote "future,"* he thought, and in so thinking, he experienced a vague sense of guilt. Unbidden, images of saints and martyrs he knew to be hanging on the other side of that wall intruded on his thoughts. What if … God and his angels did exist? What if—as Nonna and the priest said—they really knew his every thought? Could God prevent his father from returning because of his blasphemous thoughts?

The fleeting notion was quickly displaced by the singing splashes of the fountain in the *piazzetta*—the little square. Those crystalline pearl-like droplets shooting toward the azure blue sky and falling down in a luminescent shower spoke to him of life and happiness, restoring his confidence and pleasure in the here and now.

He stopped for a moment, bobbing lithely around its splashing jets to get a sip of the iron-tasting water. After a final sprint, he entered the dark vestibule that led to his teacher's apartment. As he blindly began to climb the stairs, holding onto the handrail, he wondered why town dwellings like this, or others he had visited with his nonna, were either barely illuminated by a miniscule lightbulb or completely dark.

He could detect the stale smell of Mrs. Parini's apartment even before reaching its door. Sometimes he tried to reduce his breathing for fear of what he might ingest. In the tiny entrance, the few garments hanging on an old coatrack looked shrunken and withered. They reminded him of the raisin bunches his nonna hung in the attic.

The front room, which was the only one he ever saw, contained a wooden table, an old piano, a china cabinet with a few dishes and glassware, and several chairs with worn straw seats. A grayish painting of a bearded man—self-portrait of Mrs. Parini's dead husband—stared out from the larger wall. As he passed by it, Roberto turned his face away from the deep shades, the sad expression, and the resin-colored eyes that seemed to follow him everywhere, always triggering a sense of hopelessness within him.

A few music pages and notes were piled on the corner of the worn wooden table. Mrs. Parini slowly removed an ornamental dust cover from the piano, and Roberto adjusted the height of the stool. There was only one window in that room, facing a narrow alley, and the scant lighting was barely sufficient to read the music sheet.

The lesson started with the usual musical scale routine, when suddenly, among the waves of still-echoing notes, he detected another completely unrelated sound. He stopped playing.

"Continue, Roberto," Mrs. Parini said from the far side of the room. "What are you waiting for?"

He did not answer, and he felt his stomach turn at the recognition of the faint drone of approaching aircrafts. The familiar, sinister sound crept into the silent room and became louder. He distinctly recognized the heavy-load rumble of airplanes reverberating in the crisp morning air.

"Well?" His teacher looked at him impatiently.

"Signora Parini," he said with a faint voice, "can't you hear the airplanes? There is an air raid."

"But ... there was no siren ..."

They both became still, and for an eternal moment Roberto hoped that the rumble of the airplanes would soon diminish, indicating their passing. He wished they were meant for a distant target, that they would soon disappear behind the mountains, beyond the horizon as he had seen them do so many other times.

But the unmistakable whistling of falling bombs soon shattered his hopes and the morning stillness. It was his first experience of direct bombing.

Her voice strained with fright, Mrs. Parini yelled, "Run home, Roberto, run home!"

Then, as if her simple command sufficed to discharge her own responsibility, without a second thought for Roberto, she ran toward the exit door. He saw her dashing by, arms waving in the air, and heard her crying hysterically, "Oh my God, oh my God!"

With the first explosions, the ground shook violently, the electric light failed, and pieces of plaster rained from the ceiling. Roberto stood in the middle of the room, almost paralyzed from fear. He heard people screaming and running down the stairs. He heard the commotion in the street below, but he could not see anything, as darkness and the thick dust made it difficult for him to get his bearings. There was a final series of explosions, followed by the receding sound of the airplanes.

Somehow, just finding himself still alive and unhurt gave him the courage to move.

He walked in the darkness, his hands outstretched, until he reached a wall. Moving ever so cautiously, he found the door to the corridor and then the stairs. With his arms still extended, his feet testing for obstacles, and guided only by instinct, he came to a landing, more steps, a turn, and then another landing. Finally, at the end of the ground floor corridor, there was a faint patch of light.

He burst out onto the sidewalk, only to find himself mowed down by the stampeding crowd of people running toward the square.

He pulled himself up, shocked by the hazy images of destruction that lay before him in a grotesque composition. Smashed roof tiles and other debris were spread all over the ground. Enormous clouds of dark smoke hung overhead, filtered only by a single, reluctant, pale ray of sunlight. People frantically called the names of relatives or friends: *Mario … Gina … Elena.*

Roberto moved a few steps forward but quickly realized the street was completely inaccessible and filled with a mountain of smoldering rubble. Entire facades had crumbled to the ground, and sections of old tenements were still falling in a hailstorm of bricks. Clouds of plaster dust blew violently outward, as if avoiding being crushed by the weight of collapsing walls. An entire building block was sliced open, its contents violently spewed onto the street below, its rooms sectioned as if by a giant cleaver—their ordinary details incongruously exposed to view.

A wrought iron bed hung precariously from a splintered landing. In the next room, an ornate fireplace stood intact, centered against what was now a freestanding wall, without floor or ceiling. Several rectangular patches on the walls revealed spots previously occupied by paintings, mirrors, or family portraits. An electric cord swung limply from a cupola ceiling, suggesting the previous location of a chandelier.

On one side of the street, an old woman sat on the edge of the side-walk, sobbing and laughing at the same time. When Roberto went by, he was horrified to see that she was holding a naked, bloodied foot that was protruding from the rubble, repeating what sounded like words of reassurance, as if to coax the body to which it belonged back to life. He caught sight of a ghostly figure, whose face seemed stark white in contrast to the blood splattered all over her body. She ran holding her left arm, which was only attached to her body by a shred of skin.

"Maria …"

"Carlo …"

"Mamma …"

"Nonna …"

Everyone was calling for someone, but no answer came back. Those anguished cries brought Roberto back to his own reality. Suddenly, the devastating thought that he was lost in all this chaos, that his house might be hit, that his mother and grandmother may be dead, crossed his mind. He started to run in the opposite direction, determined to find another way.

"Nonna … Nonna!" he cried, as if saying that alone would have the power to save him. People ran in all directions, but no one noticed a young boy scrambling through that chaos, his eyes full of tears.

Roberto did not recognize anything, so he ran and climbed at random, aiming toward whatever open space he found in front of him. Through his clouded eyes, he could only see his feet: jumping over the rubble, touching the sparse, clear patches of cobblestones, his shoes occasionally hit by his falling tears. They were, more than anything else, tears of frustration.

At last, he came to a small square that was still recognizable. He stopped to think. He stared eagerly through his misty eyes. He rubbed them with his hands to be sure that what he saw was real. There, not thirty yards away, a nebulous shadow broke through the smoky air. Pale, as if her veins had been totally drained of her blood, her face hardened by sheer determination, Nonna Luisa was picking her way through a pile of rubble almost a story high.

"Roberto!" she yelled upon seeing him, her voice choking with emotion. "Roberto."

He ran toward her, and their bodies collided. They embraced and kissed each other, fear and frustration suddenly dispelled, and for a long instant, the old woman held the boy against her knotted body. "Roberto *mio,* Roberto *mio …*"

- XXXVII -

1944

In the following weeks, Castelvecchio, like most other similar towns, witnessed increasing air raids, more alarm signals, frequent reports from the south of famine and destruction.

Luisa realized that most people, be they artisans, shopkeepers, or clerks, desperately clung to the irrational belief that their lives, and those of their immediate family, would somehow be spared from the destruction. Deeply troubled by recent events, but not yet desperate, the average person seemed to deny that war was about to become the texture of their daily existence.

In the countryside, this feeling was less evident, as farmers derived a sense of security from the distance that separated them from the more dangerous urban areas and from the bridges over the Arno River. After the initial shock, they began to regard the ever-increasing number of airplanes overhead as unwelcome temporary visitors, disappearing as quickly as they had unexpectedly arrived.

Amidst the worsening conditions, the bishop seized the opportunity to channel this unfounded hope toward heavenly horizons and fill his church again. Since the local soccer game, bocce, or other forms of entertainment often diluted Sunday mass attendance, he decreed a special nine-day evening function—a novena—to gather his diminishing herd to pray for the return of peace and safety. Those who attended these special worship sessions had their own reasons. Some truly believed that prayers could facilitate divine intervention, while others found that the proximity of people gave them more courage—*mal comune mezzo gaudio,* a shared misfortune halves the damage, as they said. Some felt that a visit to the church or even a silent prayer could do no harm.

Luisa attended every one of these ceremonies, as her own deep devotion demanded. Others did it because it was said to be of maximum benefit when one attended them all.

Patrizia never went. She seemed unaffected by the wishful thinking that moved other people. She did not posses any faith, and she could not fathom a God who took time to listen to the mumbling of a person or a group of people imploring to be spared. Why? Because they assembled in a particular place, lit candles, and recited litanies? What was He supposed to do? Kill others instead? Appealing that it might be in these terrifying times to put trust in a supernatural being, she had the courage not to succumb to the temptation. She stayed home, played the piano, read, or listened to music from a hand-cranked record player.

Sometimes her lack of religious feelings was so obvious that she provoked Luisa's reproach. "It wouldn't hurt you if you came once or twice," she said to Patrizia, "at least as an example to your son, if not for the benefit of your own soul."

"Mother," Patrizia replied patiently, "you are giving him sufficient exposure to the church, and I won't interfere if he decides to follow your example rather than mine." She smiled to soften her firm reply. "As for me, remember what Riccardo said the first time we argued about religion; we should respect each other's beliefs and leave it at that."

Both women were careful not to discuss these matters in Roberto's presence. However, he heard bits of conversation, and he had drawn his own conclusions based on his observations.

Unless detained because of his homework, he was glad to accompany his nonna, as he liked the opportunity to be somewhere other than the house. He knew that if he remained home, his mother would compel him to do additional homework.

In church, Roberto surveyed his surroundings and watched the crowd around him with genuine curiosity. He was puzzled by the festooned figure of the bishop, covered in ceremonial regalia—burgundy satin with heavy gold borders. *On all accounts, Jesus didn't go around Galilee clothed like that,* he thought. He looked at modestly dressed village or country people kneeling at the priest's command and mumbling the memorized sounds of Latin prayers, so obviously unintelligible to them.

He was amazed. Some of them, particularly older women, seemed to put into their prayers such an intensity and fanatical ardor that he knew would be impossible for him to feel or even fake. What was the source of that ardor? Why did he not experience it?

"Faith!" the priest said during one of his sermons. "It is the essential ingredient of our life as Christians. Its strength lies in the fact that it does not depend on our faulty human reason. Reason is arrogance, the presumptuousness of finite creatures. Faith is from God."

Roberto felt confused. His father always said that human reason was the highest attribute of man. The teacher said that reason and a rational mind was what distinguished man from animals.

So why did the preacher say that man was better off without those attributes? And provided one wanted to have faith, how did one get hold of it? Roberto looked around. How could he distinguish between those who had faith and those who didn't?

And why were many of these people not as pious and contrite outside the church confines? Did they lose their faith as soon as they left the church? How could the owner of the grocery shop look so saintly here but cheat on the weight of the groceries, as Nonna discovered while checking her shopping on her precision scales at home? Or their neighbor Mrs. Zini, who had the look of a martyr just now, but was known to raid the neighboring gardens and orchards of early fruits and vegetables at night? And who had told the fascist about the old copper pitcher? Or the farmer who was caught adding water to the wine he sold? Did God prize faith—which, according to the priest, was the highest attribute—more than honesty, generosity, sincerity, and other human qualities? What was so special about faith if it came entirely from outside?

"*Errare humanum est*," said the priest. If it could all be excused because "it is human to err," then what was the point? Besides, one could see from the vacuous expression of the faces around that no one knew what that meant anyway. Perhaps they could surmise by the tone and expression of the priest that the Latin phrase connoted resignation to the human imperfection and therefore forgiveness, and they shook their heads in submissive unison.

Does God understand only Latin, he wondered. How did the farmers and townsfolk know what they were saying in their prayers? Or what they were told by the priest? Did all these people, including his nonna, really believe that prayers were more effective than bomb shelters? Was she accepting the "faith" notion as well? Somehow, it was all so confusing, but though his inner questions remained unanswered, he trusted his intuition and felt that, in time, he would find his own suitable answer.

Intermittently, everyone joined in singing the hymns, and, at the height of the ceremony, the swelling tide of notes and chants penetrated the thick walls of the church and flooded into the neighboring streets and piazzas. When the organ fell silent, the sole, delicate voice of a violin floated among the stony heights of the church. Its notes, light as a butterfly playing among the flowers, glided over the faux-marble columns and the plump stucco cherubs, and then slowly descended, like the white petals of an almond tree, over the lowered heads of the attending crowd.

Roberto listened in delight. The joyful voice didn't speak to him of sins, pains, repentance, and death. To him, that pure, restful sound was a message of pleasure, joyfulness, and life.

Nearby, two women whispered to each other, clearly untouched by the beautiful melody. They talked about tomorrow's market; the price of chicken; the scarcity of meat, milk, coffee, and sugar. Roberto threw a nasty look toward them, and when the melody was repeated, he covered his eyes. He did not pray, but let his soul fly away with the notes, envisioning sunny beaches along the ocean, pine trees swaying in the summer breeze, glowing sunsets over mountain crests …

*****

A few days later, Luisa was returning from the cemetery after taking fresh flowers to her husband's grave.

"Where is your mother?" she asked Roberto, who was playing in the garden.

"Upstairs, Nonna. She is ironing some clothes."

"Don't wander off; we are going to have lunch soon."

She had barely climbed the stairs when Roberto heard a distant rumble. He stopped playing to search the sky. At first, he couldn't see anything. Finally, barely visible at the far horizon, he saw them like a flock of silvery birds advancing in his direction.

"Nonna … Mamma … airplanes!" he immediately called, and the two women rushed outside.

Fortunately, a week or so earlier, a shelter had been built at the confluence of two draining ditches, not far behind the Lanzis' property. It had been a strange experience for Roberto, who, hearing some shouts, had run to the end of the orchard to see what was happening. He crossed under the vineyard line that marked the property border and saw half a dozen men and women standing around the draining ditch with spades and shovels. They were yelling at a farmer, obviously the owner of the property.

"You fucking idiot," said one, "we know it's not our land. We're not taking it away, are we? We're just building a goddamned shelter for everyone."

"We are not stealing anything," said a woman. "We're only trying to stay alive."

"You're not gonna do it on my fuckin' property," the farmer protested.

"This is the deepest and most suitable ditch around. It is central to most of our houses, and we'll do it right here."

"Over my goddamn dead body, you will."

"So be it," shouted a middle-aged man, who had quietly observed the scene from the side. He threw the shovel to the ground and advanced toward the farmer, who came at him with fury. A fight broke out.

Everyone seemed taken by surprise. In the few seconds that followed, Roberto captured a sequence of images: the farmer frothing at the mouth; women standing aside, pale and startled; frightened children crying and clutching their mothers' legs and skirts; spades and shovels lying on the ground. Then the fight was over, with the farmer obviously subdued by the smaller man.

"He was a wrestler in his youth," someone whispered. "He could've hurt him if he wanted to." Other people soon intervened.

"The steam is off the kettle," said an older man. "Let's try to reason this out."

"It won't be any good to you," they said to the farmer, while helping him on his feet, "if you are killed by bombs."

The farmer wiped his bleeding nose and finally conceded. He helped excavate the ditches deeper. Then they placed wooden planks across the top and covered them with about three feet of compressed earth.

"Don't worry," they told him, "at war's end we'll help you put it back as it was."

It was the first time that Roberto had experienced violence at close quarters.

Today, the Lanzis hurried toward the shelter, followed by the Gianis and other passersby who were caught in the open and were urged to follow.

Roberto hurried toward the end of the pit, and after a few moments, everyone was inside. The heavy overhead portal was pulled shut, and darkness was complete.

Overhead, loud explosions that made the earth tremble—causing Roberto to hold his breath, as if waiting to discover if he was still alive—punctuated the whining sound of falling bombs. Then the litanies and lamentations started, sprinkled at times by thankful comments, for the sudden realization that yet another volley had spared their lives.

Some of the older women mumbled prayers; others cried or muttered broken phrases.

"Oh my God, save us from this inferno."

"Oh, Madonnina Santa, look after us."

"My poor husband went downtown; I hope he is safe somewhere."

"I don't remember if I closed my door …"

As his eyes adjusted to the darkness, Roberto began to distinguish the opaque oval faces of people sitting across from him on the step carved out of the mud wall. They seemed like faces without bodies, floating in midair. He searched for Lucia, but saw that she had been pushed far away. He kept his head turned toward her, as the woman beside him continued to pray and cry, the foul breath exhaling from her mouth making him want to throw up.

Fear was in every voice, and every word or invocation seemed to hang in the thick air like a curse. Suddenly, Patrizia began to sing:

> *Partirono le rondini,*
> *dal mio paese triste e senza sole,*
> *cercando primavera di viole,*
> *sogni d'amore e di felicità …*

> *Departed are the swallows,*
> *From my cheerless land without sun.*
> *They're looking for springtime and violets,*
> *Dreams of love and happiness …*

Softly at first, and then with her full soprano voice, the lyrics and the joyful sound forced through the space and seemed to push away the fear and desolation that had filled the refuge only moments earlier. It felt so strange that everyone fell silent for a moment. They seemed stunned. Then Luisa joined in the singing, and others followed, even Roberto, and soon a new confidence seemed to fill everyone with hope and courage; his mother had broken the spell.

Finally, when the stillness outside indicated that the raid had passed, the lid was pushed aside, and people began to spew out from the underground with renewed hope. The immediate danger had passed.

"Let's go. Let's see if our home is all right," someone said.

The undaunted sun was shining in the blue sky, but a dark mushroom-shaped cloud rose near the bridge.

411

"They missed again!" yelled an old man on a bike pedaling away from the town. "The bridge still stands, but some bombs fell on the Riccioni apartments nearby ... and also downtown. Many dead there."

The chorus of *Mamma, Madonna,* and *Oh God* started again. Roberto could not help wondering if God had allowed only sinners to die, or if, like previous times, innocents had been killed as well.

He remembered the saying "For one sinner, the whole ship will sink," and he was mystified that most people thought it divine "justice."

At home, there were a few unpleasant surprises, but no major damage. Some of the windowpanes were shattered, pots and pans cluttered the kitchen floor, and the handblown glass of an old gas lamp had disintegrated around its metal stand.

The women began to clean up, and Roberto, after helping pick up some of the larger glass and china fragments, returned to the garden. Several pieces of shrapnel were scattered on the ground, and he stooped to pick one up. Its heat shocked him, but its ragged iridescent edges captivated him. He heard chattering and saw a crowd gather around a large crater no more than forty yards from the house. His nonna peeked from the first-floor window to observe the scene, and he heard her exclaim, "That was close!"

"Too close for me," echoed Patrizia decisively, behind Luisa.

"Why do you say it like that, Mother?" Roberto asked, detecting a collateral meaning in his mother's tone.

"Because, as your father predicted a long time ago, I am afraid we will have to leave the house. Find a safer place."

"And where would we go?" he asked. The thought scared him, but he wanted to appear brave.

"Somewhere in the country. I don't know for sure yet. I will discuss it with nonna; she has an idea."

The German occupation forces reacted immediately in the days following the raid. Using the undamaged bridge, they evacuated men and light equipment from their position at the southern part of the river. At twilight, several Tiger tanks crossed at the west bend of the river, where the water was no more than a foot high. They climbed the high right banks, leaving behind the deep marks of their tracks.

Though it seemed unlikely that the Americans would hit the bridge soon, the Germans made sure they were not going to be trapped on the other side. They began to fortify the north side, digging machine gun nests and mortar emplacements along the riverbank and establishing fulcrum points in the old Medici mill and nearby farmhouses. One area command post was established in an old villa, three kilometers from the Arno Line. Batteries of 88 caliber cannons and spotters were spread atop the woody hills that ran parallel to the river five or six kilometers to the north. In just a few hours, all the strategic movements had been accomplished in total order, and far too quickly for the Americans to impede them.

"Where are the Allies when you need them?" someone said.

"Allies? Why do we call them allies, anyway?" said an older woman. "So far, I'd bet they have killed more Italians than Germans!"

The area between the Arno and the hills fell immediately under complete German control. Whatever was left of the so-called "local authorities" had disappeared. A new type of soldier, yet unseen in those parts, was now amidst the regular *Wehrmacht* contingent, soon becoming part and parcel of a new, greater fear. They were the infamous SS brigades, easily recognized for the stylized double *S* and the skull symbol they wore on their uniforms, as well as the ferocity of their actions. They were responsible for the repression of the Naples uprising. They were also guilty of the Fosse Ardeatine massacre, near Rome, where they shot 335 innocent people. This last action was a reprisal to avenge the death of 32 German soldiers killed in Rome's Via Frattina by a bomb detonated by anonymous Italian insurgents.

Presently, among other unsavory activities, they were hunting for Italian males of military age. Those who were caught out of uniform, with or without plausible validation, were arrested and never seen again.

An evacuation order was posted at the town hall and on many other walls around town. No one knew for sure if it applied to the town and its immediate countryside, or only to the front line area adjacent to the river.

During the following days, all along the Arno Line, the remainder of the German army, which had retreated across the river, marched in a northerly direction. It was a continuous thin line of foot soldiers, loaded with knapsacks with dangling cantinas, tools, armament, and a host of other assorted equipment.

Some of them were only carrying shoulder weapons, having thrown their belongings over horses, farm carts, wheelbarrows, bikes, or other strange implements all stolen or, as officially characterized, "requisitioned" along the way. People who lived along the main road witnessed the passing of this endless procession either from a distance or hidden behind the semi-closed windows of their houses. Others, like Pia Zini or Luisa—if for completely different reasons—openly watched the retreat from the front of their respective gardens.

Pia, waving her scarf, shouted encouragingly, "Come back soon! Bring back victory …"

Luisa, leaning forward over the laurel edge, derisively echoed each phrase with, "Yes, in the stolen wheelbarrows. Of course, and don't forget the bikes!"

Roberto feared the soldiers would take exception to his nonna's open exultance for their retreat and report her to the authorities or take her away. He remembered hearing about the linseed oil "purge," the beatings, and worse. He knew that, as mother put it, in matters concerning her principles, his nonna was capable of exaggeration. He also remembered the fight she put up when, months earlier, two Blackshirts had come to the house to recommend that she, like all good citizens, should fly the flag to honor the anniversary of "Conciliation Day." In spite of her Christian beliefs and affiliation to the church, she had never approved of the reconciliation between the Holy See and the fascist regime, which, in her own words, was like getting into bed with the devil.

"I would have nothing to do with it," she shouted to the fascists. And not satisfied with just a simple refusal, she chased them off of her property, slammed the gate behind them, and for the next ten minutes, shouted her disapproval for "the hypocrisy of the Roman Curia, the Pope, and all those … *black-robed* men of God …" Then she added under her breath, "So to speak."

"Nonna," he now called, pulling her gently away from the laurel edge, "let's go, please. I need help with my homework."

She turned around hesitantly. She seemed to resist the request, but then she read the worried stare in the boy's eyes.

"All right," she finally conceded. Her body, which had gradually stiffened during her heated discussion, seemed to relax. She took Roberto by the hand and turned around. "You are right, my sweet boy. Let's go home."

*****

That night, as both Luisa and Patrizia were about to go to bed, they heard a noise. It seemed produced by a hard object hitting the Persian shutter of the kitchen door. The two women looked at each other in silence.

"What can it be?" Luisa whispered.

The shutter was hit again, and this time they distinctly heard the sound of a stone bouncing back on the terrace floor and then rolling down the stairs.

"Switch off the oil lamp, Mother," said Patrizia, approaching the door. She then unlocked it and cracked it open. "Who is it?" she whispered.

"It's me, Patrizia ... Antonio," said a voice from the garden.

She opened the shutter, and in the moonlight, she observed the dark outline of a man abandoning the protective shadow of a tree and approaching the terrace. "Please come out," said the man from below the terrace.

"Stay put, Mother," said Patrizia, closing the shutter behind her and moving to the terrace. The man remained at ground level, and she bent down, below the banister, to see him through the ornamental pilasters. "You're not Antonio," she said.

"No, *signora*, I'm his comrade. I mentioned his name to get you out here without delay. I'm risking my life."

"What can I do for you?"

"I've got something for you," the man said, opening his coat. A shiny metal object came into view. Patrizia experienced a moment of trepidation seeing an automatic pistol tucked under his belt.

"Here," said the man, pulling a large envelope from an inside pocket. "We got hold of this a few weeks ago. It took us some time to verify identity and address and pass it through the lines. It's your husband's journal."

"Riccardo's?" Patrizia exclaimed. "Is he alive? Is he well?"

"We don't know that, *signora*. He was when he gave this envelope to an officer who claims to be his friend. He was trying to deliver it to you when … the partisans took him prisoner. This was over a year ago; we don't know what happened to your husband since."

"How can I find out more?" Patrizia asked, clutching the envelope. "Can you suggest anything?"

"Not at this moment, signora, but we are still communicating with people. I'll keep an ear open. Now I must run; I am on the wanted list."

"Thanks," Patrizia whispered. "Do you need anything? Are you hungry? Do you need to rest?"

"Thanks. No. Perhaps another time. By the way, keep this matter to yourself, as we are all at risk."

She pushed her arm through the pillars, and the man held her hand for a long instant, warmly.

"Good-bye," he then said, and quickly reentered the shadow, disappearing beyond the laurel edge.

It all seemed so unreal. Patrizia stared for a moment at the space vacated by that mysterious person; then she looked at the worn-out package in her hand and swiftly went back inside.

"You can light the lamp again, Mother," she said in a hushed voice.

"Who was it?" Luisa asked.

"I don't know, exactly. Antonio's comrade, he said. He gave me this," she said, tearing the outside paper. "He said it's Riccardo's journal."

"Oh my God. Riccardo?"

"Yes, Mother, I recognize it. It's the one I gave him when he left."

Both women sat down beside each other, and Patrizia flipped the cover open and began to read:

Spring, 1943

My dearest Patrizia, Roberto, Mother:

I hope you will receive this note together with the diary you gave me at my departure; such a long time ago! Since then, I've lived of memories. Cherished images that I rewind and play in the reels of my mind any time I need the strength to continue. You, Roberto, Mother, have been in my mind and in my heart every day and night, and will continue to be there for as long as I live.
I hope the moment will soon come for this crazy war to end and

for me to rejoin you and share your love in a lasting peace. I miss you all and I pray that the dangers of war will remain as far as possible from our home.

I don't know if or when I'll have another opportunity to communicate with you, but I'll try my best. Please keep in good spirit and spare a prayer for an old soldier, and one for my brother.

All my love,

Riccardo

Both women fell silent, looked at each other, and fell into a spontaneous embrace.

"I knew he was alive," said Luisa, drying her eyes.

"I hope so, Mother," Patrizia replied.

Half an hour later, they had gone through about half the journal.

"It still reeks," said Patrizia, smelling the pages. "It must have been in a fire; some of the sheets are burned at the edges."

Luisa sat in silence while Patrizia got up to get a glass of water. "Are you tired, Mother?" she asked.

"Read on, please, I'm all right. I want to hear what happened after El Alamein."

A moment later, Patrizia started again:

November 8, 1942

The Ariete Division, the most senior fighting unit in Africa, has been encircled and destroyed at about five kilometers from Bir El Abd.

419

Even the German High Command recognized the valor of this unit, which, given the deficient armament, had always given more than seemed humanly possible. The few survivors march on foot through endless stretches of desert, without arms, food, or water, under constant harassment from the air and from the ground.

Berlin and Rome have launched the joint radio decree of "Victory or death."

"Victory or death!?"

We hear through the grapevine that Rommel has no intention of heeding to this lunatic appeal. He doesn't want to see the total destruction of his remaining Panzergruppe—another Stalingrad catastrophe. He has ordered a strategic retreat.

Had he done it twenty-four hours earlier, many men and much equipment would have been saved.

We travel mostly after sundown, thankful for the occasional moonless night that prevents the Allies from bombing us all the way to the next defensive line. Grateful as well for the heavy rain that precludes those hunting us from surrounding our lines.

Nonetheless, it is carnage all the same as many more men are killed on the road, by mines, air strikes, and cannon shells. Since I usually travel at the rear of my battalion, my path is invariably littered with burned-out tanks and vehicles, charred corpses, and other relics of war. The men are left where they fall. No time for a decent burial or even a prayer.

They will remain there, and vultures and jackals will desecrate their bodies. Then the blowing sand will cover what's left of their mortal remains. Sometimes it is evident that the cadavers, their throats and faces torn to shreds by scavenging beasts, have also been robbed of their guns and personal belongings by marauding Arabs.

I've ordered my men to shoot looters on sight.

May God forgive me!

November 9, 1942

The Americans have landed in Northwest Africa, Morocco, and Algeria. Now we will be attacked from two sides.

Not even with Rommel's bravery and brilliant strategies will we be able to bear the brunt of their industrial power.

I hope our … leaders will see the futility of our sacrifices and put an end to our tribulations.

December 19, 1942

These days, we seem to receive just enough fuel to manage a retreat, always with the British on our heels.

Today we reached the position of Buerat. The entire front risks collapse. We are badly outgunned, short of fuel and food. We even lack basic transport vehicles, and the British are getting stronger every day. The rapport with the Germans—always strained at best—is now getting worse; we no longer trust each other.

As of today, all our troops are behind the lightly fortified position of Buerat. It is surprising that with all the equipment and manpower available, the British have not even tried to force the line.

January 3, 1943

We are crossing again the desolate region of the Grande Sirte. Here is where my African journey began, and here is where it will probably end. This time, we are moving in a westerly direction, most likely for the last time, for at the end of the line, the Americans and the remaining French forces shall meet us.

Will we have time to escape?

When the time comes, I hope I will be among the first to be evacuated and return to Italy.

I miss my family.

January 10, 1943

Despite the risk on the west, and despite the unrealistic views from Rome, we must move our foot soldiers westward, exactly as we did at Mersa El Brega, or face the risk that they fall victim to an immediate British encirclement from the south.

Resist on this front for another month, the politicians ask. They don't understand that the retreat will be determined by Montgomery and not by their wishful thinking. Fortunately for us, the British general is more cautious than brave, and often gives us more time than necessary.

The front has been calm in the last few days while we build new fortifications. I've used this welcome break to explore the terrain and memorize its configuration in order to find better defense lines or escape routes when that becomes necessary.

During one of these excursions, we came across the ancient Roman city of Leptus Magna. I must confess that I didn't remember when it was built or by whom.

One of my officers, a history professor in his civilian life, took us through the remains of the city—temples, statues, squares, theaters. For a few hours, I was able to forget about war. I wish my little Roberto were with me, asking his usual questions.

January 20, 1943

The pressure has started again, and again we retreat. Last night, from my position on a hill north of Tarhuna, I heard the reverberation of the explosions from Tripoli. Before abandoning the city, German engineers mined the harbor facilities and all its major equipment and arsenals. Despite Rome's dogged requests for further resistance (with which men? with what equipment?), the position there had become untenable.

Often, coming across those towns and places we passed by last year, I cannot avoid comparing the hopes of those days with our feelings now. Not that I've ever been convinced that the final outcome would be in our favor.

However, the enthusiasm of victories, transitory that it be, temporarily puts out of our mind the inevitable eventual ending.

It's human nature; who can possibly consider or fret about next week's storm forecast, when today is bright and sunny?

February 16, 1943

Three days ago, together with the rearguard of the 15th German

*Division, we reached the terrain adjacent to the defensive position
of Mareth. The Germans, taking advantage of the inexperienced
Americans in this theater, attacked their lines.*

The strategy worked.

*My unit supported the attack with artillery, and after the battle,
I visited the battlefield. Many American tanks were destroyed or
disabled. Some of those Lee, Grant, and Sherman tanks were filled
with smoke and still burning. Some had wounded or dead soldiers
still inside.*

*We moved to the town of Gafsa, just evacuated by the Americans.
Bands of Arabs had preceded us and were looting the buildings
abandoned by the military. Before leaving, the Americans had blown
up the ammunition dump in the citadel of Gafsa without advising
the civilian population, and the gigantic concussion caused about
thirty-five homes to crash over their inhabitants. The bodies of over
forty Arabs (old men, women, children) were extracted from the
rubble and left rotting in the sun.*

*My thoughts went to my family; they too may suffer from similar
circumstances. I mustn't think of this, as it would destroy my hopes.*

*Inspecting damaged armament and tanks left behind by the
Americans, I had the opportunity to assess and verify their splendid
equipment. Besides the overall superior quality—especially compared
with the Italian equipment—what I found particularly impressive
is the consolidation of their transport vehicles with the unification
of spare parts. Parts that can be interchangeably used in different
models, therefore facilitating repairs with a minimum inventory.*

*I wonder if this is a distinct American trait, or if they based this
manufacturing organization on the experience of the British in this
theater.*

February 21, 1943

*We have attacked the Americans and created a break in their line
of defense. They have abandoned the Kasserine Pass.*

We now proceed toward Thala.

*However, after losing some ground to the lightning thrust of the
motorized German brigades, the Americans and the British quickly*

*reorganized their forces. Their lines are now too strong, and we must
desist.*

We return to Kasserine.

*These, I think, are the last moves we have left. The bulk of the
Italian corps—its superior officers dead or escaped to Italy—is by now
prisoner, or completely exhausted and ready to surrender.*

In Rome and Berlin, they are still waiting for a miracle!

*Even the Germans, although still a significant fighting unit, are
being squeezed by the pincer-like movements of the Allies, who are
too strong and well armed to resist. Only the vast experience of their
generals and field commanders have kept the DAK together as a
fighting force. Soon, however, they will have to evacuate this theater
or be destroyed by the overwhelming Allied forces.*

March 15, 1943

*General Bastico (called "Bombastico" by the troops) has renounced
the command of whatever is left of the Italian-African contingent and
has returned to Italy.*

*General Cabalero will soon leave as well. None too soon, I
think. For as adequate as he may be as a desk officer, he is certainly
unimpressive on the battlefield. The losses at El Alamein could have
been minimized had he given a timely order to reposition our troops
as soon as obviously necessary.*

"Goddamned armchair generals!" Luisa cried out.

"Bastards!" Patrizia exclaimed.

Had they known the details of the last encounter between Riccardo
and the reviled general, they would have had harsher remarks.

April 1943

I believe the Germans, although burdened by the same restraints and problems as us, are preparing to evacuate the remainder of their army in order to save the salvageable. In the final hour, they'll abandon what's left of the Italian contingent to its destiny.

In the meantime, we retreat toward the northeast corner of Tunisia. Soon, unless we are dead, we'll have no other alternative but to surrender.

May 6, 1943

Finally, the Americans are attacking near Medjez el Bab. I say "finally" because, at this point, a quick physical death on the battlefield would be better than the slow psychological one we undergo every day.

They have opened with a deadly artillery barrage, followed by air bombardments of an intensity never seen before.

These soldiers from the New World are unencumbered by useless theories and traditions, and they seem to possess a good dose of practical sense. This, plus their vast assortment of armament and equipment, makes them particularly suited to the exigencies of a modern war.

(This seems to confirm my opinion that the future will be determined not by the people with the most illustrious and ancient traditions, but by those with natural resources, modern laboratories, and an efficient industrial apparatus.)

P.S. It strikes me as ironical that the fate of Mussolini's new Roman Empire will be sealed exactly where Rome obliterated its ancient enemy, the Carthagineans, in the year 146 BC.

May 8, 1943

Everyone in the field now understands that the end is near. Only in Rome and Berlin do a few people, devoid of morals and intellect, still act as if wishful thinking were a suitable substitute for weapons and equipment … as if unworkable orders were a valid surrogate for strategy. We have lost tens of thousands of men. We have little water, gasoline, ammunitions.

Since El Alamein, we have fought an enemy infinitely better armed and equipped than we, but we were forced to do it with the plans and myopia of incompetent people—politicians a continent away from the war theater, with strategies and delays dictated by their own political necessity, unrealistic desires, lack of common sense and vision.

May 10, 1943

We have received news that the 15th German Division has been totally destroyed. Our flank is now completely open, and nothing is left between us and the advancing Allied troops.
I am sure that this is the end.
It is sad to think of all the youth needlessly sacrificed over the sandy shores of Africa. Even sadder, in this fatal hour, is hearing our leaders shout over the airwaves (from the safety of their shelters): "Resist! Resist! Resist!"

Patrizia read the last phrase and took a sip of water, but she had difficulty swallowing it. Her throat seemed to have suddenly shut. There was silence inside her soul and silence outside. Beside her, Luisa cried noiselessly. She understood the pains her son must have endured, and only tears seemed to give her some kind of relief.

"Thank you, Patrizia," she whispered at last. "Thanks for reading it to me. I'm going to my room now. I'll go and pray."

"Good night, Mother. I'm going to bed as well. By the way," she said, spinning on her heels, "not a word to Roberto for now. There isn't much we could tell him. And the little there is," she added sadly, "it's better if he doesn't know."

"I agree, Patrizia," Luisa answered after a moment. "Good night."

Patrizia closed her bedroom door, but she did not turn on the light. She threw herself over the bed and clutched the journal against her body. She pressed her hands over the pliant cover as if it were his hands, caressing it as if it were his skin. "Riccardo," she repeated over and over. "Riccardo *mio*."

With her mind's eye, she followed his journey, imagining a two-thousand-kilometer-long trail over the desert, the battles, the dangers, the casualties. Her eyes open, she stared into the darkness as if expecting to see him appear. She tapped a spot beside her, as she had the first time by the river. "Sit here beside me, my love," she said, her voice choked with emotion. "You'll tell me all your troubles, and then we'll make love."

After a long, long while, she finally fell asleep, and then she awoke with a shiver. She was cold, and she slipped under the covers without undressing, the journal tightly tucked under her body.

- XXXVIII -

The following week, the Germans issued additional orders; the hours and parameters of free circulation were further reduced. It was verboten to assemble in public places or hold any kind of meeting except for church services. It was absolutely verboten to approach the riverbanks. No one could cross the Arno River. German soldiers now guarded both sides of the bridge. Tanks were positioned nearby, in the shadows of the horse chestnut trees, with camouflage nets and tree branches completing their concealment.

One morning, Luisa and Patrizia were picking vegetables in the back garden. Roberto had come down the side stairs, jumping several steps at a time, and now held the basket where tomatoes, green beans, and eggplants were nestled. He took a ripe tomato and placed it under his nose. He liked its subtle smell, fostered by the warmth of the sun. He put it back in the basket and rubbed a large eggplant. "Such smooth skin and beautiful color!" he exclaimed.

"Yes, but you don't like them," his mother said.

"It's the last crop for this season," said Luisa, probing under the leaves of bean plants for hidden ones. It has been a good one, though."

"We still have some potat—" Patrizia couldn't finish her sentence. A prolonged explosion shook the earth, and the windowpanes vibrated within their frames. There were no airplanes in the sky.

"What on earth was that?" Luisa said.

Roberto placed the basket on the ground and ran to the front garden, with the two women following. They looked toward Castelvecchio and then toward the bridge, but no smoke was visible there. They looked all around, but no trace of bombs was detectable.

"Did you hear that?" yelled a man going by with his bicycle.

"We certainly did," Luisa replied. "But what was it and where?"

"I haven't the faintest idea," replied the man, continuing on his way, "but it seemed to come from around the train station."

At those words, Patrizia climbed the stairs of the front terrace, a presentment painted over her face suddenly drained of color. She looked south, and Roberto saw her cover her mouth with her hand as if to stop a cry. Her face was suddenly pallid, her eyes filled with astonishment.

He ran up the stairs and took her hand. "What is it, Mother?" he asked.

She did not reply. She took him under his arms. "Climb here," she whispered, helping him on top of the banister of the terrace. "Can you see the chimneys of the distillery?"

He looked toward San Romano. "No, Mother," he said, "there's a cloud of smoke where they used to be."

"They have blown the place up with mines," she said. "That's what those explosions were." She shook her head in dismay, shattered by the realization. She thought of the time and effort Riccardo had spent there, his successes, his hopes for the future. Now everything was reduced to a pile of rubble. And with the distillery gone, so were their jobs. Would they rebuild it after the war? If not, what then?

"Poor, Riccardo, "Luisa moaned. "If he only knew." Tears were falling down her cheeks. "His dreams all up in smoke."

Roberto looked at the two women and felt a knot in his stomach. "I hate war," he said, running toward the back of the house.

In the following days, other facilities of actual or presumed strategic value were razed to the ground. Finally, the last of the German troops, who had remained behind to attend to these destructions, mined the main roads and evacuated the area south of the river. As soon as they arrived on the north side, they attended to the positioning of machine gun nests and mortars and then started to dig L-shaped trenches in strategic positions. Others proceeded to requisition all the farmhouses adjacent to, and protected by, the massive riverbanks. Hundreds of additional German soldiers poured into the town and took over public buildings and private homes for lodgings, often chasing away the owners or rightful occupants. The officers were billeted in the larger, more comfortable houses or villas spread through the countryside. A larger red flag, centered by a black swastika, now hung from the pennant of the city hall—and sentries with submachine guns guarded the four main entrances of the town. Castelvecchio had suddenly acquired the look of a German town. A cavalry contingent took over the football field. The soldiers tied their horses to the wrought iron rings that hung from the walls, and raised field tents in the middle of the turf.

Roberto could see the soldiers from his classroom window, moving around the field, tending or exercising their horses, or washing themselves in a large metal basin, their bare torsos shining in the midday sun. On his way home from school, he now often encountered platoons marching to or from the main square or entering one of the intersecting side streets roofed by archways tunneled under the older tenements of the town, called *chiassi.*

Sometimes he even stopped to watch those soldiers in olive green uniforms march, and listen to their rhythmic cadence. The sound of their booted feet, striking the paving stones, echoed and magnified under the *chiassi,* transforming it into a menacing thunder.

One day, as he was playing in the garden, Roberto noticed several German officers sitting under the pergola of the Zinis' garden. They were playing various musical instruments and merrily singing what sounded like German songs. Pia Zini and her daughter Fernanda mingled about and seemed to enjoy their company. The older woman was serving them a strange-smelling brew. "That's the best I can do," Roberto heard her say. "It's a long time since we saw real coffee around here." Roberto learned from his mother that those officers were billeted there.

"Thank God the Germans haven't come to our house yet," Luisa said. "I would find it impossible to live with them."

*****

Patrizia thought of her husband, imagining him in the same state as those soldiers, or even worse—perhaps prisoner, corralled like an animal in a stretch of desert enclosed by barbed wire, with little food or clothes. Poor Riccardo, what he must have been through since the end of the African campaign. Such a long time had passed, over two years already. Sometimes one of his last phrases echoed ominously in her mind: *And if I shouldn't return …*

"They are just men with a different uniform, Mother," she finally said in a moment of compassion.

Luisa did not reply.

*****

A few days later, a Volkswagen car stopped in front of the house, and three officers and a local fascist came up the stairs.

"These officers will need to stay here," said the fascist.

Clearly afraid to betray her feelings, Luisa walked away and slammed the door behind her. It was up to Patrizia, after a fruitless argument, to show them around and come up with an accommodation that would allow the reduced family quarters to be separate and independent from the Germans. "They can use the front stairways," she said to the fascist. "The key is already in the door."

The man related the matter to his comrades in what sounded like a hesitant, stumbling translation, which was nonetheless acknowledged by *Ja* and *Jawohl.*

One of the soldiers lifted the picture of Riccardo in uniform that rested on the piano. "Artillery officer," he said. And then, observing it more closely: "Afrika Korp," he added.

Dated March 14, 1941, it was an enlargement of Riccardo's ID card photo.

"My husband," Patrizia said.

She took the picture away from the German and held it for a long moment. Memories tore at her relentlessly. At times, the hope that grew inside her seemed too large for her heart to bear.

*****

When the fascist left, Roberto left the room and looked for his nonna. He found her in her bedroom, kneeling on the floor, her elbows resting on top of her bed, her head inclined toward the picture of the Madonna that hung over the far wall.

"Dear Mother of Jesus," he heard her plead, "please help us in this desperate hour."

"Nonna," he said, placing his hand on her shoulder. "Don't worry, we will be all right."

She made the sign of the cross, turned around, and hugged him. "You're such a considerate boy," she said, pulling herself up. "Your father would be proud of you."

The Germans picked up their rucksacks and personal weapons and moved into their agreed lodgings, consisting of kitchen, corridor, two bedrooms, and the attic. The Lanzis had the front hall with two adjacent bedrooms and the subterranean floor with its small kitchen.

The movements of the soldiers could be heard through doors and heating vents.

"The scent of their sweaty clothes and unwashed socks has infiltrated the entire house," Luisa lamented. "It's an alien odor for this house. It incessantly reminds me of their presence. I can't stand it."

Roberto could smell it too as soon as he entered the front hall, but he didn't say anything for fear of aggravating his grandmother.

The soldiers usually left the house early in the morning and returned toward the evening. At night, they could be heard talking and laughing or pacing in the adjacent rooms. Sometimes they played records on what sounded like an old Pianola or sang. Once, when she could no longer stand their noise, Patrizia started to play the piano herself. She started humming a song and then began singing at full voice. She had not played much since Riccardo's departure.

Suddenly, there was silence from the other side. Then there was a knock on the door that separated them from the German quarters. They didn't answer at first. There was a second, more insistent knock, and Roberto looked at his mother. She nodded, and he unlocked it. Roberto observed with some trepidation the three soldiers advance into the family room and toward the piano. One of them was shirtless, while the other two wore open shirts outside their olive green uniform pants. Their sleeves were rolled up above the elbows, and the one with dark hair had his suspenders dangling from his pants. Luisa, sitting in a corner knitting, glanced at them from above her glasses. Roberto saw her grab a large knitting needle as if it were a weapon.

Patrizia continued to sing:

> *Vieni, c'è una strada nel bosco,*
> *Il su nome conosco, vuoi conoscerlo tu?*
>
> *Come, there's a path in the forest …*

When she finished her song, the soldiers applauded. "*Gut, gut!*" they exclaimed. "*Sehr gut.*" They gestured that she continue, and the blond shirtless one went around the piano, closer to Patrizia. Roberto felt his body tense, wondering what he would do. The soldier bent forward and turned the page of the music book.

Patrizia, her body erect and seemingly undistracted, rubbed her hands a moment and then started to play again. It was Mozart's *Eine kleine Nachtmusik*—slow, melodic, and more melancholic than other times she had played it. The three soldiers did not move or talk. They rested their sunburned hands on the piano, looking fixedly at Patrizia, their faces now covered by a veil of sadness. At the end of the piece, Patrizia did not stop. She played an arpeggio, and then switched to the leitmotif of a famous Italian song of the times.

Then she began to sing:

> *Mamma, solo per te la mia canzone vola …*
> *Mother, only for you soars my song …*

The soldiers were visibly affected by the words they recognized, and even more so by the evocative music and Patrizia's emotional interpretation. Homesickness and nostalgia could be read on their softened facial expressions. By the time of the finale, their eyes were glazed with tears. With the last notes still echoing in the air, Patrizia closed the piano and smiling softly said, "Good night." She pointed at Roberto, saying, "He must go to sleep now." She closed her eyes and bent her head over her joined hands. The soldiers understood and moved slowly toward their rooms.

"*Danke schön,*" uttered the youngest. "*Ja, danke,*" echoed the others.

Poor misguided souls, she thought. At that moment, with their uniforms and military badges removed and their cheerless countenance, rather than feared soldiers, they seemed ordinary young men, longing for their parents and their home.

That night, they heard no more music or talking from the German side.

*****

Days later, toward sunset, as the soldiers returned from their daily tasks, Patrizia looked at them from behind the Persian shutters. From their sunburned skin, she had already guessed that some of them might have been veterans of the African front. She thought of Riccardo and wondered what his appearance and state of mind might be by now: Humiliated by a defeat that he anticipated, or happy for it? Would he be in a field hospital? A POW camp? Dead or alive?

She heard the Germans going to the back, and she moved to the rear bathroom window to observe them. The one that looked the youngest had taken a spade from the tool shed and was walking toward the Gianis' property.

He returned shortly after, holding his shirt as a sack; it was full of potatoes. They started to peel them in the kitchen, where Luisa had given them a pan. She was about to leave when one of the soldiers started to eat some of the potatoes uncooked.

"Barbarians," she cried, slamming the door shut.

The situation was even worse for the Gianis. In addition to forcing them to accommodate several soldiers in their house, the Germans installed a large tent right in the middle of their backyard.

"That's just what we need," Erina said to Patrizia that afternoon.

"We might as well hoist a sign for the Americans and say, 'Please drop your bombs here!'"

"I know," Patrizia replied. "It's tough. Mother has just about had it too. She can't stand the thought of sharing her roof with them. During the Great War, they killed her husband and destroyed her house …"

"Yes, I know. What should we do, Patrizia?"

"Let's all meet at our place tonight. Come through the side door. Ask the other neighbors too. We'll come up with something."

Early that evening, several people gathered at the Lanzis' to discuss what action should be taken.

The last bombing raid, the total German takeover, the ensuing evacuation order and martial law, and finally, the forceful intrusion into their very lives had wiped out the last illusions about the relative safety of the village and its immediate neighborhood. Now some people suddenly remembered Luisa's past references to Riccardo's predictions.

"Your son was right, Luisa," Erina whispered. "We're going to be in the front line because of that darn river. We should have crossed to the other side when we were still able to. But … we didn't want to abandon our homes. They're all we have left."

They seemed to hang around Roberto's mother and grandmother as if they held the solution to their fears.

"Oh my God, Luisa," moaned a woman whose spouse was known to be a deserter. "What are we to do? My husband … I wish my husband were here. I don't know what to do. I am scared. I pray to God that …"

"Please stop whining," Patrizia hissed impatiently, "and leave your Heavenly Lord in peace. He can't help us; we've got to help ourselves."

Roberto looked at his mother, clearly puzzled. He seemed to think she had been too harsh with the old woman, who now cried quietly. He also observed Nonna's reproachful glance at his mother when she mentioned the Lord.

"You are not the only one," Patrizia added pointedly, "whose husband is not here to hold your hand. Mine went to the African front! Anyway," she said, in a lower, calmer voice, "one thing is for sure: it's too dangerous to remain here. We are too close to the bridge, too close to the main road. German vehicles and soldiers will be seen around our houses ... Sooner or later, we'll get fired on from the other side."

"But the meaning of the evacuation order is still unclear," commented Pia Zini. "Why should we leave our homes now? The Germans might counterattack, cross the river again, and the Americans might not—"

"Do us a favor, Pia," Patrizia snapped. "You can think whatever you want, but don't try to make us see things with your eyes. I don't care about politics; I have a child to think about. Anyway, if that is how you see it, why did you come?"

"You are right. I might as well go home."

Luisa opened the door and let her out, but remained a while longer near the window to hear Pia's receding steps. "We all know why she came," she said.

"Yes," said Erina, "to know what we were doing or where we're going."

"Anyway," Patrizia said, "we need to find a place away from obvious targets, somewhere deeper in the countryside. Anyone can do whatever is right for her family. My mind is made up." She stopped, as if searching for softer words than those that surfaced in her mind. "And then," she finally affirmed, "whatever will be, will be."

- IXL -

1944

Later that night, there was a light knock at the side door. Patrizia switched the light off and let Gemma and Erina Giani and her twelve-year-old daughter Lucia into the house. They had heavy coats, and the pockets seemed stuffed to capacity. Nina held a large bundle. "We are ready," she whispered. "No one else will be coming. Pia and Fernanda are still hoping for a German victory, and the Barsottis may come in a few days."

"The fewer the better," Patrizia said.

"I'll go wake Roberto," Luisa said.

He had been put to bed partially dressed. His nonna helped him into a light jacket, while Patrizia gathered the two bundles with clothes and other necessities prepared in advance. She gave a last-minute look inside them, to make sure she would be carrying the one with Riccardo's journal and his picture in uniform.

They could hear the muffled conversation of the Germans in the other rooms, and they moved quietly, walking barefooted to avoid detection. Luisa had a last look at the living room, her eyes sweeping over her cherished possessions: the piano Patrizia had brought from her house, the brown settee that Riccardo had purchased after his engagement at the distillery, and the milk glass oil lamp—the last and only thing remaining from her old bombed house. "Twenty years of hard work," she uttered sadly. "A lifetime."

Damn war! Now it even swept them away from the comfort of their home, the solace and familiarity of their hard-earned belongings.

Patrizia made it clear that she was of a similar mind, but even while it happened, she had already let on that she placed it in the past. She said that if they now wanted to have a future, they should be strong and only think of the immediate needs.

"Come on, Mother," she whispered, pulling gently on her arm. "We really must leave now. Our lives are more important. Besides, we will be back soon." Patrizia resisted the supine acceptance that suffering was an inescapable attribute of life, believing that such a mind-set would only serve to encourage life contrarieties. "This is only a temporary setback," she concluded. "You'll see, Mother."

Luisa's anguish seemed to subside at last. She tightened her black cotton shawl around her head, surveyed the room one last time, and lifting her eyes heavenward, she made the sign of the cross and bid the house good-bye.

They left by the side door, and before it was shut, a loud laugh crept through from the German side of the house. It was just a laugh, followed by a few high-pitched words, but at that moment, it sounded ominous. The women huddled quietly for a long instant, and Roberto held his breath to hear better.

"It's all right," he whispered. "They are just talking among themselves."

At the bottom of the stairs, they put on their shoes and moved stealthily toward the path in the back fields. At the end of the orchard, Luisa turned around once more and looked at the pale shape of the house. Roberto noticed her eyes shine with tears as she made the sign of the cross, spun on her feet, and walked away in the night.

She directed them toward a narrow opening in the vineyard, holding aside the bunch of green grapes that hung low. It was calm and clear, and an infinite number of bright stars punctured the sky above. Every now and then, the sound of a night bird or the flutter of its wings broke the silence. The only other sound was that of the cadenced, muffled steps of the small group on the damp ground.

"Let's move," Patrizia urged. "In less than an hour, the moon will rise, and we could be spotted by a patrol."

"Where we are going?" Gemma asked.

"We've decided to try the Banchini farm," Patrizia answered. "Luisa knows where it is; she gets something for her rabbits there. I've also seen these people a couple of times. They brought dregs to the distillery."

"They're decent people," Luisa said. "They won't refuse us for the night. Tomorrow we shall see ..."

They snuck across the field behind the Lanzis' house in a northerly direction. They walked in silence, one after the other, in the narrow and shallow ditch that divided two wheat fields, wrapped in the dark of the night, connected only by their anxiety and common determination to find a safer place.

*****

Roberto walked behind his grandmother and was closely followed by Lucia. He soon realized that he had never been so far in that direction. Everything seemed strange and unfamiliar. They were leaving their house, to go where? To do what? When would they be able to return? How would Father find them if he suddenly returned? How did his grandmother know where to go? He realized that without his mother and grandmother, he would be completely lost. "You are the man of the house," his father had told him, yet at this moment, he knew he was of little, if any, help.

He looked at his nonna with the light bundle and his mother with the heavier one. "Can I carry that?" he asked.

"No, thank you, cucciolo. I'm fine."

"And you, Nonna?"

"I'm fine too, Roberto," said Luisa, turning around, "but help me climb the ditch."

He promptly jumped up and pulled his nonna with all the strength he could muster. "Easy, boy," she said. "You'll pull my old arm off."

They had climbed the edge of a narrow, winding country road that seemed to disappear in the distance at either end. Everyone waited until Luisa said, "To the right. I know a shortcut."

Roberto tried to decipher the dark, mysterious world around him, wondering when they would return home.

He was now beside Lucia, holding her hand. As his mother had predicted, the moon rose silently from the far horizon. He noticed their dark shadows cast against the lighter gravel surface of the road. To him, it looked as if ghosts were following them, images that frightened him a little. After a while, he noted the long, thin shadows that seemed to be hinged to their feet slowly shorten, pivot to the left, and project images in line with their bodies.

"We've changed direction," he said.

"You are right," answered Lucia, looking back. "I didn't realize we had gone around a curve."

"Shhh," hushed Patrizia.

The appearance of the moon was an unwelcome witness to their escape. Roberto closed his eyes and inhaled deeply, detecting in the fresh night air the scent of the countryside: freshly mowed clover grass, rosemary bushes, strawberry grapes.

They walked in silence for what seemed a long time, and now they were facing a long stretch of straight road.

"Ouch," Lucia whispered. "I think I'm getting a blister on my heel."

"We're almost there," said Nonna Luisa. "See those tall trees in the distance? Behind there is the Banchini farm."

Roberto looked ahead, but all he saw was a dark, cloudy mass that was barely distinguishable from the shroud of the night.

As they approached, the barking of a guard dog broke the silence. He felt Lucia's hand squeeze his tighter.

"Don't worry," he said, discerning a metallic sound that went with the barking. "I think he is chained."

They passed the tree grove, and the farm appeared as a compact mass cut against the dark background of the distant hills. As they got closer, the huge dog barked angrily, jumping and straining on its hind legs. Luckily, as Roberto had guessed, its threat was held in check by a long chain looped to a steel cable that ran the width of the yard. Its barking became more menacing.

"Banchini," Luisa called out. "Banchini."

Shortly after, a man in a white undershirt opened a creaking window as the dog continued to bark. "Who's there?" he asked, his hoarse voice confirming the interruption of sleep.

"Gino, it's me, Luisa Lanzi."

"Tito," he then yelled to the dog, "shut up and don't bother them people."

When the dog quieted down, Gino listened to Luisa and told her that, given the hour, they would have to make do with the shed.

"By the morrow," he added, "we'll see if we can do somethin' better." He withdrew from the window and closed the shutter again.

The children huddled in the middle of the yard as the adults made some space in the shed.

Roberto looked around. He was tired, as he had never been up so late at night. He was confused by the unfamiliarity of his immediate surroundings. On the left of the vast yard were two buildings—equipment sheds, he thought. At the far end, three conical haystacks; and opposite of them, a water well with a brick wall about four feet high, with a winch on top.

"Let's get some straw," he heard Lucia's mother say.

As his nonna turned toward the strawstack, the dog moved with a simmering growl that echoed from the back of his throat. Then he jumped and barked furiously, yanking at his chain. On his hind legs, the dog seemed taller than the two women, who stopped and fell back a few paces. Lucia tightened her grip again, and Roberto wondered whether the chain was going to hold that huge, maddened dog.

Everyone except Patrizia seemed to freeze. She placed her bundle down and walked toward the beast. "Tito," she called with the calmest voice, "don't be a bad boy." She advanced slowly but without hesitation. "Quiet, boy, quiet! We're just going to get some hay."

To Roberto's surprise, she extended her hand, and the dog sniffed it. Then it quieted down and began to lick it. She clutched his thick leather collar, and with the other hand began to stroke his head.

"Now sit, you big naughty boy. That's it. I know, I know, you just want some attention."

She began to scratch his thick neck, and the dog lay flat on the ground. "That's it. That's my good boy." In the same soothing tone that she'd spoken to the dog, she said, "Now, Mother, walk slowly to the stack. Don't run or make any sudden moves."

Roberto was amazed. It was the third time in the last few days he had witnessed the surprising calm and confidence of his mother. He thought of her singing in the refuge, playing the piano and singing "Mamma" to the Germans, and now this! The presence of danger seemed to bring out qualities he did not know she possessed. Who else could think of singing as bombs fell from the sky? Who else could calm a mad unmuzzled dog like that? In these dangerous circumstances, he reasoned, she seemed to be even braver than his nonna! Perhaps there were many things about her that he didn't yet know or understand. The memory of the slap she had given him a long time ago did not seem to sting as much tonight.

"Are you sleepy?" Lucia asked, feeling his hand go limp.

"A bit," he confessed.

"What's that dark mass beyond the haystacks?"

"I don't know," he answered. "I can't make it out. It's a tall hedge or something."

"Come on children," Luisa called. "Let's try to get some sleep."

Given the circumstances, everyone welcomed the opportunity, even the spartan comfort of the makeshift beds. The floor of the shed was just compacted earth, and for Roberto and herself, Luisa made a nest of hay in a low cart found in a corner.

"This way, the kids won't be on the humid ground and close to insects," she said.

"Or nasty rodents," Patrizia added.

Roberto lay on his side with Lucia close beside him. He felt the warmth of her body and her hand over his shoulder. He liked that feeling and didn't even mind the prickly straw or the strange odor rising from the cart.

As he drifted off to sleep, two vague notions floated in his mind. One was the pleasantness of Lucia's proximity. The other was the fear that his mother and his nonna, good as they were, would be unable to negotiate the troubled waters ahead and eventually land him on a safe shore.

· XL ·

When Roberto awoke the next morning, he was aware of the pungent freshness of the air stinging his face and the sweet smell rising from his straw bed. He stirred without opening his eyes, and the strangeness of his bedding aroused memories of the night before. His arm instinctively pushed toward the space Lucia had occupied. It was empty. He sat, listening for cues. He heard her voice and that of another boy and rejoiced at the thought of playmates.

Brushing off the bits of hay sticking to his shirt and pants, he walked through the maze of farm implements. He heard the hustle and bustle of the grown-ups. It sounded as if they were moving furniture and rearranging things, perhaps making space to accommodate the newcomers, as Gino had promised. He reached the open yard and looked around. The early morning sunshine robbed the farm of its mystery and revealed its true peaceful nature. What had looked strange and unfathomable at night looked clear and inviting in the daylight.

The thick dark mass he had seen beyond the doghouse was a

section of river cane almost ten feet high. It swayed in the morning breeze, beckoning memories of family excursions to the Arno River. He, rushing down to select a sandy spot near the water, his father following with the food baskets, his mother helping Nonna Luisa down the steep incline.

The main building, though rudimentary compared to his home, had the definite charming character of many Tuscan farmhouses. Strongly built, it was painted in the typical yellow wash, with doors, window shutters, and the trim in dark green. An overhanging red clay roof stretched out to protect the outside stairway that ended at the top in a wide terraced space. It gave access to the living quarters on one side, and on the opposite, it opened to a view—by means of two arched windows—of a flat countryside that extended to the hills. The long south wall was interrupted at ground level by several massive doors, hinged directly on their gray stone frames.

These were the entrances to the stable, the wine cellar, and other utility rooms. A rustic bench carved out of a tree trunk rested on two stone pillars near the stable. A tall pear tree, its front and back branches trimmed so that it would grow flat against the wall, had acquired the appearance of a botanical menorah. Behind the branches, the wall surface had a bluish hue, evidence of frequent spray of copper sulfate. On the western side of the house, a fenced yard promised vegetables and other edibles. Farther away, several fruit trees were laden with plums, peaches, and other fruits.

Beyond, just across the narrow country road they had come from, a large cement washbasin was now visible beside the artesian well. Above it overhung the leafy head of a gigantic walnut tree. A narrow footpath led toward the vineyards and the open fields.

"Hi, kid! Who are you?"

A slim dark-haired boy, approximately the same age as Roberto, stood behind him. He wore a ragged shirt and a pair of worn-out trousers with multicolored patches, and he was barefooted. Despite his scruffy attire, his manner was confident, and his eyes had an intelligent expression. His skin tone was dark and healthy.

"My name is Roberto. I came last night. We moved from our house because of the bombing."

"So I hear. How old are you?"

"Thirteen, and you?"

"Thirteen and a half. Boy, you are tall for thirteen …"

"What's your name?"

"Mario."

"Is this your house?"

"Sort of. We can stay as long as my pa works this here farm. Come, I'll show you around."

Roberto hesitated a moment. The temptation of being able to enjoy a moment of freedom contrasted with the sense of discipline instilled by the family, which suggested that he should report to his mother and grandmother immediately.

"Come," Mario repeated. "I'll show you my cows."

He led the way toward the stable. Once inside, Roberto stopped briefly, trying to distinguish his surroundings.

"Isn't there any light?" he asked.

"Nope. But in a minute, you'll get use to it." He took a pitchfork and opened one of the high windows at the far end of the stable. A strong, sweet smell saturated the warm air, and a swarm of flies buzzed around his head.

"It smells like the cart where I slept," Roberto said.

"I bet," said Mario, through his laughter. "It's the cart we use to carry manure from the stable."

Roberto was not amused. "I slept there with Lucia," he said promptly, as if this statement could somehow mitigate the circumstances.

"She and her family went somewhere," said Mario.

"Why? Where?" Roberto's sudden disappointment filled his voice.

"I heard my mom say we don't have room for everybody. She told them folks to go to the Buti farm. A few miles yonder." He read Roberto's disappointment. "They'll be back though, to pick up the rest of their stuff," he continued. "That's why them guys didn't say good-bye."

Roberto didn't have time to appraise the impact of this information, as Mario immediately called, "Vieni qui." *Come here.*

He gestured encouragingly for him to advance toward the middle of the bare concrete floor. A thick layer of straw covered the slightly elevated sections on either side of it. There, several large *Chianine* cows, ruminating on the morning feed, remained oblivious to the intrusion.

"Come," Mario urged, getting between two of the large animals. "You can feed them hay."

Roberto advanced slowly, hesitant to walk through the narrow pathway between those monumental animals. Determined not to show his fear, he slowly moved forward and reached the manger.

"See that one?" Mario asked, pointing to the one on the left. "She's Bianchina—my very special one. I saw her born and gave her that name 'cause of her coat. She's whiter than the others." He pointed to the next cow. "That other one is Viola, because of that color ringlet under her neck. And the other one …" Mario proudly continued to name all the other cows as if he were introducing his own family members.

"Do they give milk?" Roberto asked.

"No. Only when they've calves. Now they don't. Besides, we work them too hard in the fields. We get our milk from a farm near here."

When they finally returned outside, the sun was already blindingly bright and hot. Roberto removed his pullover and rested it on the wrought iron railing of the stairway.

"Take your shoes off too," Mario told him. "I bet you can't run like me without them shoes. City kids are sissy."

"Castelvecchio is not a city. It's a town," Roberto corrected, "and I am certainly not a sissy. I'll demonstrate it to you."

"Oh boy, you talk funny."

"Do I really?" He removed his shoes and socks and followed Mario, who'd run away, taking a course over graveled and rough areas to test the endurance of his new companion. Roberto followed closely, accepting the challenge and ignoring the discomfort to his tender feet. After a while, Mario stopped and, breathing heavily, said, "You know, for a city kid, you're doing all right."

"Why did we stop?" Roberto asked, faking his desire to continue, in spite of his burning feet.

"Time to go back. You wanna have some breakfast together?"

They started to walk toward the house, Mario's arm resting on Roberto's shoulder. Given the brief time they had known each other, Roberto found this gesture a bit overly familiar for such a new acquaintance, but he did not withdraw.

Maybe this is the way it is in the country, he thought.

They were already friends.

*****

As the two boys were crossing the country road, Roberto heard a strange noise coming from behind the curve. He stopped to listen.

"Don't worry," Mario said. "It's old man Buti."

An old farmer, coming from the direction of Castelvecchio, pedaled toward them on a bicycle without tires. The crushing sound of the metal rims over the fine gravel of the country road had revealed his presence even before he had come into sight.

"He took the tires off; otherwise, the Germans take his bike," Mario explained. Anything new?" he then yelled in the farmer's direction.

"The usual rumors, kid. They say Leghorn was bombed again. And not just the harbor—the whole city. In town, I saw more people who ran away from there. They think it's safer here, I reckon."

"I hope so," said a voice behind them.

The man on the bike waved his hand in salute and continued his journey.

"This is my pa," Mario said.

"Good morning, sir. I am Roberto, Luisa's grandson," said the boy. He recognized the man who had answered the night before and held out his hand. "How do you do, sir?"

"I'm doing well for an old man," said Mario's father, "and by the way, they call me Gino." He shook the boy's hand. He had a calloused, strong hand. He was of average height, but his chest, shoulders, and arms were large and muscular. He was rugged and healthy looking, with cheeks round and red as Delicious apples. Thick eyebrows shaded his greenish, quick eyes. He wore dark trousers that were mended in several places, and a gray sleeveless woolen undershirt, probably hand knit by a family member. A shiny pair of clippers was tucked under his belt.

"Let's go for breakfast," he said jovially. He sounded so friendly and natural that Roberto felt immediately at home.

Later that day, the adults argued pros and cons of space and sleeping arrangements, as well as the fairness and necessity of some shared contribution, especially in food and kindred matters.

After a short discussion, the ground cellar was deemed the most suitable space. In fact, though exposed to probable cannon fire from the American side, it afforded the protection of massive double walls. And on its far side, against another wall, was the added shield of several concrete wine vats that would be empty until grape gathering.

Roberto followed his nonna and Gino to the cellar, "But," he wondered, "where will we sleep?"

"On the floor, my child. Don't worry, though," Luisa answered. "Today, when our uninvited German guests are away, we will go to our home with Gino, and we will take mattresses, blankets, clothes, and all we'll need for a while."

"Everybody here in the same room?"

"Yes. Everybody together, and even with more people if necessary. This is war, dear child, not a summer vacation. When my house was destroyed," she said, "your Uncle Lorenzo and I slept under the stairway for several days. And when it rained, we had rats for company ..."

He didn't ask any more questions.

Luisa and Patrizia left with Gino and returned after several hours.

"Did everything go well?" Roberto inquired.

"Yes, cucciolo," his mother answered. "The Germans were away, as expected, and just a few people went by the street when we were loading. Many people, I gather, have taken to the countryside."

The two boys helped unload the mattresses from the cart. As directed, they then took preserves and food supplies Luisa had gathered to the cellar, concealing them in cool, hidden corners.

The day after, Luisa and Gino went for another load, which mainly consisted of wooden cages in which chickens and rabbits had been gathered.

"I closed all the doors and Persian shutters," Luisa told Patrizia, "but I left the inner glass windows open so they won't shatter from concussion."

Luisa paused, her cheeks red from the intense heat. She had unfastened the first two buttons of her shirt and now began to loosen the knot of her perennial headscarf. The sun was fiercely hot, and at this hour of the day, it shone almost perpendicular. The chickens had all

456

disappeared from the yard and found refuge and comfort inside the cane thicket at the edge of the courtyard. Even the dog was flat on its stomach in the narrow, shadowy strip beside his doghouse, his tongue falling from the side of his mouth. A few birds crossed the air space and then disappeared into the thick foliage of the chestnut tree, while a persistent chorus of tree frogs pierced the air. Luisa wiped her forehead and looked at Patrizia as if wanting to say more, but she hesitated.

"What else, Mother?"

"I took advantage of Gino's presence and buried a few things in the orchard. I'll tell you more later...." Her expression made it clear that she did not want to go into detail with the children nearby.

*****

Despite the spartan communal sleeping accommodations, the smelly latrine, and the lack of running water, the farm soon became a new dimension of personal freedom for Roberto.

Though he still enjoyed studying and learning, he did not miss his regular lessons and the time with tutors. He enjoyed Mario's company, the playtime, and even the daily chores, like feeding the pigs and the chickens, or picking fruits and vegetables, or pulling pails of water out of the artesian well.

He enjoyed relearning the farm environment he had known and then forgotten as a young child, and sharing with his new friend what he knew from school or from his readings.

One day, Mario stopped at the corner of a field and said, "In this field here, we can't plant Colombano vines on account of the soil bein' sandy. Figure that out. What's sand doing this far from the sea?"

"You see those hills?" Roberto asked, pointing south. "And those others?" He swung and pointed north.

"Of course I see 'em. I'm not blind. What about them hills?"

"Millions of years ago, those hills were probably the natural outer limits of the river. When it flooded and then receded, it left deposits of sand and silt on some areas of the plain. That's why there's sand over here."

"How do you know that if it happened millions years ago?"

"I read about it. I mean, not necessarily about this, but about the Nile and many other rivers and lowlands …"

"I'm stupid. I don't know them things." Mario shrugged his shoulders. His hands were open as if to say, *What you see is what you get.*

Roberto laughed cheerfully, "No, Mario, you are not stupid at all. You just haven't read about these things, that's all."

Mario didn't seem convinced. He twisted his mouth and raised his eyebrows, seeming to have lost some of his confidence.

"I didn't know that you cannot grow certain things on sandy soil until you told me," Roberto said. "So we are even. Before I came here, I had only seen river cane growing in the riverbanks, near the water, or at least in marshy soil."

"You are right, you know. Normally they do, but my great-grandpa planted some a long time ago. In time, they grown to what you see now—'bout fifty meters span by twenty or more deep. What you don't know is that on the south side, there's a deep ditch that fills with water when it rain and keeps the roots … moisted."

"Moist, you mean. But what are they for? Just for looks?"

"No! We don't do things just for looks at the farm. In the fall, when the canes are full-grown, dry, and strong, we cut them and use them for all kind of things. To steady tomato plants, long green beans plants, and even young grapevines. Look," he said, pointing nearby. "Over there, you see them vines? Then, in the spring, the canes grow again."

"Now I understand."

Mario went on his knee and picked up a handful of soil. "Look at this," he said, crushing it against his palm and letting it drop to the ground, "it's like dust or dirt, but if you put a good seed or a plant in it and get plenty o' rain, you get all the food you need." He got up and looked beyond the wheat field, his eyes caressing the blond heads "It is so beautiful."

"I envy you," said Roberto.

"Why?"

"Because you talk of the beauty of nature as if it were a palpable thing. Don't misunderstand; I like nature as well."

"So? What's the diff'rence?"

"I like it superficially—how can I say it?—almost at distance. But you, the way you talk about the trees, the wheat, the soil, you seem to have a personal, intimate relationship with it, like with a friend or a relative. Do you know what I mean?"

"Sort of, but as I already told you, you kinda talk funny for a thirteen-year-old kid. Anyway," he said lightheartedly, "You see that other field over yonder?" He pointed north. "That land, we don't work as sharecroppers. It belongs to us. My ma brought it in when she got married to my father."

"As a dowry, you mean?"

"I don't remember the word, but it sounds something like that. Anyway, my pa says one day we'll build our own house over there. It's good land, good for vineyards, for fruits, and almost anything. He says that if you treat the land good, she is good to you too. She can feed you and your family."

Another day, as they lay in a field, Mario taught Roberto the common names of several varieties of grass and edible leafy plants. He explained that some were used raw in green salads and were pleasing to the taste. Then he took a blade of grass, held it vertical to his lips, and blew air through it, creating some musical sounds, only three or four notes that were repeated over and over by both boys until they were out of breath from blowing and laughing.

Mario could imitate the musical call of the bullfinch and the scratchy voice of a blackbird. He knew where tortoises liked to nest, as well as the types of seeds they preferred to eat. He knew most birds by their calls and by the color of their feathers.

Then came the play with the slingshot, sometimes aimed at field mice and other rodents that damaged the fruits in the melon patch. Other times, it was used to knock down the reluctant walnuts from the unreachable branches of the tree.

Soon Roberto became an expert sling shooter, which gained him additional admiration from Mario, who was impressed with the dexterity of his friend.

"Not bad at all, for a city boy," he often exclaimed.

The next day, it was Roberto's turn to be surprised by Mario's ability and sound judgment. They were driving the cow-driven cart, loaded with grass from the field. Roberto had taken the reins and enjoyed this new experience. It seemed very easy. They reached the turn from the road into the farmyard, and he pulled the left rein with some strength. It was a narrow passage, and when he looked down, he realized that he had pulled the reins too soon. The left wheel would not clear the ditch, which, from the height of the cart, seemed even deeper. He quickly pulled both reins and stopped the cart. "Now what?" he asked Mario.

Mario calmly took the reins from Roberto, gave them some slack, and said, "My pa always says that on occasions like this, I should trust the good sense of the animals. Look, I'm gonna let them guess the distance." Unrestrained by the slackened strap, the left cow moved to the right and forced the other to do the same. The cart rotated on its wheels on the spot, crushing the fine gravel to dust. Then it moved forward with a slight jerk, crossing safely over the narrow bridge.

"Fantastic," Roberto said with relief.

He liked to learn these new things. He liked the open, straightforward spirit of his playmate. He felt as free as a bird in the almost boundless vastness of this farm. Its subtle charm spoke to him, bringing back fading memories.

He especially liked the evenings. Particularly suppertime, when lulls in the cannon fire allowed them all, farmers and refugees alike, to gather in the large, rustic kitchen, waiting for supper.

La Rossa, Mario's paternal grandmother, and his mother, Giulia, attended to the cooking, which was done over the side of *fornelli,* the ash pits of the large redbrick fireplace. Afterward, when the cooking was done, they promptly gathered the ashes and covered the red embers. In the morning, they reversed the procedure and scooped the ashes aside,

lifted the embers, and added enough coal or dry bits of wood to start the new fire, saving time and precious matches.

While La Rossa cooked, Luisa and Patrizia set the dishes on the solid walnut wood table, and everyone else sat on the straw-seated chairs, ready to share the frugal meal. The orange flames of homemade candles and acetylene lamps flickered behind the covered windows and cast their orange light on friendly faces.

The first supper at the farm had been a revelation for Roberto. He heard Mario suck broth noisily from his spoon, and his grandfather, Amato, almost touched his plate with his nose. Gino smacked his tongue against his palate after sipping the wine, and others brought their mouths near the food, rather than the opposite, as he had been taught. Spoons and forks scraped noisily against the surface of the plates, and almost everyone spoke with food in his or her mouth. He looked up at his mother in astonishment.

She nodded slightly and allowed her lips to curl in a little smile.

He knew that she understood, and furthermore, that he shouldn't make any comment. With his next spoonful of soup, he produced the same sound as Mario. He then looked up again at his mother, who now shook her head and frowned. He got the message. Contrary to the farmers' saying, what was good for the goose was *not* good for the gander, insofar as where table manners were concerned.

"Look," said Mario poking at Roberto's arm, "my grandpa has fell asleep."

Roberto looked toward Amato. His eyes were closed, his head had fallen down, and his chin rested on his chest. A faint snore came out of his toothless mouth.

As days passed, Roberto soon recognized that their diversity—in table manners, education, or background—was balanced by their generosity and spontaneity, and by the spirit of camaraderie they were forming, including their common feelings, such as fear of the American bombers, of Germans reprisals, of the potential loss of family members, of death. Even fear of starvation if the war front remained at the Arno Line for too long.

In addition to Amato, Mario's grandfather, another man soon joined the group. His name was Francesco Bertinelli, but he was deferentially called "Professor." He was a distant cousin of Amato's, and he had been teaching literature at a Lyceum in Pisa until the first bombing of the city and the closure of the school. Roberto liked to listen to him, as both his vocabulary and the incisiveness of his comments reminded him a bit of his own father.

At suppertime, the kitchen became animated by the conversation of these men and women who passed the food to each other, ate eagerly, and, with a muted twinkle in their eyes, forged their common bond at the sound of the cutlery striking the stoneware dishes.

"You heard the latest?" Amato asked one evening. "The Americans bombed Livorno again."

"You know why?" asked the professor.

"I do," Roberto volunteered, when no one else replied.

The professor turned toward the boy. "And what would that be, young lad?"

"Because there is a harbor, and it could be used by the Germans to bring in reinforcements, weapons, food …"

"And what else?" the professor challenged him.

"Or evacuate their troops if they want to escape."

"Well said, Roberto, and where did you learn those things?"

"From my father," the boy answered proudly. "He said many things … which are now happening."

The professor smiled. "Clever fellow, your father," he added a moment later.

"Let's hope them Germans don't stay long," Gino said. "I hear they're doing lots of diggin' in the riverbanks. It don't promise too well."

"With every day that goes by, I hear more bad news. I don't like their mood," the professor concluded with a sigh.

"Like at the Piave and the Tagliamento rivers during the Great War," said Luisa, "I hope that my son's prediction will not come true…"

"What prediction was that?" Gino asked.

"That we could have an Arno Line, just as we had a Piave Line during the Great War. Twice in a lifetime," she said to herself. "One was more than enough for me!"

"I heard," said the professor, lowering his voice, "that the Germans have arrested several men of military age in Santa Chiara and other towns. They shot one of them and took away the others. I'm told they did a lot of bad things in the south."

"I have heard it too, and from pretty reliable sources," replied Luisa. "Young and not so young."

"Every man between sixteen and sixty would be better off hiding for a while," concluded Patrizia, "at least until we can assess how the SS are going to behave around here."

"La signora is right," echoed Gino's wife, Giulia.

"Giulia," said Patrizia, faking impatience, "I already told you not to call me signora. We are all the same here."

Giulia blushed visibly.

Roberto could see that it wasn't easy for her to change what had been a lifetime habit. She couldn't treat as equal someone who was above her social and educational standing. She seemed confused and lowered her head without answering.

"But where will they hide?" Bruna asked.

"That," Luisa quickly intervened, "we shall discuss later. Besides, Patrizia made a mistake; she didn't mean *hiding*; she meant going far away …"

Roberto noticed his nonna's cold look of disapproval at Bruna's question, her sideways glance at Patrizia, and the almost imperceptible nod toward him and Mario. Obviously, she did not want the topic discussed in front of them.

The professor understood the message too. "Gino," he said, more loudly than necessary, "this is a mighty good wine." He then lifted his glass in a silent toast, and Gino acknowledged the compliment, repeating the gesture.

"It's a young wine," the professor continued, "but it has the flavor of last summer, and if I close my eyes, I can still evoke its beauty; remember the hopes; feel that hot, dry sun burning over my skin. Now I can feel it in my palate." He smacked his tongue knowingly and looked at his half-full glass against the acetylene flame. "Bright as a ruby," he said, bringing the glass to his lips. "*Salute.*" He drank the wine in one long gulp.

- XLI -

1944

As news about the war situation continued to worsen, the people at the farm seemed to draw even closer to each other. In the comfortable proximity of their shared home, they smiled, frowned, and showed their emotions as openly as children did. Just like in the shelter, where even strangers brought together by chance and enveloped in a few feet of darkness shared intimately the common feelings of fear or hope. One moment sharing the possibility of immediate death, and the next, the exhilarating feeling of its reprieve, praying to their gods, crying, singing.

These feelings seemed to make them say or do things seldom said or done in the light of ordinary circumstances. As Luisa said, the situation had become a drama. A drama that could easily turn into a tragedy in which they had been unwillingly cast.

*****

"Nonna, Nonna," Roberto cried, "please come down."

Moments before, he had heard the grinding sound of wheels over the graveled country road and had crossed the yard to see what it might be. From behind the curve suddenly appeared the silhouette of a middle-aged man pushing a wheelbarrow. Something was spilling over the edge. Roberto squinted and focused his eyes. As the man got closer, he recognized old Barsotti, the Giani's neighbor to the east. The items over the edge of the wheelbarrow appeared to be a pair of dangling arms and legs.

"Nonna," he called again.

"I'm coming, I'm coming," she said from the stairway, "but what are you so excited about? What is it, Roberto?"

"Old Barsotti is coming this way, Nonna, and he has someone in a wheelbarrow. I think he is crying."

Luisa crossed the bridge over the drain ditch and walked toward the visibly distraught, teary-eyed man. "Orlando," she said, as he reached the area shadowed by the walnut tree. "Orlando, what happened?"

The man gently lowered the wheelbarrow and began to sob. "My beloved wife, my poor dear Marina," he said. "Look at her, Luisa. She seems asleep, but she's dead. Not an hour ago, she was alive and well, feeding the chickens in the yard. Then the shelling started, and we ran to the cellar. She sat in a corner over a short barrel, behind a heavy door, resting her head on her hand and praying." His voice cracked with emotion. Luisa looked at Marina lying inside the wheelbarrow and then put her arms around him, gently patting his back, "Poor

Marina," she said. "She was such a nice human being. How did she die?"

"When the shelling stopped, I called, 'Marina, let's see what they hit this time.' She didn't move. 'Marina,' I called again, 'with all that racket, you can't be asleep.' As I got closer, I saw a tiny stream of blood and gray stuff pouring out of her temple." A loud sob interrupted the account. The old man dug a striped handkerchief out of his side pocket and wiped his sweat and his tears, and then he blew his nose loudly.

Roberto, who had remained a few meters away, was stunned and sickened at the view of that poor man and the heartbreaking end of his wife. He too thought she was a nice person. She had always been kind to him and the other kids when, during their play, they had encroached in her garden; instead of scolding them for trespassing, she had given them apricots and other fruits. And now she was dead. Why?

"I touched her," Barsotti continued, "and she was as dead as a stone."

"Oh my God, "Luisa said. "She was such a gentle soul."

"Yes, she was!" the man cried with anger. "It's not right. It's not right that a person like her is dead while so many swine go on living."

"You are right," said Luisa. "Unfortunately, my dear Orlando, such is life. My poor husband was taken from me the same way, during a bombing; believe me, I know what you're going through. Perhaps God wants the good people near him."

Roberto heard her voice crack and saw her hand wipe her eyes. He stood there, unable to do anything but stare at the face of death and the face of pain—looking silently at that inert body that had been, only hours earlier, a healthy human being. One of her arms had fallen to the side, and her hand was almost touching the gravel. Luisa noticed it, took it gently, and raised the arm over Marina's chest. Then she removed her light scarf and wrapped it around her bleeding head, pulled down the skirt raised by the breeze, and asked, "Where are you taking her?"

"I'm going to the cemetery. I'll find a place for now. Then later..."

"Do you need a spade?"

The man looked at Luisa as if he could not understand.

"A spade," she repeated, making a digging motion.

"Oh, a spade. Yes, of course, I do need a spade. You see, I can't even think straight anymore."

Luisa nodded toward her grandson. "Please get one, Roberto. Bring a white bedsheet as well. They are drying on the clothesline on the other side of the shed."

The boy ran away and returned with both items, handing them to his nonna.

"Don't worry, Orlando," she said, covering Marina's body. "I'll hold the spade; I'm coming with you to the cemetery." Then, turning to her grandson: "Roberto, please tell your mother that I'll be back in a while."

"Thank you, Luisa. I wouldn't have had the guts to cover her face with dirt. If there were a God," he then said, shaking his index finger toward the sky, "he wouldn't allow unfair things like this to happen."

"*Coraggio,* Orlando," she said, clearly not wanting to acknowledge his conclusion. "Let's go."

The old man moved between the shafts, lifted the wheelbarrow, and began to walk on the sun-beaten road toward Castelvecchio with Luisa.

Roberto watched them disappear behind the first curve, the sound of cracking gravel still audible for a long time.

Barsotti is right, he thought. *If there is a God, He is not a righteous being.*

That night, as he lay in bed awake, Roberto thought once more of death and destiny. He tossed and turned, unable to wipe out from his mind the calm and serene image of Marina, the visible pain on her husband's face, his nonna's ache at the memory of her dead husband. Life and death, he concluded, seem at times determined by imperceptible movements, irrelevant distances: meters, centimeters, even millimeters. You sit on a barrel, as Marina had done, and you die! You stand a meter away, and you are saved. No one realizes, until such a thing happens, how slim the margins of one's existence truly are. Regardless, and without any doubt, death was a serious thing!

During the following weeks, more German vehicles were seen moving along the country road, and the soldiers' expressions seemed more tense and dour. One began to hear news of reprisals in the occupied towns … of more people being shot or taken away to German labor camps. Even children and old people were said to be shot or burned inside their houses by the infamous SS, sometimes in retaliation of partisan actions, and others, without any provocation, just to intimidate the population. At times, the details seemed so far-fetched and cruel that Roberto had problems believing them.

The Americans were said to have finally advanced to the area immediately south of the Arno River. However, despite their vastly superior forces and domination of the skies, they seemed to lack the desire or ability to cross it and break through the German defenses.

The *Wehrmacht*, though demoralized and with depleted armament and resources, made the best of the terrain and held fast.

German engineers mined the most direct approaches to the Arno, and, as foreseen by the professor, they put their first line on the fortified trenches of the right riverbank. They held some reserves in the immediate countryside, lodging in solid farmhouses that had been forcefully freed of their rightful occupants.

Finally, strategically positioned in the back hills, which flanked the river for almost its entire course—at a distance that ranged between four and six kilometers—they placed their notorious batteries of caliber 88 mm cannons and heavy mortars. From those heights, protected by the forest growth, trenched terrain, and natural grottos, they covered the entire valley with lethal precision.

Shortly after, SS troops began to make house incursions and countryside mop-up operations, often with the consequent arrest of all able-bodied men. Internment or summary executions for those Italians of military age found without uniform or regular permits became a normal occurrence. More and more people were seen every day, a few bundles of mere necessities hanging from their shoulders, walking toward the hills or just away from the town, in search of a refuge. Their woeful faces revealed many unspoken stories.

The Americans responded to the German strategic withdrawal in what many people called their "usual way": abundance of aerial bombing of likely retreat routes—like bridges, railway lines and mountain passes—and frequent flights of spotter airplanes to cover the area, often followed by seemingly random barrages of cannon fire. Their "usual way" was their unwanted contribution to the growing misery of the civilian population.

"They must have too much ammunition," the professor commented after one such protracted bombing seemingly aimed at nothing specific. "I think they shoot at anything that moves. By the law of averages, they may even hit some Germans."

Not too many people found it humorous!

Roberto listened to the words of the grown-ups and tried to draw his own conclusion.

"These comments," said the fair-minded professor to Roberto, "may seem rather uncomplimentary to the Anglo-Americans. However, one must accept that, at least on the Italian front, they certainly have not demonstrated much aptitude for fighting."

Every now and then, Luisa would voice her concerns about the abandoned house. "I wonder what we'll find when we go back …" "I hope those Germans won't pinch our possessions …" "I wish we had taken some of the good linens with us."

"Let's not trouble ourselves with those thoughts, Mother," Patrizia would say soothingly, trying to deflect Luisa's worries. "We have enough on our plate as it is."

In fact, in addition to the already serious situation, other happenings became part of the daily concerns; killings and other types of violence perpetrated by the SS were confirmed. More bombing and destruction were reported. The scarcity of food had reached dangerous levels in the cities, and people were known to have fought over a crust of bread.

The element of fear increased.

By now, all men of military age, whether exonerated from service or sick, or unless they were regular fascists or "collaborators," suddenly disappeared from sight. Some taken by the Germans, others finding refuge in the most absurd and unlikely places in town, or hiding in the countryside or in the thickly forested hills north of the river, where not even the Germans were willing to venture.

Even so, the safety of those who ran away was not assured, as the SS searched houses, farms, bomb shelters and the countryside. They randomly shot their machine guns through the cornfields and tall crops. They shoved bayonets through hay and grass bales. Often, local diehard fascist fanatics, who still believed in the final victory of the Reich, aided in their search.

At the Banchini farm, following Patrizia's advice, all able-bodied men suddenly disappeared, and the children were told they had gone to a safe place far away.

"Where?" both Mario and Roberto asked.

"A place near Pisa," was the terse reply.

"That far?" said Roberto, unconvinced. He received no answer and understood that he should leave it at that.

The women had now taken on all the necessary chores of the household. Luisa and Patrizia helped organize the growing group and relieved Giulia of those decisions that seemed beyond her ability. Eighty-four-year-old Amato kept looking after the vegetable patch and feeding the animals. The children, often out in the open, should use their better hearing and eyesight, and advise the adults of approaching German patrols.

"But how?" Giulia asked. "Calling to us from outside?"

"No, that would be too obvious," said Patrizia. "Let's see. Yes, I've got it! Have them shout something to the dog. Something like, *Tito, a cuccia!* Tito, heel. And we'll understand."

*****

Around the middle of August, other relatives of the Banchinis arrived at the farm, among them Gino's sister Floria with her twenty-eight-year-old son Ivo; his wife, Angela; and their six-month-old baby. They lived in the nearby town of Santa Chiara, but after the third air raid over the town, in which the bridge and several town blocks were destroyed and their house rendered inhabitable, they decided to come up to the farm.

Ivo, though exonerated from service, as the sole financial supporter of the family, was advised to join the other men "near Pisa," and he soon disappeared from sight.

The last person who came was a sixteen-year-old girl called Lina. She was one of Giulia's cousins, whose father was at the Russian front, and whose mother had recently died. All her other relatives lived on the south side of the Arno River, and she was now cut off from them.

"She is beautiful," Mario whispered in Roberto's ear at her appearance. "I hadn't saw her in a long time."

"She is," Roberto replied, letting his eyes journey over her features. Her face, framed by a healthy crop of brown hair with copper reflections, was a perfect oval. Her mouth had narrow and inviting lips with a gleaming set of teeth peeking from behind them. Her nose was small and delicate. Under thin, slightly arched brows, her chestnut brown eyes held a hint of a smile that made her look strangely compelling. Her voice, clear and cheerful, was like the first notes of a happy overture that unconsciously enters one's heart and fills it with joy. It enhanced the overall feeling of wonder Roberto felt as he stood near this wonderful creature. A wisp of wind blew a strand of hair across her face, and Roberto imagined it soft to the touch. He was attracted to her even before he understood the reasons. It was the first time that he experienced a strong feeling like this.

As she stood there talking to Giulia, Lina seemed suddenly conscious of Roberto's attention. She turned around and saw his appraising stare resting on her face, her body, expressing approval. A smile flickered in her eyes.

Giulia seemed distraught by the new arrivals. She seemed to want to say yes to everyone, but was afraid that space and food would soon be insufficient.

"Don't worry, Giulia," Luisa told her. "After all, thanks to God, we are luckier than most. Downtown, it's much worse already. We still have chickens and vegetables and fruits. Besides, they are your relatives, and they need help. We'll squeeze a few more into the cellar, and if need be, we'll add water to the broth."

In addition to the Lanzis, there were now six more people sleeping in the cellar, plus the occasional passerby without a roof over his head who was sheltered for a night or two.

Initially Roberto, who was used to his own private space, disliked this forced fraternization. However, he soon realized that the adults came to bed when he was already sleeping and were often up and away by the time he awakened. Therefore, he adjusted to the idea.

During the day, the straw mattresses were lifted and placed on edge, and then held against the far wall with thick ropes. Bedsheets and blankets were folded and placed in a corner inside wicker baskets. In the darkest place, there was the whitish shape of a porcelain chamber pot, or urinal, as Giulia called it.

A scene had been rehearsed: if during the night, someone knocked at the door, Ginevra, who was the plumpest and least appealing, was to discard most of her clothes, take the pot to the center of the room, and pretend to be defecating, accompanied by appropriate sound effects and visual efforts. Roberto hoped never to witness such a scene.

Just before supper, which—shelling permitting—was around eight, a couple of women would go to the cellar, sweep the floor, place the mattresses in the usual circular arrangement, and ready the sleeping accommodations.

Roberto discovered with joy that Lina, whose pleasing features he had observed, was to sleep to his immediate right. *I like that,* he thought. He did not know precisely why, but he did know that her presence caused him to experience a sudden inner joy, a desire, which made his days more exciting.

*****

Day by day, the fighting intensified. Yet during the more or less predictable bombing lulls, normal activities resumed; life had to go on. The gathering of food was one of the main chores at the farm. Everyone was assigned specific duties appropriate to his or her age, strength, and experience.

Lina had to gather ripe fruits in the orchard before they fell or spoiled or were stolen by roaming vagrants. Every other day, she repeated the task. She fetched two large woven cane baskets, one for the fruits for immediate consumption, the other for the inferior ones used for preserves. On these occasions, old Amato replaced the boys watching the country road to signal oncoming Germans, if necessary, and Lina took the path through the fields with Mario and Roberto in tow.

The two boys were happy to help her. Young, pretty, and high-spirited, she joked with them and allowed them to eat the ripest fruits, in spite of Luisa's strict instruction not to let them spoil their "regular" meals.

Roberto and Mario walked toward the place where they had left the wooden ladder. They carefully removed the tree branches that hid it from view and placed it right against the sturdy branch of a fruit tree. They took turns climbing the ladder, picking the fruits and tossing them to the other two below, who caught them and placed them into the baskets. After collecting enough, they hid the ladder again and returned to the farm, each helping with the baskets.

This particular day, Lina wanted to climb up the tree. She rolled up the sleeves of her shirt, dropped her clogs, pulled up her skirt at the waist, and began to go up. Mario steadied the ladder as it rested on uneven terrain, and Roberto lined up the baskets. With a sneaky smile on his sunburned face, Mario called Roberto to his side.

"Look," he whispered, nodding upward. "Look at them yummy legs."

Roberto glanced upward. His eyes slid along Lina's stunning legs, all the way up to the small white triangle of her underwear. He laughed under his breath, but not as knowingly as Mario. Yet that sight gave him some kind of pleasure, the source of which he could not completely understand.

When Lina came down, the two boys were still giggling, and she squeezed them playfully in a bear hug. "You little rascals," she said. "I know what you're up to."

Roberto did not resist the embrace, and he kept his body tucked against her supple softness, his nostril touched by the pleasant scent of her skin.

"Can we have another plum?" he asked.

"Or something better," Mario added with a wicked grin.

"Here is what I'll give you," said Lina, gently slapping him in mock anger. "And now stop it, or I'll tell your mother ..."

Whenever there was the opportunity, the two boys were happy to help Lina with whatever chore she had to do.

Before supper one night, when the sun was ready to set behind Monte Serra, their eyes followed her as she approached the well to wash herself. She used a pail of water pulled earlier from the artesian well and now sufficiently warmed in the sun. Like most people at the farm, she washed without undressing. She unbuttoned her shirt, folded her collar inside and washed her face, her neck, and the upper part of her chest. Then she pulled up her skirt and washed her feet and legs.

The boys, pretending to be at play and hidden behind the vines, snatched frequent looks at her well-toned legs and thighs shining under a thin film of water. They were splendid under the setting orange sun.

"Her legs remind me of those of Venus ... I saw her in my history books," Roberto said.

"What a dumb thing to say," Mario replied.

*****

One day, just after the morning cannonade, the two boys emerged in the front yard just in time to see Angela turn in the path past the orchard. She turned around once, as if to check if anyone had noticed her, and then she quickly turned around and disappeared behind the foliage.

"Let's follow her," Mario suggested.

Roberto noticed his secretive smile and followed him. Lina, who had already fetched the empty baskets and was walking in the direction of the orchard, joined the two boys. They jogged between tall rows of vines, in a course parallel to Angela, making sure they were not detected. Every now and then, they saw her turning around, as if making sure that no one had followed her. Finally, she quickened her pace and then ran until she reached a field with tall grass undulating in the morning breeze. Near the middle of the field, she sat down and almost completely disappeared from view.

"Now what?" Roberto asked.

"*Vieni*" said Mario. "We'll climb that tree over there. Don't make any noise."

They moved under a tall peach tree and helped each other climb until they reached sufficient height to regain full view of Angela, who now lay flat on her back, her hands behind her head and her skirt well above her knees. The two boys were standing on the same tree branch, with Lina sitting a few feet below them.

"What is she doing?" Roberto asked.

"Wait ... you'll see. Look ... he's coming," Mario whispered, pointing in a northerly direction, toward a young man who had just emerged from the foliage.

"Who is that?" Roberto asked.

"It's Ivo, her husband. Don't you recognize him?"

"Wasn't he near Pisa with the others?"

"Pisa, my ass. They told us that 'cause they are afraid we'll talk. I heard my mom say to granny," Mario continued, "that they shouldn't do those things in the daytime. If he gets caught by the Germans ... he is risking his life for a screw."

"What screw are you talking about?"

"Gee whiz, you town kids are kind of dumb sometimes. A screw, a fuck ... you know?"

He saw Roberto's baffled look and covered his mouth to muffle his laughter. "Not that kind of screw, you dummy," he said, his hand descending toward his crotch. "I mean the ones you do with this. You put it into the girl thing, and then ..."

Lina was laughing silently, and Roberto looked at her and then at Mario with an expression of surprise and embarrassment.

"And then what?" he asked hesitantly. He wanted to know, but he was afraid to show Lina his lack of knowledge in these matters.

"Then you move back and forth. My cousin Lorenzo told me. He is nineteen, and he's done it a few times. He says it feels good. People do it just like cows and other animals. I've seen it done ..."

Lina was holding her hand over her mouth, but a muffled laugh escaped.

"Do your parents know you saw it?" Roberto asked in a whisper.

"Sure they do. It's natural, they say. And then ..."

"Shhh!" Roberto hushed.

Ivo had reached the spot where Angela lay. He looked around to make sure no one had seen him, and he promptly knelt between her legs.

Angela pulled her skirt even higher. He began to kiss her neck and her now exposed breast, squeezing the other with his left hand while pushing against the ground with his right hand.

After a few moments, his hand descended toward her abdomen, and seconds later Angela's white slips were tossed aside. Ivo pulled his pants down with some urgency, and the boys giggled when his white buttocks flashed under the morning sun. He lifted himself above her, his arms now outstretched beside her shoulders. He lowered his body over Angela, who had spread her legs wider and was now embracing him. Then they started what seemed to be a back-and-forth movement.

Roberto looked down toward Lina and saw that she was still holding one hand over her mouth, her eyes wide open.

Even at that distance, with every movement, they could hear Angela writhing and moaning while she kept pace with the crescendo of Ivo's thrusts. Soon the rhythm intensified, and after slower, more deliberate movements, it suddenly subsided. Ivo seemed completely exhausted, and he rested his head in the cavity of Angela's neck in complete abandonment, as if he had fallen asleep.

"Let's go," Lina whispered from below.

The three descended from the tree, and she faced the boys. "Now, not a word to anyone about this, you hear? Otherwise we'll get scolded, and I, as the oldest, much more than you."

The boys nodded in response, and Roberto looked into her eyes and moist red lips, wondering what it would be like to do "back-and-forth" with her.

"I certainly won't tell," he said.

Lina gave him a hug. Once more, he marveled at the pleasure of that soft contact.

During lunch, Roberto could hardly take his eyes away from her face. He wasn't sure if witnessing the act together had added anything new to his relationship with her.

On the one hand, he was pleased to share with her the secret of previously unknown possibilities. And on the other, witnessing that "act" seemed to cause her status as a goddess to be somewhat diminished. His mind was definitely engaged by two conflicting feelings. He chewed his food unthinkingly and abandoned himself to the stream of confused images, facts, fantasies, and ideas floating at the periphery of an almost dream-like state. The softness of Lina's embrace and body scent, the fragrance of freshly cut grass, and Angela's mysterious moans mingled in his mind.

It was particularly hot that day, and the cannons were silent. After lunch, the boys were told to go take a nap in the cellar.

They adjusted the blankets on top of their respective places, closed the door, and darkness ensued.

After a while in silence, Roberto called, "Mario, are you sleeping?"

"Not yet. What do you want?"

"I was thinking … how does one ask?"

Mario turned around. "Ask for what?"

"Sex, or a screw, as you call it."

"You don't ask for it." Mario thought about it and then said, "You kiss the girl; you caress her, and then …"

"You still need her permission to kiss her, don't you?"

"No, you don't. Who do you want to ask, anyway … Lina?"

"No. No one, really. I was just wondering."

"I betcha you never even saw a pussy."

"You are quite wrong, my friend," Roberto answered swiftly.

"Oh yeah? Why don't you tell me about it, then?"

"Not now."

"Why not?"

"I want to sleep."

"Sure, sure, but you'll have to tell me later. I won't forget …"

Roberto remained silent, pretending to fall asleep immediately. His thoughts went back to Lina. He closed his eyes and thought of the mysterious pleasure she must enclose in her supple body, in that soft-looking bulge covered by the white triangle of her underwear.

Something stirred inside him, and he rolled over and pressed his body against the mattress. The unexplored desires, unknown yet pervasive, mingled confusedly in his mind and in his body, and now, for the first time, a potent if yet unfamiliar urge wakened inside him.

It was undoubtedly connected with Lina.

- XLII -

The morning had seen more activity than usual. Several troop carriers had gone by with camouflaged artillery pieces in tow. And then a military truck with some civilians and a few armed *Camicie Nere*— Blackshirts. One of them was the podesta of Castelvecchio. From his place on the truck and his rather grim face, it was difficult to know if he was a prisoner or an oppressor. Perhaps, at this stage of the war, he was a bit of both.

Soon after, the Americans started to shell the countryside, and everyone went to the dugout shelter. Two German soldiers had come in as well. Everyone was apprehensive, but after a few moments, the soldiers had moved on.

Later, the boys were told to take advantage of the shelling lull and go turn the grass cut the day before while the sun was still high.

"Why?" Roberto asked as they worked.

"To dry it on both sides and move the dampness. Otherwise, the cows get bloated and sick."

Then Mario suddenly said, "So what's the story?"

"What story?"

"The one you don't tell me yesterday, you fool, about pussies, screws … you know?"

"Ah, that one … I'll tell you another time," Roberto said. "It's too long and boring."

"I knew it. You never saw a pussy, that's why."

Roberto did not answer immediately; he just continued to turn the grass over.

"So …?" said Mario planting his fork on the soft soil. "Am I right?"

"Of course not," Roberto said with a smirk, "and now that we are finished, I might even satisfy your curiosity."

They sat in the shade of a large poplar, their backs against the tree trunk, their legs stretched over the soft grass. Patches of sunlight came through the foliage and played over the parched ground. Choirs of cicadas repeated their monotonous summer mantra, while chaffinches and canaries carried on their chitchat in their lyrical abandon. Mario laced his hands behind his head and waited patiently.

"Let's see," Roberto started in a mocking professorial tone, "over three thousand years ago, the Etruscans had some of the best toilets in the ancient world. And some of the worst ones." He noticed Mario's astonished face and went on, imitating the exact words and tone his teacher used. "In fact, while nobles and rich merchants gave free play to their bodily needs in the ample confines of their alabaster and marble lavatories, their slaves and common devils did it in a squatting hole."

"You talk funny, and I dunno who the Truscans is … and what that has to do with pussies."

Roberto laughed. "I am trying to satisfy your curiosity, Mario, and at the same time review some history. Bear with me."

"Okay, but don't talk that away."

"This story goes all the way back to my kindergarten days. The washrooms at St. Joseph's kindergarten, where I was, were the same as those of our ancient predecessors—the Etruscans. You follow?"

Mario clucked his tongue and shook his head, clearly still unable to see the connection.

"In plain words, Mario, the nuns' bathrooms at St. Joseph's were equipped with modern, ceramic seats; the children's were just plain squatting holes."

"Like the latrines at our farmhouse, you mean …"

Roberto had not intended to draw unfair comparisons. "You see," he said, ignoring his faux pas, "not that anyone ever saw much of the stone since it was always covered by near misses. In order to unload our burdens, we children had to persuade those nuns—black-clad inveterate soldiers of the faith, as I call them. Then we had to race the endless corridors of the monastery, outrun the competition on the final stretch, pull down our pants, find a clear spot for our feet, and take aim. For those, like me, who, for an additional sense of security, wore belts and suspenders, the chance of hitting the center on arrival was almost nil."

"I dunno … It's kind of funny, but it hasn't nothing to do with sex."

Roberto gestured for patience with his open hands and continued mimicking the tone of a storyteller. "During one of these sprints down the corridors, I reached the first toilet door and slammed it open. Astonished by what I saw, I came to a stop. The stall was already occupied by this creature, red in the face from the exertion, who, instead of a dangling penis, had a vertical slit between her legs."

"That was the first time you seen a girl's pussy?"

"Exactly. Up to that point, I had presumed the only difference between them and us was in the length of our hair and the shape of their clothing. No other detail had ever come to mind."

"So what did you do?"

"I moved to another stall, and as soon as I got home, I shared my discovery with my grandmother. However, she didn't seem impressed. When my mother came home and heard the story, they looked at each other, and back at me, and then my mother opened her mouth, but the words seemed stuck on her lips. After another side-glance with my nonna, she finally said, 'It's a secret, you know. But since you have discovered it, we'll explain the reason."

"And what she tell you?"

"She told me that the creature I had seen had probably been a boy. But one who frequently urinated in bed, and the doctor who had been consulted about remedying this nocturnal inconvenience had likely decided to cut off the penis."

"What a dumb answer!" Mario exclaimed. "And what did you say to that?

"I thought for a moment, and then I asked, 'If he … she … still was to pee anyway, how could the operation prevent her from doing it in bed?'"

"You was alreday a smart ass, wasn't you?"

"If that is your definition," Roberto answered with a smile. "The explanation didn't sound truthful. So, later on, I asked a few friends and finally came up with a new account. This particular older boy, who knew *everything*, not only told me that the difference was natural, but also that babies were made by joining of the male and female genital organs. Imagine that!"

"You mean screwing?"

"Whatever you call it."

"How old were you when that happened?"

"Four or five, I'm sure. However, I was already in second grade. Unfortunately, my parents had predetermined that I should be a genius, the next Guglielmo Marconi, I think."

"Who's that?"

"The man who invented wireless radio." Roberto laughed at Mario's puzzled look. "And not only that," he added in self-mocking fashion, "in the afternoon, I had to take piano and French lessons. Some from regular tutors and some from nuns."

"Tell me about them nuns."

"What about them?"

"Anything you want. I never gone to kindergarten … I'm curious."

"What can I tell you? I never really liked them. My recollection is that they fed us intolerable food, made us recite lot of prayers, conducted long and dull lessons, and punished us frequently—in my opinion, also unfairly."

"What do you mean by that?"

"It didn't matter what you did. You were punished by standing in front of the nun's desk, facing the class and holding a chair upside down over your head. You were only allowed to hold the back with your hands, so it wouldn't fall."

"Not very nice ..."

"Not nice or gentle. These chairs were solid oak, and in addition to being heavy and hard on the skull, the bars of the chair right in front of your eyes created a terrible sense of captivity."

"You were punished too then," Mario observed.

"More than once," Roberto admitted. "In fact, I remember one time that sister Amalia caught me drawing airplanes unloading bombs over an imaginary Garden of Eden. She was the one I disliked most, and she seemed to sense that and was harder on me than on other students."

"And what she did to you?"

"This time, besides the upside-down chair punishment, I was given a tongue-lashing. I still remember her words, something like: 'Regardless of your intelligence,' she said, 'which of course is not your own merit but a gift from God, unless you redeem yourself, you shall follow in the path of Lucifer and go to hell!'"

"Was you scared?"

"No, I wasn't," Roberto answered, smiling. "I didn't think I was that bad. By then, I had already learned to ignore people I didn't trust, or like. In the case of Sister Amalia, not only didn't I trust her, but I couldn't stand the sight of her. But to tell you the truth, the worst part was having to look at the grinning faces of my staring classmates."

"They do that?"

"Yes, Mario. Even those I thought were my friends made me feel they were enjoying my punishment. So, I searched for other escapes."

"Like what escape?"

"One of my favorites was the large yellow and blue world map hanging on the far wall. There, I could be with Caesar's Tenth Legion at the conquest of an empire, or with the Vikings discovering distant lands, or with Columbus landing on the beaches of the New World. My arms may have been numb, my skull aching, my leg muscles in pain from the forced immobility, but I was happy in my own world, and almost invulnerable to the outside."

"Wahooo!" said Mario.

The two boys fell silent, their thoughts seeming to wander solitary paths.

A car approaching from the north finally interrupted the tranquil feeling. The two boys peeked through the vines and then shouted to warn the others, "Heel, Tito! Heel!" An open-top Volkswagen, its spare tire bolted to the top of the front cowling, went by at full speed, and the boys sat down again with a sigh of relief. When the noisy engine was no longer audible, Mario asked, "Which country was you escaped to just now?"

"My very own, Mario," Roberto answered, giving him a friendly slap on the back.

*****

"Roberto," Lina called, "come give me a hand. We've got to get a bale of hay in the far field.

"I'll fetch the cart," said Roberto, glad to comply with the request.

"It's already there."

"Let's run, then," he said taking Lina's hand. He sprinted forward and dashed toward the clover field.

It was mostly sunny. A few ragged clouds sailed overhead. Their shadows traveled silently from field to field, darkening the green contourless surface at their passage. Then the sun suddenly reappeared, inundating the area with its bright rays. The earth seemed to smile again, as if rejoicing under its warm embrace.

Roberto and Lina worked at a good pace, and the cart was quickly loaded, but more hay remained on the ground.

"What about the left over hay?" Roberto asked.

"Which one?"

He turned around to show her, and Lina pushed him down on the mound and then threw herself on him. They started to wrestle, and Roberto rolled over, held her by her wrists, and, encouraged by her initiative, was about to kiss her. Suddenly, he stopped, raised his head, and pulled away.

"What are you doing?" she said.

Roberto placed his hand above his eyebrow to shield the light and looked toward the blue sky.

"What are you doing?" Lina asked again.

"Shhh … listen. Airplanes."

"Let's run back."

"No time for that. Come."

Right then, two fighter planes plunged from the sky and swooped in their direction Roberto dragged Lina to the closest gully and threw himself to the ground. He looked up as the airplanes arched smoothly in a northerly direction and began to fire. Lina looked at Roberto and made the sign of the cross.

"Why did you laugh?" she asked, when the burst of machine gun fire ceased.

"Oh, nothing," said Roberto, keeping an eye on the planes. "Look, they are coming back. Don't worry, though, they are shooting at something on the hill."

The airplanes made another pass, banking right above Lina and Roberto's provisional refuge. They were so low that the clear profile of the pilots, their heads wrapped in leather caps, was quite visible. They took yet another swoop and then disappeared. A dark column of smoke rose from the hill.

"They must have hit a truck or a tank," Roberto concluded.

Lina propped herself up and sat on the edge of the shallow ditch. "I want to know why you laughed when I made the sign of the cross."

As the planes flew away, an unbelievable peacefulness seemed to replace their sound. It suddenly spread its wings and filled the vacated area.

"It was an innocent smile, Lina," said Roberto defensively. "I didn't mean to be impertinent."

"Don't you believe in God?" she insisted.

"I don't know."

"Don't be silly. How can you not know?"

"Well, if you want me to answer yes or no, then I'll say no."

"When did you first realize that?"

"When I was four years old. But it didn't start with God … but with the guardian angel."

"What?"

"Yes," said Roberto, suddenly aware he could prolong Lina's company, "and if you promise not to say anything to anyone, I'll tell you the story."

"I swear," said Lina, placing her right hand over her chest.

"As I said before," said Roberto, as his mind replayed in puzzlement the ancient incident, "I must have been just over four. My parents were about to return from work when Nonna called me in to wash and prepare for supper. I had been playing at the back of the house with my toy soldiers, and as I entered the kitchen, Nonna looked at me and then at the box of toy soldiers I held in my hands. She promptly noticed that many of them were missing, and most of the remaining ones were damaged.

"'What happened to them?' she asked in a stern tone.

"'Nothing,' I said in reaction to her aggressive tone.

"'What do you mean "nothing"? Where are the missing soldiers?'

"'I don't know,' I said. I was starting to feel uneasy.

"'Listen, Roberto, you'd better tell me the truth right away, or else I will ask your guardian angel, and He, as sure as heaven, will tell me! But then there will be no forgiveness.'

Lina made a face and put her hand in front of her mouth as if to stop a comment.

"I was stunned and didn't know where to turn," he continued. "My beloved Nonna was chiding me, and the special angel who was supposed to defend me was, at least according to grandmother, ready to turn into a squealer!"

A sound of suppressed laughter escaped Lina's lips.

"'Roberto...,' Nonna Luisa insisted, 'for the last time, tell me what you did with the missing soldiers.'

"'They were dead, Nonna. I buried them in the garden.'

"'And these?' she asked, lifting a damaged one from the box.

"'They're just wounded ... I'll mend them and make them better.'"

Now Lina burst into laughter. "You little rascal," she said jokingly, and then passed the tip of her tongue over her lips while changing her posture on the edge of the gully. Her skirt caught the stubble of dry grass, leaving her legs uncovered to mid thigh, and Roberto's eyes roamed over her velvety skin. He resisted the temptation to put his hands there, caress them, and then let them glide all the way to that mysterious triangle of her underwear and beyond. But the moment had passed, and now he lacked the courage. So he forced his glance away and carried on.

"My nonna bit her lip, kept a serious face, and used the occasion to teach me what she thought to be a useful, moral lesson. She told me to place the box on the table, and then she sat on a chair and asked me to stand in front of her. 'Now listen,' she said waving her index finger under my nose, 'first of all, when I ask you a question, you must tell me the truth immediately. Second, you must learn that money doesn't grow on trees. Your parents and I work hard for it, and destroying things is like destroying money. Last, remember that I had to argue with your father to buy you these toy soldiers. You know how much he dislikes anything that has to do with war, and now you repay me with this!'

"By then, I had stopped listening. I was mortified and tried to make sense of it all, reviewing the events that had led to the scolding. I had taken my toy soldiers, with Nonna's permission, and gone to play in the garden. When I tired of marches, parades, and other static contests, I tried to make the game more interesting. I divided them in equal numbers and placed them in shallow trenches I dug out in the soil, as I had seen in pictures of the Great War in the history books. Then, like most gods of the Olympus did in the battle of Troy, which father sometimes read aloud after supper, I had taken a preference for one side and bombarded the other with earth clods until they were destroyed. What was wrong with that? The matter of money had not entered into my consideration, nor had the possibility of a scolding or the implied participation of my guardian angel.

"'I am sorry, Nonna,' I said without excessive conviction.

"'Repentance ... that is a good beginning,' she said. 'However, it's not enough. You must learn that in life one has to pay for his own misdeeds, one way or the other.

"'But I have no money ...,' I told her.

"'No, but so you'll remember, there will be no dessert for you next Sunday or the following one. *Qui bene amat, bene castigat*—who loves you much, punishes you much—as the Romans said!'

"So," said Roberto taking Lina's hand, although I suffered the punishment without complaint, I remained unconvinced about the role of my guardian angel. After all, I did tell Nonna about the soldiers. So, the next time the matter of my presumed spiritual protector came up again, I decided to take a chance."

Lina listened attentively to the caressing tone of Roberto's voice. She looked at his eyes, which seemed to speak of love.

"What did you do then?" she asked at last.

"It was a few weeks after the first incident. I was running in the garden, pretending to be riding a horse. I jumped over a flower bed, and then another, but at the third one, I misjudged the jump and landed on a plant with both feet. Two large begonia buds that Nonna Luisa had nursed for some time were irreparably smashed, their petals spread over the ground. I was desolate and terrified. I knew how much my nonna cared for her flowers. I picked up some of the petals, removed my footprint, and tried to minimize the damage, and then I went to play at the back of the house, as far away as possible from the site of the accident. Minutes later, my nonna, ever so attentive to each and every plant of her garden, noticed the damaged flowers.

"'Roberto,' she shouted.

"I heard her angered tone and ran to the front. 'Yes, Nonna,' I said, as innocently as I possibly could.

"'What happened to my begonias?'

"'What begonias?'

"'Don't toy with me, my boy. You know very well the ones I mean.'

"'No, I don't.'

"I held grandmother's stare, and as I anticipated, immediately came the now habitual phrase: 'Tell me the truth, or I'll ask your guardian angel.'

"Mindful of the previous event, I wanted to avoid another scolding or punishment. Therefore, I opted for an alternative that, in my mind, if nothing else, postponed the consequences. From where I stood, hell was rather far anyway.

"'If you are talking about those flowers,' I said, pointing at the begonias, 'you can ask my guardian angel, but I didn't ruin them.'

"'Who did, then?'

"'I saw a big dog jumping all over the garden, and then he ran away...'

"'But the gate was closed; where did he come from?'

"'It must have come from the back. He ran away that way ...'

"My heart was pounding. I expected to hear a thundering voice from above contradicting my story, or a cloud in the sky spelling the word *liar*, or an evil spirit whispering my name into Nonna's ears. But nothing of the kind happened.

"Nonna Luisa looked into my eyes for a long moment, and though feeling uncomfortable, I knew I had to hold her stare.

"'I believe you,' she finally said. 'I wonder whose darn dog that was.'

"Later that night, when Nonna tucked my covers and left my room, I tried to assess two possibilities out of the day experience. Either my guardian angel is not a squealer, I concluded, or else he doesn't exist. And if he doesn't, does anyone else?"

"You were a gutsy little guy, weren't you?"

Roberto smiled but did not answer. Lina's top button of her blouse had come undone. His eyes had fallen inside the hospitable opening and were journeying over her swelling bosom.

Oh, how I'd like to slip inside that shirt, he thought.

"And that is the reason you don't believe?" he heard her say.

"Of course not. That was only the beginning ... and an excuse to stay with you longer," he added with a sly smile. "I'll tell you more some other time. But now we'd better go, before they wonder what happened to us."

- XLIII -

1944

La Rossa and Lina had gone to a neighboring farm with a few eggs and a small bag of flour, to barter for some oil, lard, and other commodities.

Roberto and Mario were near the stack, gathering fresh straw for the stable, when a German truck sped into the yard. It stopped in front of the farmhouse, a low cloud of dust settling around the tires. Four soldiers climbed down from the vehicle and walked briskly toward the stable, as if executing a pre-planned action.

Roberto felt a sudden twitch of fear and noticed that their uniforms differed from those of regular *Wehrmacht* soldiers. They wore no helmets, and their weapons were minimal. In fact, only one of them held a machine gun, and another, who, by his behavior, seemed in charge of the group, had a revolver tucked in his belt holster.

He ran with Mario ahead of the soldiers, just in time to see the door kicked open, a black boot jutting across the opening, briefly interrupting the stream of light intruding from outside. Small particles of dust and straw whirled into the air under the vortex created by the movement of the door. When the door slammed shut, the stable temporarily fell into absolute darkness and silence.

The soldier in command shouted a command, and immediately one of the soldiers reopened the door. Four *Chianine* cows, which had scrambled to their feet when the door was kicked, looked at the intruders and then turned to the manger, considering the sweet-smelling hay.

"*Welche kuh nehmen vir?*" asked one of the soldiers, caressing the plump hind of the first cow. "*Diese?*" Then, placing his sunburned hand over Bianchina's snow white mantle, he touched her and patted her appreciatively, from her high neck to the hind legs. "*Oder diese?*"

"*Das da.*" That one.

The boys didn't need to understand the language of the soldiers to deduce that they wanted to take one of the cows.

The animals turned their heads curiously and then continued to munch at their usual slow pace. When the soldier touched Bianchina again, the animal tensed, then retracted slowly.

Mario stood near the door, frozen, fear painted on his face. His brown, soft eyes were widened in an almost hypnotic stare.

Bianchina kept crunching hay, and she grunted softly, her huge profile an immaculate bas-relief against the dark gray wall of the stable.

The soldier finally stopped and slapped her back. "*Ja,*" he said with satisfaction, moving toward the manger to loosen her rope.

Mario's mother entered the stable, dropping her gaze immediately when she encountered the arrogant stare of the soldiers. It was obvious that she was afraid of any reaction from them, and not seeming to know what to do, she sat quietly on a low barrel near the door. Mario walked to her. In one fluid, natural gesture, she put her arm around her son and drew him closer to her until he was cradled protectively between the folds of her long skirt. Tears began to fall from the boy's eyes as he whispered, "Not Bianchina. Not my Bianchina."

Giulia was crying too, but she seemed unable to utter a single word. She was clearly frustrated, feeling incapable of fulfilling a role that the culture and the times had always reserved for menfolk.

"Roberto," she finally whispered, "go call your mother. Please tell her to come right away."

When Roberto returned to the stable with his mother, one of the soldiers was already pulling Bianchina out of her stall.

Patrizia walked slowly toward the officer and, assessing the situation, demanded with authority, "Who said you can do this?"

The German plainly did not understand and therefore did not reply.

"*Papiere*," she insisted, her outstretched hand more eloquent than the spoken word.

The officer stared at her in surprise; she did not betray any nervousness.

Roberto was surprised. Even he knew that the soldier did not require any particular authority.

Patrizia no doubt recognized this undisputable fact. It was a wartime act perpetrated by an enemy who was now frustrated by a war that was clearly lost—a war that he must continue fighting to its bitter end, while at the same time striving to survive. The act of a German soldier who, among other things, probably perceived all Italians as betrayers of his own cause since they had surrendered prematurely to those who had been their common enemies.

Perhaps she was counting on the Germanic sense of discipline more than on the logic of her request.

Roberto looked at his mother, then at the armed soldier who started fidgeting with his machine gun. One of the soldiers said, "*Order Kommandanten Vomt.*"

"Show me," Patrizia insisted. "*Papiere.*"

The officer nodded, spoke a few words, and one of the soldiers left the stable and was heard getting into the truck.

Silence and the stillness of the moment were everyone's accomplices.

For a while longer, Patrizia could pretend to have made a logical request; the soldiers could act as though they had made a legitimate demand.

Roberto saw his mother's jaw tighten in her effort to remain calm and composed. No one talked. The only sounds audible in the stable were the cows ruminating with calm deliberation and the flies buzzing in the still, stale air.

The soldier returned, waving a piece of blue paper, which he held in front of Patrizia's face.

"The ink is still wet, you bastard," she uttered between her teeth indignantly.

Roberto was stunned. "Living in times of conflict," he had heard his father say, "one must recognize the moment and qualify actions and reactions according to the context." He knew it to be reasonable to defend one's rights, but wiser to ensure continuity of life. He hoped his mother would not argue beyond reason.

Patrizia looked at the cold, cruel stare of the soldier who was point-ing his gun, now in her direction, then toward Roberto.

*****

No! Not my son! she yelled in her mind.

Stay calm, Patrizia, her thoughts screamed. *Don't overreact! Acknowledge your temporary state of weakness. Subordinate your sense of justice; survive!*

So long as we live, she repeated to herself, *we can always regain that which is temporarily lost. But death precludes it forever!*

She knew that too many people driven by an abstract sense of justice or attachment to their property tried to defend their material possessions and ended up losing it all, and their lives as well. Only days before, she remembered, a poor farmer was cut down by gunfire when, blinded by anger, he had chased, with a pitchfork, a German soldier who was killing his chickens.

No! she said to herself. *Neither a chicken nor a cow is worth our lives!*

Terrified at the thought that she could lose her son, she tore the piece of paper from the hands of the soldier and blurted in repressed anger, "You win! Your piece of paper for our cow!"

"*Schnell!*" shouted the soldier in charge.

The others began to move quickly, pulling Bianchina by the short rope and directing her toward the ramp lowered from the truck.

The cow seemed reluctant to obey, and the armed soldier poked her with his gun. The animal looked back as if able to perceive the touch of death emanating from that shiny, cold instrument. A visible shiver of fear traveled the length of her body.

Roberto looked at his mother's ashen and tense face. She held the piece of paper in her hands and looked at Giulia and Mario, who were crying.

"I'm sorry, Mario," she whispered, and gently stroked his soft, dark hair. He responded with a feeble smile, his eyes brimming with tears as he stared at her with a look of mute supplication.

Patrizia's eyes were dry and unflinching. Her expression was now blameless; it seemed to say, *What can we do? It's the bloody war!*

She looked at the blue sheet of paper still in her hand; she folded it and pushed it into her skirt pocket. Perhaps she could report this unauthorized action to the commandant. *To what avail?* she thought. *What would that accomplish?* She realized that not even the commandant could bring the cow back. Furthermore, pursuing the matter could result in reprisal to the farm and its occupants.

She turned toward her son, who was still mesmerized by the events, and placed her hand protectively on his shoulders. She wanted to respond to his inquiring look, but she did not know what to say.

Suddenly, the image of that black instrument of death pointed toward him, her only child, only moments before, hit her like a lightening bolt. She felt a sharp, deep pain travel through every cell of her body, as though it was not until this precise moment that she fully comprehended the danger just passed.

Impulsively, she turned toward the boy and enfolded him in her arms. "Cucciolo," she whispered in his ear, "even parents are sometimes powerless, unable to protect what they hold dear. But an act of submission is sometimes necessary for survival. For life!"

She shook him gently. "Do you understand?"

He wanted to answer her. Tell her that he understood, that he was proud of her, but the words remained frozen in his mind. He pulled back enough to look her in the eyes and nodded vigorously. He then smiled and finally said, "I know, only donkeys nod. I ought to say, 'Yes, Mother, I do.'"

"I'm glad you remember," she whispered.

Her tone and look of affection said much more than that.

She pressed her boy to her bosom, and he responded with the tightest hug that he had ever given her. At that moment, she felt the need to cry.

*****

A few days later, Roberto stood on the stairway landing of the house, keeping an eye on the winding road ahead and the activity in the yard. Mario still looked sad for the loss of Bianchina. He had been near his mother during most of the last few days, and he was now feeding the pigs in the east shed. Lina was washing her hair beside the water well, humming a song. The hem of her skirt fluttered in the breeze and rose behind her legs as she bent forward. Her bosom threatened to overflow from her camisole. Roberto leaned over the porch to have a better look.

Amato was crossing the yard with a small load of hay on his back. "If there was a God," Roberto heard him mumble, "that's how a woman should always look, at least until ninety. Instead," he continued with a disappointed tone, "she'll marry, get pregnant, nurse her children, and get fat. That beautiful tight skin will become a pile of wrinkles." He spat from the side of his mouth. "But look at her now. God bless her."

He pushed the stable door with his foot and swore; the crepuscular fantasies in which his mind had just indulged crashed into the thick, smelly air of the stable and brought him back to reality.

Roberto had followed Amato's monologue unseen. He leaned over the banister and took a long look at Lina. Then, after being sure no one else was in the front yard, he came down and walked in her direction. His eyes fixed on the supple movements of her slender body and the rising hem of her skirt as she leaned forward, toward the metal basin.

No one was near, and he experienced a sudden determination to say something about his feelings for her. His heart beat faster and faster, and he could not decide what to say or what to do.

"Roberto," she called from behind the fluid screen of her dark, shiny hair.

He did not answer at first. His eyes were diving toward the smooth surface of her legs and mentally climbing slowly toward that mysterious, soft-looking triangle at the vertex of her thighs.

"I can see your feet," she said. "Please come here and pour some water over my head. Do it gently, though."

Roberto did as requested and then said, "I could rinse it thoroughly if you want … and even massage your scalp …" It seemed an innocent enough proposition.

"Do you know how?"

"Yes, I do. I'll show you if you let me." And in saying so, he began to massage her scalp slowly, as his mother always did to him, only more gently, more deliberately. He casually pressed his body to hers, pretending that it was necessary to reach her height. He moved his hands rhythmically, with supple movements, his fingers penetrating the thick, silky mass of hair until in contact with the smooth, white skin.

"Uhhhh," she moaned, reminding him of Angela's unusual sounds. "This feels good. You have a magic touch, you know?"

"Because I like touching you, Lina. You are so beautiful …"

"Thank you, Roberto, but I think it's enough for now. We don't want people to talk." She burst into spontaneous laughter. "You know what I mean?"

"No, I don't," he answered, resentment in his voice. *After all,* he thought, *why did she push me on the hay and roll over me?*

She swung her head upward, and a fine shower of droplets fell over the boy. He did not retract, but stood there staring into her eyes in a strange way. She held his gaze. He hoped she'd glimpse there all that his lips couldn't say. Words were not necessary when his feelings were loudly declared by the expression on his face, the tender look in his eyes, and the loving touch of his hands.

"It was only a joke. I didn't mean to offend you," she said with a tone of concern, and she reinforced her assertion by caressing his face. He spontaneously returned her caress, and she turned toward his hand, gently touching his palm with her tongue. He didn't understand the gesture, but he liked the feeling of it.

"Lina, I wish we …" He was unable to express his feelings with words. He hoped she could read it in his eyes. *Please, Lina,* he wanted them to say, *read it in my heart.* But his unspoken words seemed to bounce against her silence, like pebbles against a concrete wall.

"I'll go and set the table now," she finally said, "I'll see you at supper."

Her gentle tone restored a bit of hope.

Around the supper table that evening, people voiced their growing concerns about the future.

"The food supplies are dwindling," said Luisa.

"Yes, and bartering with other farmers has also dropped off," added La Rossa. Everyone is holding on dearly to whatever is left. Besides, they're even afraid to say they've got something, for fear of bein' robbed."

The two old women had stewed some vegetables and a few potatoes. That not being enough, they had sliced some stale bread, soaked it in cold water, and then placed wedges of tomatoes and basil leaves over it. Olive oil, salt, and pepper were the finishing touch.

"I like this *panzanella,*" Giulia said.

"For one thing," Mario's grandmother said cheerfully, "it won't be heavy on your stomach."

"Besides," Luisa added, "we'll have to be frugal with the few chickens and rabbits left. We don't know how long this darn war will last."

Everyone sat at the table and ate avidly, stopping only to listen to the odd cannon shell whistle in the distance and then explode far away. The targets were far, and while eating, the people around the table indulged in routine conversation, tending to the practical aspects of life: what to cook tomorrow, what to feed the animals, who would fetch this or that. They ate and drank, and at the end, they exchanged some of the usual war news.

"I heard the Germans have retaken Volterra …"

"Yes, and the Americans have bombed the harbor of La Spezia again …"

"Some people from the south who crossed the lines said lots of Polish and Canadians died at Cassino. The Americans bombed the place from the sky, but the dirty work on the ground was done by others."

Roberto listened to the adults and sometimes participated in the conversation. Mostly when, due to the absence of the professor, he was asked to clarify some geographical detail or historical data. *Is Cassino south or north of Rome? What are Polish people doing there? What language do Canadians speak?*

"French if they come from the province of Quebec," he said in response to the last question, "and English if from the other provinces." He always answered promptly, with his usual politeness. His knowledge, language, and seriousness at times seemed to make adults forget that he was only thirteen years old.

When he felt Lina's eyes upon him, he enriched his answers with details and information far beyond need or expectation. Truly, though, Lina was all the audience he needed, and when, through the soft glow of burning acetylene flames, he encountered her smiling eyes, he held her gaze. He hoped she could understand that the extra performance was just for her.

She'll know that, Roberto thought. Her generous, romantic heart could decode the intensity of his protracted looks and the words trapped in his eyes.

The look of desire she read in his face seemed to give her a certain amount of pleasure. Roberto was almost certain of it, but he would have liked to eliminate all doubts.

If only I were a bit older…, he mused.

When the conversation returned to commonplace matters, Roberto did not participate, but continued to follow every move that Lina made. He frequently glanced in her direction and was jubilant when she held his stare longer than expected.

Toward the end of the meal, Lina got up from her chair to distribute the last morsels of food left in the pan. She walked around the table spooning out the last bits of stewed vegetables and potatoes. "Let the kids have the rest," said old Amato. "They still have to grow."

"Just a potato and some sauce," said Mario, pushing his plate to his right. Lina scraped the bottom of the metal pan and served Mario, and then she moved behind Roberto. "Here," she said leaning forward to reach his plate. In so doing, she rested her bosom on his shoulder. It was but a moment, yet Roberto had the distinct impression that it had been deliberate and definitely longer than necessary. He did not move but just looked at the faces around the table to see if anyone was looking his way.

"Thanks, Lina," he said, turning his face toward her. Her lips sketched a fleeting smile that he promptly returned.

When it was time to go to bed, he said good night to everyone and kissed his mother and Nonna. Then he picked up a small candle, and, shielding the flame with his hand, he quickly went down to the cellar. He undressed, blew out the candle, and pulled the blanket up to his chin. Thoughts of the past day roamed in his mind.

He was about to fall asleep when he heard someone descending the stairs. Moments later, the large cellar door opened and a slender figure moved across the dark panel of the night. His heart jumped. He heard the muffled movements, the gentle slap of naked feet on the bare cement, the rustling noise of discarded clothes, and finally the movement of the straw mattress near his.

Lina! he thought. It was the first time that he was alone with her in a dark, enclosed place. His heart started galloping again.

"Roberto," she said in a soft voice, "are you awake?"

"Yes, I am."

He felt her movements, and then her hand touched his body searchingly.

"Give me your hand," she whispered.

He pulled his left hand from under the blankets and extended it toward hers. She pulled it gently toward her body and made his fingers journey leisurely over her breast. He was surprised by its softness and the changing hardness of her nipples. She guided his hand toward the flat of her belly. Moving downward over her navel was, for him, like crossing the unknown frontier of a wondrous land.

She guided him farther down, and as his fingertips encountered her soft tuft of hair, he realized that she was completely naked under her nightgown. His penis had come alive and pushed his blanket upward. His left hand reached the middle of her pubic area, and he felt a wetness he did not expect. He almost retracted his hand, but Lina's gentle pressure kept him there, and he began to stroke her softness with a movement dictated by her wants. He did not know the reason for that caressing stroke, but he enjoyed her closeness, her excitement, her sudden intake of breath, the heat of her flesh.

After a while, he sensed a new energy possess her body. Her movements accelerated. Her breathing became heavier, and muffled sounds escaped her lips. Soon she seemed to feel an excitement similar to the one he had witnessed with Angela. Her grip tightened, and her body arched upward to meet the stroking hand. Finally, she uttered a final sound, exhaled noisily, and then let her body relax on the mattress. He slowly pulled his left hand away, changed his position, and put his right arm over her bosom. Her hand reached for his aroused organ.

The sound of footsteps down the stairs indicated that other people were coming to bed.

They listened silently for an instant, and then she said, "Let's pretend we're sleeping."

He liked her conspiratorial mode. He promptly turned on his stomach and pulled his blanket over his head. He slowly moved his hand near his nostrils, and for the first time, he inhaled the scent of womanhood. He remained in this position for a long time, listening to the people settling in for the night and to Lina's regular breathing.

Every now and then, he slowly moved his hand near his nose and breathed in. Finally, he fell asleep.

He dreamed that he was in the middle of the wheat field, his body on top of Lina's, moving back and forth as she caressed his neck and his face. He kissed her mouth while hushed, sweet sounds escaped from her parted lips.

- XLIV -

1944

A few days later, two trucks with camouflage colors arrived at the farm with a small contingent of German soldiers.

"Tito, heel!" the boys shouted to the dog. The code alerted the occupants of the house.

Roberto knew instantly that this was not "regular" *Wehrmacht* either. In addition to their more brazen behavior, the conspicuously large medallion hanging on each of their chests loudly declared them as SS troops. He felt his bowels about to dissolve.

With them came a German-speaking Italian dressed in a black fascist uniform.

The dog barked and pulled on his chain, coming dangerously close to where they stood. One of the Germans pointed his gun toward the beast, and Mario moved protectively near the dog, held him by the collar, and calmed him down. "It's okay, Tito. It's all right. Good boy, Tito."

This time, the interest of the Germans was not in the cows, but rather in the people.

"*Raus!*" shouted two or three soldiers, pushing everyone out into the yard. "*Evakuierte zone!*"

"This is an evacuated zone," barked the Italian, addressing the small group. "You must leave, or you will be taken away by force."

"And where do you suggest we go?" Patrizia asked dryly.

Everyone had now gathered around her, following the exchange with apprehension.

"Lady," he replied, "that is not my concern. The people behind me are not known to be very patient or charitable. Please don't complicate my life and yours."

"But we have nowhere to go," pitched in Luisa. "Besides, as you can see, there are only women, children, and an old man here. What danger could we ...?"

"Listen, I don't make the rules. I just follow them."

"All right," replied Patrizia, "but please ask the German in charge if the eldest can stay. After all, they cannot abandon the animals and the few possessions they have left."

The man turned around and spoke at length with the German officer in charge. His reply sounded harsh and indifferent. The fascist spoke again, turning toward Amato, who was leaning on his walking cane, looking older and frailer than ever. Finally, he turned toward Patrizia and asked, "How old is the old man?"

"Over eighty-five."

"*Fünf und achtzig*."

The German nodded.

"All right," said the Italian. "The old man can stay, but only him. If you value your life, don't try anything stupid. The SS will come back in an hour to check the premises. If they find you here, they'll shoot you."

"But he's too old to stay alone," cried his wife. "Who'll take care of him? He'll die …"

"Only him," repeated the soldier, unmoved by her anguish.

"What the hell, La Rossa?" said Amato, spitting between his feet. "Don't worry … I'll keep busy. Besides, I'm not alone. I've got to take care of them animals, and there is the melon patch to water. Them things don't know a war's going on."

Even before the soldiers had disappeared behind the curve, the people quickly began gathering a few items of immediate necessity and placing them on top of two small carts. They debated where to go as they grabbed some loaves of bread, flasks of drinking water, blankets, plus a few extra pieces of clothing.

Roberto observed the scene from a corner of the cellar. They were about to leave their haven, with its thick brick walls and sufficient food, to take the road with a skimpy cart, two or three blankets, some garments, and only enough food for the night. It didn't seem to be possible. *Where will we go?* he asked himself. *Who could be as nice as the Banchinis and share their home with us?*

Roberto noted that Mario's mother had begun to cry. I'm *glad my mother hasn't. What would it be like if everyone did?*

"We are too many to be taken in by any single farm," said Patrizia. "We'll have a better chance if we split up."

Roberto's heart nearly stopped when those two words were pronounced: *split up!* So now, in addition to leaving the comfort of the farm, they had to separate; and who would go with whom? This had been home, his sanctuary, the place where Lina and Mario lived. Was he going to lose everything? For a moment, he felt like screaming. The final blow came when he realized that Lina was not going to be with him.

He was bitterly frustrated, as he hadn't even considered that she would not be included in his group. Earlier that day, he had hoped to have another night with her alone. To touch her again and ... who knows what else? Now he looked at her leaving and felt totally dejected. When she turned around, he waved his hand in her direction. She seemed to understand his plight. "I'll see you soon," she yelled.

South of the Banchini house was the Arno front line. Running east and west, it was merely the extension of the territory declared as no-man's-land. Consequently, the only direction open was north, leading toward the German back lines and the hills. Yet there was a strong reluctance to move too far from the farm and into unfamiliar areas where probably not one of them would be known, not even as a distant acquaintance.

Roberto's group was ready to leave as well. La Rossa embraced Amato. Managing to hold back her tears, she said, "Be careful, old fool. I want to find you here when I come back!" Then she positioned herself between the shafts of the old cart, took a deep breath, and began pulling the cart forward, assisted by the other women, who were pushing it from behind.

Roberto never imagined that walking away from Lina would be so painful. That single event troubled him more than the risk and the uncertainties. He walked beside the cart in a melancholy mood, and his sadness swelled when he realized they didn't even have a specific plan or destination.

"We'll stop when we find a place beyond the forbidden zone," his mother said.

"Or when we're too tired to go on and need a shelter for the night," his nonna said.

They had covered the distance of three or four kilometers when an intense shelling from the American side began. There was a moment of shock, and then Patrizia said, "Let's move, we must get to a safer place. We are too exposed here."

They began to walk more quickly. Luisa and Rosa mumbled prayers, while Mario held his mother's hand. Roberto listened to the creaking noise of the cart on the graveled ground and wished it could be loud enough to overcome the rumbling of the artillery and the whining noise of the shells whistling overhead. The thunder of nearing explosions rang in his ears, vibrating in his bones. He wondered if the tightness in his chest was caused by the explosions or by his own anxiety.

He looked at the downcast faces of the adults. Only his mother's expression resembled a stone sculpture. He wondered if she was really that fearless … or pretending for his sake.

This was by far the most relentless cannonade he had ever experienced, and its intensity seemed to increase minute by minute. He was also hungry, but he did not dare say so. All the same, the comfort of a warm meal and the alluring sight of Lina sitting across from him or moving gaily around the table, would not abandon him. It added to his ache. The notion caused him to remember a passage from *Dante's Inferno*:

Nessun maggior dolore che ricordarsi del tempo felice nella miseria ...

No greater affliction in misery than to evoke happier moments in time ...

Up ahead, on the south side of the hill, farmhouses and villas were being blown to pieces. At every explosion, a litany of saints escaped from the mouth of la Rossa or Nonna Luisa: "*Sant' Antonio, Santa Rita, San Severo,*" and finally: "*Santissima Vergine, Madre di Dio*"—"Oh Most Holy Virgin, Mother of God." But none of them seemed to have any desire or power to help the situation.

"Don't be afraid, cucciolo," Patrizia said, reading concern on Robererto's face. "They are bombing far ahead of us. By the time you hear the bang, the damage is done. Just like when you hear thunder after a lightning ... remember?"

"Today the Americans seem to be targeting the high ground," said Luisa.

Nightfall had displaced daylight as the group reached the foothills. They stopped a moment to look around, and then moved toward a massive farmhouse at the edge of a dense thicket. Other refugees were hiding in the bushes. They had come into the open after their shelter had taken several hits. All around them now, the entire area was bursting with explosions.

"We can't go any farther," yelled Patrizia. "We'll have to stop here."

She had barely spoken when a shell erupted like a thunderclap a few meters away, and shrapnel hissed through the smoky air, fortunately without hitting anyone. A farmhouse nearby suddenly became part of the targeted areas. They soon realized that the random nature of the American shelling made it impossible to pick any secure spot or predict a safe escape route.

They pushed the cart toward a slight depression in the ground. Patrizia wrapped Roberto and Mario in heavy blankets and told them to huddle under the cart. The adults took shawls and other blankets and lay them as a protective perimeter around the boys.

Roberto thought the bombing sounded like a firework finale, but infinitely more dangerous. He thought of the hell described by Kurt, the young German officer who had fought in Cassino. He thought of his father, who must have experienced bombing like this. Yet, the continuous exposure to these bombardments had conditioned him almost to the point where, after a while, he felt a kind of numbness to the real peril. It made sense to him when he heard his mother say, "In time, one can get used to almost anything."

He raised his head and peeked through the spokes of the cart's wheels. In a startlingly brief moment, his eyes registered never-to-be-forgotten images that flashed in sudden bursts of light from an explosion, only to vanish instantly into the utter blackness that followed. From start to finish, the explosions occurred with lightning speed, ravaging the quiet and darkness.

It was an infernal scenario, in which one could picture the birth or end of the universe. A primordial chaos of unleashed forces, with flames and choking smoke, light and pitch-black darkness, silence and cacophonous blasts, life and death.

There were a few breaks in the bombardment during the night. However, they were soon shattered by artillery barrages of redoubled fury and intensity. Orange flashes of fire briefly illuminated and silhouetted people and objects and then disappeared as if they never existed.

Roberto saw his grandmother in one of these moments, her silver hair shining against the unearthly light, her lips moving as though she was reciting a prayer.

Prayers, he thought. *What is God doing at this hour? Why is He allowing all this? Why don't his angels descend from heaven and put a stop to this? But what if there is no God? What if there is, but He doesn't care?*

He deplored that unbidden inner voice, which continually asked questions beginning with *What if* … On the other hand, he could not silence it.

With every new explosion, Roberto involuntarily shut his eyes. In the ensuing darkness, he retained the indelible impressions etched in his memory: a human form running in one direction, another diving into a hollow in the ground, a tree blown into the air. Like the high-speed shutter of a camera, one quick flash, an image pierced the lens, capturing and imprinting forever in the fraction of time before the shutter closed.

Who did his family and friends have now? If only one God existed, whom was He rooting for? Was He using evil people to punish other people who had committed some sin or another? What sins? Against whom? Against what?

Shortly before dawn, there was a pause in the bombing, and finally Roberto fell asleep. He dreamed that he was caught in an earthquake.

Once, after tucking in his blankets, his nonna had told him about one of her experiences: "It was nighttime," she said, vividly recalling the scene. "I was alone in the house, about to go to bed. When I felt the first tremors, I wasn't sure what it was. I stopped for a moment, and then the ground shook violently. I fell down as if I were completely drunk. Plates and glassware came crashing down from the cupboards, and the light went off. I don't mind admitting that I was scared. I heard people screaming and running in the street below, and I, too, instinctively wanted to run out of the house. I kept my hands and arms stretched in front of me. I kept bumping into chairs and other things that had shifted out of place. Finally, I reached the stairs, and holding onto the handrail, I don't really know if I fell or flew, but I did find myself on the ground floor ... and then in the middle of the street. Dozens of people were running about, calling, and crying. The ground was covered with roof tiles and plaster."

Right now, Roberto was living that same experience. He had fallen to the floor, and the earth shook convulsively beneath his body. At first, he was alone, but then he heard a voice nearby. "Roberto," someone called. "Roberto."

He opened his eyes. The first thing he saw was the cart above him. His nonna was moving nearby without apparent hurry or fear. He knew he was no longer dreaming, yet the earth kept shaking. A rumbling noise coming from somewhere behind caused him to turn around. A huge Tiger tank maneuvered beside the crumbled walls of the farmhouse, its large treads pulverizing the rubble. The earth shuddered again ... and again. *It's a man-made earthquake,* Roberto thought, even more frightening, as in this case, destruction and killing were man-made and intentional.

The Tiger tank was in place, and the Germans were now ready to do their own shelling.

They had to move again.

Rosa, Giulia, and the Lanzi women and children left under the watchful eye of the Germans.

"Did you see how big that tank was?" Roberto asked his friend.

"I certainly did," Mario replied. "It was scary big."

The boys helped pull the hand-driven cart loaded with a few essentials, and dragged their feet through the dusty country road to the next farm. It was overcrowded with other refugees and they could not stay. Then, in desperation, the small group decided to try the town. They walked the semi-deserted streets scattered with rubble and dead cats and dogs killed by shrapnel until a man from whom Nonna Luisa bought chicken feed recognized her and offered them shelter for the night.

They placed blankets and bedding on the cement floor. Roberto noticed the streaked thin layer of corn flour and feed spilled over it. It had been partially swept off the ground, probably, with the millet broom that rested against the wall. It was a small windowless warehouse, which, during the day, received some light from the double door that he remembered always open. Roberto had seen it before, but it had been filled with burlap sacks piled up to the ceiling in tall pyramids. Now it was empty, with only the smell of feed in the air. It was a comforting scent, reminiscent of better times: when nonna shopped there for her domestic animals and Father was home ... and the war was a distant sound.

"Come here, cucciolo," Patrizia said, patting the space beside her. "Let's try to get a few hours of sleep. We're all dead tired."

When everyone lay on the floor, Patrizia snuffed out the candle.

"May God look after us," Luisa whispered. These were the last words Roberto heard before falling asleep.

Soon, though, a violent shelling started. Some of the explosions occurred so close that the acrid smell of cordite filled the air and burned his throat.

They did not move. Despite the devastating effects of the bombs, the dread of their uncertain destiny and the unpredictable actions of the SS squads was even greater than the fear of their own physical death by bombs. They were interminable hours, but dawn finally came. In the morning, now desperate and demoralized, the adults discussed the few options left.

"If I have to die," Luisa concluded, "I want to do it in my own house. I'm tired of moving without aim or hope."

"Don't say that, Mother," Patrizia countered. "There is absolutely no food there, and we would be completely alone."

"What happens if we go back to the farm and the SS come?"

"I don't know, but right now, it seems the only thing to do. And if we have to defy the Germans in the process, so be it."

"I miss my house," Luisa insisted, "and if have to ..."

"Mother," Patrizia barked, "please refrain from saying that you want to die in your house. Let's think of living instead. Believe me, it makes no difference where we die." Then she moved closer to the older woman and whispered, "And do me a favor: stop mentioning dying when your grandson is near. You know how much he loves you. Why do you want to worry him for nothing?"

Luisa was visibly stunned by Patrizia's aggressive tone and by her saying "your grandson" rather than "my son" or "my child." Also, by her own egoism in not considering Roberto's feelings and concern.

A while later, while the two women seemed to reflect on their feelings and differing views, Giulia mildly asked, "Are we going back to the farm?"

"Yes, we are," Patrizia calmly stated.

- XLV -

It was now a week since they had returned to the Banchini farm, and so far the SS had not molested them. In fact, to Roberto's delight, after experiencing an odyssey similar to the Lanzis', Lina and her group also returned to the farm.

Today it was another sunny day and the momentary peaceful-ness of the countryside seemed to soak up the distant sounds of war. The muffled noise of military trucks rolling over the far-off highway resembled the purr of a cat. The odd scout plane flying up high was like a tiny grasshopper lost in the immensity of the sky. Its drone did not seem to disturb the lethargic stillness and silence of the fields around.

Roberto and Mario were playing in the yard as Patrizia walked by, a towel in her hand, humming a song. The others were inside the house, attending to their chores. Roberto had just waved to his mother, when a Volkswagen car suddenly came from the road behind the farm and stopped nearby, in the shade of the chestnut tree. A German officer got out of the car, adjusted his jacket, and looked around.

We are in trouble, Roberto thought when he saw him.

"Tito, heel!" he shouted to the dog.

Tito began to bark even harder.

The German smiled at him with an unusually mild expression. Also, he did not seem to carry any weapons, and he had a rather sophisticated air about him. Mitigating though his appearance was, the boy repeated the signal to the dog: "Tito, heel!"

He shouted even though the dog had stopped barking.

He noticed his mother next to the water well, washing her hair. She had unbuttoned the front of her dress and pulled down her collar. She must have heard the car and the warning, but she continued to rinse her hair, humming one of her favorite songs:

> *Oggi e' una Magnifica giornata,*
> *E goderla voglio sempre più*
>
> *Today is a beautiful day,*
> *And I want enjoy it more and more …*

Roberto looked at the German approach his mother, and he began to walk in their direction.

"*Buon giorno, bela signora. Or is it signorina?*" he heard him saying. Good morning, beautiful lady. Or is it miss?

"Either one will do, *Herr Kapitän*," she said. "Can I help you?"

"What *is* your name?"

"You speak Italian well, *Kapitän*. My name is Patrizia Lanzi. And yours?"

"I am Otto Bredis. You live here?"

"What does it look like?"

She swung her head around, and some spray fell on the officer's uniform. He backed up one step. His annoyed expression changed as his eyes took in her youthful beauty.

"You *grande kapitalist*," he said, gesturing to her silk dress.

"What should I save it for?" She grinned. "I could be dead by tomorrow."

"You very weise or very crazy."

"Wisdom and madness are so close that sometimes they coincide." She moved toward a sunny spot to dry her hair.

"Is there something you want?" she asked, seeing that the German was staring at her.

For a moment, he seemed to have forgotten his official business. He mumbled a few incomprehensible words and then put his hat back on and straightened. "Actually, I come to say 'tis evacuation zone. You cannot stay here. Very dangerous."

"Here we go again! Captain, neither you nor the Americans will make me move one more time. Not alive, anyway. If I have to die, I'll die near my friends, in this farm, wearing my best dress. Not among strangers and not on the road or in a dirty ditch like a stray animal." She tossed her head back and her hair swayed and shone in the sun like a silk skein. "You have deprived us of the dignity of living," she said. "At least leave us the dignity of dying."

He seemed to be taken back by her strong words. And even Roberto, who had moved closer and followed the scene, feared the German's reaction. Meanwhile, Mario came out of the shed and walked over.

"I see if can convince commanding officer to let you stay," the German said. "I can't decide myself."

Patrizia's eyes, full of fire only an instant before, softened again at the look of his contrite face.

"I am sorry," she said. "I know it's not your fault. It's the bloody war."

Airplanes were heard in the distance. Mario counted nine silvery shapes in groups of three, cut against the blue sky.

"It's a formation of nine," Roberto confirmed.

Suddenly the two boys saw tiny cylindrical shapes detach from their bellies. "Bombs!" they exclaimed in unison.

"Mother, Mother," Roberto yelled, running toward her. "They are for us; they are for us."

The ground shook as if in an earthquake, a series of loud explosions shattering the calm morning air.

Otto stopped Mario and Roberto and put his arms around them protectively. When the airplanes passed overhead, he said, "It's all right now. They going away." Then he looked at Patrizia, who had hardly moved, and exclaimed, "You not afraid? You definitely crazy!"

Just then, the air raid alarm of Castelvecchio rang in the distance.

"Too late as usual!" Patrizia exclaimed. "Darn idiots!"

They moved away from the trees and stopped in the middle of the yard, looking toward Castelvecchio. A tall column of dark smoke was already rising near the bell tower. A while later came the faint, rhythmic tolling of funeral bells, spreading to the countryside the news of death.

"They are never too late with that," Patrizia said.

"They mistake again," said Otto. "Altitude too high. They play war, but don't like risk." He shook his head and smiled. "*Auf Wiedersehen, schönes fräulein.*" Good-bye, beautiful signorina.

"Signora," she said.

Otto ignored the correction and saluted. "I come again." He looked back at Patrizia for an answer, but Roberto only saw the white flash of her teeth.

*****

Days later, Captain Otto Bredis returned as promised.

The boys shouted the "Tito, heel!" signal. Then, having recognized him, they walked toward him.

Patrizia, who had heard the signal, came to the porch and went down the stairs. She was now behind them.

"I have permit," said Otto, waving a document, stamped and signed by the commandant. "But I need somesing from you."

"Now what?" Patrizia snapped suspiciously.

"I investigate. People tell me you vork in distillery and are also good first-aid nurse."

"So?"

"Need help for vounded soldiers. You help; we help. You can bring your mother too if you wish."

It was an open secret that the Germans, in preparation for their next strategic retreat toward the "Gothic Line," had already dismantled their field hospital and transferred all non-combat personnel to the back lines.

"I'll let you know tomorrow," she said.

Otto saluted. "Till tomorrow, then." He clicked his heels and left.

Later that afternoon, Patrizia took her turn at the sink, washing dishes and pots while Luisa dried them with a soft, checkered cloth. No one else was in the kitchen.

"Mother," she said, "Otto told me that we can stay here, if we help with their wounded people."

"May God forgive me," Luisa said under her breath, "but I hate the Germans with all my heart. I will not help them in any way. Because of them," she said, banging an aluminum pot over the sink, "I lost my husband and my house, and Italy lost over six hundred thousand men."

Besides her personal grudge, which went back to the Great War, she believed the Germans to be people without compassion, "real heirs to their Vandals forefathers," as she had voiced at times.

Patrizia did not reply immediately.

She noticed that Luisa was breathing with difficulty. Her appearance had changed drastically in the last few months: she did not eat properly, she hardly slept, and she was often in a state of anxiety. Only nerves and willpower, everyone said, were giving her sufficient energy to go forth. Plus her love for her grandson, whom she wished to see safe and grown into a man.

"Would you rather go back on the road under shelling? Or sleep in ditches, risking the kids' lives and ours?" Patrizia countered at last. "I don't like it either, Mother, but we have no choice."

Luisa finally conceded. "Perhaps I should practice some of the compassion mentioned in my church books. Besides," she said attempting a smile, "I wouldn't let you go alone."

As Luisa would soon find out, her wish for compassion would benefit more than just the Germans. In addition to *Werhmacht* soldiers, the wounded included American and other Allies prisoners taken at the Arno Line, as well as several Italian civilians, who were often unable to find the local doctor, not known for his courage or his faithfulness to the Hippocratic Oath.

The decision to help would enable them to maintain a roof over their heads and, hopefully, give them some protection against the type of marauding soldiers who had taken Bianchina and could return for more looting.

*****

Weeks went by, and indeed the unusual arrangement benefited both parties. Sometimes Otto gave them some brown bread and a small bag of cane sugar … "*Fur die kinder,*" he would say. For the children.

Luisa stubbornly refused to eat anything that came from the Germans, and she gave her portion away to people with fewer resources. Under cannon shelling, she often delivered whatever she could to the Buglioni farm, where many *sfollati,* or refugees, had found shelter and were said to have run out of food. Her heart filled with fear, but also with hope that God would lead her safely to her destination and back.

Now and again, when off duty, Otto visited the farm at night. Occasionally, he shared a home-cooked meal with the family, played with the children, and, when Luisa was busy with the chores, he tried to converse with Patrizia. As the shelling intensified, he suggested the reinforcement of the bomb shelter they had improvised. He laughed when Patrizia showed him the paper left by the soldiers who had taken Bianchina.

"It says next German soldiers should take away rest of cows," he explained in his heavy accent. "I vill procure proper paper from *kommandant.*"

A few days later, he posted a decree that officially extended the protection of the area command to the Banchini farm. Now they would not suffer further losses from the scurrilous incursions of the retreating army.

Otto was kind to the children and let them use his binoculars to visually explore the hills of San Romano and the unlimited sky.

Despite this, Patrizia remained rather cool toward him.

"So, *German,* what other news do you bring us?"

"Do not call 'Cherman,'" he told her resentfully. "I am from Austria."

"If you wear a German uniform, what else would I call you?"

Otto seemed to reflect for a long moment. "My country suffered too after the Great War. Ve vere the capital of an empire and became impoverished state, vidout access to sea … and surrounded by new hostile states. No other country suffered as much as ve did after the war. My family, my father … Anyvey," he then said, changing to a quieter tone, "since you have to call me somesing, call me Otto. Otto is my name, not bad connotation; some Italians called Otto too."

"All right, Otto, tell me, when are the Germans going to leave?"

"You hate us now. But Allies not all good either. You'll see. You don't know vat they did in the South. Moroccans and other color troops very bad, no discipline. They raped women and children, killed husbands."

Patrizia looked at him incredulously. She had not heard anything like that before. "And how do you know that?"

"You do not believe—I see it in your eyes—but it is true. I heard it from Italian populations when ve reconquered lost towns. Also, from prisoners captured in the area of the Gustav Line. Also heard it from communications of the French Army, under vhich Moroccans soldiers fight. And from Polish soldiers who heard the terrible screaming of women from their positions."

"This sounds too strange to me. What are the French, the Moroccans, the Poles, and all the other people doing in Italy, anyway?"

"That is a good question," Otto said with a sad smile. "With Americans and British are many other nationals fighting for one reason or another. Some of them," he added after a short pause, "perhaps for no reason at all."

"What do you mean?"

Otto let out a long sigh and then said, "War is bizarre. Sometimes ideals, objectives, perceived national interests, hatred, and unrealistic hopes make for strange cocktail, *ja?* Leaders make promise to have more people fight vith them. Men chose to believe it; they fight, they kill, they die."

Patrizia looked at Otto in silence, and he went on. "The Poles, for instance, fight on the side of the Allies—who are same side as the Russians—hoping to regain their country at the end of war. But I think Russia, if vinner, vill keep Poland. The French fight to regain honor of their army, defeated and humiliated at the beginning of war. The Canadians and New Zealanders and other young countries hope shedding blood will make them more ... how to say ... more legitimate in eyes of larger nations. Many people ... many different, sometimes absurd reasons ..."

"Is this so?"

"It is so, Patrizia. Yet you hate us the same."

"I wouldn't call it hate, Otto. It's just that until you go, we are in danger. Bombs from the top, damned SS Truppen on the ground ... I'm sure the SS do as many bad things."

"Shhh." Otto put his index finger to his lips. "Don't say those things aloud," he said in a hushed voice. "Yes, they do—it is war—but have you ever heard of them raping women and children?"

- XLVI -

The shelling had started again. This morning the Allies were pounding the farmhouses on the distant hills. The projectiles whistled overhead without representing any immediate danger to the Banchini farm compound.

The usual spotting plane, or *cicogna,* as everyone called it, was flying overhead, and the children, used to these routines by now, played in the yard and watched the country road for German patrols.

Ivo's wife, Angela, sat on a low wooden stool near the tool shed, trying to breastfeed her child. It was a painful effort because her once-abundant milk had nearly dried up.

"It's the fright," someone told her. "Sometimes it happens that way."

The child was hungry but try that he might, he was unable to draw sufficient milk from his mother's breast to be satisfied.

From the hiding place that Gino had carved out inside the haystack, the men could clearly hear, interspersed with the whining whistle of the shelling, the voices of the children at play; those of the women shouting comments and instructions from the front porch; the clanking noise of the chain that Tito pulled along the wire line; and now, the cries of the baby.

"I don't know what to do," Angela said to Giulia, who had come to see her. After a while, the baby's cries became increasingly louder, taking on a tone of desperation.

"I can't stand it anymore," said Ivo at one point. "I must go and see if I can find some milk."

"Only place you'll find a milk cow is at the Buglionis'. Last I heard, they still had the Holstein. But it's way too dangerous."

"I'm sure Angela is desperate. I've got to do something, *Zio*. I'll be careful. Besides, the Germans stay put during the shelling, especially while the *cicogna* is overhead."

"I don't know, Ivo, but …"

"The little guy is hungry. I've got to go."

Gino nodded, concern written on his sunburned face. "Go through the fields and vineyard," he said. "Then turn to the path, but don't stay on it. Take the shallow ditch that runs the same way, till the end of the field. Cross the next wheat field, and from the other side, you'll see a large reddish complex. That's the Buglioni farm. Be careful."

"Do you have any money?" the professor asked.

Ivo touched his back pocket to make sure that he had his wallet, "Enough," he answered, getting to his feet.

Everyone fell silent. Gino cupped his hand behind his ear and listened. Judging by the sound of their voices, the children seemed far from the haystack. He began to undo the access panel by turning the two wooden latches that held it shut; then he opened it a crack and listened again.

"It seems okay," he said. "No one is near."

He raised the heavy lid from its lower open hinges and lowered it to the ground. Ivo patted his uncle on the back and promptly lifted one leg over the edge. When his foot was firmly on the ground, he bent his body, swung his head out, and then lifted the other leg. He was now in the open.

Gino lifted the lid into place and turned the knobs. "How does it look?" he whispered.

"Perfect," Ivo answered. The thick, rough texture of the straw-padded lid blended perfectly with the surrounding area of the haystack. No one could have suspected the existence of that hiding place.

The entry hole was positioned in a place not visible from the house, and once out, only a few meters separated a person from the cane thicket. All seemed calm and secure around the farm as Tito lay quietly in the shade of the kennel, enjoying a midmorning nap.

Ivo followed Gino's recommendations and weaved carefully through the river cane, following a longer, indirect path through the vineyards, ditches, and wheat fields. Every now and then, he lay on the ground and listened carefully for any suspicious noise. Then he started again or sought the safety of a ditch when the whistling of a shell announced the dangerous proximity of an explosion. After about an hour of this painfully slow advance, he was finally near the Buglioni farm.

Suddenly, the shelling stopped. Shortly afterward, he heard the voices of children who emerged from their hideout and began to play in the yard. He heard a woman telling them not to stray away, just in case the shelling started again. Everything seemed normal. Ivo took a last look through the grape leaves and then crossed to the other side of the field and into the yard.

"Signora," he called as he walked toward the old woman moving in the court. "I come from the Banchinis'. I have a few-months-old child who's starving, and I need some milk. I can pay for it … Can you help me?"

"*Gesù mio,* son, I'm sorry, but the Germans took our last cow two days ago. We got no milk ourselves."

"Oh my God!" Ivo exclaimed in disappointment. "What am I to do now?"

"Wait," said the woman with a sudden afterthought. "I heard the Spallettis still have a milk cow. It's that orange farm over there; you can go and see …"

Her words were still hanging in the air as Ivo followed the direction of her outstretched arm, and the screeching sound of brakes shattered the relative silence of the moment. A German vehicle turned in to the yard, and everyone froze.

Three or four soldiers jumped to the ground before the truck even came to a halt. They hurried toward the two adults. They were SS soldiers in camouflage uniform, machine guns in hand and stick grenades hanging from their thick leather belts.

"*Halt! Still gestanden.*" No one moves.

"Mother of God!" the old woman exclaimed.

Ivo's mind froze; his mouth went dry. He could not form or utter a single sound.

"*Komm, komm,*" a soldier gestured with his gun. "*Raus auf den LKW.*"

Ivo was petrified.

"*Komm!* You deserter!" he yelled, implying that Ivo was of military age and should have been at some war front or other. "*Schnell!*"

"No!" Ivo finally cried. "Me no deserter. Yah, *esonero*, I orphan … me have esonero. Look!" He extracted a sheet of paper from his back pocket and began to unfold it to show the soldier.

"*Schise!*" the soldier barked, hitting the paper with his gun muzzle and causing it to flutter to the ground. "*Schnell!*" he repeated, poking Ivo's rib cage with the gun. "Italian *esonero* no good vere ve going!"

"Let him be," implored the old woman. "He has a small bambino to feed …" She tried to push herself between the two men, but the SS soldier gave her a violent shove that sent her rolling to the ground.

"Bastard," Ivo hissed through his teeth, "she is an old woman." He moved toward her to help her, but a second SS kicked him and pressed the muzzle against his chest. The old woman had slowly rolled her body and was now sitting on the ground, blood dripping from her knees and from her nose.

"Don't worry, son," she said with teary eyes. "I'll be okay."

"Please go tell my wife at the Banchinis'," Ivo pleaded, as he was pushed toward the military vehicle.

In the back of the truck, guarded by two soldiers with pistol machine guns, stood about thirty or so Italian civilians, crammed against each other. Their apparent ages ranged from around twenty to over fifty. The common element was the fear and hopelessness written in their eyes.

One of the older men helped Ivo climb aboard. "Welcome to the meat wagon," he said.

He had light gray hair and pale blue eyes. The open expression on his face inspired confidence.

When the last soldier on the ground climbed into the cab, the truck started, swung around the yard, and reentered the country road, taking a northerly direction.

Ivo looked with despair at the road they were leaving behind, at the growing distance between him and his young wife and his little Renzo.

"I just needed some milk for my baby boy," he said to no one in particular. Tears ran down his cheeks, and his lips trembled.

"*Coraggio,*" said a voice beside him. "Have courage."

After a short ride through the valley, the truck began to climb the tortuous road to the hills, hazy with heat waves under the hot midday sun. The smell of sweat and fear permeated the air. At the top of the hill, the road continued through the woods. It was suddenly much cooler, and the air, spiced with the scent of the pine trees, made the situation more bearable.

Here and there, stationed in small clearings beside the road and fully camouflaged, Ivo noticed several armored vehicles, tanks, and other equipment. Soldiers stood nearby. They drove for about an hour, and then, just before reaching the town of Monsummano, the truck stopped under the shade of a large oak tree, and the men were told to get off the truck and sit on the ground. "*Runter von Laster.*"

The soldiers formed a perimeter around the resting area and one remained on top of the truck to man the machine gun mounted on top of the cab.

Ivo sat on a chunk of Pietra Serena stone, and the man who had helped him onto the truck, after relieving himself against a tree, walked toward him. "Wanna share a smoke?" he said, breaking his last cigarette in two. He sat beside Ivo who accepted the cigarette. "I heard you say that you have a young son. How old is he?"

"Seven months. He's our first one."

"Are you from Castelvecchio?"

"No. I am from Santa Chiara, but after several bombing raids, we got scared and moved to my uncle's farm in Castelvecchio. I went to that other place looking for milk for my son."

"Myself, I'm from Fucecchio. I was born in Empoli, but I left a long time ago. They got me as I was returning from the cemetery …" He blew a puff of smoke. "Today is the first anniversary of my mother's death. At first, I thought of running away, but they were all over the place, and after the first warning shot, I wasn't going to try again. A young guy did …" He paused and swallowed the lump in his throat. "They cut him down. His body was riddled with Schmeisser bullets, and they left him in the middle of the street like a goddamned dog." He shook his head and brought the cigarette to his mouth again.

"What do you think they'll do to us?" Ivo asked.

The older man let out a deep sigh. His face became even more clouded with concern.

"What's your name, son? Mine is Bruno."

"Ivo. My name is Ivo."

"Well, Ivo, you heard the saying *Finché c'e vita, c'e speranza*—While there is life, there is hope." The corners of his eyes held a sad smile. "I guess they mean that there isn't much of it afterward."

"What can we do?"

"Listen, Ivo," Bruno said, leaning closer to him, "it looks as if they are taking us toward Bologna. I hear the Germans are building their next line of defense, and they need us to do the work. I also think that after they've used us … they …" He paused a moment as if to search for the right words. "Kaput—they'll kill us," he finally blurted out with some effort. "And if my legs were as young as yours, when we get to the mountain pass and the truck slows down, I'd take my chance and jump."

The conversation was interrupted by the arrival of several other trucks and two armored vehicles, all with the SS cross lightning bolts painted on the doors, all with the same mix of prisoners and soldiers.

Soon there were the usual guttural shouts of *Komm!* and *Schnell!* Sometimes they were followed by *Italiener schweine*—Italian pigs.

Ivo and his new companion joined the others aboard the truck.

One by one, the vehicles continued toward the north in an orderly, evenly spaced column, sandwiched between two armored cars topped by heavy-caliber machine guns. Ivo began to wonder how he could ever have a chance of escaping.

*****

By midday, the shelling had subsided. The boys noted a heavier-than-usual passage of military vehicles and foot patrols, and they shouted the usual signal—"Heel, Tito! Heel, you bad dog!"—whether the poor beast was barking or lying quietly in the shadow of his kennel.

When the men in the haystack heard the signal, they did not move or talk. In the late afternoon, when Patrizia and Luisa returned after completing their chores at the command post, all seemed calm. Even the baby, after being fed a boiled concoction of finely sifted mashed beans, had finally fallen asleep.

Supper was prepared and then served as usual, after sundown. The women, children, and old Amato sat around the wooden table, and La Rossa and Luisa began to serve the food. Tonight they had created some kind of vegetable concoction in a tomato sauce. Patrizia called it *ratatouille.* "It tastes better in French," she said. La Rossa called it vegetable stew, but regardless of its name, everyone dunked the crusty bread into the dense sauce and ate eagerly.

Comments such as "And even today we shall not starve" and "Thank God we have not run out of food yet" were made around the table.

Taking advantage of a moment in which everyone seemed distracted by the food, Luisa sneaked out of the kitchen holding a bundle. Downstairs, she walked a wide circle around the house and entered the cane patch at its western end. Cautiously, she made her way through the thicket until she was in front of the haystack. There, she paused for a moment, and when she felt sure that no one had seen her, she whispered, "Gino, it's me, Luisa. Open the latch; I have your supper."

Gino opened enough to receive the bundle, and Luisa asked, "Is everything all right?"

"Yeah, we're all right, but where is Ivo?"

Luisa looked at him through the opening. A faint glow was shed from the homemade candle that rested on a wooden box at the center of the confined space.

"Ivo," Gino repeated. "Where the hell is he?"

"We thought he was here with you, Gino. Where else would he be?"

"In the morning he was, but then he heard Renzino cry, and he went to the Buglionis' for milk. He didn't come back."

"Oh my God. When did he go?"

"Around ten, I reckon."

"I hope nothing happened. Otto told us that many hostages were taken today. The SS are all over the place; even the regular German soldiers are jittery. Listen, eat and be quiet. I'll go to the Buglionis' and see what happened." Then, as an afterthought, she added, "Maybe he was smart; he saw a lot of patrols and hid there. Anyway, I'll go check. Be calm."

She stopped at the kitchen door and with a casual voice called, "Patrizia, Giulia, please help me with something here."

Patrizia looked up from her plate. For a moment, she seemed on the point of asking why, but the look on Luisa's face must have made her stop. They joined Luisa outside, where she told them what had occurred.

Giulia exclaimed, "The Germans got him! I know they got him." She bit her hand as if to stop expressing her next thought.

"We don't know for sure," said Patrizia, touching her arm.

"I'll finish supper, and then I'll go to the Buglionis'," Luisa said. "Not a word to the others."

545

They returned to the table, but Giulia stared at her plate without eating.

*****

Roberto had followed the scene, wondering what the look on her face meant. Nonna seemed to rush through the rest of her supper, and his mother's face held no decipherable expression. He knew something was wrong, and he wanted to know what. Could it be bad news about his father?

Luisa gulped a sip of watered wine, got up, and, without uttering a word, made for the door.

"Where is Nonna going?" Roberto asked his mother.

"She is busy with something. She'll be back soon."

"But where is she going? She didn't even finish her supper …"

"Roberto!" Patrizia gave the boy a stern look. "You know what happens to curious people. They grow a nose as long as Pinocchio's. Now finish your supper and go to bed!"

*****

Counting on her faith in God and the fact that regular *Wehrmacht* soldiers were generally respectful of women and lenient with older people, curfew or not, Luisa walked to the Buglionis' farm.

Everything seemed quiet, and from the outside, the place looked deserted. Luisa went to the front door and knocked lightly. No one answered. She knocked another time and called in a low voice, "Anybody home?"

Finally, she heard a soft shuffling of feet, and a voice answered, "Who is there?"

"*Amici* … friends. Open the door, please."

The old woman who had spoken to Ivo and witnessed his capture cautiously opened the door, a suspicious look on her face. The light of the candle shone over Luisa's face and the silvery band of hair around her head.

"Oh, it's you," she said with relief. "You are the one who brings food to our refugees." She began to cry even before Luisa could tell her the reason for her visit at such a late hour.

"I was supposed to come and tell you, but I was afraid. They pushed me to the ground. They took that young man away with a bunch of other people. Look," she said, uncovering her knees, which were all scratched and swollen. "I can hardly walk. Poor boy … I pray to God that he'll be all right. I was just telling him that the Spallettis' might still have a milk cow, when them soldiers plunged in here and took him away …"

Luisa listened to the details and then said, "They drove north, you said?"

"Yes. I went upstairs and watched them take the route to the hills."

"Thanks for the information. Now I'll have to find a way to tell his poor wife." Then she turned back and added, "Look after those knees or you'll get an infection."

"I will. I'll pray that the poor boy will be safe."

"Yes," Luisa answered from the door. "Let's pray to God, and let's hope He is listening tonight!" Then she added in her mind, *Forgive me, God, if I am beginning to sound like my daughter-in- law.*

She walked into the night, in the direction of the Spallettis' farm. On the one hand, she was still determined to find milk for the baby. On the other, she was frightened by the news of Ivo's capture and searching for words to soften the blow for Angela.

When she finally returned to the Banchinis', she was holding a small bottle of milk capped with a plug of corncob.

Patrizia and Giulia looked at her questioningly. She avoided their stares, and turning toward Angela, she said, "Go boil the milk, so when the baby awakens it will be ready." Then she told the bad news to the others and suggested that they keep it to themselves for the night. "One never knows," she added, without too much conviction. Upon hearing the news, Giulia was visibly shocked. Her eyes filled with tears, and she was barely able to choke back a moan.

"For God's sake, Giulia," Patrizia whispered, "let's not add to the problem." She took her arm and pushed her gently toward her bedroom. "Please go dry your eyes."

The night was relatively calm until a loud knock at the cellar door woke everyone. Through eyes veiled by sleep, Roberto observed the well-rehearsed pantomime fall into place. At the second or third knock, Patrizia lit a match and Nonna Luisa shouted, "I'm coming, I'm coming!" The acrid, sulfur smell of the match snaked through the stale air, and when its flame grew large and bright, Patrizia lit the candle stuck to the cement floor with molten wax.

Everyone was awake, and as preestablished, Ivo's mother, with much of her fleshy body purposely uncovered, sat on the porcelain chamber pot in the middle of the room. Angela pinched her baby awake so that he would begin to cry and scream. Nonna Luisa walked to the door, her normally straight figure now bent, her silvery hair undone for greater effect. She pulled the latch and opened the massive door just a crack.

The soldiers entered the provisional dormitory, and the orange flame of the candle revealed the scene. Their expression was one of utter revulsion. They seemed disgusted by the look of sickly humans. After an initial hesitation, they advanced carefully among the drowsy bodies of the refugees as though walking through a minefield. They looked under the concrete vats and behind the row of old oak barrels, aimed their torchlights in the darkest corners and the far walls, and ensured there were no hidden doors. Having ascertained that no one hid in the cellar, they quickly retreated to the fresh night air. Their visit was predictably short!

Nonna Luisa shut the door again, returned to her makeshift bed, and noticing Roberto's wide-open eyes said, "Don't worry darling; they have gone away." She pulled the woolen blanket up under his chin and told Patrizia to extinguish the candle.

When it was dark again, Roberto reached for Lina's hand under the blankets, and then he fell promptly asleep again, but his slumber was frequently laced with disturbing nightmares. He saw his father far away, walking in a sandy desert, and tried to run after him, but regardless of how fast he ran, he couldn't make any progress. He could not reach him. He then tried to call at the top of his voice, but the howling winds carried his calls away. He tried again, but no sound came out of his mouth. Now he could hardly see him, a vague silhouette near the horizon, inexorably marching away from him.

When all seemed lost, the image returned. It was that of a man in a fresh khaki uniform at the far curve of Castelvecchio, just like the time

Riccardo had left for Africa. Then, as in the sequence of a short feature film, that reel ended and was followed by another, where Roberto saw himself in the narrow country road that led to the Banchinis. He was running and running, and behind him, German soldiers were trying to catch him. He tried to run even faster, but his legs did not seem to respond to his commands. He knew he could run faster than this, but something was impeding his movements.

Later, the dream continued, and in this sequence, gunshots were fired behind him, and his right arm was hit by a bullet. It didn't hurt as much as he thought it would, but now he could no longer move it, and his running was further hampered. Soon he would be caught. He pressed on, sweat now running down his forehead. Although he had been running toward the Banchinis', somehow he suddenly found himself in the center of Castelvecchio. The Germans had disappeared, but a bombing raid was in progress.

He was alone, and dozens of people ran in all directions, crying and calling the names of their dear ones. Then they stopped and began to sing, and they looked at Roberto and laughed. The world did not make any sense!

He began to run and cry as the bombs kept falling and houses crumbled to the ground in a hail of bricks and dust. Finally, he stopped in front of a hill of rubble blocking his way.

From its top, his nonna, white as a ghost, descended toward him, her feet floating above the rubble. "Roberto," he heard her shout. "Roberto!"

Someone shook him gently, and the voice repeated, "Roberto! It's time to wake up and have breakfast."

He opened his eyes, and through the partial obscurity of the room, he saw his nonna leaning over him. He tried to move, but his right arm was asleep under his body, and his legs were entangled in the heavy blanket.

A bright glow filtered from under the uneven cellar doors, and a sharp blade of light with dancing particles of dust crossed a large keyhole and hit the cement floor.

"I'm coming, Nonna," he said.

Though it had been only a dream, Roberto was disturbed by it. He worried for his father, but he did not say anything.

Later in the morning, Luisa, Patrizia, and Giulia finally told Angela that Ivo had been taken prisoner.

Roberto and Mario witnessed her desperate crying and became aware of the bad news as well.

"God, what have I done to deserve this? My poor innocent child without a father. What am I going to do?"

"Calm down, Angela," Patrizia pleaded. "Let's wait and see; he may be all right. I'll ask Otto, see if he knows anything."

Angela finally quieted down and held her baby closer to her chest. "My poor baby, my poor husband …," she muttered.

The boys were told to redouble their vigilance of the country road and to shout the "Heel, Tito" signals louder than ever before.

"Didn't they say he was taken at the Buglioni farm?" Roberto asked Mario.

"Yes, but let's pretend we bought the Pisa story."

The atmosphere in the house was tense, and when Luisa and

Patrizia left to perform their usual duties at the command post, the two boys sat quietly on the porch and kept their eyes glued to the winding country road.

*****

That afternoon, taking advantage of a moment when the commanding officer was away inspecting the front lines at the Arno River, Otto came to the kitchen. "Patrizia," he whispered, "I hear SS units found men in haystacks in farmhouse near Santa Chiara. The men were burnt alive. If men hide in hay at your farm, tell them go away. SS now burn other suspicious places."

"Have you heard anything about a young man taken at the Buglionis'?"

"No. But I know many people taken avay to the North."

As soon as they returned home, the two women told Giulia about Otto's comment. Then, with a plausible reason, they called everyone into the house while Luisa took her usual long detour through the cane patch. She advised Gino and the professor that it was no longer safe to remain inside the haystack, and it was now necessary to find safer refuge.

In addition to the intensified Allies' bombing and mop-up operations by SS storm troops, food became insufficient, and townspeople without resources, or refugees from other areas, were breaking into the abandoned houses, looting or vandalizing the properties.

Luisa was worried about their abandoned house, but Patrizia discouraged her from wandering so close to the front line. "Let's think of our safety first, Mother," Patrizia said when Luisa suggested they visit the house. "It shouldn't be long now."

552

Rumors began to spread that a small contingent of German troops had begun to abandon the Arno Line, and that the general retreat was "imminent." The only certainty, however, was that the bombing continued, and the SS was becoming wilder and more unpredictable by the day. Two young men of military age were said to have been shot in Castelvecchio, and a third one was hung from a lamppost. Several more, young and not so young, were taken away to the North.

"Good as the imminent retreat of the Germans will be," Patrizia said. "If it comes a minute after we're dead, it won't be imminent enough!"

Almost two weeks had elapsed since Ivo's disappearance, and with each passing day, the hopes of his return became fainter and fainter. Angela and Giulia were more and more depressed and in need of encouragement, which Luisa and Patrizia usually supplied.

Patrizia continued to ask Otto to speculate as to Ivo's whereabouts. Finally, in answer to her prodding, he confirmed that the supreme commander of the Italian campaign, General Kesselring, had ordered another line of defense in the Appennines.

"All able men are taken there," he said. "It's called Gothic Line. Many people taken there for hard vork, trench excavation, carry ammunitions … I don't know; maybe Ivo's there."

"I hear there are partisans in the mountains," said Patrizia, in an attempt to elicit further information."

"Yeah, not so goot. Partisans kill Germans. Germans kill partisans. Sometimes civilians die too. It's war."

"What's the chance of his return?" she asked pointedly.

Otto hesitated, then, his eyes fixed to the ground, he whispered, "I don't know. I honestly don't know."

*****

A few days later, in the middle of the night, while everyone was asleep, a knock was heard at the cellar door. It didn't seem to be the usual decisive knock delivered with a rifle butt, and Luisa, who was a light sleeper, pulled gently on Patrizia's arm.

"What is it, Mother?"

"I think there's someone at the door. Light the candle, please."

Another light tap was heard, and Ginevra turned around, supporting herself on her elbow.

"I'm coming," said Luisa.

She turned around to make sure that everyone in the dormitory was ready to assume the usual positions, and when Ginevra, threading through the sleeping bodies, pulled up her skirt and reached the pot, Luisa yanked on the latch, and asked, "Who is it?"

A dark shadow fell over the threshold of the cellar. The soft orange glow of the candle reached outward and spread faintly over the human figure emerging from the dark night like an apparition.

"Who are you?" Luisa asked. "What do you want here?"

Everyone's eyes were aimed at that man who stumbled forward, hardly able to stand on his feet. He had a dark beard, and his long, sticky hair partially covered his pale face. His clothes were torn, his military shirt ripped in several places, and a small canvas bag hung from his bony shoulders. He took a step and then leaned against the wall. His deep dark eyes shone with tears, his open mouth unable to produce a sound.

"Who are you?" Luisa asked again. Then, getting closer to the man, she exclaimed, "Oh my God!"

The man threw his arms around her and whispered, "Yes, Luisa, it's me."

"Ivo!" she finally said.

"Ivo, Ivo!" Angela cried, jumping over the mattresses.

"Ivo, my son!" Ginevra shouted, trying to get off the pot, which stuck to her bare buttocks.

Everyone was up and wanted to see and touch the bearded man to be sure he wasn't an apparition.

Roberto propped his body up to look and then turned toward Lina. She was sitting on her bedding, smiling. Then she reached for his arm. "This is good news, isn't it?" she said, shaking it gently. Then she threw herself down again.

Roberto pulled closer to her and slowly reached for her hand under the blankets, his heart filling with joy when he realized that she was waiting for him.

"It's me. It's me," Ivo kept repeating. "It's really me!" He laughed and cried and caressed Angela's shoulders, as she wouldn't let go of him.

"Hallo, people … everyone," Patrizia called a moment later. "Let's not forget who is out there. A German patrol could be here any minute. Ivo, take a couple of blankets and go with Angela somewhere. We'll look after the baby."

Renzino was still sleeping, as Angela had forgotten to pinch him. Ivo knelt beside him, inhaled the sweet scent of his soft baby skin, and gently kissed his forehead. "My baby. My beautiful angel," he whispered. Then turned toward Patrizia and said, "You are right, Patrizia. It's even more dangerous than you think. Can you get me something to eat? I'm starving."

"I'll get the food," said Luisa.

The candle was snuffed out, and everyone tried to return to sleep, while Ivo and Angela followed Luisa and got some food.

*****

After Ivo had eaten, he moved with Angela toward the patch of river cane, walking toward the middle and spreading the blanket in a small clearing.

Angela lay on it, a sliver of moon reflected in her dark eyes. Ivo rested on his side, very close to her, his body propped on his left elbow, his right hand journeying over Angela's body. Her bosom had never felt softer, her body never so inviting. He couldn't take his eyes away from her face. He kissed, caressed, and made love to her. Then, resting his head in the hollow of her neck, his breathing still heavy, he began to cry. The weeks of tension, fear, and horror suddenly melted inside his chest, turning into warm, salty tears that fell silently on the woolen blanket.

Angela stroked his head, his neck, and his shoulders, whispering sweet words, as she did when soothing her baby. After a long time, Ivo returned to his previous position; dried his face on his arm; took Angela's hand in his; and in a soft, even voice, began to tell his story.

At dawn, when the tremulous light of the stars began to fade and disappear into the pale vault of the sky, Ivo joined the other men in the new hiding place. Angela picked up the blankets and returned to the house to recount in detail the dangers Ivo had endured, the horrors he had witnessed, and his final escape. Everyone, including the children, listened with intense interest.

*****

The convoy with Ivo and the other prisoners headed toward the higher ground of the Tosco-Emilians Apennines. There, as Otto had related, the Germans were preparing their next line of defense and used slave laborers to excavate trenches, move rocks and construction materials, and carry shells and armaments. Toward the evening of the first day, the convoy reached a narrow passage through the mountain road running from Florence to Bologna. In many places, the road ran parallel to the torrent Reno.

A *cicogna* was seen overhead for some time. It drew circles in the tranquil sky, its casual motions reminiscent of a bird of prey. However, recognized as an unarmed craft, the soldiers ignored it. Some of the Italian prisoners followed its overhead flight apprehensively.

"*Keine Angst; es ist ein Aufklarungsflugzeug*, said a young German soldier derisively. Don't be afraid; it's just a spotter plane.

After a while, no one paid much attention to its aerial maneuvers. Suddenly, it disappeared, and from behind a mountain peak, two fighter planes came hurling down like hawks swooping for the kill. Engines screamed, machine guns rattled, and two bombs detached from under their wings and dropped with a sinister whine.

The convoy came to a sudden halt, and soldiers and prisoners alike scrambled off the vehicles and dove into the nearest ground depression or behind rocks. Ivo and Bruno ran a few meters along the road, diving into a patch of tall grass just as the first bomb hit one of the vehicles, which burst into flames. Several prisoners were caught in the open and were mowed down by machine-gun fire.

A second bomb exploded, and the soldiers fired their rifles back at the airplanes, but without visible results. After the first pass, the planes regained altitude, swung around, and came back for another strafing run, causing more death and destruction. Then, tracing a wide semicircle in the crepuscular sky, they disappeared again behind the mountain crests. No sooner had the roar of their engines died in the distance than the Germans started to bark their guttural commands: *Shnell ... Komm, komm.*"

Ivo's eyes burned. His nose filled with the pungent smell of smoke from the burning trucks, mixed with the gases of the exploded shells. He did not get up. Instead, he slowly raised his head, and through the grass, he took a quick look at his immediate surroundings.

The German soldiers had quickly regrouped and were urging the hostages to climb onto the remaining trucks. On his right-hand side, forty to fifty feet below the road, were the turbulent waters of the Reno torrent, and across were thick bushes and chestnut trees. On the left side, for as far as he could see, the road was walled in by the mountain that rose almost vertically toward the sky, without crevices or recesses.

There did not seem to be an easy way out. He pulled on Bruno's sleeve, but he didn't move. He then reached farther, to his shoulders, and his hand felt wet and sticky. When he withdrew it, he saw that it was covered in blood, and a dark red rivulet ran beside Bruno's body.

He looked up again. The Germans seemed to be leaving the dead civilians wherever they lay. Overcoming his revulsion, Ivo forced his body over the widening puddle of blood. When he felt the mucky wetness reach his skin, he rolled back to his previous supine position.

His left arm stretched forward, partially covering his face, while his right arm lay limply beside his body. He heard someone approach and held his breath. He saw the boot of a soldier poke at his companion. "Kaputt!" shouted the soldier, probably to the sergeant. "*Zwei kaputt.*" He then swung around, and after what seemed an eternity, Ivo heard the trucks depart. He remained flat against the blood-soaked ground until the only noise he heard in his ears was the residue ringing from the explosions and the rush of the torrent.

Finally, he sat up beside his unfortunate companion, whose inert body was riddled with several holes oozing with a dark red bubbly substance. Farther up the road, other bodies, all civilians, were strewn on the side of the street. A column of dark smoke rose from the two smoldering vehicles. He was alone, tired, hungry, far away from his family, far away from the farm, but he was alive!

He had to get away from there before another convoy came. Ivo looked again at Bruno, and pulled him farther away from the road. He turned his body over, closed his eyes, and thought that if he was lucky enough to make it back, he would go and tell Bruno's family. After all, Fucecchio was not too far from Castelvecchio. He found Bruno's driver's license with his picture in his old leather wallet; it read, *Bruno Veraci, born in Empoli June 12, 1894.* He was barely fifty years old.

Angela fell silent. As she finished telling the story, her eyes filled with tears, and her lips trembled, revealing the mixture of emotion trapped inside her chest. Luisa stroked her back soothingly.

"What happened next?" Roberto asked. He had not missed one

word she had spoken. His fervid mind had pictured the scenes, creating his own version of a modern odyssey.

Patrizia gave him an eloquent side look and shook her head.

After another moment, Angela continued the story.

*****

Ivo meanwhile, had rejoined the other men in the new hiding place. "What the hell is this?" he exclaimed, crouching down. His voice echoed in the hollow space.

"After Otto's warning about the SS burning them haystacks," Gino said, "we tried to think of a safer place to hide."

"And the most unlikely place," chipped in the professor, "was this old septic tank."

It was a concrete cistern, large enough for three or four men, placed deep below ground and accessible only through a narrow manhole and a short shaft.

"We emptied it at night," the professor continued. "The job was painstakingly slow and rather unpleasant, as it had to be done with pails and other small vessels pulled from the top and emptied in the surrounding ground. The stench was sometimes unbearable. But it had to be done."

"The professor almost threw up several times," Gino said, with a smile in his voice.

"'It has to be done,' I kept saying to myself," replied the professor. "With every pail I unloaded, I repeated that."

"A night later," Gino took up again, "we disinfected the whole thing with spirits the Lanzis had brought, and then we whitewashed the walls with lye. After a couple more days, when all was dry and safe, we moved in."

Ivo made no comment. After a long moment, he began to narrate his story from the very beginning. He talked in a hushed voice, at times loaded with emotion. Particularly when he pronounced his son or Angela's name, or when he spoke about his ill-fated companion. Gino and the professor listened quietly, their bodies leaning toward Ivo's voice.

"I left the driver's license in the front pocket of Bruno's shirt for identification," he said. "I took his wristwatch and pocketed the rest of his things with the intention of returning them to his family, and I was ready to leave. I looked around once again—no way to climb the mountain. No way to stay on the road either, as the only traffic to be expected was that of German convoys. So, I carefully descended toward the torrent, drank some water, and washed out the blood with the freezing mountain water. Then, jumping from rock to rock, stumbling and falling, with the help of a long wooden stick, I finally made it to the other side.

"Night was approaching, and I had to find a place to lie down and rest. I climbed through the undergrowth, and finally I found a grassy spot under a chestnut tree. I gathered some leaves, lay down, and before I could think of anything, or say amen, I fell asleep."

"Quite an eventful day!" commented the old professor.

"What kind of a man are you?" Gino said jokingly. "Luisa came back with the milk without getting into trouble! And you …"

"What can I tell you, Zio?" Ivo answered in good humor. "And that was only the beginning!"

A sliver of moonlight shone in from the camouflaged opening above. Gino and the professor saw the pained expression on Ivo's face and waited patiently for him to continue.

"I was awakened by somebody kicking my feet," Ivo said, adjusting the blanket under his buttocks. "I opened my eyes, and several armed men stood above me, staring at me suspiciously. They weren't fascists, but who the hell were they? They asked me lots of questions and made me repeat my story several times.

"At a certain point, a young man spun off from the group and ran toward the torrent. When he returned, he approached the one who appeared to be in command and said, 'He is telling the truth, Lando. There are two burned German trucks and many dead bodies on the road.'

"'Go to San Giorgio,' Lando told him. 'Tell the priest to send someone with a cart, and then take the bodies and bury them. Afterward, you can rejoin us at the usual rendezvous. And you,' he said to me, 'come with us for now. Later, we shall see. By the way,' he added, 'when did you last eat?'

"'Yesterday morning,' I answered.

"He pulled a chunk of bread and a slice of pecorino cheese out of his knapsack and handed the food to me. Then we started to climb along a narrow mountain path."

*****

Gino and the professor sat almost motionless, except for the odd movement of their legs. Movements that, given the narrow confines, had to be coordinated with those of the other companions. The outlines of their dark bodies were sharply in contrast with the white walls.

The moon had traveled some distance, and its pale light now shone on the faces of the two older men.

"Who were those men? Where did they take you?" Gino inquired, rocking on his buttocks to stimulate the blood flow.

"Fighters. Fighters or partisans, Zio. They belonged to a Garibaldi partisan brigade operating in those mountains. But the Germans and a fascist band belonging to the X Mas battalion was raking the area, and for the next ten days, we went to hell and back several times. We climbed a mountainside, descended another. We ran away from large German patrols, ambushed smaller ones, killed German soldiers, left some of our dead behind. We passed through abandoned villages burned and pillaged by the Germans and fascists in reprisal, and stared into the face of death every minute of the day.

"At night, when we didn't escape to the highest part of the mountain or join another partisan group in the opposite one, we slept a few hours—in an abandoned shed, under a chestnut tree, inside a rocky crevice."

Ivo paused for a moment. Then, in a voice strained with emotion, he said, "A few days later, a group of partisans surprised and killed a couple of young German soldiers who had stopped to smoke a cigarette and rest beside an old deserted farm. But they didn't just kill them, they shot them and then hung them from a pergola and covered their bodies with shit.

"When a German patrol discovered them, they sent word to the area command, which promptly dispatched a battalion of SS troops to even the score. The closest town was completely surrounded. The Germans got twenty people at random, shot them, and left them in the town square for the others to see."

Ivo fell silent, and no one spoke. Outside, the gentle rustling of the canes and the odd barking of a dog could be heard in the distance.

Gino shifted his weight uneasily and asked, "But, Ivo, why did the partisans let it happen?"

"The Germans were many … and better armed. They had armored cars, mortars, machine guns. They kept coming, and if we had stayed to defend the town, they would have killed us all."

"But," Gino insisted, "they must have known the Germans were going to get crazy over it—"

"It's hard to explain, Zio."

"Yes, it is," the professor agreed. "It is the madness of war. The inevitability of the old biblical dictum: An eye for an eye … a tooth for a tooth. Then the whole head and body, and then hundreds or thousands of heads and bodies. It becomes a play of numbers, a madman's equation, like a game of poker, where the stakes are raised in the vain hope that the adversary will quit the game first, that he won't see your hand, and so you'll win by default. But war is not played with cards and colored chips; it's played with bullets. And innocent people, even if not involved in the match, become part of it, and they are pushed to the center of the table, like chips in a game of poker, and they get killed."

Gino looked at the professor with awe. "But," he asked again, "who are these partisans?"

"Anybody, Zio. Even people like you and me."

"Yes," said the professor, "people like us. Some may be patriots, willing to risk their lives for the liberation of the motherland from the German joke. Others, soldiers who did not want to fight beside the

Germans. Mostly, I would guess, just simple mortals like us, pushed together by different circumstances …"

"True," Ivo confirmed. "Some of the men I came to know were simple mountain people who had escaped the draft. Some were deserters who had abandoned their units after the armistice. Others had escaped their towns to avoid persecution from fascist diehards. A few, I am afraid to say, were opportunists who seemed more interested in looting abandoned houses and towns than fighting the Germans." Ivo had a strange tone in his voice when he continued. Some were just called communists …"

"And I bet," the professor promptly interjected, "that they were the only ones motivated by some kind of ideology."

"What do you mean?" Gino asked.

"The communists," the professor said, "like it or not, are people inspired by Lenin, Marx, and the Russian Revolution. They hate the fascist regime and see this guerrilla warfare as the opportunity to arm and be in a strong position after the war. If you ask me, they are the only ones with a long-term plan, not just avoidance of military service or the killing of a few stranded Germans. For them, this fight is a stepping-stone toward power and a new political system in post-war Italy. Like Mussolini said to Ciano when entering the war, they too need a few dead, and a few heroes, to justify and validate their cause!"

"Who gives *them* people the weapons to fight?" Gino asked again.

"The Americans do, as well as the British, Zio. At the beginning, I'm told the partisans had only old Italian army stuff, like the ninety-one rifle, low-power pinecone-shaped hand grenades, and even twelve-gauge hunting rifles like yours. But then the Americans started to make parachute drops, and the partisans got automatic weapons, machine guns, explosives, and other materials. But you know what? The Garibaldi brigade, being of communist leaning, always got fewer supply drops than the others."

"Yes," the professor uttered, "The Americans!"

"Why do you say it that way, Professor?"

"Because I doubt they know what they are doing. Or ...," he continued after some hesitation, "they do know it and have already calculated some kind of favorable return."

The other two men remained silent. From the puzzled look on their faces, it was evident they were wondering what the professor was trying to tell them.

Finally Gino spoke. "For God's sake, Professor, I'm a poor *contadino*. I don't understand them things ..."

"You see, Gino, we were saying that the Americans are giving the partisans weapons and other materials. We were also saying that, most probably, the communist wing of the partisans may end up in a strong position after the cease-fire. Therefore, we can conclude that either the Americans don't realize they are potentially arming their political opponents, or ..." He hesitated again, as if to confirm in his mind the validity of his next statement. "Or they do realize it and are choosing temporarily what's the best of a bad situation."

"And what might that be?"

"They let partisans and Germans fight and kill each other, as many as possible, so they will save more of their own lives. It's once again the logic of war, which is a bit of a contradiction, but I hope you get my meaning."

Ivo nodded quietly, and Gino's furrowed forehead indicated he was still trying to digest all those strange concepts.

"But," Gino finally snapped, "they must know the Germans are stronger, and that they kill many civilians too ..."

"They most probably do. After all, they're advancing over terrain previously occupied by the Germans. I'm sure some of the stories must have gotten through to them: Naples' street fighting, Rome's Fosse Ardeatine ... But, dear Gino, as we were saying before, this is war, and in war, the casualties of your enemy—military or civilian—don't receive the same considerations as those of your own side. Look at the carpet-bombing the Americans do over our cities in order to 'liberate' us! Anyway, Ivo," he said, turning to the younger man, "I'm sorry we interrupted your story. Tell us more of your odyssey."

Ivo hesitated for a long instant, as if to mentally rewind the reel of recollections that had brought him back to the mountain.

"On the second day, they gave me an automatic gun too. A Thompson gun, they called it, but as you know, Zio, I have problems even shooting your twelve-gauge at sparrows, let alone human beings."

He stopped, scratched his neck, swallowed a couple of times, and then said, "The following evening, two partisan groups joined forces, and we ambushed a small convoy of German trucks. The Germans must have expected it; they fought back and caught us in a cross fire.

"They hit us with heavy machine-gun fire, mortars, grenades ... you name it. Several of our men were hit, and then the guy beside me—a man in his forties, I think—got hit right between the eyes and fell into my arms. I rested him against a stone and looked downhill. I saw these green uniforms crawling uphill toward us, and I started to shoot at them like a madman."

"Strange," commented the professor. "You said *uniforms* instead of men or soldiers."

"Yes, Professor, the moment I saw that poor man die, I thought I could be the next one. I went into a frenzy. The black instrument in my hands became the only hope I had of survival. I pointed it at those advancing uniforms and shot repeatedly. I wanted to kill them, all of them, before they killed me.

"After a while, someone grabbed my arm. 'Let's get the hell out of here!' he shouted, 'There are too many of them.'

"Later, as we climbed to higher ground, Lando, the chief of our group, moved beside me, 'You did well,' he said, smacking his hand on my back. 'How many did you kill?'

It was the word 'kill'—pronounced aloud with that indifference—that brought me back to reality. It was men I was trying to kill, not uniforms.

"A few days later a terrible thing happened, and then I knew for sure that this whole fighting situation was not for me."

"What happened, son?" Gino asked with a soothing voice, as his arm extended toward his nephew and gently stroked his shoulders with his work-calloused hand.

"From the height of their hiding place," Ivo started in a soft tone, "a sister group saw a small German patrol coming up to a mountain pasture. The partisans took position behind rocks and other natural barriers and ambushed the Germans.

"They killed several soldiers, and the three or four remaining, seeing that they were completely surrounded and exposed to cross fire, gave up the fight and surrendered. 'We take no prisoners,' said the man in charge of that group. He ordered the Germans to toss their uniforms, and he marched them to the nearest woods. There, he shot them one by one. Apparently, one of the soldiers was barely twenty, and after seeing the first of his comrades shot in cold blood, he began to cry like a baby.

"I was told he held a piece of paper in his hand and tried to show it to the nearest partisan. When he was shot and tumbled to the ground, the piece of paper escaped from his grip. Someone picked it up. It was the picture of his wife and baby."

Ivo stopped, overcome by emotion, his eyes filled with tears. "I thought of Angela," he cried, wiping his eyes with the back of his hands, "and my Renzino. I thought I could smell his sweet, delicate skin … I couldn't stand it any longer! I had to find a way to come back. But how?"

He sniffled a couple of times and cleared his throat. The others remained silent, spellbound by the unfolding drama.

"The day after," Ivo said after a long pause, "one of our informants, a middle-aged man they called 'the postman,' told us a large contingent of SS troops was coming up from both sides of the mountain.

"We were ordered to split into smaller units, abandon Monte Croce, find refuge in the opposite mountain, regroup, and wait for further orders. As you can imagine, some of the partisans were local people and knew every inch of those paths, woods, and inclines. Therefore, despite their close formation, we were somehow able to sneak through the ascending German line. In several places, paths ran almost parallel to each other, at times separated only by a few trees, a thick bush, a boulder mushrooming out of the earth. We heard their voices, shouts, commands, the noise of their shuffling feet. Now and then, through sparser foliage, I even saw the sparks of their cigarettes—like fireflies in a wheat field—which appeared and then suddenly disappeared into nothingness.

"We marched downhill for many hours in complete silence and then began to climb toward our destination. Midway to the top, we reached a small clearing in the thick vegetation and looked across, in the direction of Monte Croce. On its dark slopes, a dozen or more fires were burning. The valley echoed with the explosions of mortar shells and the staccato burst of machine-gun fire. Every now and then, a tracer shell pierced the darkness.

"'Those bastards are burning our villages,' someone whispered in horror. 'Look, there goes Petrara … and San Giovanni … and Nerbello.' 'They are burning everything in sight,' echoed another man. 'Houses, school, churches … everything is on fire!' A young man had to be forcibly held as he started to shout, 'My mother and sisters are there; I gotta go back. What's gonna become of them!'

"It wasn't long before the news reached us.

"At dawn, a couple of old souls who had escaped the massacre reached our little group. The SS, they said while they sobbed, surrounded each and every village and hovel. Not finding any partisans or men of military age, they gathered everybody else. They shut the people in stables, schoolrooms, churches. Then, at a certain signal, they began to shoot everybody. Afterward, they hurled hand grenades onto the piles of corpses, and finally they torched the buildings with flamethrowers.

"They slaughtered every living soul they found, Zio: old people, women, children. Even priests and animals. The few who survived were either in the woods at the time of the SS's arrival, or had been covered by the falling bodies at the start of the shooting and had somehow remained undetected. As if by miracle," he added.

"Or rather by virtue of the strangest circumstances of life," said the professor.

Ivo did not reply immediately. He paused for a moment to regain his composure, his hushed whispers laced with trembling and strain.

"One of these men," he then continued, "told us of how he remained under a pile of bleeding corpses for several hours. A pregnant woman, two of her children, an old man … all lying on top of him. The cries and laments of wounded people were silenced by additional gunfire. Then there was silence. After a long while, his mind benumbed by fear and bewilderment, he started to disentangle himself from that hecatomb. He managed to free one arm, then another; he pushed back those bodies and then passed his hand all over his own body. Once … twice … incredulous to find no wounds or feel any physical pain. '*I am alive,*' he thought in wonderment, and began to move among those corpses that had been, only moments before, live human beings, who were now reduced to a mass of inanimate, fetid flesh.

"He crawled over bodies and over the wreckage of the demolished building. When he finally reached the open air, he looked toward the sky and exclaimed, 'Why me? Of all those poor people, those children, why did you save me? What's wrong with you, my God?' Then he began to walk in wide circles, drifting aimlessly until he met another old man whose family had been completely wiped out.

"Somehow, by midmorning, they reached our plateau. Exhausted, they fell to the ground, weeping and telling stories that were beyond description.

"They killed them all, Zio. Every single one of them. I saw one of these places myself. I think it was the village of San Pietro a Monte. In the old elementary school building, there was nothing left but smoldering rubble and mutilated corpses—all riddled with bullets and blown to pieces by grenades, half-burned and made unrecognizable by the scorching fire of flamethrowers. I felt as if my mind could not believe what my eyes were seeing. I sat on what had been the front steps of a demolished house, my gun on the ground, and I became possessed by a silent rage. I held my head in my hands and cried like a baby."

"'What the hell are you doing?'" Lando asked me. 'You aren't even from around here.'

"'I want to go home,'" I said. 'I want to go back to my family.'

"I didn't tell him that I was confused. That in some cases I thought the Partisans had behaved as badly as the Germans. That I saw no merit in killing a few enemies and then watching them kill so many innocent civilians, women, children … That I couldn't anymore distinguish good from bad, friend from enemy … man from beast.

"'It's okay, kid,' he told me. 'This war is tough on everybody. Wait a few days; it's too dangerous now.'

"And wait, I did. As I think back, I couldn't even tell you if it was hours, days, or weeks. My mind recorded most of the events, and now that I am here, they pass in front of my mind's eye like a fast film run backward.

"One day, Lupo told me that the Americans had broken through somewhere south of us. There was lot of confusion on both sides, but if I wanted to try to go home, I had to do it before the lines stabilized again and the fighting resumed. I thanked him. He gave me that knapsack you saw, with some bread, cheese, and rations. He also gave me a scarf with a map printed on it. American pilots use those in the event they are shot down, to recognize the terrain and plan escape routes. He showed me the best way, and I began my return."

"Where were you at the time?" the professor asked.

"Half a day's walk north of Florence, I think, but it took me much longer."

"What happened?" Gino asked.

"I was able to escape from the area still occupied by the Germans, but I almost got shot by the Americans."

"Oh my God!"

"Really, Zio. I came across an advanced American emplacement, and they started to shoot at me—sight unseen. After a few minutes with my head and body in this hole in the ground, I waved my white kerchief … and someone shouted for me to come forward with my hands up. They saw my Thomson gun and my military map and accused me of shooting an Allied pilot and stealing his belongings.

"They kept me for three or four days, locked in a nearby farmhouse with little food and no one to talk to. Finally, someone came from the front lines and said that the pilot who was shot down was safe with the partisans, and he vouched for my release. So, toward evening, they put me in a car they call a jeep and took me toward Empoli. There, they told me that if I had any brains, I would wait until the Americans arrived before I tried to cross the Arno River."

"Well?"

"Well, Zio, as you know, I haven't got any brains, and I crossed to the German side again."

"Either you haven't got any brains, or you love your family more than you love yourself." Gino slapped Ivo's back amicably. "You are a hell of a nice fellow," he said. "I don't know if I wouldn't have waited."

"Where did you cross?" the professor asked.

"At the bombed Santa Chiara bridge. I know the area well, and with all those chunks of concrete and metal frames sticking out of the water, it's not difficult to cross."

"What if the Germans had taken you again?"

"I don't even want to think about it. As I got closer to this place, I thought I was dreaming. Every noise, every shadow, and the whisper of the wind were enough to scare me to death. I walked like a zombie on the grassy side of the country road, sometimes thinking that I was almost there, and other times thinking that I would never arrive. Once, I crossed several fields, and I even stepped on a mine. Fortunately, it must have been an anti-tank mine, and my weight didn't make it go off. I was so tired and desperate that I almost didn't care anymore. Shortly after, I saw the house, and the thought of Angela and my little son so close to me brought me to tears."

His voice faltered, and Gino again rubbed his nephew's back with his hand.

"The rest," said Ivo, "you already know."

- IIIL -

End of August 1944

The sun was blindingly bright this morning, the sky clear blue, the air stifling. The country road was free of traffic and of Germans, and Roberto and Mario left their observation post to sneak into the cellar.

After a long time spent comparing their collections of shrapnel bits and used up machine-gun shells, they heard Tito barking. They stopped to listen. The barking was immediately followed by a sharp knock on the door that made them jump. They quickly unbolted the door. The heat slammed into the boys from the opening, announcing the power of the midmorning sun. At first, all they saw was a dark, tall shadow sharply cut against the blinding brightness of the day. Then, as their eyes adjusted to the light, they recognized the silhouette of a tall German soldier in a sweaty and disheveled olive green uniform. Two rifles hung from his shoulders, a stick grenade stuck out of his right black boot. For a long moment, he stood motionless in front of the two boys, who were paralyzed with fear.

"*Trinken,*" the soldier commanded. "*Vino.*"

Mario fetched a flask from a shelf as fast as he could and handed it to him. In that heat, it was not unusual for German soldiers to stop and ask for a drink, but it was usually water.

"*Zu trinkst zuerst,*" he said, pushing back the flask.

The boys understood that he wanted them to drink first. It was the habitual request from the Germans, who were afraid of being poisoned.

Mario raised the vessel to his mouth and swallowed some wine, then handed the flask to the soldier, who drank for a long time. He rested and then drank again, his head tilted back, his eyes squeezed shut. His Adam's apple went up and down with each gulp; the wine spilled and ran down his sunburned neck, wetting his shirt.

He drinks a lot, Roberto thought. Certainly more than any German soldier he had seen before.

Finally, he gave the flask back and left.

"Strange," said Roberto. "Normally they ask for *wasser.*"

"Yeah," Mario echoed, "and he had two rifles instead o' one."

When the soldier was past the yard, the boys decided to follow him at a distance. The soldier walked by the well, crossed the vineyard, a field, then another field. After a while, convinced that he was directed toward the Buglioni farmhouse, they decided to return home. They raced partway. Mario, acknowledging Roberto's running superiority, invented shortcuts though passages and corners yet unknown to his companion. Or led him through patches of sharp wheat stumps, which Roberto's bare feet could not manage too well.

Suddenly, the calm of the moment was shattered by a loud detonation—the crisp smack of a firearm. The boys slid to a halt and listened to the reverberation still echoing in the air, while flocks of birds sprinted toward the sky. They looked at each other as if to verify what they heard.

"It's a rifle shot," said Mario, terror in his eyes.

"It came from the direction of the German soldier," added Roberto.

Although they were used to explosions caused by long-distance shelling, the sound of a shotgun so near to them added a new source of fear to their experience. They started running again, this time shoulder-to-shoulder, stealthily moving from the cover of one vineyard row to the next, quickly returning to the safety of the farm before the adults noticed their absence.

Shortly after, the boys spotted three men coming their way. Two old farmers held a German soldier by the waist to support his walking. They crossed the yard in the direction of the German command post. It was the very soldier who had asked for wine a while earlier. He was evidently wounded in the left shoulder, and he bled profusely through the white cloth used as a temporary bandage. The trio crossed the yard without even looking at the two boys who now stood askance near the cellar door. Their direction was definitely that of the command post.

About an hour later, two German light trucks full of SS infantry soldiers sped ominously by the country road, leaving a cloud of dust behind them and racing toward the Buglioni farm. When they returned, they had a group of about twenty Italians—a few were kids who were barely teenagers, and the rest were above fifty. They were forced to walk in single file between the trucks. Machine guns pointed at them from every direction.

Everyone instantly knew this was going to be a tragic day.

*****

Patrizia was summoned, and she looked at Otto in puzzlement. "What happened to that soldier?" she asked. "And why are all those Italians held at gunpoint?"

"Vounded soldier told commanding officer Italian partisan shot him and then ran away," Otto explained. "Please patch vound as quickly as possible."

"What did you say?"

"Shot by partisans."

Given the context, her loud, unexpected laughter sounded all the more inconceivable.

"He is a liar," she told Otto, who looked at her in disbelief. "Tell your commandant there are no bloody partisans around here. These people are even afraid even of their own shadow. Partisans," she repeated. "Don't be ridiculous."

The angered commandant demanded an explanation. He insisted that she start doing what he had requested, and he ordered the Italians against the wall. Five Germans, pistol machine guns aimed at point-blank range, were ready to open fire.

Patrizia's face looked like a sphinx. She was standing in the middle of the room, a few steps away from the wounded soldier. Her thinking process seemed to have stopped. Her brain did not respond to her commands. Incongruously, she found herself numb to the situation at hand. She lost consciousness of everything around her except for the singing of the birds outside.

Luisa's eyes seemed to be begging for a miracle.

The wounded soldier was starting to falter as the massive loss of blood began to take its toll. It was evident that he required immediate attention.

"Schnell!" yelled the commandant.

Patrizia shook herself from her frozen state. *If I take care of him without challenging his statement,* she thought, *we'll all be dead.* She took a step back and said to Otto, "Tell the commandant that unless the soldier tells the truth, I'll let him bleed to death!"

"You crazy! Don't do this, Patrizia," Otto shouted. "I know this officer; he kill you too!"

"And I know these people," she insisted. "Listen to me, Otto. There are no partisans in this part of the country. He is a liar."

"But who shoot him, then?"

"Ask him."

The commandant was out of patience, and he asked Otto to explain the situation. He then took his revolver from his holster and placed its nozzle at Patrizia's temple. *"Schnell,"* he barked angrily. *"Schnell."*

Just then, the wounded soldier emitted a strange, agonizing sound. It sounded like a cry for help, except it lacked words.

Otto, at grave risk for his own life, stepped toward the wounded soldier, grabbed him by the front of his shirt, and shook him. "She'll help you only if you tell the truth. *Mach shnell sonst bist du in weniger als einer minute tot.*" Hurry or you'll be dead in less than a minute.

The soldier's shrinking eyes and contorted facial expression depicted his physical pain and his internal struggle. He opened his mouth, but no sound came out. He closed his mouth and swallowed with effort. The others all watched, holding a collective breath. Finally, three words exhaled from his parted lips. Then he collapsed to the floor.

Patrizia did not understand his words, but she knew the danger of the gamble she had undertaken. In her mind, she was already saying good-bye to her child, to Riccardo, to life! Her eyes, blurred by the strain, saw the officer lower his Luger pistol and Otto smile. For an eternal moment, her mind refused to make the linkage between those two actions.

"What's happening?"

"He said he shot himself," Otto replied.

When Patrizia realized the danger had passed, she looked at Luisa, who stood there mute and white as a statue, apparently praying to God to prevent what seemed inevitable. She walked to her, hugged her, and said, "Don't worry, Mother. It's passed."

Then she went to the soldier and began to cut his shirt and dress his wounds. The bullet had penetrated his chest about ten centimeters above the heart and exited between his left shoulder and neck. She removed his shirt and noticed that a rib had been splintered. On the neck side, the bullet had exited with extensive superficial damage. As she began to clean the wounds, it became evident to her that they were worse than initially imagined.

"I can try to stop the bleeding," she curtly said, "but he'll need a real doctor later. I don't know what kind of internal damage he has suffered."

"When stronger, he send to back lines. Maybe send to eastern front," Otto said. "Or maybe …" He never finished the phrase.

The news of the German *rappresaglia*—retaliation—had spread throughout the countryside. Two hours later, when the two women were finally allowed to return home, Giulia and Rosa ran to embrace them, crying from the pent-up fear and sudden relief.

The Germans still kept the hostages for the next several hours, and the Banchinis' farm became a continuous pilgrimage, with their relatives seeking reassurance that they would soon be released. All the while, they thanked Patrizia and Luisa for what they had already done.

"We shall never forget this," one woman vowed, holding her hand over her heart.

"My Fabio is there," said another. "Sometimes he makes me mad, but he is so young. I would have died if they killed him."

"May God bless you," echoed a third one.

It was a strange procession of people. Patrizia was beginning to understand how close she had been to being shot. Her mind went blank as she heard words such as *husband, son, saved, gratitude*; it didn't seem to make sense. She looked at the next person with blank eyes. "Go home now," she whispered. "There is nothing more I can do. I'm sure the hostages will be released soon. Go home, please."

*****

Two days after, the wounded soldier recovered sufficiently to sign his confession.

"Ich habe mich selbst angeschossen," he told his commandant. "I wanted to go home to my family," he added to justify his action. "Why are we still fighting …? It makes no sense. The war is lost."

True to his sense of Teutonic discipline, the German commander ordered the Italian hostages to assemble in the front yard of the farmhouse. He wanted them to see the "fair" sense of justice he applied to one and all.

He had the wounded soldier placed in front of a haystack, spoke a few words to him, and then turned around and walked about ten paces. He slowly extracted his Luger pistol from its leather casing and personally shot him through the head.

The soldier's body fell to the ground with a fluid motion impossible for a live person. Those who had closed their eyes heard the shot, immediately followed by a muffled thud. The body twitched for a moment—its limbs jerking as if pulled by invisible wires—and then it stiffened. A moment later, all signs of life abandoned the body. A small red puddle formed on the gravel beside his head. A few hacking sounds indicated that someone among the Italian prisoners was throwing up.

The officer looked distractedly in their direction, and with a gesture of contempt, he finally ordered their release.

- IIL -

End of August 1944

After the shooting episode, Otto visited the Banchini farm more often than before. In spite of his German uniform, he was now welcomed as one of the family, as everyone knew that he had sided with Patrizia and tried to free the hostages.

"He is an enemy," said old Amato, "but a good man all the same."

It had never occurred to Roberto that Otto was an enemy. He had protected the farm, sided with his mother at his own risk. Sure, he wore a German uniform, but according to what he saw and heard about many Italians—including priests, doctors, and soldiers—he had behaved better than some of them.

This became even more evident a few days later. When returning from the front line on the Arno, Otto climbed the stairs of the command post, relieved himself of his weapons, and immediately approached Roberto's mother.

"Patrizia," he said with an anguished sigh, "I vent by house as you ask, and ..." It seemed as if he could not continue.

"And what, Otto? What happened?"

"Bad news. I found Italian people inside. They broken through vall vere you hidden things; they stole vatever they like."

"But," said Patrizia hesitantly, "when we left, there were German soldiers there, not Italians."

"Germans left veeks ago. Italians forced doors and entered house. We stopped them and sent avay, then locked doors and windows and posted notice, but many things already gone. I'm sorry."

"Bastards," Patrizia hissed. "Did they take the piano?"

"No, Patrizia, but I think it's damaged."

Luisa heard the news as well. She loosencd her headscarf and pulled it away from her neck. She breathed with difficulty, and her face was pale and tight. For a long moment, it seemed that the news had drained her of all of her strength, and in a few moments, she seemed to have aged ten years. She rested her frail body against the near wall.

Patrizia put her hand on her shoulder and slowly helped her move to a chair nearby. "Don't worry, Mother," she said.

"We worked so hard for those things," Luisa said in a voice barely louder than a whisper. "As if we didn't have enough trouble with the Germans. Now even our own people behave like brigands."

"Don't worry," Patrizia repeated. The dark of her eyes deepened, and her face changed into a mask of anger. "We'll survive even this experience, but I'll promise you this: if I ever recognize my clothing, my jewelry, or anything from our house on someone else, not even God will save that person from my rage."

"Patrizia *cara*," Luisa breathed out. "As you told me sometimes, don't bring God into this. Please."

"I'm sorry," Otto said. "I keep eye on house, I promise." He then clicked his heels and left.

He returned the next day. "Tito, heel!" he shouted in jest. Roberto and Mario heard the call and ran out of the kitchen. Otto had already climbed the stairs to the portico. *"Guten morgen, kinder,"* he said to them.

"Guten morgen, Otto."

Cannon blasts put a stop to the exchange. They were followed by the whining sound of shells piercing the calm morning air. Roberto and Mario looked at Otto questioning, but his unchanged serene expression was reassuring.

"That's our eighty-eight cannons," he said. "Can tell by the sharp, dry sound." He took his binoculars and searched the southern side of the horizon. "Look." He handed them to Roberto. "Our batteries are shelling the San Romano bell tower. Americans use it as observation site."

Roberto adjusted the sight and soon found, among the green hills—now seemingly at arm's length—the well-known redbrick tower adjacent to the San Romano cathedral. He saw the flames of the exploding shells, chunks of brick wall falling, and then, about three seconds later, he heard the actual sound of the blast. He saw tiny human figures scrambling for safety, running down the road to the station. Another salvo passed overhead, and he aimed his binoculars over the tower again. Several shells hit its base at the same time. The tower leaned to the left in slow motion and then crashed to the ground in a cloud of dust.

It had seemed like a game. A long-distance shooting competition seen through the filter of a kaleidoscope.

"Look, Mario," said Roberto matter-of-factly, "the tower has been destroyed."

*****

A few nights later, along with the usual canteen of food, Otto brought a Victrola player and several records. After supper, taking advantage of the calm of the hour, the people carried their straw-seat chairs outside and sat against the south wall, still warm with the accumulated heat of the day. They breathed the fresh night air and stared at the dark blue sky. Nothing could be heard except the typical sounds of a perfect summer night: the strident serenade of crickets in the trees, the reassuring croaking of the frogs in the nearby ditch, the rustling of the bamboo cane swaying in the gentle summer breeze.

Otto cranked up the Victrola, and after a few scratchy sounds, a soft, lyrical melody started to pour out of the speaker. Everyone stopped chatting and began to listen to the music as if it were a soothing balm. Just a few of those melodious notes seemed to erase from their minds and from the air the reverberations and echoes of the explosions. That moment of peace and music held no sound or recollection of war. A pale full moon illuminated the yard and rendered the scene almost surreal—a perfect image of peace and contentment, like a picturesque impressionist's painting of farm life.

When the music stopped, there was an abrupt silence. No one moved to change the record.

It wasn't a normal silence, but one laden with thoughts, questions, even fear. It was as if everyone had become suddenly afraid of having enjoyed a moment of peace and oblivion, allowing themselves to forget yesterday's pains, tomorrow's perils. For a brief moment, all thoughts of war had subsided.

The music had fostered the illusion of a world at peace, of a life that was beautiful. The melody had been the thread upon which their fantasy had walked. And now that the line was broken, they fell back to reality.

Roberto was the first to speak. He was near Otto, and he noticed the engraving, in Gothic letters, on his belt. *"Gott mit uns,"* he read aloud. "What does it mean, Otto?"

"God is vith us."

The boy looked at him strangely. *Only in mythology did the gods of the Olympus take sides in people's wars,* he thought.

"Do you truly believe that God is on your side?"

Otto looked at Roberto and messed up his hair jokingly, "Everyone hope that God is vith him, but no one knows if He is."

"How can God possibly be with the Huns?" Luisa muttered, playing on the word.

*****

Patrizia thought this conversation shouldn't continue. "How long yet, Otto?"

"How long …?"

"For the front to move north. For the Americans to come. For this bloody war to end."

Otto's face became sad and serious. He turned his head away; his eyes seemed to be transfixed on a distant point. "I don't know," he said in a low voice, "but not very long now. Soon ve must retreat, but Americans not in hurry to advance … and soon ve …" He didn't finish the thought. "I vill miss you, Patrizia," he whispered.

"Thank you, Otto." She'd felt the sadness in his tone, and she touched his arm gently. When he turned his head, his mouth offered a little smile, but his eyes were shining with tears. It appeared as if he had to make an effort not to cry.

"I tell you something, Patrizia," he said, when no one was close enough to hear. "You risked life for your people, but they don't deserve it."

"What are you saying, Otto?"

"Some people came to the commandant to tell him your husband is on the English side."

She looked at him without seeing him. "That's a bloody lie!" she whispered to Otto. "His sympathies may lie with them, but he was at the African front, with the Pavia Division … fighting side by side with the Germans … In Tobruk, in Bengasi … and then …" Her voice was failing her. "After the retreat from El Alamein, I never heard again …" She tried to remember the last time she had received his letters. *Over two years ago,* she thought. More than seven hundred long days of silence, of loneliness. Even longer since her body had felt his caresses.

"I not say I believe them. I just say they don't deserve you. Be careful."

*****

A few days later, after sundown, the Germans began to move north with the last motorized vehicles they had left in the area. Demolition squads came down from the hills and began to place charges under the bridge and mine the riverbank and the main road to town.

It looked like the prelude to the end, but nobody dared to hope, for fear of yet another disillusionment—like the eighth of September the year before, when Marshall Badoglio, temporary caretaker of the "vacated" government of King Emmanuel the Third—or "Pimp Emma the Turd," as Patrizia used to call him—declared an armistice with the Allies. And just as the naïve, hopeful Italians rejoiced in the streets and squares of their cities and villages, the Panzer Divisions descended from the north, disarmed the Italians, and occupied the peninsula.

A few days later, the Americans dropped leaflets over towns and countryside, and some fell near the farm. They declared the "imminent" end of the war. Nonna Luisa, excited by the blissful message, picked up a few to distribute to the neighboring farms. Halfway to her destination, a heavy American shelling began. A real barrage, which seemed directed to the very area.

Patrizia had remained at the command post to take care of several wounded Allied soldiers taken prisoners at the Arno. Mario's mother, grandmother, and old Amato were caught out in the fields. At the first whistling sound of oncoming shells, they ran to the closest ditch and burrowed into the ground.

Mario was playing in the yard with two boys who had come from the neighboring Falaschi farm. "Let's go to the cellar!" he yelled. "We'll get into the vat."

At the same time, Roberto, who was helping Lina draw fresh water from the well, dropped the pail to the ground. "They are falling close!" he shouted. "Run!" He took her hand and ran toward the cellar.

"Not here, stupid," said Mario, from inside one of the concrete vats. Roberto pulled Lina away and quickly moved toward a vacant one.

"You first," Roberto said.

Lina bent forward and entered the vat headfirst, unintentionally showing a good part of her rear end. Roberto quickly followed. They were now in complete darkness, huddled against each other. In the intervals between the explosions, muffled by the thick concrete walls, Roberto could hear Lina's rapid breathing. His own heart was going at galloping pace. "Are you all right?" he asked her.

"Yes, yes, I am." A louder explosion broke the verbal exchange, and bricks and mortar buried their fateful shelter.

*****

When the barrage began, Luisa cursed her naïveté. "At my age," she reproached herself, "still believing in fairy tales … believing propaganda leaflets." Then she quickly turned around and began to run. When she was about one hundred meters from the farm, she stopped abruptly. Her mouth half-open, unable to draw air, she instinctively raised her hands to her mouth, as if to suppress a scream. She stopped breathing, for right in front of her own eyes, the smoldering remains of the roof of the Banchinis' farm suggested the worst.

"Take my life but save my Roberto," she said, beginning to sob as she ran the last meters toward the farm, crying, "Roberto, Roberto!" She relived again the terrible moments of 1917, when the entire house had collapsed over the staircase under which she and young Lorenzo had taken shelter from the American bombardment.

"Dear God," she said, "what have I done to deserve this?"

At that moment, Patrizia ran into the yard, from the opposite side.

"Where is he, Mother?" she said in an unsteady voice. "Have you seen Roberto, Mario … anyone?"

"No. I just arrived. The roof was burning … No one is around. They are all dead."

"Please, Mother … they might be in the fields."

"No," said Giulia from behind them. "Me and La Rossa were there; the kids and Lina were near the house." She was crying uncontrollably and dripping at the nose.

"Let's calm down, please," Patrizia urged. "If they are in the cellar, they are going to need our help. Let's get to it."

They started to move the fallen bricks and smoldering wooden beams from the area adjacent to the massive wood door. Luisa dragged away a large piece of burning wood without even feeling the pain. Giulia, still crying, pushed away a charred window frame.

"It should be enough," said Parizia, after kicking the last piece of large rubble. "Help me yank the damn door; it will sweep away the small debris."

They finally opened enough of the door to squeeze through. From the last rays of sun filtering through the gap, they saw a cloud of smoke and dust particles still dancing in the air. The sleeping area seemed undamaged except for lingering dust and small debris that had fallen from the ceiling.

"I can't see anyone," Patrizia said, her voice denoting a mixture of relief and concern.

She advanced toward the back, where vats and wine casks lined the peripheral walls. She looked at the pile of bricks and rubble in front, at the still-smoldering fallen beams, and then toward the ceiling, where, through a large gaping hole, an imperturbable piece of blue sky peered through. The open door created a downdraft that blew smoke and dust toward her.

"Watch out," Patrizia warned. "More rubble may fall from the ceiling yet."

*****

"Wow! That was close," Roberto said, when the first shell hit the roof. Mortar, bricks, and debris rained over the top of the vat. "They hit the house. I hope my nonna and mother are safe."

This was the first time that he was separated from them during a cannon barrage. Previously, they had always been together—huddled inside a shelter, burrowed in a ditch, under a wooden cart, or even just stretched over a cement floor, but still together.

"I'm sure they're all right," said Lina. "Are you afraid?" She drew closer to him.

"No. Gino said these vats are very strong. And then … you are here with me, so how can I be afraid?" He was glad his voice had sounded reasonably firm. *No, I'm not afraid,* he repeated to himself. But, then, what was it that caused him the vague anguish he felt inside? Was he troubled for himself or for his mother and grandmother? It seemed to be for them, yet, if he looked hard inside his heart, his sentiment seemed shaded by a certain selfish feeling … an inner question repeating *What would I do without them?*

Lina drew closer to him and placed a kiss on his cheek. A thick fog of dust began to come in through the narrow opening of the vat; other shells exploded nearby, but the only thing that he felt was Lina's soft lips on his face—like a seal over a future promise. The reality of Lina's presence and that sweet kiss erased the fear and fed his hunger for Lina. He moved nearer and felt her move even closer to him. She adjusted to the circular shape of the vat, curled up, and rested her head on his lap.

The outside world suddenly disappeared.

He put one arm around her shoulders, and with the other, he began to caress her knees and thighs while inhaling her scent. Bombs continued to fall; his mother and grandmother were still unaccounted for; and the vat trembled as if shaken by the hands of a giant. Yet Roberto felt only joy as he held Lina's soft body in his arms.

"I love you, Lina," Roberto whispered in her ear. He let his hand slide over the smooth, soft skin of her thigh. The bombs, and the narrow confines of the dark vat, had made him more daring and brave. He finally made contact with the hem of her slips and the opening movement of her legs signaled her approval. He was about to reach his objective when, in the tense moment of silence that followed, Roberto heard a muffled sound coming from the corner of the cellar, and then several voices.

Once again, he had to postpone the realization of his desire.

"Mario," he heard Giulia call.

"Roberto," Luisa said. "Lina? Where is everybody?"

Answering shouts resounded from the arched opening of the vat where Mario and the Falaschi boys were hidden.

"We must go too," Lina whispered.

"I'm afraid so."

One by one, the children came out of their refuge and crossed the smoldering wreckage.

Roberto was happy to see that everyone was alive and safe, but he also regretted that the bombing had come to an end at such a crucial moment. *But ... how could I have experienced pleasure while my nonna and mother might have been in harm's way?* he asked himself. And laced with bliss and contentment, he felt a vague feeling of guilt for his having pleasure while his loved ones were in danger.

"We are all here," Mario said with a trembling voice.

"Such a beautiful thing to be young and carefree," Luisa said, laughing and crying at the same time.

*****

The ordeal had not yet ended.

During the last days of German occupation, the special troops tightened security even more. One risked being shot for as little as breathing too hard, or at the wrong time.

One day, the SS caught two young men in Castelvecchio. They

were barely eighteen, but lacking military exoneration papers, they were taken to the hills, ordered to dig their graves, and buried alive at the edge of a pine forest.

Old Falaschi, from a nearby farm, was hiding behind bushes in close proximity, and he saw the entire horrid scene. As soon as the Germans left, he ran to the burial spot, and forgetting his own safety, he feverishly began to scrape the loose soil with his bare hands.

When he returned to the farm, his wife could hardly recognize him. In a matter of hours, he had aged ten years: his sparse, white hair fell lifelessly over his forehead; his eyes were red from crying; his arms hung by his side as if pulled out of their sockets. "What happened to you?" she cried.

"Every instant an hour," he mumbled, looking at his mud-encrusted hands. "Every minute an eternity."

"What are you talking about?"

"They killed them but didn't shoot them."

"Who?"

"They buried them alive," he said, and he began to cry again. "The bastards … they tied their hands and feet and buried those poor boys alive. They were boys. Just boys they were …"

His wife put her arms around him, trying to console him.

"I couldn't save them," he continued between sobs. "I knew it would be too late for one of them, but I tried to save the other. I had to make a goddamned choice, you understand?" he almost yelled.

Unable to calm him down or understand the full story, his wife began to cry as well.

"I went for the one who looked younger," he said, "trying to forget the other poor fellow, and scraped and scraped with my bare hands, swearing at every fucking god in heaven or hell for allowing heartless, cruel, murderous fucking slaughters like that." He shook his head as if no longer able to comprehend the world around him.

"After a while, I got the hand of the young man, then the arm. I pulled and scraped; I wish I could've eaten the goddamned earth. I yanked his arm again. It felt still kind of warm, and I worked my way toward his face, hoping and hoping." He wiped his eyes and nose with his shirtsleeve. "But when I got to it," he said, "it was too late. His mouth and eyes and nose were full of soil. His face was red like a ripe tomato, the veins of his neck ..." Unable to go on, he fell into his wife's arms.

A farmer who had verbally attacked the soldiers taking away his last pig was shot on the spot. Even those older people who were marshaled to dig ditches and prepare the defenses on the Gothic Line never returned.

- IL -

September 1944

One evening, Otto returned to the farm. He walked as if he were carrying too heavy a weight on his broad shoulders. His greeting, normally lighthearted, seemed shaded by a veil of sadness. He casually placed his automatic rifle against the wall and let his body drop on a chair. He hugged Roberto and Mario, who had come to greet him.

"Good evening, Otto."

"*Kinders,*" he answered in a soft voice. "How many planes did you count today?"

"Twelve."

"And how many times you shouted 'Tito, heel'?"

"Not many because the Ger ..." Mario realized what he was saying and bit his lips.

"Don't vorry," Otto said. "I not say."

He knows, Roberto thought.

Otto smiled knowingly and hung about with them for a while longer, as if avoiding the adults in the room.

Finally, he took a big breath, exhaled, gently patted the boys on the head, and walked away from them.

Following him across the room with his eyes, Roberto saw him stop in front of his mother.

"Promise not repeat vhat I tell you," he told her. He paused for a moment. *"Bald rücken wir ab,"* he said, as if to himself. "Patrizia, tonight is ven ve leave."

Roberto had abandoned his play to witness the scene.

He saw his mother instinctively hug the soldier in front of her and hold him for a moment. He returned her embrace.

"Why don't you stay? We'll hide you. Give you civilian clothes. We'll testify that you did nothing wrong, that you protected us. You'll see ..."

"No, Patrizia *cara*. Ven called to arms, I promised my father ... I swore vhatever circumstances, I not betray. I must go."

She thought of her husband—the words he had used to justify what he perceived as his duty. Now she was hearing these same words from this man who stood in front of her.

"But this is not 'your' betrayal, you fool. Hitler and his henchmen betrayed you and everyone else, with their dream of Lebensraum, their sickly quest of glory, their evil."

"I am sorry, Patrizia. I can't. Maybe one day … ven this is finish … I come back to see you." He dug an old leather wallet from his pocket and took out a small picture. "Here," he said, "Please keep it, so you remember."

She took it. On the back, he had written *My dear Patrizia, I shall never forget you.*

They embraced, tears flowing down both of their faces.

Then Otto tore himself away. *"Auf wiedersehen,"* he said. "Please say good-bye to everyone for me. I… can't" He clicked his heels and then walked away. He waved a salute to Roberto and Mario. His shoulders now square, the fine gravel squeaked under his heavy boots, marking the fast cadenza of his military pace.

Roberto looked at his mother questioningly. "Au revoir, mon amie," he heard her say with a trembling voice. But when Roberto met her eyes, her face returned to a calm and composed expression that camouflaged her true feelings, and her countenance said, *Don't ask questions.* He was surprised at her display of emotions. He too was sorry to see Otto go, but less if his leaving meant the German soldiers were retreating from the area, that the front would move north, that his father may return.

With Roberto by her side, Patrizia walked up to the road to wave a last farewell. Otto never looked back.

He had barely reached the cornfield and was near the old poplar tree, almost out of view, when cannon shells whistled overhead. Mother and child instinctively dropped to the ground, Patrizia covering her son with her body. The earth shook violently under them, and at the same time, deafening explosions lacerated the calm evening air. Debris rained over them. With his ears still ringing, Roberto opened his eyes.

He saw the large poplar tree, which he had climbed so many times with Mario, now reduced to a burning trunk, its broken limbs spread all over the road. A few leaves were still lazily fluttering in midair, their deliberate, slow fall a defiance of the violence of war. His mother still held him, but he raised his head, and where Otto had just disappeared, there was only a dense cloud of smoke.

"Look, Mother," he said, pulling away from her hold. "Otto …" He ran toward the smoke, his mother following. His heart filled with a terrible premonition.

Otto lay at the bottom of the ditch, his face turned toward the sky. A narrow stream of blood ran from his temple, over the contour of his face and his neck, finally forming a murky little puddle on the parched ground. His deep blue eyes were wide open, his eyebrows slightly raised, and his face frozen in an expression of pained astonishment. It seemed to be asking *why.*

A few steps ahead, a ginger-colored dog also lay dead in the ditch. "Slaughtered, like a bloody dog." Patrizia's face was tense with anger and pain.

"Go, Roberto. Run and go tell Nonna we're okay. Tell them to come with a cart."

She looked at the dead soldier with eyes fogged by tears. A protracted shiver crossed her body before she descended into the ditch, knelt near Otto's body, and gently closed his eyes. Then she sat on the grassy bank and cried, her sobs audible from a distance.

*****

Now that Otto was dead, Patrizia no longer felt bound by her promise to him. So, she assembled all the people living at the farm and told them that tonight the Germans would evacuate the area.

"Be careful, though. This could be the longest night of the war."

Few slept that night. Everyone waited impatiently. For, if Patrizia was right, these were the last hours of the German occupation of the Arno Valley. They could be hours filled with excitement and the anticipation of approaching freedom. But they could also be hours fraught with the danger of a sudden retaliation from a vulnerable yet sufficiently potent army in retreat.

Gino and the other able-bodied men had to spend the night huddled inside the septic tank. The professor, claiming he'd rather die than stay one more hour in that dungeon, had joined the rest of the household. Enveloped in absolute darkness, he stood by one of the high-back windows and took turns with Luisa and Patrizia peeking through the wooden slats. Around midnight, the exodus of the retreating army finally began. A few men at first, walking noiselessly on the grassy sides of the road, their ready weapons pointed forward or toward the fields. Then came solid formations, their rhythmic steps ticking away with the minutes and the hours.

"The Germans are really leaving this time," Giulia whispered hopefully.

"Look at those poor defeated souls," added Luisa.

"Strange people, the Italians," contemplated the professor. "Who else could look at this scene and feel even a hint of pity for those who were, only moments before, feared enemies. Who else, I wonder, could find enough room in their hearts for compassion toward those men who have been, until yesterday, the very cause of our own suffering?"

His words incited thought, but no one replied.

The Italians had despised these men in their finest hour. When, handsome, in their sharp uniforms and Teutonic armor, they triumphed over the armies of Europe. When, full of pride, confidence, and arrogance, they goose-stepped like masters in the streets and squares of conquered nations, looking at the vanquished people with contempt and spite. They had nothing in common with those bellicose demigods, burning with the spirit of war.

Now it was different, though. For these were the days and hours preceding their final defeat. Their tired feet pounded the Tuscan soil for the last time, and the black night weighed over them like a lead mantle. Their spirits were broken by a reality they could no longer refute. Now, reduced to the state of common mortals, they could only inspire pity.

The Italians could relate to them now ... and spare an ounce of compassion.

And so, once again, the people stood behind windows and shutters, looking at the retreat of the once-mighty *Wehrmacht*. The metallic glitter of the soldiers' weapons was dulled and camouflaged by paint and foliage. Shadows that seemed to form and detach from darkness at one end of the country road, only to melt again into the night at the opposite end, the retreating army was swallowed by the dark night like a flock of birds disappearing into a cloud. Every man marched silently in the solitude of his own thoughts and fears, broken by five long years of senseless campaigns laden with violence, suffering, and death. Each face was hidden under a heavy steel helmet as the mean marched in a last silent parade.

*****

Roberto was unable to sleep. He slowly pushed his hand under the blanket toward Lina. He reached for her warm hand and held it tightly. She emitted a muffled sound, shifted her body a little, and squeezed his hand in return. Then her slow, regular breathing indicated that she had resumed her sleep.

Roberto didn't want to fall asleep, and he was satisfied to be holding Lina's hand and silently share the repressed excitement, the tense atmosphere of expectation exuding from the adults around them. He listened to them whispering their feelings throughout the long night.

Regardless of his efforts, he fell asleep and dreamt of his father, Uncle Lorenzo, and Otto. They were all together, laughing and joking, having supper over the white sands of the Arno River.

Toward dawn, he woke up. The atmosphere of the place seemed strangely unnatural; what was it?

There was absolute silence, and it felt as if time stood still, as if silence itself had miraculously enveloped and obliterated all other sounds, making itself become louder than any explosion.

Roberto couldn't lie down any longer. He had to get up and see for himself.

It was September 10, 1944.

*****

At first, the sky turned pale. A sliver of sun peeked from the high crest of the Apennines, hung briefly over the summits, and glanced at the landscape. Then the incandescent disk seemed to levitate briefly over the spine of the mountain like a bright orange balloon. It detached itself from the crest and began to glide toward the sky, bathing the valley below in a flood of light.

The new day was born.

As if to confirm it, a rooster crowed in the yard. Then another. Then an entire choir emerged. Birds chirped, and the domestic animals stirred in their stables. Dog barked in the distance, but theirs was no longer an alarming sound.

The first window was cracked open by a daring yet hesitant hand. Then a door was pushed ajar, then another window. Then all windows and doors sprang open as people rushed outside to join in the laughter and cry as they jumped and sang and hugged and kissed.

The church bells began to toll, and then those of the main bell tower, adding their festive strikes to the general sense of happiness of the new day. Dozens, hundreds, and then thousands of people filled the streets and squares of the town. Reborn to freedom, people celebrated what was, at least for them, the passing of the front … liberation … the end of the war.

At the Banchini farm, as in the rest of the immediate country-side, the men came out of hiding, and for the first time in months, they rejoined their families. They embraced and kissed their women. They hugged their kids, tossing them up in the air and then catching them and holding them tight against their bodies, or rubbing their rough faces against the soft ones of their children. Occasionally, they even hugged and smacked their calloused hands on each other's backs, congratulating each other for the escaped peril. Often starting their phrases with, *Do you remember when …?*

Patrizia and Luisa hugged each other and then Roberto.

"Cucciolo," said Patrizia, affectionately resting her arms over his shoulders, "for us, the war is over. No more running to the refuge. No more bombing."

"We shall return home soon," said an exultant Luisa. "Home sweet home." Then adding forlornly, "Or whatever is left of it."

"Don't be sad, Mother," said Patrizia. "Riccardo and Lorenzo will return, and life will be beautiful again."

A cautious smile dawned on Roberto's sunburned face. He didn't want to disappoint them, but he couldn't partake in their joy. Did they really believe that Father would return, or were they saying so for his benefit? And Lina … how was he going to fill the void left by her?

Roberto looked at the people around him, listened to their sudden optimism, the voicing of new hopes. Though sharing in the general sense of relief, deep inside his heart, he also felt a desperate, urgent hunger for news of his father's fate.

-L-

September 1944

By midmorning, the country road was a constant procession of people going to town to check on relatives or friends, or returning from there with the latest news. Ivo, Gino, and the old professor were at the edge of the yard, talking with as many people as possible to compare the various reports and get a clearer view of the situation.

Old man Buti, as Mario had called him, came by on his bike, now fully equipped with tires.

"Hallo, bunch of hooligans!" he shouted in jest. "I'm gonna go and tell the Americans to move on. I don't wanna see them Germans again."

"Good for you, Beppe!" Gino shouted back. "Give them Americans a ride on your bike."

Another man reported that in Castelvecchio, several hours after the departure of the Germans, not seeing any sign of the Americans, scores of people headed for the riverbanks. For several hours, they called and waved their white bedsheets, towels, and scarves, hoping to draw attention from the Allies.

Eventually, several soldiers in khaki uniforms were seen moving carefully on the high plateau adjacent to the opposite riverbank. They advanced slowly, dashing only through the open spaces to then stop and hide behind bushes and tree trunks. After what seemed an eternity, a few finally made it to the edge of the riverbank. As they began to descend toward the water, explosions were heard here and there. Clouds of smoke, sand, and body parts blew up in the clear morning air, marring what should have been only a happy event.

Ironically, those soldiers too cautious and distrustful to take the direct approach stepped on the mines strategically placed by the retreating Germans, and they were blown to pieces.

"Come down straight, for God's sake," an old farmer yelled from Castelvecchio's side. "The paths are not mined. What are you playing warrior for? The Germans have gone!"

Finally, an American soldier of Italian origin came within talking distance. "What's up?" he yelled. *"Dove sono I Tedeschi?"* Where are the Germans?

"They gone … last night!" someone yelled.

"Son partiti," someone else repeated. "They have left. What in the hell are you waiting for?"

The soldier finally got the message and sent word back to his superior, but a new problem arose when the first contingent of troop carriers approached the old bridge.

Neither the American bombing nor the German mines had been able to demolish the sturdy bridge pylons built hundreds of years before—when Cosimo Dei Medici reigned the city state of Florence. However, its surface structure was damaged and weakened. Besides, it would take time to verify and disarm residual demolition charges, so it was deemed too dangerous to cross.

After consultation with local people and visual inspections of the site, the Americans confirmed it safer to wade the river at a place known as "Shallow Point," just southwest of the town.

By late afternoon, the men of several infantry platoons, their weapons held above their heads, the placid river water lapping around their waists, finally reached the north side of the river.

Hundreds of villagers came to the riverbanks to greet the liberators. They sat on the grassy banks or strolled up and down, watching with curiosity and wonder as these young men from the New World smiled, chewed on something constantly, and offered candies and cigarettes.

The Italians countered with wine, fresh eggs, and whatever else was available, trying to communicate with broken phrases, gestures, and body language.

Most of the heavy equipment came across the second day, when big powerful machines with frontal scoops called Caterpillars were used to carve a ramp on the riverbank. In fact, neither the Ford nor the Dodge trucks—not even the Sherman tanks—could negotiate the high ridges on their own power.

"Look at that, Marino!" someone yelled at the sight of such a powerful piece of equipment. "And that fool Mussolini wanted to do war with shovels and bayonets. What can I tell you?"

"It's true," another replied, "but you know what's strange? I saw with my own eyes German Panzers climb the bank without any problem. These Americans seem to have quantity, but not quality."

A third one chuckled. "Yes, but with that quantity, quality can't prevail. What can a Tiger tank do against the twenty or more Sherman tanks the American can send against it?"

Three days later, tanks, trucks, and heavy equipment never seen before filled all main roads from Castelvecchio to the woods and beyond. The townspeople began to wonder why, with such an abundance of armament at their disposal, it had taken so long for the Allies to dislodge the last ill-equipped Germans.

On this same day, after hearing so much from those who had ventured to town and returned with varying descriptions, Patrizia took Roberto by the hand and said, "Come on, cucciolo. Let's go and see for ourselves what these long-awaited Americans look like."

They walked at a fast pace through shortcuts and paths in the fields, carefully avoiding certain ones. "Why do we go around those, Mother?" Roberto asked at one point.

"Mines. There are mines buried under the soil …"

"How do you know?"

Patrizia looked at her son, and with a voice that betrayed sadness, she whispered, "Otto told me. He showed me a few places where they were. He didn't want us to be accidentally blown up."

"He was a nice man."

The sun was hot, and every now and then, they stopped to cool off in the shade of leafy trees.

"Look, Mother," said Roberto during one of those pauses, pointing at a vineyard nearby, "those grapes will be ready in a few weeks. Ours will be too, I think."

"Yes," Patrizia laughed, "and I am sure your nonna will let you have all the *primizie*." Then, in a somber mood, she added, "And hopefully Father will be there to enjoy them too."

Roberto had not mentioned his father very often since his departure. Even when he had the opportunity, he did not want to cause pain to his mother or his nonna, and, honestly, he was afraid he would break down. What man of the house would he be then? He had heard all he needed to know, and he was aware of their worries. Asking questions would not benefit anyone. He had silently listened to their speculations after the fall of the African front and the absolute lack of correspondence: "I wonder if he is still alive …" and "I wish we would get word of his whereabouts. Is he a prisoner … wounded … dead?"

Dead? he repeated silently to himself. This was not the first time he had considered this possibility, and more than once, he had experienced the moment as if it were real. Overtaken by emotion, he had been unable to chase away the thought. Making sure no one would see him, he had surrendered to the feeling, which brought tears to his eyes. Once or twice, he had run in the fields, stopping behind a bush or a tree to sob loudly and let the tears drop uncontrolled.

"What do you think, Mother?" he asked. "Do you expect he'll return soon?"

"I hope so, cucciolo. I really do."

For Roberto, familiar with the old Tuscan proverb *La speranza e' la fede degli stupidi*—Hope is the faith of ignorant people—he considered his mother's response a non-answer.

"I do too," he charitably conceded.

He visualized his father in the desert in his uniform. Or in his denim suit, back from the distillery. Or in his gray suit, during his suppertime discussions with his colleagues. Or the times that he had sat on his father's lap in front of a map and learned about other countries, other peoples, wars, and the mysterious motives that seemed to move human beings. He wondered why his father's ideas seemed always so different from what he heard from others. He remembered with a smile the last time they had gone for a picnic at the Arno River—and his elaborate description of what a true artist was. He had liked his drawing, and that made Roberto happy. For some reason, his opinion seemed to be more important to him than even nonna's.

Finally, they reached a country lane that led to the Via del Bosco— Road of the Woods—at a point just north of the old cemetery. The road was jammed with trucks and tanks and smiling soldiers waving and shouting compliments at his mother as they went by.

"Ciao, bella signora!" … "I'm from New York, signorina ... Wanna come with me to Chicago?" … "Hallo, beautiful!"

A few whistles were followed by other comments in English. Roberto started to resent the attention his mother received from all those men. He looked up at her expression and concluded that she did not seem to mind. They kept on walking along the line of tanks and soldiers.

The Americans are really here, her face seemed to say. *They have crossed the front line, and the Germans will not return. Not now and not ever.*

"They are so young," she said. At the sight of those youthful and cheerful liberators, the months of worry and fear and danger seemed to dissolve. Tears began to pour from her soft, chestnut-brown eyes.

"What's wrong, Mother?" the boy asked her. "Why do you cry?"

"It's nothing, cucciolo. I cry because I am happy."

He did not understand. He had never heard or seen anyone cry for happiness.

She quickly dried her tears, and they walked up the street, where the scene was the same: vehicles bumper-to-bumper and young soldiers, their smiling faces a strange contrast to the dour, unfriendly faces of most Germans he had seen. Some of them were dispensing candies and chocolates to children and women, or offering perfectly rolled cigarettes to the local men who, now that the danger had passed, had suddenly reappeared.

Roberto noticed a couple of soldiers, their skin as dark as coffee. He stared at them, and they smiled, their teeth glaring in the dark frames of their faces. "Look, Mother, black soldiers."

"They are Americans too," she replied.

"Yes, of course, Mother," he answered with some indignation. "I read they were brought as slaves from Africa a long time ago. But I only saw them in pictures; I didn't imagine them quite so ... in real life."

"I should have known that you knew," she said, smiling.

"One day," he stated seriously, "I think I'd like to go to America."

"And leave your family?" Patrizia asked jokingly.

He couldn't give her a verbal answer; instead, he squeezed her hand twice.

It was extremely hot, and the incandescent disk of the sun seemed to stop at the zenith of a deep blue sky. The leaves of the horse chestnut trees lining the road cast their deep shadows over the dusty ground and over the Sherman tanks, as if part of their camouflage. Heat waves rose from the unshaded soil, and distant images appeared distorted and out of focus.

Like many other villagers, at the incredible sight of all the equipment, Roberto too wondered why it had taken so long for the Americans to advance.

"What kept you?" Patrizia finally asked an American who spoke with a southern Italian accent.

"Signora," he replied, "in America, we have this saying: *To make a tank one day, to make a man twenty years*. And tanks can be replaced. There is no merit in rushing forward if it costs more of our lives."

"You have a point there," she admitted. "But you didn't take that into consideration when you bombed the hell out of us. It takes just as long in Italy to make a man, you know. Or a woman, for that matter …"

The soldier did not reply.

*****

So much time wasted. So many lives lost for nothing! Patrizia thought of the two young men shot by the SS just two days before—such an irony! How many more senseless casualties were there throughout the front?

When the initial frustration began to subside, she slowly began to recognize the inescapable reality of it all. Their families were safe and secure in their homes and their country. America intact and far from the dangers of war, theirs, was not an unreasonable perspective.

Unquestionably, Patrizia thought, *it is our war, our land, our urgency. Those in greatest danger are our people. Why, then, should these soldiers from a faraway land—well fed, well clothed, and secure—risk their own lives to abbreviate our suffering?*

*****

Patrizia returned to the farm with Roberto and told everyone that the Americans had arrived. It was time for everyone to shake the fear of war, she said. For those who were lucky enough to still have a house, to start thinking of returning home, to live again, as her favorite song stated. Everyone rejoiced, embraced, ate, and toasted to the arrival of their liberators and the passage of the war front.

"Patrizia is right!" Ivo shouted. "Let's have some fun."

At those words, Gino, who had been quietly listening to the conversation, began to run toward the shed, returning moments later, his face lit by a strange smile, flaunting a spade.

"I'll be back in a minute," he said. He ran toward the artesian well, then turned on his heels and began to take long, regular steps in the direction of the walnut tree. There, he swung ninety degrees and paced toward the first row of vines. He stopped at the count of seven, spat on his calloused hands, and began to dig a wide circle. He began at a frenetic pace, but as he went deeper, he appeared to be careful and concerned for the safety of his prize. Roberto and Mario joined him. They knelt at the edge of the excavation, scooping the loose soil with their bare hands.

Finally, the top of a large box appeared. It was wrapped in a heavy canvas that had been sewn perfectly all around. Gino pushed the spade away and knelt in the damp soil as if to pray. He then leaned forward, jerked the box a few times, and lifted it out of its temporary grave.

"What's that, Pa?" Mario asked.

Gino did not answer. He got up, shook the loose soil from the canvas, and silently pushed it toward his son. Mario pressed his hands against the canvas and moved them around to feel the contour of the box. After a moment of hesitation, he finally cried, "It's the accordion; it's the accordion!"

That evening, the kitchen buzzed with activity. The women intended to prepare a supper worthy of the occasion. La Rossa pulled feathers from a couple of chickens; Giulia pan-fried battered zucchini and zucchini flowers. Franco and Roberto washed salad leaves and red tomatoes, and Lina peeled potatoes, while Luisa improvised a sumptuous dessert. "I'll make the best crème caramel you ever tasted," she told everyone. "Tonight we deserve a treat."

"I need more sage and rosemary," La Rossa said to no one in particular.

"I'll get it, I'll get it," Roberto and Lina replied in unison.

They ran downstairs and across the yard, racing at first and then holding hands. Lina pulled to one side and then stopped near the jasmine bush. She crumpled a bud between her fingers and inhaled eagerly. "Smell it," she then said, raising her hand toward Roberto's face. He took her hand and held it near his nostrils. It was so alluring. A gentle breeze blew from the vineyard, and the wide leaves rustled and danced and whispered unwritten songs.

"I'm so happy when we are together," he said suddenly. They seemed appropriate lyrics to add to the sound of nature.

"So am I," she replied, and she seemed about to add something else, but she bit her lip instead.

"Where is my sage?" La Rossa called from the portico.

"Coming!" Roberto hollered back. He ran to the bushes and began picking sage leaves and small branches of rosemary, which he placed on Lina's apron pocket. His hands were redolent with the spicy scent of the herbs. He inhaled eagerly and then placed one hand close to Lina's nostrils.

"It smells so nice," she said, closing her eyes. Then she held his fingers and touched his palm with her tongue.

Roberto looked at her, studied her expression, and noticed, passing over her face, impressions of conflicting impulses.

When they returned to the kitchen, La Rossa was squatting in front of the open pit, poking the burning coals and blowing on them as showers of sparks burst against the black background of the fireplace. She had spread some of the red-hot coals over the stone rim of the pit to warm up the extra pots elevated by wrought iron stands. Her red cheeks reflected the light of the fire. "What took you so long?"

The men had already begun to consider the immediate needs of the fields.

"Them Germans left just in time," Gino said. "Another week and the wheat would have started to fall to the ground."

"We'll have to harvest as soon as possible, Zio," Ivo added. "We'll help."

That evening, supper was an event to remember, and the women outdid themselves preparing all kind of food. There was roast chicken, ducks, pigeons, three different vegetables. In addition to the promised dessert, Luisa had even managed to prepare almond cookies and *pinolate*. A few flasks of special wine, which Gino had buried behind the shed, found their way to the table, to the great appreciation of the adults.

Everyone consumed more food and wine than usual, and that seemed to contribute to the joyous atmosphere of the evening. During that supper, Roberto's eyes never tired of looking at Lina. In the soft, orange glow of the candlelight, she appeared even more beautiful than usual. Her faded blue shirt was tight around her slender waist but its front was undone up to her soft bosom, and when she bent forward, it showed parts never touched by the sun. It invited Roberto's eyes and imagination to descend even further, toward the very spot he had journeyed with his hand not so long before. He envisaged her bare legs beneath the tabletop, her sculpted thighs, and at the very end, that mysterious softness that he had caressed, and which still intrigued him. When his eyes met hers, and when she held his gaze, the people around them receded. A heat wave crossed his face. The fork he held in his hands began to shake, and rivers of unspoken thoughts flowed out of his soul.

I love you, Lina. Can't you hear me? Please don't turn your eyes away from me. Take me through the doors of physical love.

After supper, everyone went out in the yard. The night was pleasantly warm, and the air smelled of jasmine, sage, and rosemary.

After yet another glass of wine, Gino embraced his beloved accordion, and after loosening his fingers with a series of musical scales, he began to play. He played for hours. Sometimes he sang old songs and ballads with an unexpected beautiful baritone voice. Other times, everyone sang or danced, sharing a moment of unbridled happiness. Ivo danced with Angela, holding the baby between them. The old professor invited Luisa and Rosa for a few steps of "old-style waltz," as he put it. Mario had suddenly disappeared, and when he returned, he held three aluminum pots and two wooden spoons, which he placed on top of a table, and began to accompany his father as though it was a battery of drums.

"Very, very good, Mario," said Roberto. He was happy to be left to dance with Lina, and the two managed to stay at the periphery of the dancing area. Luisa saw them, and touching Patrizia with her elbow, said, "Look at the two lovebirds."

"I know, Mother. He is not a child anymore. Somehow I suspected it; now we know for sure."

Luisa looked at her with bewilderment. Patrizia's matter-of-fact statement seemed to surprise her. "Roberto mio," she whispered.

The young couple held each other tightly and spoke softly into each other's ears.

"I am going to miss you," she said first.

"Me too," he answered, "more than you can imagine. "

"I know."

"I wish I were older," he continued, his voice choked with emotion, "then I would ask you to be my girl."

"In a way, I am your girl. I've never let anyone else touch me there."

A full moon had made its way to the pinnacle of the sky and poured its reflected light over the earth below. People's shadows were sharply defined on the clean-swept yard, and were it not for their movements, one would have thought them etched on the ground with China ink.

The yard was filled with exuberance and gaiety. Months of fear and apprehension seemed to dissolve suddenly in the air with each note of Gino's accordion. Even the dog seemed to bark in tune with the music. No need to shout the coded message tonight: *Tito, heel!* No need to signal oncoming German patrols. Tonight Tito barked at the moon, or perhaps he sang, and other dogs at farms near and far joined in at his call. Like the bells of neighboring towns had done the day the Germans had left.

It was getting late. Some of the people started to tire, and they sat on the straw-seat chairs they had dragged outside. Mario sat beside his mother, his head resting on her lap. Patrizia, who had not accepted any invitations, claiming to be incapable of dancing, signaled to Roberto that it was time to go to bed. He nodded, but he held on to Lina even tighter.

"I must help clear the tables soon," Lina whispered, "but if you unbuckle your belt, I'll steal it from you and run away."

Roberto looked at her without understanding. "What for?" he asked.

"You'll chase me to get it back."

He still looked puzzled.

"We'll meet behind the shed, you silly," Lina said. "Get it?"

He smiled and nodded, and as soon as she pulled his belt, he began to chase her. They stopped in a place where they were completely concealed from view by a cluster of bamboo cane. They faced each other, her features bathed by the white light of the moon. She bent forward and kissed him on the mouth. He stood still at first, feeling astonishment and pleasure at the same time.

"What's the matter?" Lina asked, feeling his reluctance.

He told her what his parents had always said to him about kissing on the mouth. "'There are germs in the mouth, Roberto. Don't let anyone kiss you there.'"

"But I am young and healthy. Don't worry, Roberto."

She kissed him again, and this time he felt her tongue play against his lips and her soft body press against his.

"Let your mouth open," she said. "Some people call it French kissing, like they do in the movies."

Roberto remembered one such scene in one of the rare movies he had been allowed to see. His mother had told him to cover his eyes during the scene, but he had peeked through his fingers.

Lina's kisses felt so good. He had never suspected that a simple kiss on his lips could resonate throughout his entire body. It was worth defying Mother's guidelines. *Most probably,* he thought, *Lina's germs are compatible with mine anyway.*

"Kiss me again," he said.

– LI –

"Tomorrow we'll return home," Patrizia announced two days later, while having dinner.

It was the logical conclusion to a long inner deliberation, a simple statement casually tossed out to everyone. But together with the obvious reality, its forced nonchalant tone denoted more complex feelings.

The departure would be an emotional moment for everyone, as the bond created in such a short but intense period was stronger than anyone could have imagined. They had shared shelter, food, dangers, fear. Together they had experienced enough emotions to fill a lifetime.

Together they had endured; they had survived.

The joy of freedom, alongside past perils, was clearly present in their minds. But in their hearts was the sad realization that they had to part from the special friends who had become an integral part of their daily lives during such trying times. Also, that other danger may lay ahead. In town, there were already rumors of partisans' revenge against the fascists. There had been beatings and other violence. Food was still scarce and jobs inexistent; commercial activities would take some time to resume.

"All the same," said the professor, "the Germans have retreated behind the defensive positions of the Gothic Line. The front may remain static throughout the coming winter, but at least ..."

"But at least," said Gino emphatically, "the goddamned Germans won't return."

"True. The Americans are well positioned along the entire front. The Germans will not come back."

"Yes," Patrizia confirmed, "but I hear that many people returning home found their places destroyed or looted, that unexploded bombs and mines are killing as many people now as during the actual fighting." She paused, looked around the table, sighed, and concluded, "But the sooner we pick up the pieces, the sooner we can glue our lives back together again."

When Roberto heard his mother's conclusive comment, the food stuck in his throat. He felt his heart beat faster inside his chest. A sudden rush of blood went to his brain, for although he'd known this moment would come, he had hoped it would not be so soon. He looked across to Lina's face, and their eyes expressed what words could not. He felt tears press hard behind his eyes, and he fought to stop them. Then he looked at Mario, his first real friend, and they exchanged a look of understanding.

Regardless of circumstances, the moment had finally come for everyone to begin on a new path. Patrizia had stated it in the simplest manner: "Tomorrow we'll return home."

"The morrow?" Giulia asked. "Isn't it too soon?"

"No, Giulia. As the professor said, the sooner we go, the sooner we begin with our normal life. If life is ever going to feel normal again," she added, almost to herself.

"But in these times," Gino attempted, "without a man in the house, why don't you wait until your husband or your brother-in-law returns?"

"You'll come back for the *vendemmia*"— harvesting of grapes , said Mario. "Won't you?"

"Of course I will."

"We'll all come," said Luisa. "We'll be glad to help and spend time together."

Patrizia nodded in silence.

Roberto noticed in the faces and body language of the people around him how much they had appreciated his mother's influence. Through the last long months, she had been their leader, their rock, and now they had come to the end of that period.

For a while, everyone around the table fell silent. For together, with their common thoughts, everyone was surely caught in the web of personal feelings that they could not share: their own beloved far away; people they may not see ever again; the uncertainty for the future; unknown risks …

*****

The next day, as Patrizia had announced, the Lanzis were ready to leave. Patrizia and Luisa reminisced one last time with Giulia and

La Rossa, summoning up episodes that now seemed remote and extraordinary.

"Remember that time they sent us away from the farm?" said Giulia.

"Patrizia, remember when that German shot himself?" said La Rossa.

"What about when they hit the house and we thought the kids were killed?" said a teary-eyed Luisa.

"Fortunately," said Patrizia, "it's all behind us now."

Questions, assertions, smiles, and then long silences. Silences pregnant with thoughts and feelings that did not need to be spoken.

It could so easily have happened that, like many less fortunate souls, they would not have been lucky enough to be there talking about these things.

The silences were filled with nostalgia for those happier, fleeting moments when, after the fear, they had experienced the joy of finding themselves alive.

"Promise me you'll return and see us," said Giulia at last, "and bring Roberto. Mario will miss him."

"We will, I'm sure," Luisa answered.

Roberto saw his mother and grandmother say a last good-bye to Amato, the old professor, Lina, and all the other refugees, while Gino took two cows out of the stable, connected their harnesses to the cart, and loaded and secured their belongings.

Finally, they were ready to leave.

Once the two women were safely aboard the cart, Gino yelled cheerfully, urging the team forward.

"Via, yhuh, we're gonna go to town."

He cracked the whip in the air and the cart pulled ahead with a jerk, grinding the fine-graveled road under its huge ironclad wheels. Roberto ran in the opposite direction.

"Roberto, we're leaving," Luisa called. "Where are you going?"

*****

He heard the call from a distance but did not reply. Taking advantage of a moment when everyone seemed occupied, Roberto and Lina had run to their rendezvous.

The bamboo cane whispered in the morning breeze, the sun shone high above, and two young lovers stood face-to-face; words were not necessary. They kissed—a long, sensuous kiss that sent waves of pleasure shimmering through Roberto's body.

Shortly afterward, Lina pulled away, tears falling from her eyes, "Good-bye," she said. "I'll miss you." And she ran off, disappearing behind the shed.

Roberto stood motionless for a moment, looking at the empty space in front of him. He listened to the faint sound of her steps, muffled by the grass, soon disappear. In a matter of instants, nothing remained of her but the sweet scent of her skin in his nostrils and the patch of flattened grass where her feet had been. He leaned down and laid his hand on the ground, caressing the tender grass softly, as though he were touching her. Then he let his body slump over the gray boulder nearby. He was devastated at the thought of losing her; he had become attached to her more than he thought possible.

Is this how Mother felt when Father left? Was it this pain?

He gazed at the spacious surroundings as his mind leapt all the way back to the night they had abandoned their home and walked to this farmhouse. Something inside told him that he was still the same person, and yet he was not. How was he going to return to the old school routines, to piano lessons, to the old tutors?

"Roberto."

It was his mother calling now. She suddenly appeared behind him. "We are leaving, darling," she said.

How did she know I was here? he thought.

"I understand, cucciolo," she said, placing her hand on his shoulder, "but now we must go."

Her eyes and sad expression told him that she did understand. *But how did she?*

And why did she look sad as well? Was it the thought of her missing husband? Was it a feeling she had felt for Otto? He wished to know but did not dare to ask. Perhaps it was better that way.

He put his hand over hers. "Please, Mother," he said. "I'll catch up with you in a moment."

He felt her hand clutch his shoulder, then pull gently away. He heard her hushed steps slowly fade away, and finally he heard the whisper of the following silence.

His eyes lingered one last time over the familiar shapes of his wartime haven, as if to imprint those images into his memory, capture the essence of the feelings he had experienced.

"Roberto!" Luisa called again from a distance.

From an opening through the bamboo cane, he saw the cart slowly disappear beyond the first bend.

He got up and began to run through the open fields. He ran with a motion as fluid as the flight of a bird.

Good-bye, Lina, his heart cried, as he passed by the shed. "Good-bye, Mario," he whispered, ducking under a vine. Good-bye, fields.

He reached the moving cart, jumped on, and climbed confidently over crates and furniture. At the top, he sat on a soft bundle of clothes and leaned back, allowing the warm sun to embrace his body.

"Finally!" Luisa exclaimed.

He did not answer, instead closing his eyes to hold his memories a while longer.

The adults sat in the front of the cart, the cheerful tone of their conversation expressing a confident mood. Despite the troublesome political and economic future of the country, despite all the unknown, they seemed to be happy.

Happiness! Roberto thought, as if the deepest meaning of the word, or its effect, could be promptly evoked merely by uttering it.

Happiness! he repeated internally, as if to summon the emotions he had read in the faces of the adults. He had even seen people cry from happiness, and that he could not comprehend. His mother for instance, at her first sight of the Allies. How could someone as strong as she was cry from happiness? How could anyone?

He could have cried now, if he had been alone, to loosen the tight knot he felt in his throat, but that was not caused by happiness. Rather, it was from the profound feeling of loss imprisoned in his chest. The sadness in departing from Lina mixed with the persistent feeling that, with the passage of the war front, the moment that would reveal his father's fate was near.

The presentiment lodged in his mind did not sit well, and that is why, in his heart of hearts, his own feelings did not seem to compare to what the adults expressed. His seemed to carry a tinge of sadness, an element of doubt. After all, for him, the war period at the farm—despite all its perilous moments, fears, and hardship—had been eventful and not without pleasant moments. Mario and then Lina had brought into his life something previously unknown. Despite the many dangerous trials and near misses, and the sight of actual death—including Ottto's—he had seldom thought that his personal life was endangered by the frightful events. The extraordinary had become a condition to which he grew accustomed to, a simple matter of survival. He had felt alive! Mario's friendship, Lina's attraction—could it be called love?—his personal freedom, the easy chores, and the warmth of all the people around had, during the last months, all played such an important role in his life.

Now they had all gone.

He sensed the cart change direction, and he opened his eyes. From his vantage point, he could take in the whole countryside at a glance. He saw vineyards, trees, and red-roofed farmhouses emerge from the uniform green patches of their gardens, the yellowing open fields. And then, beyond all that, as in so many hazy backgrounds of Renaissance paintings, lay the typical rolling hills of Tuscany.

Roberto thought it strange that entire towns and cities had crumbled to the ground under the evil of man. Yet here, in the countryside, a few short days after the cease-fire, nature was already recovering from the wounds of war. The soft rustle of leaves and fluttering of birds' wings seemed to gently sweep away the memory of the whining whistle of falling bombs and the lacerating echo of deadly explosions.

He was amazed and awed at the extraordinary regenerating power of nature, at the tolerance of the deep injures inflicted. At its ability to absorb the abuses of man, at the innate generosity, as Mario put it on their first outing into the fields, in giving back plentiful fruits in return for man's work.

He smiled, remembering the time they had gone to cut some grass for the cows and noticing his friend completely absorbed in his task. His arms moved in harmony with the swing of his body, and the scythe was a mere extension of his limbs. His feet were solidly planted on the soil, as though he was one with the earth. It was a picture of contentment, and sometimes he had admired his friend's uncomplicated nature, a few times even envied him. But if he asked himself whether he would have liked to be like him, the answer came as a resounding no! Yes, it was a beautiful, straightforward life. However, Roberto felt incapable of staring at the scenery around him, striking as it was, and thinking it'd be the only one he would ever know. Or planting vineyards and waiting for years for them to grow and bear fruit—and then waiting or praying for God to send the right amount of sun and rain to make the grapes grow. No! He aspired to something else, something more. He wasn't sure yet what that would be, but he knew that one day soon, he would.

"Yap," said Gino, as if hearing Roberto's thoughts about nature, "the vines are loaded with beautiful bunches of grapes, plentiful and high grade. It's gonna be a very good year."

Realizing he had been thinking of nature almost with emotion, Roberto laughed at himself. It had never happened before. For him, flowers, trees, leaves, insects, the earth, and the sun had, up to this moment, been inseparable elements of an unquestionable whole: the universe. Indivisible and always there, like the distinct elements that formed the air he breathed, existing regardless of emotion or acknowledgment. *Perhaps,* he thought after a moment, *there are other feelings mixed in my mind.* A little voice whispered to him, *Or in your heart?*

Lina, Lina, Lina, he silently screamed, cursing at the perverse lucidity of nostalgia. He closed his eyes and recalled her ivory face, hearing her voice whispering to him, "I'll be leaving tomorrow. We may never see each other again … or perhaps we will. But either way, I won't forget you."

He remembered the kisses exchanged behind the shed and felt his spine tingle again, as it had at that first unexpected magic contact.

French kiss, she had called it. Were all French people truly kissing that way? He had thought it strange at first. Especially after being told for so many years, by his mother and his nonna, to avoid being kissed on the mouth for reasons of hygiene.

But Lina had reassured him that she was healthy—and that he would like it. She was right. He had liked it a lot, more than he could even tell, and now he wished it was that night again, behind the haystack, and he could ask Lina for more. Perhaps even touch her again where no one else had.

Obviously, parents were wrong sometimes … or else they lied, trying to hide from their children those things that they would learn anyway. He had to stifle a laugh thinking of his parents attributing the different anatomy of girls to a "cut-off penis." Then his thoughts returned to Lina. Would she really disappear from his life? Would she in time become only a faded memory, like Amelia and Rosina?

"Look at that!" he heard Gino exclaim. "There, beyond the curb."

It was a German armored car, its left side leaning on the ridge of the field, the right side ripped open by an explosion. Tall weeds already grew beside it, almost climbing over the steel. Leaves covered the flat part of the gun turret, and insects buzzed in and out of gun holes and twisted iron. A bird had relieved itself over the black swastika. A yellow butterfly flapped its delicate wings and rested on the tip of a gun muzzle. Its grace and fragility seemed a mockery to the futile efforts of men, to the ephemeral traces of war.

"That bird knew what it was doing," Gino said, as they passed the disabled war machine. "Shit on them bastards!"

"Alive today and dead tomorrow," Luisa commented with a sigh, "all according to the will of God."

*****

Patrizia was not in any mood to listen to Luisa's fatalistic views, be they preassembled in heaven or concocted in hell. She thought of Riccardo, whose destiny was still unknown. She thought of Otto and the millions of people who had died for nothing. She looked at the road that rolled from town to town, parting the countryside in softer slices of green. She listened to the whisper of the rustling leaves, to the carefree singing of birds. She pushed away all the sad thoughts from her mind, stretched her arms toward the blue sky, and abandoned her body to the warm embrace of the sun.

The day was beautiful, and she was alive. There was still life to live, and nature seemed to shout at her *Sing … sing … sing!*

She heard nature's voice and began her favorite tune, as she had done many times before:

> *Vivere finché c'è gioventù. Perchè la vita è bella e la voglio vivere sempre più.*

*****

The words were appropriate; regardless of circumstances, life is meant to be lived … and lived fully. *Particularly when young,* Roberto thought.

They reached the outskirts of Castelvecchio, and a small group of men and women passed by the cart. Roberto sat up to observe them. They were mostly peasants and seemed to be returning from some sort of assembly. They were singing a kind of martial song he had never heard before.

"They are singing the '*Internazionale*,'" Luisa commented. "We are passing from one 'ism' to another, and I don't think I'm going to like communism any better than I did fascism!"

"What hymn is that, Nonna?"

"It's a revolutionary Russian song, Roberto. I'm afraid we'll have to hear it as often as we did the fascists' 'Faccetta Nera.'"

Most of the people, whether men or women, donned red scarves around their necks. One man wore a bright red shirt as the followers of

Garibaldi had done during the War of Independence, almost a century before.

"Clever touch," said Patrizia. "The new contenders are already draping themselves in patriotic clothes."

A toothless middle-aged woman was waving a red flag with the hammer and sickle emblazoned in the upper corner.

"The professor knew what he was saying," Gino commented at that sight. "Them communists seem to know how to get what they want …"

Roberto had heard snatches of conversation between the professor, Ivo, and Gino, and he was beginning to make sense of those talks.

He was surprised, though, at the sudden transformation of those people. Mild-mannered, submissive peasants only weeks before, they were now marching in a political parade, following a waving red flag and a small band playing the tune of the '*Internazionale*'. Praising Lenin and this new party called communism, while defying church and provisional authorities that frowned upon this new political philosophy that seemed to undermine what had been, for as far as one could remember, the traditional values of Italian society.

It must have been, as the professor stated, mainly as an open rebellion against the injustice of a system that had been condemned, from time immemorial, to a state of misery and hopelessness from which they were now trying to escape.

The silhouette of the church dome and the old bell tower came into view. But other familiar outlines—among which was the bell tower of the Badia church and its octagonal cupola, the stone tower of the municipal palace, and the higher floors of the Carmelitane convent—had disappeared. They were erased forever, as if by a capricious hand, from the imaginary canvas of the sky, victims of the many air raids, which, though aimed at the bridge had, more often than not, hit the town.

"Oh my God!" he heard his nonna exclaim. "What will our life be like now? Am I to live again the time of San Donà? Will our house be in worse condition than Otto told us?"

Roberto thought of the house as well. The idea of having his room all to himself didn't seem as appealing as it once had been; he would rather be at the Banchinis', with Lina by his side.

Yes, Roberto thought, *what is our life to be now? And will Father ever return?*

He remembered and treasured the feeling he experienced when he sat on his knees, looking at maps, reading, inhaling his cologne or aftershave, wishing to be grown-up and shave and wear the same fragrance. *Will I feel the same way at his return?* he wondered. Despite his nostalgia, he doubted that. With the war, like everyone else, he had lost his innocence, and as Nonna put it, once gone, innocence cannot be regained.

The relationship would be different now. He would have many things to ask him, about the war in the desert, winning and losing battles, life and death. But also many things to tell him about his own experiences. He couldn't imagine sitting on his lap again, after seeing people die, after kissing Lina. No, he was too old for that. Perhaps they'd sit at a table and discuss things, or go fishing together, just father and son, like Mario and Gino at the farm. Like the time they went to the river and sat closely together, his father studying his blueprints and him drawing a picture. Now he could walk side by side with him, without having to stretch his legs so much as he did that time going home from the river.

But what if he did not return?

Heartrending as the thought was, he could not avoid considering the possibility. What would he do then? He would do his best, but would that be sufficient to protect the family or provide for it? Certainly not immediately. How could he, then, become the worthy man of the house his father wanted him to be? And what did he himself wish to become, anyhow?

In a way, he envied the adults. They were well acquainted with the lives they lived before the war, and they were happy to return to it. They had husbands, wives, children, careers, old-time friends, and hobbies, and they seemed to know exactly what to wish from their existence. But what about him? He had parents, a grandmother who loved him dearly … It was a lot in a way, and yet, at this moment, it didn't seem enough.

"Roberto," Luisa called, "how come you are so quiet?"

"No reason, Nonna. I have nothing to say."

"Don't worry, my dear. Soon you'll sleep in your bed, start the old routines, go to school. Everything will be as good as before."

Roberto attempted a smile. He felt no great desire to return to the old routines, school, piano, French lessons, church …

For a brief moment, he even wished he were like Mario, uncomplicated and seemingly content with what life had given him. Ready to renounce what he might have glimpsed outside the realm of the farm for the tranquility and peace of mind his life had promised.

The day had begun as a joyous one for all, holding the promise of a new beginning. Yet, for him, with the first good-byes, the mirage had soon turned into grim reality. He suddenly realized that, regardless of his father's return, the road ahead was now going to be quite different. As the journey toward his home progressed, he felt that it took him away from both the farm and his childhood. The farm now seemed the symbolic milestone that marked and separated his past from his future. Regardless of how he felt, that seemed to be what destiny had assigned to him. But if fate had marked the direction, *he* had to be the one who chose the way.

If my father is dead, he then thought, without a shade of self-pity, *the way will be more difficult, but I will try to be worthy of his trust. I will not give up. But what exactly would the man of the family need to do?*

The chanting sound of the communists gradually subsided, and Roberto thought he heard the faint hum of an engine in the distance. Instinctively, he searched the sky as he had done so many times before, holding his breath to better detect the distant hum of airplanes.

No. Above him, and for as far as he could see, there was only the imaginary façade of a deep blue sky, and no airplanes.

It must have been something mixing with the noise of the iron-clad wheels grinding the gravel of the country road. Yet a shiver went through his body, and his skin rippled like the surface of water from a sudden gust of wind.

He closed his eyes again. And in the blurry image that flashed behind his eyelids, he saw an immense ocean of sand, a desert scorched by the midday sun. In its midst was the lifeless figure of a fallen soldier in a khaki uniform … his father.

The weighty feelings he had held for too long poured out of him with a deep sigh. Tears escaped from his closed eyelids. They were tears of deliverance, for in his mind, he had already traveled the road ahead … alone.

He felt a new energy inside, and his heart cried out two silent words: *Good-bye, Father.*

LaVergne, TN USA
25 August 2009
155819LV00006B/1/P

9 780595 526994